## Moccasin Track

*Book Four*

## What Authors and Reviewers are saying about the *Threads West* series:

"Whoever would have thought that a fourth-generation cattleman and rancher would have the imaginary zeal and literary prowess to bring to fruition a series of novels of sweeping grandeur.

"Rosenthal's incisive and dramtic revelation of the core elements of spiritual and moral fiber that have contributed to the making of the American nation makes for an unforgettable saga that is favorably compared to Larry McMurtry's bestselling Pulitzer-Prize-winning *Lonesome Dove* (with the promise of Rosenthal's work surpassing the other in both scope and extent), James A. Michener's inviting glimpses into the history of North America in *Centennial* (the Threads West series allowing for greater in-depth exploration of character. Rosenthal's epic masterpiece will come, in popularity, to rival even some of Louis L'Amour's best-loved work.)

"Threads West, An American Saga has already garnered a host of awards in the Western, Historical Fiction and Romance categories. Rosenthal's command of the nuances of the English language is fluent and strong. His descriptions range from the sensual and evocative to the harsh and dramatic. Rosenthal is as aware of the intricacies of his own language as the characters are of themselves...and their surroundings...conscientious and painstaking attention to details of the setting in which he portrays his wide-ranging cast."

~Lois Henderson
*Bachelor of Arts in English with Honors, Higher Education Diploma, Higher Diploma in Library and Information Science—indexer of more than one hundred thirty books; editor of dozens of theses and university and college level study manuals.*

"Just want to say how much I like this story. Johannes is a rascal, and I love rascals! Epic storytelling, detail and dialogue. Rascals! Passion! Action! Real! Keep writing the Threads West series!"

~Max McCoy
*Author of the four Indiana Jones and eighteen other novels, Screenwriter for Steven Spielberg's Into the West, Multiple National Award Winner, and Professor of Creative Writing*

"Diverse characters...highly visual prose...a journey of gathering suspense...delicious and devastating results. Rosenthal delivers!"

~Josephine Ellershaw
*Multiple #1 international bestselling author*

"Reid Lance Rosenthal outdid himself with this novel. His settings and descriptions are stunning. The weaving of the stories together and apart flows easily, creating an incredible depth of experience for the reader.... But it's Reid's people that just blew me away. (I hesitate to call them characters—that would insinuate that he made them up....) They are as real—if not more so—as most of the people I have ever met. I know Rebecca better than most people I have ever gone to school with. People I worked with for years have never solidified in my memory the way Sarah and Zeb have.... I love that—running into people I know."

"I felt a surprising sense of appreciation for the diversity of the author's people and plots. Every group—cultural, religious, racial...following Eagle Talon's journey, Israel's escape, Black Feather's tragedy, as well as the Europeans, all of whom come from even more layers of origin, makes for a rich blend of experience, perspective and understanding. Americans may have started out on a million different paths, but it's the strength, determination and perseverance that all American ancestors had in common, regardless of where they came from and how, that created your purpose. We describe our country, Canada, as a mosaic, but we see yours as more of a melting pot. There's a lot to be said for that. And Rosenthal says it beautifully."

~Alexandra Brown
www.RomanticShorts.com

Threads West
An American Saga

# Moccasin Track

# REID LANCE ROSENTHAL

*BOOK FOUR*

*Fourth novel of the Maps of Fate Era (1854–1875)*
*of the Threads West, An American Saga series*

*ROCKIN' SR PUBLISHING*
Cheyenne, Wyoming

**Moccasin Track** © 2010–2019 Writing Dream LLC
*www.threadswestseries.com*

Also available on NOOK, Kindle, iBookstore, Smashwords, Kobobooks.com, and Audible.com

Book design by TLC Graphics, *www.tlcgraphics.com*
Cover by Kelli Ann Morgan; Interior by Bob Houston eBook Formatting
Proofreading June 2019 by WordSharp Editing, *www.wordsharp.net*

Map by Caroyln Nelson
Cover painting by nationally acclaimed artist, Debbie Sampson
©iStockphoto.com/Blueberries leather
©iStockphoto.com/colevineyard leather tooling
©iStockphoto.com/belterz scrolled leather
©iStockphoto.com/billnoll
©iStockphoto.com/ranplett (parchment paper)

Printed in the United States of America

ISBN: 978-0-98215764-0-0
Library of Congress Control Number: 2019909618.

To my mother, June, who, among many gifts, passed on to me a love of, and talent for, writing. To my father, Rolf, the epitome of the Greatest Generation, who lived the American dream, embodied the American spirit and defended freedom as a sergeant in the United States Army.

To my editor, Page Lambert, who continues to remind me just how much there is to learn about the wonderful craft of prose.

To Jordan Allhands and Devani Alderson, whose unsurpassed computer and web design skills make access to this series possible for so many.

To Rebecca Jean, tireless, senior publisher's assistant and master of all trades.

To the characters—my friends and countrymen—who live in these pages.

Finally, to America, her values, history, people and the mystical energy and magical empowerment that flow from her lands.

# TABLE OF CONTENTS

Threads West
An American Saga

Book Five

PREVIEWS

An American Saga

This is the fourth novel of the Maps of Fate Era
books, (1854–1875) of the *Threads West,
An American Saga series.*

# INTRODUCTION TO THE EPIC AMERICAN SAGA, *THREADS WEST*

*Threads West, An American Saga,* is a monumental epic
series that tells *our story.* The lives of men and women of
uncommon cultures, differing origins, and competing
ambitions, woven through time and threaded into the cloth
that is our American Spirit and our Nation. *E Pluribus
Unum.* Historical events—the love, enmity, triumph and
tragedy of eleven lineages, spanning five generations and
hurtling through American history beginning with the first
book, *Threads West,* set in 1854, and arcing to the last book,
*Summits,* bringing the epic forward to the present.

The Epic Saga will consist of five series—each series
consisting of three to eight novels. Each series represents a
time frame or Era in the tale and a distinct period of
American History.

The five series of the *Threads West* Epic Saga are:

Maps Of Fate Era: 1854-1875;

North To Wyoming Era:1875-1900;

Canyons Era: 1900-1937;

Coming Thunder Era: 1937-1980;

Summits Era: 1980-2027.

Enjoy our story. Because it is *your story.*

*Threads West*
*An American Saga*

# INTRODUCTION TO
# *MOCCASIN TRACK*

## Book Four of the Maps of Fate Era Novels
### From the Epic American Saga, *Threads West*

The year is 1855. America is on the cusp of her great westward expansion and on the threshold of reluctantly becoming a world power. The lure of the vast territories and resources beyond the Mississippi explodes the population of St. Louis, gateway to the frontier, to almost one hundred thousand, an eight-fold expansion from just a decade prior.

One thousand miles to the west lie the Rocky Mountains, the lawless, untamed spine of the continent. The power of their jagged peaks beckons the vanguard of generations—the souls of a few adventurous men and women of many cultures and separate origins, to love and struggle in the beautifully vibrant but unforgiving landscape of the West. America's promise of land, freedom, self-determination and economic opportunity is now known worldwide. Immigrants from many continents exchange the lives they know for the hope and romance of a country embarked on the course of

greatness.

These immigrants drawn from the corners of the earth are unaware of the momentous changes that will shape the United States in the tumultuous years between 1854 and 1875, sweeping them into the vortexes of agony and ecstasy, victory and defeat, love lost and acquired.

The personal conflicts inherent to these brave, passion-filled characters—the point of the spear of the coming massive westward migration—are spurred by land, gold, the conquest of Mexican territory by the United States, railroads and telegraphs. Their relationships and ambitions are tempered by the fires of love and loss, hope and sorrow, life and death. Their personalities are shaped by dangerous journeys from far-off continents and then across a wild land to a wilderness where potential is the only known reality. But their lives will be forever altered by those who are yet unknown but destined to join them in the fiery forge of American Spirit upon the anvil of American History.

The epic saga of *Threads West* begins in 1854 with Book One. We meet the first of five richly textured, complex generations of unforgettable characters from America and Europe. The separate lives of these driven men and independent women are drawn to a common destiny that beckons seductively from the wild and remote flanks of the American West.

In Book Two, 1855, *Maps of Fate*, they are swept into the dangerous currents of the far-distant frontier by the mysterious rivers of fate, the power of the land and the American spirit. An elderly slave couple with faith in the passport of the Constitution, spread their wings to the winds of Freedom; the black hearted renegade leads his band of killers in acts of horror, but is about to face a possible dark redemption when he takes a young, vulnerable captive. Secret maps, hidden ambitions, diverse cultural traditions, distrust, lack of understanding and magnetic attractions shape their futures and the destinies of their lineage.

In Book Three, 1855, *Uncompahgre, where the water turns red,* the, men and women of the saga, having reached their initial destination of Cherry Creek, near what will become Denver, are faced with life-altering decisions. Some must decide to pursue or abandon torrid love affairs that have flowered on the dangerous journey from Europe and across America. Shaken by events they could not foresee and converging with souls they could never imagine, they begin to build a nation that's essence is in transition. The life threads of characters of uncommon cultures and competing ambitions meld through fate and history. The people of the Sioux Nation struggle to cope with the inevitable changes that cast shadows upon their lands, culture and sacred traditions. A family from the Oglala band of the Sioux Nation, fierce with pride, is filled with trepidation about the intent of the hairy faced ones. The elderly slave couple, and a renegade with his young, traumatized captive also introduced in *Maps of Fate,* are bound ever more tightly to the arc of the story—their tragedy and triumph-filled tales weaving into the fabric of a collective destiny. Mormons, including families with whom the *Threads West* characters have intersected in the course of their journey, stream west in the Great Exodus escaping persecution, searching for Zion, and establishing their homestead's in the Utah

Territories. Driven north by the Texas Rangers, an outlaw vaquero with royal blood quests for a new sense of self and place, embittered by the loss of his *estancia* to the Americans in the Mexican War. The black-hearted renegade is unknowingly catapulted by his tortured past into deep internal conflict, long held beliefs warring with confusing, new found empathies, the outcome of the battle within his soul unknown.

In this, the fourth, and the upcoming fifth books of the *Threads West* novels (*Moccasin Track, 1855-1856* and *Footsteps, 1857-1861*), new *Threads West* characters are born of the brave men and courageous women who have come so far and risked all. The budding enmity between North and South flares into the winds of war, and the remote fringe of the frontier is destined to descend into virtual anarchy as most of the meager army troops are withdrawn to the east.

On the Front Range of the Rockies, Cherry Creek will be renamed Montana City, then Denver City and finally Denver, as the city booms with the effect of gold discoveries in the Pikes Peak area and the Ouray, San Juan and Uncompahgre Mountain Ranges. The first newspapers in the West roll off the presses in Leavenworth and Lawrence, Kansas, and Platte Valley, Nebraska. A young man, drugged then kidnapped in his Chinese homeland, is forced into labor on the railroad but his determination to escape remains undaunted. The Sioux Nation will grapple with the terrifying realization that they cannot compromise with the disdainful and greedy hairy faced ones, and the Sioux warrior may be ordered by the tribal Council to make the dangerous journey into the lands of the enemy Utes to learn more of the hairy faced ones from those with whom he has bonded. The Ute Chief, in the throes of personal tragedies, will determine peace and sacrifice are the only roads to survival.

A massive, unfeeling tide washes over the ancient traditions and lands essential to the existence of both tribes. The renegade learns the meaning of sacrifice in a final desperate attempt to compensate for his acts – and failures to act – decades prior. The elderly black couple find home and family they were sure had ceased to exist. A military heart finds the full circle of its destiny and a love he thought forever lost.

Momentous changes continue in Books Six, Seven, and Eight (*Blood at Glorietta Pass, The Bond,* and *Cache Valley*), igniting further greed and compassion, courage and treachery, rugged independence, torrid passions, and fierce loyalties. The Civil War erupts, and the fires of deadly tumult sweep west. A young Irishman, Gulf Coast fisherman by trade, unsure of the course but eager for the pay dons a grayunfirom. A Confederate Army mustered in Texas, and the newly formed Denver Militia, neither aware of the existence of the other, are mutually surprised when their forward columns collide with one another at Glorieta Pass, North of Santa Fe, in one of the least known but critically important battles of the Civil War, known there after as "The Gettysburg of the West." The Mormon family contends with the demands of the church and surprise visitors from the past while creating a legacy in the Cache and Salt Lake Valleys, the fate of their lineage to be dramatically affected by those they have met long before.

A tidal wave of hopeful souls, some displaced by the

devastation of the Civil War, add to the torrent of humanity flowing west following the trail of the strong men and women of *Uncompahgre*. The meeting of the tracks of the Union Pacific Railroad from the east and Central Pacific from the west in 1869, underpin the rise of the robber-barons, cattle empires and commerce, drawing hundreds of thousands to the Rockies and beyond.

The first *Threads West* generation born in the remote and sparsely settled west, and introduced in *Moccasin Track,* begins to mature and contend with this cauldron of events, their lives unsettled by personal tragedies, triumphs, love and loss, their individual personalities irreconcilably opposite. Colorado, Wyoming, Utah and Montana evolve into separate and distinct territories and then achieve statehood. Law and order struggles as outlaws linger on the outer edges and range wars erupt between the landowners and the landless, sheepherders, cattlemen and sodbusters. The clash of cultures, creeds and beliefs, and bitter rivalries over the control of scarce water resources, fuels further violence and cruelty.

Railroads and telegraphs pierce even this wild land. The broken treaties with Native Americans spread into bitter and contagious conflict throughout the West. The "resolution" of the "Indian problem" leaves families and hearts broken, a dark stain on the pages of American history, and the foreboding visions of the Sioux in Book Two, *Maps of Fate,* sadly fulfilled.

You will recognize the characters who live in these pages. These brave, passion-filled men and women face conflicts exacerbated by a country in transition and the accelerating melting pot of diverse cultures that mark this magical moment in American history. They are the ancestors of your neighbors, your family, your co-workers, their lives the woven threads of men and women from different locations, conflicting values, disparate backgrounds, faiths and beliefs. Forged on the anvil of the land, they are bound by the commonality of the American spirit into the tapestry that is our nation.

These decades of *Maps of Fate* Era novels of the *Threads West, An American Saga* series become the crucible of the American Spirit, forever affecting the souls of generations, the building of the heart of the nation, destiny of a people and the relentless energy and beauty of the western landscape.

**The adventure and romance of America, her people, her spirit and the West.**

*Threads West, An American Saga.* This is *our* story.

*www.threadswestseries.com*

An American Saga

*Threads West*

# THOUGHTS FROM REID
# ABOUT BOOK FOUR

I AM OFTEN ASKED WHY I HAVE "TIGHTENED THE CINCH" on this immense story of America set in the West. True, I love to write, and yes, I am vested in these characters. Their personalities are compilations of people both you and I have met. Each carries a part of me. They are my friends. You are about to continue the journey within *Moccasin Track*. They have obviously become your friends too, which pleases me!

I am infatuated with America's people—the hands, hearts, feelings, origins, personalities and spirit that built the United States, but my enthusiasm is also fueled by my love of country, liberty and my bond with the land. I have always believed that a nation's essential elements are its people and its lands, and the common spirit that unites us all and binds us to all things natural. It is the interaction with, and between, each that determines the direction and, eventually, the destination of society—its freedom, values and exceptional qualities. The trail behind leads to the path ahead.

I am delighted and humbled that this epic saga is being avidly devoured by readers from ages thirteen to ninety-six, with readership almost evenly split between male and female book lovers. I am told this is highly unusual. Perhaps it is due in part to the affinity readers develop for the unique, distinctive personalities of the men and women who live in these pages—some brave, others cowardly, all independent, the vicious offset by the kind, conflicted yet resolute, laced with fears yet persevering. All are passionate, though the passions of some are infused with bitter thoughts and dark actions. Perhaps many of you turn these pages because you feel as I do—the touchstones of the past are the guideposts to the future. *Moccasin Track* is the continuation of this tale of America, her people and the West—new lineages and the first generation of Threads West characters' offspring join the many threads of uncommon cultures, differing origins and competing ambitions that entwine into the American spirit; lives and generations woven on the loom of history, propelled by fate and freedom to form the tapestry that becomes the whole cloth of the nation. It is uniquely American, this meld of the mosaic.

My life has been spent on the lands of the West. I am fortunate to have felt the ancient energies of sun-warmed canyons. My soul has heard the whispers of Spirit carried on mountain breezes that once caressed the leathery, bronzed skin of ancestors. Logs hewn by hands long before our time have shared their energy of history, hope and courage of years long past. I'm compelled and honored to tell this tale—driven to capture the visual and memorialize the singular passions of our individual paths merging to form the shared trail of our American spirit.

I am gratified your eyes see these words and your fingers touch and linger on these pages. I hope your American soul

is as touched by the reading as mine was by the writing. Feel the spirit. Think of the history. Remember the struggles. Be proud—we are all Americans and together, we comprise America. This is our story. Thank you for reading *Moccasin Track*, Book Four of the Threads West, An American Saga, the epic saga of us.

AUTHOR

*An American Saga*

# PRELUDE

To the great readers of the *Threads West* epic saga:

The following 52 pages, xxx - lxxxi are known as front matter in the book world. In *Moccasin Track,* they consist of three primary components:

1) The *Threads West* saga maps are presented by popular demand—first time ever. Enjoy!

2) The men and women of the *Threads West* epic saga provides an in-depth listing of all the major and secondary characters for books one, two and three. Listed alphabetically by first name in both major and secondary character categories by book for easy reference, their physical characteristics, dress, backstory, personality traits and motivations are the essence of the character studies.

3) The arc of the tale runs the gamut of most major actions, events, passionate rendezvous, tragedies, triumphs, geographical movements and plot points from the first page of book one to the final page of book three. Almost fifteen hundred pages of number one bestselling, award-winning novels boiled down to a

quick, enjoyable overview in 29 pages!

Presently, our readers are in one of four camps along this epic trail: those who have not yet started the *Threads West* saga but will!; those who are currently immersed in turning the pages of this story of us in book one, two or three; those who have read all three books and have neither the time nor inclination to read the first three again to prepare for number four (though many of our readers turn the pages of the series two or three times gaining better understanding, detail, nuance and foreshadowing with each reading); and finally, those readers who have recently completed or are about to complete their delighted devouring of the first three novels.

The *Threads West* story is a vast tale—because it *is* our story. The tale of America and Americans of uncommon cultures, divergent origins and competing ambitions has always been, and continues to be, epic.

The maps will bring a smile to all. However, neither the character listing nor the arc of the tale needs to be read to enjoy book four. Whether a reader chooses to read one or both is an individual choice. However, we strongly recommend that if you have not finished the first three books, you do not read *any* of the following 52 pages. They are rife with spoilers that could undermine your enjoyment of the unfolding intricacies and surprises of *our* story.

Likewise, those readers who have recently finished the first three books, the characters and plot relatively fresh in their minds, might enjoy the character listing as a refresher and reference and skip the arc of the tale.

Finally, there are those readers who reached the back cover of book three some time ago, and though anxious to begin book four, would likely find both the character studies and the arc considerably helpful in getting immediately back in the saddle of the *Threads West* saga.

Whatever your choice—enjoy!

*An American Saga*

# The Men and Women of the Threads West Epic Saga

*Listed alphabetically by novel*

Book One, *Threads West, An American Saga—The Vanguard of Generations*

## MAJOR CHARACTERS

**Inga Bjorne**—There are few men who are not arrested by the intensity of Inga Bjorne's pale blue eyes. Tall, beautiful, curvy and athletic with long blonde hair, her life has been contentious. She suffered the painful loss of her Norwegian parents when she was eleven. That trauma was exacerbated by a lazy, alcoholic uncle who dragged her to New York. When she was thirteen, his final abuse afforded her the courage to escape from his perverse control. For seven years, she has done what she must to survive in the bustling diversity of squalor and luxury that characterized mid-1800s New York City. The timely application of her charm, looks and wit is finally about to land her a comfortable job with the mayor of New York, Ferdinando Wood, on his house staff at Gracie Mansion. Unknown to Inga, that stroke of fortune will tip the next domino in her life and will shake the foundation of her experiences and her caustic view of men.

**Jacob O'Shanahan**—Feisty, stocky, cunning and violent, Jacob grew up in the grimy streets of Dublin, Ireland, living hand to mouth, his focus only on the egocentric satisfaction of the day at hand and backroom poker, which is the mainstay of his livelihood. His quick temper and greed are about to thrust him over the precipice of a major life alteration. The coarse fabric of his existence intertwines with the threads of others in a quirk of dark, unknown destiny that neither he nor they can contemplate or prevent.

**Johannes Svenson**—Both irreverent and charming, his military service in the Danish Heavy Cavalry as a decorated officer instilled in him a quiet but mischievous worldly confidence. Tall, lean, blond, roguish, adventurous, restless, he and his Don Juan life are adrift. Johannes, in his search to find himself, is about to be swept by the mysterious rivers of destiny into the unknown currents of an unanticipated romance and a far distant frontier.

**Rebecca Marx**—A dark-haired beauty with ravenous eyes and a figure that turns heads, Rebecca is petulant, clever, demanding, spoiled and reluctant to give up her creature comforts and stature in English high society. Prior to her father's death, she shrewdly assisted him for years in the family trade. She finds the decline of the business her grandfather founded demeaning. Her last hope is a mysterious family asset rumored to be of great value somewhere in rugged, unsettled land across the Atlantic

thousands of miles to the west. She has only a map, her father's deathbed whispers and his bequeath of a far distantSpanish land grant as guides. She leaves her mother Elizabeth, frail and elderly, to sail to America and the thread of another life begins to spool toward an unknown future.

**Reuben Frank**—Lives and helps operate the family cattle farm with his wise but ailing father, Ludwig, and brothers Erik, Helmon and Isaac. For twenty-one years, he has led a sheltered existence on the outskirts of the little town of Villmar, on the serpentine banks of the Lahn River in eastern Prussia. Though of medium build, his frame is toughened from working cattle and the farm. His agile mind, good business sense and quiet strength have not gone unnoticed by his father, whose health has been in decline since the death of Reuben's mother several years prior. Though the family has prospered, the expansion and perpetuation of their livestock operation is confined by lack of land and the rigid social structure of 1800s Europe. The heritage of Reuben's family and the future of their cattle business are about to be placed in his hands. His ability to rise to the enormous responsibly in an untamed land he has never seen and a county not yet his, is unknown, even to him.

**Sarah Bonney**—Youngest daughter of Richard and Nancy, Sarah is a curvy, petite young woman with lustrous blue eyes, flowing red hair and a determined dream. Following the death of her mother the Old World holds little promise. The glowing letters from her Aunt Stella in New York, an ambition and wonder that can be satiated only by exploration, and a strange pull that flows from the unknown continent across the sea, is about to collide with the realities of life, and personalities more jaded, far more cunning and infinitely less innocent than hers. Sarah has made her choice, but will it prove to be the right one?

Zebarriah Taylor—Weathered, wiry and wily in the ways of the wilderness, this tall, thin loner seeks the solitude of quaking aspens, sun-drenched canyons, gurgles of rushing high country creeks and the still waters of beaver ponds that supply him with pelts for trade. Zeb is not partial to people, intensely dislikes settlements and towns, and distrusts most who share his skin color. He is plagued by a tragic past— orphaned as a teenager by a renegade band led by the notorious vicious killer, Black Feather. Trying desperately to forget, he succumbs to the call of the West, living for a time with an Oglala Sioux tribe learning the survival ways of the wild. His few friends are members of the Arapahoe and Shawnee tribes with whom he trades. Unknown to him, his tough and leathery path will inexplicably intersect with the life journeys of others, resulting in generational influences far more broad and long-term than his lone wolf nature can foresee.

## BOOK ONE—SECONDARY CHARACTERS

Adam—Freed Aborigine slave, now voluntary servant with his wife and daughter to Rebecca and Elizabeth, Adam possesses a strange and powerful ability to sense the future but how accurate will his predictions be?

**Aunt Stella**— sister of Sarah's mother, Nancy, is plump, matronly, fussy and naïve. She has promised Sarah a job in her New York seamstress shop.

**Elizabeth** —Rebecca's frail and failing mother distraught over the death of her husband, Henry, terrified by and opposed to Rebecca's journey to America to try to rescue the floundering family finances.

**Emily, Nancy and Richard Bonney**—Sarah's sister and beloved, deceased parents. Emily, the co-owner of their seamstress shop in Liverpool, is heartbroken and concerned with Sarah's departure for America.

**Erik**—The youngest of Reuben's four brothers and Reuben's closest sibling, he is emotional, a thinker and a student of music and the arts. Soft-spoken, slight of build, scholarly and thickly bespectacled, he is greatly influenced by their father, Ludwig, and his respect and admiration for Reuben.

**Ludwig Frank**—Patriarch of the Frank family and Reuben Frank's father. Deep-set brown eyes, hardworking, wise and devoutly Jewish, he built a highly respected cattle enterprise in eastern Prussia but is convinced America is the future.

**Uncle Hermann**—Reuben's uncle, Hermann left the farm and joined the Prussian army when he was twenty-two. After being wounded, decorated and discharged, he immigrated to America with his wife, corresponding with his brother Ludwig often—eventually hiring a scout to search and map the perfect location for a cattle ranch in the West. With wavy, salt and pepper gray hair, and of medium build, he struggles with a noticeable limp—a lingering badge of his former service. After his wife's death, he has lived alone outside of New York City with his servant, Mae, a kind, heavyset Negro woman.

*An American Saga*

**Threads West**

Book Two, *Maps of Fate*—New Characters Weave
into This Story of *Us*

## MAJOR CHARACTERS

**Black Feather**—Bitter, aggressive killer with a band of like-minded followers and renegades, with a tall, angular frame, swarthy features and a thin white scar above his lips, his reddish bronzed features are framed by an explosion of long, dirty brown hair. Originally named Samuel Ray-sun Harrison, Black Feather grew up on the family farm. His father, Jonathan Harrison—white, older and lanky with graying hair—traded with the Osage Indians using milk, eggs and vegetables from his Missouri garden as barter. Black Feather's mother, Sunray, was a full-blood Osage, statuesque and beautiful. Her athletic body was proportioned perfectly with a thin waist flared to hips made for childbearing. Her perfect white teeth were always displayed in a broad and friendly smile that complimented her wide, acorn-brown eyes. Young Samuel loved her deeply. His parents, and their faithful, gentle, old horse, Dot, were brutally killed by outlaws when he was twelve years old. Set on revenge, he tracked down the killers, taking two black feathers from their dying leader's hat and adorning his hair with those symbols of revenge from that moment forward. Haunted by a tortured past, he finds himself confused by the empathy he feels for the young, traumatized woman-child he captures.

**Dorothy**—Black Feather's early teen woman-child captive taken from an ambushed wagon train. A thin, blonde girl, Dorothy is traumatized and muted by the stress of her abduction and the unexpected violence that has shattered her life. Whether she emerges from her emotional shell depends on circumstances neither she nor Black Feather can foresee.

**Eagle Talon**—A rising young brave, leader of the younger warriors of his small, adopted Oglala Sioux tribe. The only son of war chief, Two Bears of the Northern People, he marries the daughter of the shaman, Tracks On Rock, and moves to her clan's village as tradition demands. Eagle Talon is an expert hunter and intuitive statesman, but brash. Rigidly athletic, graceful and proud, he wears eight eagle feathers in his long black hair and an ornate shield painted with the claw of a raptor fastened high on one arm, its rounded top slightly higher than his shoulder. Is he wrong to ignore the premonitions permeating his soul or doubt the visions of Talks With Shadows?

**Israel and Lucy Thomas**—Married for twenty-four years, these elderly slaves have opposite but complimentary personalities. Israel's curly hair has turned salt and pepper. He wears thick, brass-framed spectacles. Taught to read by Mistress Tara, daughter of an Oklahoma plantation owner, he has studied the Constitution and Declaration of

Independence through smuggled newspapers. As he learns of the rapidly evolving dispute over slavery, he harbors the dream of escaping west to freedom via the Underground Railroad but first he must overcome Lucy's stubborn temerity and resistance to change. Her rounded figure and worn features also speak of advancing age. Her wide-set brown eyes and high cheekbones are framed by brittle, graycurls of hair escaping the edges of a tight wrapped bandana.

**Mac (Macintyre)**—The short, wide-shouldered Irish wagon master. His full, light red beard and mop of dark red hair correctly foretell a joviality mixed with a quick temper and experienced, iron leadership. Trail wise, time toughened, many hopes depend on his skills and shrewd, steady hand.

**Walks with Moon**—Daughter of Two Bears and wife to Eagle Talon, she and her husband share love and respect. Intuitive, passionate, protective and filled with a strong foreboding about the influx of white men into Sioux lands, she is now pregnant with their first child. One friend, Talks With Shadows, has shared a frightening vision—but will this turn out to be just another silly rambling?

## Book 2—SECONDARY CHARACTERS

**Elijah and Saley**—Kentucky pioneer family, consisting of husband Elijah, sallow-faced wife, Saley and four children. Their oldest son thirteen-year-old Abraham is a crack shot and has been responsible for putting food on the table since the age of five. Two mules pull their modified prairie schooner westward. Along with Zebbariah Taylor, Elijah and his son are key hunters for fresh meat for the wagon train.

**Flying Arrow**—War chief of the Oglala Sioux village. Elderly, gray haired, still broad-shouldered but having lost the sculptured muscle of youth, he carries a long, thick staff with a heavy wooden burl at its head that has counted many coup.

**John**—Formerly a wrangler in Mac's wagon train, he was seriously wounded in the encounter with Black Feather's renegades and left in the care of doctors at Fort Kearney. Tall, neatly trimmed, brown hair and mustache that curved above his lips and ended have way to his chin.

**Joseph**—Devout young Mormon, son of Charles and heir to a future designation as an Elder, this sincere and friendly man has an unusually long pointed nose and thin face. He, his equally religious wife and their toddler son are part of a Mormon wagon train on the Exodus along to Zion in Cache Valley, north of the Salt Lake basin.

**Margaret and Harris Johnson**—A kind looking couple with ruddy faces, thick-set builds and a keen sense of American pride. Third generation Virginians, their lineage traces back to the 1600s. They proudly fly a several-foot-wide American flag, an old Betsy Ross banner sporting a a circle of thirteen stars on a field of blue, from a knotty-barked pole lashed to the side of their wagon. Margaret is handy with a musket and a mother hen to their two children, Becky and Eleanor.

**Snake**—A seedy, snarling member of Black Feather's band, he deviously sows the seeds of insurrection. His thin, wiry frame is perpetually covered in a dirty, heavy cotton pullover shirt hanging uneven and tattered below the tops of his leather loincloth. A sweat-stained leather headband with a single row of beads above dark brown, almost black eyes, keeps his long unkempt strings of hair swept behind his shoulders.

**Talks With Shadows, Pony Hoof, Deer Tracks, and Turtle Dove**—Young wives of the braves, the best friends of Walks With Moon. Though the butt of humor and doubt, Talks With Shadows may possess the *puah.*

**Tex**—A demented farmer member of Black Feather's band but with more loyalty to Snake, he is stocky, bald, cruel, round-faced with a scar on his neck. He delights in the knife and victims not yet dead.

**Tracks On Rock and wife, Tree Dove**—Wise, highly skilled medicine man of the Oglala Sioux. His wife Tree Dove, her handsome beauty marred by smallpox, is a strong soul who often gives him counsel.

**Turtle Shield, Pointed Lance, Brave Pony, Three Knives and Three Cougars**—The band of young braves of the Oglala, they are close friends with Eagle Talon.

*An American Saga*

**Threads West**

Book Three, *Uncompahgre, where water turns rock red*—The Characters You Have Come to Love and Others, Key to the American Tapestry being woven, about to Catapult into the Tale

# MAJOR CHARACTERS

**Black Mare**—Of Ute descent, she is shorter, perhaps five foot, two inches, but radiates a quiet friendly power, loving and respecting her husband, Ouray with a deep reverence, her primary goals his happiness and giving him a son. She often wears a one-piece, loose fitted, lightly tanned, leather dress, its embroidery descending from her shoulders in the shape of a "V", its bottom and sleeves heavily fringed. Her willowy build has distinctive womanly curves, her eyes large, brown and set wide in an angular face framed by long, smooth jet-black hair, carefully brushed and parted in the middle, braided on one side tapering to the bodice of her leather dress.

**Chipeta**—Of Apache descent, she is short, not much over five feet and young, just sixteen winters. She prefers a one-piece, loose fitting, leather dress, long fringe hanging from the sleeves and tapers on the lower portion. Her black hair, parted in the middle, swings about her shoulders when she

laughs, as she does often, shyly covering her mouth with her hands. The young woman is devoted to Ouray and his wife and inseparable from her mentor, Black Mare.

**Erik**—The youngest of Reuben's four brothers introduced in Book One and Reuben's closest sibling, he is emotional, a thinker and a student of music and the arts. Soft-spoken, slight of build, scholarly, and thickly bespectacled, Erik is greatly influenced by their father, Ludwig, and his respect and admiration for Reuben. Prussia has lost its appeal and now America and Erik's bond with his brother, Rueben, beckon ever more strongly.

**Joseph**—Introduced in Book Two as a devout young Mormon, son of Charles and heir to a future designation as an Elder, this sincere and friendly man has a remarkably long pointed nose and thin face. He, his equally religious wife, Roberta, and their toddler son are part of a Mormon wagon train on the Exodus along to Zion in the Northern edge of Cache Valley, north of the Salt Lake basin. Little do they know their brief, chance meeting with Mac's wagon train in Book Two will have fateful consequences that transcend generations.

**Ouray**—Son of Chief Guera Murah who, though raised Apache, was Chief of the Mountain Ute until his death in 1861. Raised in Taos, Ouray is conversant in a mixture of English, Spanish and Ute. He is stocky, ruggedly handsome, about five foot, nine inches tall, with broad muscular shoulders and commands a on air of authority. His leggings are usually of loose, dark leather, fringed heavily on the outer legs, intricate bead patterns approximately three inches wide running from the waist down to equally wide double bands of beads at the cuffs. His lighter leather shirt is likewise heavily fringed at the waist, shoulders and sleeves, an extra layer of leather sewn over each shoulder adorned with dark-colored bead patterns. His face was round with wide-set eyes set above a nose with well-defined nostrils, and high cheekbones balancing well with his rounded chin and lips, his upper lip slightly thicker than his lower. His long, jet-black hair is parted low on one side and tied in tight braids that hang either side of his chest almost to his belt.

**Philippe Reyes**—First generation Mexican of aristocratic French and Spanish descent. His good manners and disarming charm mask a hard, conflicted nature and extraordinary prowess with his brace of onyx-handled Colts. His mother and father lost most of their vast estancia in the Texas Revolt. Bitter over his family's plight, Philippe stirs trouble in Texas and is disowned by his parents. Enraged, he becomes notorious for cross-border rustling and is eventually chased north by the Texas Rangers. Though gregarious when necessary, Philippe is quiet, tough and dangerous, preferring to keep to himself. Thin, wiry, tough, strait backed, with a square jawed, handsome, finely chiseled face, an aristocratic well-spoken air, and unflinching, quick, brown eyes. He is magnetic as a cobra, which draws women to him with little protest from Phillippe. But, he is about to encounter a life surprise of the heart that will manifest both tragically and triumphantly through the course of four generations.

**Randy**—Wagon master Macintyre's brother, Randy, a resident of Cherry Creek and a shrewd trader. Randy and Mac weren't twins; Mac was a year older but there was no mistaking them as brothers. Built the same—short, wide, powerful and red haired and bearded—they had identical accents and startlingly similar mannerisms, including an Irish brogue. Fresh from Ireland in the early 1840s, the brothers were searching for adventure, opportunity and a place where being Catholic didn't matter. They began as traders and teamsters. Then, in 1844, they started the ramshackle Gart's Trading Company and Mercantile in Cherry Creek

**Snake**—A former member of Black Feather's renegade band introduced in Book Two, he is now the brutal leader of his own following of violent outlaws. Seedy, swarthy and snarling he deviously sows the seeds of insurrection amongst the renegades. His slightly statured, thin, wiry frame is perpetually covered in a dirty, heavy cotton pullover shirt hanging uneven and tattered below the tops of his leather loincloth. The slits of his dark brown, almost black, eyes never show pity or any emotion other than anger and amoral contempt. A sweat-stained leather headband with a single row of beads above dark brown, almost black eyes, keeps his long unkempt strings of hair swept behind his shoulders. Dark hearted and without compassion, he is commanding in a manipulative way, and cocky, but by no means courageous. A killer with no remorse.

# Book 3—SECONDARY CHARACTERS

**Bill Dawson**—A big cattle rancher with a sprawling spread north of the New Mexico Territories and south of the tiny settlement of Pueblo, five days ride south of Cherry Creek. Silver-white hair drapes Dawson's broad and still powerful shoulders. His eyes are slightly squinted by habit against the sun, and set wide within the frame of his darkly tanned, weathered and wrinkled face. He is fair and friendly but drives a hard bargain.

**Floyd Bummer and Gang**—Outlaws known for causing trouble in Cherry Creek. Two of his men were heavyset, one quite tall and very thin. Floyd was of medium build, the brains of the mostly two bit, but still dangerous outlaw, fierce, unrelenting and over sure of his own skills and smarts. All carried pistols in their belts except Floyd who wore his holstered. They dressed alike, dirty, torn cotton shirts of varying faded colors, their clothing looking like it had long ago outlived its originally planned lifespan.

**Goose**—An Arapahoe woman shunned by her tribe when she takes up briefly with Phillippe. Very heavy, with a round, pudgy, deep copper face, her jet-black hair hangs in greasy strings around her shoulders, to which clung a dirt-smudged, grease stained, leather pullover dress, which fit tightly to her ample form, the sagging layers of flesh squeezed into the doeskin imparting skin-filled folds to the material. Good with a knife and possessive of Phillippe, she creates quite the scene when Phillippe leaves her, without a goodbye, to ride with Reuben, Johannes and Michael.

**Johnson**—The lanky Texan with a slow, careful Texas drawl who has been with Black Feather almost as long as Pedro sharing with Black Feather the secret of golden loot just the two of them had years ago buried downstream on the Yampa. Steadfast, loyal to Black Feather, and respectful of Dot, he becomes the new second in command in Black Feather's remaining thirteen-strong band of outlaws.

**Michael Sampson**—A heavy set, sixteen year, with rounded face, sloped shoulders, frightened eyes, and a severe stutter, emotional injuries suffered at the hands of a drunken, bully father. But he knows cattle and can wrestle a steer to the ground by his lonesome. The big, heavy youth sits his saddle comfortably when riding, his sloping shoulders hunched slightly over his heavy torso, his upper body rolling with the gait of his older sorrel horse. He wears a dirty, brown wool vest over a graywool shirt. He had a .44 Colt Army revolver tucked in his pants. "*Too far towards the hip,*" Reuben had observed, "*in no position to be played quickly.*"

## The Heroic Horses of the *Threads West Saga*

**Bente**—Johannes mount. A big, bay mare that stood almost seventeen hands. She suited Johannes' height well. Her stride was just a tad clumsy, but she had powerful shoulders and haunches and was steady and fast when not loafing, her long, thoroughbred-like legs chewing up the miles. Just a little bit spooky, the mare had a habit of flipping her bay head back, perking her dark-tipped ears and whinnying.

**Buck**—The sleek, but powerfully muscled, mottled brown and white tobiano mustang, best friend, confidante and trusted companion of Zeb. Trail smart, savvy, unflappable, surefooted with more common sense then most humans. He and Zeb shared almost telepathic connection, Bucks fluid gait was typically without any obvious commands, and he often served on lookout on Zeb's back track.

**Diablo**—A overo-mustang cross, almost 17 hands high and jet black, bred by Phillippe, with the speed and long legs of a racing horse and the stamina and smarts of a wild pony. Phillippe is convinced that Diablo is faster than any horse in the territories, a notion disputed by Zeb and Buck.

**Dot's Horse**— A short, but well-built bay mare, originally Gonzalez's steed until one of the bullets from Reuben's Pearl Handed Colt ended the outlaw's life. Slow, steady, without personality but reliable the mare is a perfect match for the catatonic young girl-woman.

**Lahn**—Big, blonde, palomino, powerful and fast. Reuben's horse, and often his master's sounding board, named for the river which flowed lazily past the cattle farm back in Prussia. The gelding was not shy about snorting, shaking his head, and stomping a quarter circle dance when annoyed or startled, but has speed, heart and a love of adventure.

**Red**—Mac, then Rebecca's mount. An excitable and impatient, 15 hand high, stocky, red sorrel with an attitude. Easily excited, but fearless, Red was known for head shakes and sideway prances, a perfect match for Rebecca, who was

gifted the Spirited mare by Randy after Mac's murder on the journey west.

**Sally**—Israel and Lucy's wise grey, stocky mule, its advanced years clearly evident by its light grey, almost white muzzle. Sally had the habit, when perplexed or perhaps amused at her human companions of flicking one ear forward, one ear back and blowing through her lips.

**The Black**—black stallion, 17+ hands high, thick muscled, broad shouldered with massive haunches. He answers only to Black Feather, their renegade hearts in sync. Impatient, eager to be always on the move, The Black is a study of consent motion, not shy of showing his displeasure to sudden loud sounds or delay with pawing deep, deep whinnies and rears to his side.

*An American Saga*

# The Unfolding Saga of *Threads West* – The Arc of the Tale, Books One, Two and Three

You will recognize the characters who live in these pages. They are you. They are us. This is not only their story; it is *our* story. This is *Threads West, An American Saga*.

## BOOK ONE— *THREADS WEST*
## THE BIRTH OF THE SAGA

At the outset, none of these characters know of the others— their lives are separate, their desires unique. All are from disparate origins with conflicting aspirations. Yet, they are seduced and compelled to a common destiny that beckons from the wild and remote flanks of the American West. In January of 1855, the lives of Rebecca, Jacob, Sarah, Reuben and Johannes intertwine during the maiden voyage of the SS *Edinburgh* as it streams from Portsmouth Harbor across the Atlantic toward New York.

Seven months prior, Zebarriah Taylor, the reclusive mountain man who learned his skills from the Sioux, strikes out from his cabin in the Red Mountains of the

Uncompahgre with his tobiano paint horse Buck and three mules to Cherry Creek to peddle his pelts and buy supplies. In May of 1854, the speck of a settlement could only boast a few buildings, three hundred white men, and twelve hundred Arapaho, all living in tents and tipis.

In Cherry Creek, Zeb runs into his old friend, Jim Bridger. He warns Zeb of the low prices of beaver pelts and suggests better prices could be fetched in far-off St. Louis, a thousand miles to the east. Zeb determines to strike east.

As Zeb and Buck make the wild, lonely journey to St. Louis, Inga—who emigrated from Norway under difficult circumstances as a young girl years prior—maintains a respectable façade as a waitress in a posh Manhattan pub, fertile prospecting grounds for her second, more sordid and secret, avocation. One of her clients, a portly banker from St. Louis, claims to know the mayor of New York. Inga is skeptical until, to her dismay, an invitation to serve on the mayor's staff at Gracie Mansion is delivered by the mayor's courier. Inga eagerly accepts.

Aboard the *Edinburgh*, Reuben's immediate attraction to Rebecca is rebuffed with contempt by the brown-eyed beauty. The Prussian is only partially aware of Sarah's intense attraction to him. Yet, Jacob sets his lecherous eyes on the redhead, planning to take her by force if need be. Johannes and Reuben become friends, their opposite natures and differing skills complementing one another. But Johannes keeps his military background close to the vest.

The Europeans disembark on the shores of America in New York Harbor, each going their individual ways, unaware that their lives will interweave again. Reuben and Johannes visit Uncle Hermann, who reviews the maps drawn by scouts he and Reuben's father hired, informs Reuben that a third map was never delivered and stresses to his nephew the danger, and importance of the journey to the family. Uncle Hermann gifts Reuben a .52 caliber Sharps rifle. He directs them down to the mercantile where his longtime friend and sergeant in the Prussian army, Wallace, helps Johannes select a saber, a .52 caliber Sharps carbine, a .44 caliber Army Colt revolver and a campaign hat. Reuben selects a cowboy hat, and, despite Wallace's warnings, is drawn to a pearl-handled .36 caliber Navy squareback Colt pistol that glows seductively in the gaslight.

Mayor Wood, a friend of Rebecca's father before his death, extends an invitation to Rebecca to stay at Gracie Mansion while she decides best how to handle the disposition of the lands fifteen hundred miles to the west depicted on the maps attached to her father's will, and the rescue of her family fortunes. There, Inga and Rebecca meet, become friends and share the secrets of young women. Playing on the mayor's undeniable attraction to her, Rebecca beguiles Ferdinand into giving Inga a leave of absence, and the Scandinavian beauty eagerly accepts Rebecca's invitation to accompany her west, likely just to St. Louis, as Rebecca has no wish to go farther west into the unsettled territories with ruffian Americans.

The journey to St. Louis is long, mostly by rail. Reuben and Johannes are as startled as Inga and Rebecca when they find themselves on the same Pennsylvania Railway train hurtling west. The attraction between Rebecca and Reuben flares but then is purposely and brusquely suppressed by

Rebecca. However, Inga and Johannes fall deeply in love, consummated by passionate encounters.

To her consternation, Sarah finds that Aunt Stella's business has declined due to the impending strife between the North and the South and other economic worries in New York. There is no position for her, after all. Jacob carouses the bars and taverns in search of poker games. In one bar, with inebriated carelessness, another player named Micky flashes a map of a location far to the west ostensibly depicting hidden gold. Jacob follows Micky from the poker game and, in a dark alley, his boot knife finds the hapless man's ribs. With the bloodstained map in his possession, Jacob sets his sights on Sarah Bonney. Knowing the address of Aunt Stella's shop, he puts on his best airs and false front, stealing flowers from a street vendor, fooling Aunt Stella completely, and overcoming Sarah's instinctive concerns when he suggests she accompany him west. He glibly assures her they will travel in separate compartments, and his offer is meant only to assist her in her travels and possibly the setup of a sewing shop in St. Louis.

The train on which Sarah and Jacob embark is just several days behind that of Reuben, Rebecca, Inga and Johannes. As the cars lurch forward amidst bellows of steam, a panic-stricken Sarah is confronted with Jacob's true intentions. He brutally rapes her, escapes her attempt to kill him in retribution, and continues to rape and abuse her for the duration of the journey, holding over her head a now tarnished reputation and a threat of murder if she says a word.

In St. Louis, Reuben learns that Rebecca has decided to

travel to Cherry Creek to be closer to her lands and their disposition. Aware of Rebecca's penchant to deploy her stunning good looks and formidable charm to her manipulative advantage, Reuben coldly agrees to allow the women to accompany them, but in a purchased wagon of their own.

Reuben and Johannes head down to the docks on the east bank of the Mississippi where they meet Mac, a bull of a red-bearded Irishman, and wagon master well known for his experience and no-nonsense expertise in shepherding wagon trains to Cherry Creek, then returning with wagon loads of pelts and other western goods for sale to points farther east. With his brother Randy, he owns the little settlement's only mercantile, which Randy manages. The three men have an instant rapport.

While returning to their hotel on 4th Street, Reuben notices tall, lanky Zebarriah Taylor rolling a smoke not far from Mac's Livery, his lithe form leaning comfortably against a support post, his fringed buckskin attire showing the wear of many years on the trail. Innately trusting the trapper and confident in the mountain man's skills and experience, Reuben offers him a position. Zeb is initially adverse, but when he learns that Reuben's destination is the Red Mountains and the Uncompahgre, he agrees without disclosing those mountains are his home.

Book One ends on the precipice of an arduous journey into the unknown—the wagon train mustering on the west side of the Mississippi, barges ferrying rigs, teams of braying mules and oxen, whinnying horses and the stalwart souls looking west to their future; unforgettable, driven men and

women drawn to a common destiny that beckons from the wild, mysterious and lawless flanks of the American frontier. The story of us continues in Book Two, *Maps of Fate.*

An American Saga

# BOOK TWO—*MAPS OF FATE*
## THE EVOLUTION OF THE SAGA

In Book Two, the secrets of the maps are partially revealed, hidden conflicts emerge, magnetic attractions ebb and flow, tragedies strike and destinies are shaped. New characters weave into the tapestry of America and the West.

Book One ends and Book Two begins on March 18, 1855. As Mac shouts the command to move west and teams strain against the traces of the wagons, eight hundred miles west, on the South Fork of the Powder River, a Sioux family, fierce with pride and steeped in tradition, enters the tale. Southwest of St. Louis, an elderly slave couple on an Oklahoma plantation set their wings to the winds of freedom. Hundreds of miles south of the Sioux, at the mouth of the Cache la Poudre Canyon, the renegade Black Feather and his band prepare to strike.

On a barge loading on the east side of the Mississippi, Zeb is aboard with Buck, as a modified freight wagon, driven by a surly Jacob, rumbles onto the vessel. On the wagon is a cowering but seething Sarah, certain, but concealing, that she is pregnant. The redhead and Irishman argue, and Zeb intervenes. Blades are drawn, but Jacob retreats. Zeb finds himself drawn to Sarah. Hundreds of miles southwest in Oklahoma—the Indian Territories—Israel Thomas tries to

persuade his heavyset wife, Lucy, that freedom lies northwest, but Lucy is filled with a dread of the unknown.

Far from where the barges enter the currents of the Mississippi, Eagle Talon braces against the chill of an early spring Rocky Mountain morning, his eyes on the elder war chief, Flying Arrow, his heart with his wise and passionate young wife, Walks With Moon. Her pregnancy fills his spirit with elation and foreboding. His instincts tell him that life is changing, but his warrior spirit believes *The People shall prevail.*

A week prior, three wagons left Fort Laramie headed south, rigs bursting with supplies and family furniture. Fourteen-year-old Dorothy and her family are filled with hope and excitement.

Mac bellows down the line of wagons and prancing teams, *"Move them out."* As Reuben gallops down a quarter mile line of rigs, he's astounded to see Jacob and Sarah. Farther west, Black Feather urges his score of renegades into the mouth of the Poudre River to savagely attack the three wagons carrying Dorothy and her family.

Black Feather's men murder all the occupants except the young, cowering girl. To his own astonishment and that of his band of dark souls, Black Feather takes her under his malevolent wing.

The wagons forge westward over the lands and rivers of Missouri. Reuben's heroic actions save the life of a pioneer child. Impressed, Mac designates him assistant wagon master. The Sioux break winter camp, and the long line of women, children, travois and camp dogs begin their spring quest for the buffalo. Warriors fan out ahead as the village pushes east. Black Feather's band flees east to escape whatever Army patrol might find the scorched wagons and burned corpses along the Poudre. Another wagon train of twenty-two wagons, men, women and children, Mormons, all related on the exodus, their hearts and hopes pointed to Zion, Salt Lake, and the front range of the Wasatch, cross the Illinois state line into Missouri pointed toward Fort Kearny.

In a gathering of the wagon train, Mac lays down the rules with a bullwhip to an insolent Jacob. Sarah shoves a derringer in Jacob's face, and Jacob backs down, fearful of incurring the wrath of the others, but a vengeful fire begins to smolder.

Signs of the hairy-faced ones pock-mark the land, the buffalo are scarce, and the Sioux are restless. Scouts warn of a large enemy encampment of Pawnee moving east. Flying Arrow and Tracks On Rock, the father of Walks With Moon and shaman of the tribe, agree to veer north. The women concur. A scout spots an unusually large Pawnee war party ahead. Eagle Talon and his young warrior friends are directed to take over the advance scout positions, but their orders are strict—follow the Pawnee war party, search for buffalo and keep the Council appraised.

The wagon train is besieged by a late spring blizzard. In the women's wagon where everyone shelters, slightly drunk, Jacob realizes that the beautiful Norwegian blonde referred to by Mary, the older whore he spent time with in the city, was Inga. Jacob reveals this fact with vicious delight. Zeb is enraged, Johannes is shocked, and Inga is mortified. A damaging wedge is driven between Johannes and Inga.

Lucy and Israel make it north over the imaginary Mason-Dixon line. They head west, their destination unknown, their quest for freedom beset by hardship and the danger of discovery. At a furtive stop along the Underground Railroad, an elderly white lady shares a map of the Rocky Mountains. One location calls out to Lucy and Israel—the Uncompahgre.

Black Feather's band makes lewd approaches to his young captive. When he learns her name is Dorothy, a flood gate opens to long-suppressed memories of his family's Missouri farm and the vicious white cutthroats who raped his Osage mother and murdered both parents. One of the outlaw's bullets found his old faithful mare, Dorothy, nicknamed "Dot." His renegade band grows restless with his refusal to allow molestation of the girl—even his longtime lieutenant, Pedro, ever resentful of Black Feather's authority.

Southeast of Fort Kearney, Mac's wagons intersect with the Mormon wagon train, and Johanne is stirred by a religious service on forgiveness. His heart softens, but he's reluctant to rekindle the flame between he and Inga.

Now spread out a half-sun from one another, Eagle Talon and his fellow warriors sweep northeast, alert for bison herds of brothers, ever vigilant for enemy Pawnee and soldier patrols.

Rebecca and Reuben are astonished when they each discover the maps of the other, and share the secrets of the parchments, realizing that the trails drawn long ago by men who were strangers converge at the same point in the remote western slope of the Rockies. Their long simmering relationship is torridly consummated, but Rebecca remains uncommitted to venturing beyond Cherry Creek, and Reuben struggles to keep his expectations in check. Unreconciled with Johannes, Inga discovers she is pregnant and learns that Sarah is as well. A special bond of commiseration binds the two women.

Black Feather grows increasingly wary of his men, their lust for loot, women and murder unappeased. He turns his band southeast, hoping to find a small wagon train. Instead, they encounter Mac's train. The two outfits confront one another face-to-face, rifle bore to rifle bore. The tension escalates when Zeb and Black Feather, who murdered Zeb's family and burned their Missouri farm more than a decade before, recognize each other. Mac's Irish temper flares. Black Feather dismisses Reuben as a young fool when the Prussian dismounts. Gunfire ensues, and the renegades retreat in panic, leaving eight dead or dying, six at the hands of Reuben's deadly pistol. Zeb warns Reuben, *"You have a gift, son. Make sure it does not turn into a curse."*

Eagle Talon shadows the wagon train, intrigued by the man with the pearl-handled gun and the dark-haired beauty obviously drawn to him. Spirit whispers to him, *"Friend. Strength. Honor,"* and the dark-haired woman conjures memories of Walks With Moon several suns still to the west.

In the prairie south of the Immigrant and Mormon trails, and northeast of Cherry Creek, the wagon train begins the crossing of Two Otters Creek. Scouting the hills, Zeb runs into signs of the Pawnee. He is attacked and barely escapes. With his tobiano, Buck, stretched forward at full gallop, his legs a blur, Zeb races back toward the wagons, firing his

pistol as a warning, the Pawnee warriors on his heels like a boil of angry hornets.

From a low-slung ridge, Eagle Talon watches the drama unfold. Impelled by the mysterious connection between he and the white man, he joins the fray. His warrior band quickly joins him—screaming down the ridge toward the oblivious Pawnee.

The battle is fierce, and, to Sarah's horror, a Pawnee arrow finds Inga, Rebecca is clubbed almost senseless by a Pawnee shield. Zeb steps into a breach in the line, knives against lances, Johannes commandeers a dead warrior's horse, saber flashing in the sunlight, and the tide turns as the distant war cries of Eagle Talon's band can be heard.

The battle over, the pioneers assess their many casualties, the Sioux dispatch and scalp the wounded Pawnee, and Eagle Talon and Reuben raise their hands to one another, establishing a bridge between cultures and families.

Mac is wounded during the violent struggle. Taking advantage of the confusion, Jacob plunges an arrow into the heart of the red-headed wagon master, then tries to cover his tracks. Zeb, though, is not fooled.

Eagle Talon and his band return to the tribe in misplaced triumph. An angry Council has convened a special meeting and demands their presence. Walks With Moon, Deer Tracks and Talks With Shadows, known for premonitions, prepare dinner, speaking in whispered tones of the rumors swirling about the return of their husbands. In the flicker of the lodge fire, Talks With Shadows speaks in a voice not her own, her eyes wild, unearthly, *"I know what will happen,"* she whispers. *"How does the baby in your belly grow, Walks*

*With Moon? ...Does he feel strong?... The men have brought shame upon themselves, and Eagle Talon has bonded with a hairy-faced one. The future of The People is not bright."*

The wagon train, several weeks out from Cherry Creek and days from their first jagged view of the Rockies, is unexpectedly visited by a small U.S. Army Cavalry patrol. Sad and unkempt, Johannes greets them, smartly returning the salute of the captain, his destiny becoming increasingly clear.

Overconfident, Rebecca wanders off alone to bathe in the creek and is attacked by Jacob. About to be raped, she feels the vile Irishman sag on top of her as Sarah repeatedly sinks a knife blade into his back in spasms of pent-up rage. Sarah pulls the bloodstained gold map from his pocket. Zeb discovers the women and doctors the crime scene to appear as if the Pawnee had committed the murder. The three make a secret pact never to speak of that day's deeds to anyone.

Lucy and Israel doggedly continue west and are almost discovered by a posse, but a sympathetic rancher in the Nebraska Territories hides them in a grain bin. Breathing through straws made of reeds, they emerge covered in white dust, laughing at the sight of one another and with relief. The rancher offers them an old gray mule in return for leather and saddle repair by Israel, his first job as a free man. The pair set out again, carefully working their way west, this time with the mule.

The Sioux continue eastward, the young warriors shunned as Talks With Shadows had eerily foreseen. The shame weighs heavily on Walks With Moon and Eagle Talon, who wonders about the strange visions of Talks With

Shadows, which Walks With Moon refused to reveal fully.

Hundreds of miles to the west, Black Feather's cutthroats hole up in a canyon east of the Poudre. Black Feather gruffly nurses Dot after a potentially fatal rattlesnake bite. The men are restless, incited by serpent-faced Snake, maniacal Tex and Black Feather's long time, untrustworthy lieutenant, Pedro. During an altercation, Black Feather puts a bullet between Pedro's eyes and gives the band an ultimatum—stay or go. Led by Snake and Tex, eight bandits leave. Those who remain are among Black Feather's most loyal and oldest companions, including Terry Johnson, the Texan with whom he has ridden for more than ten years.

South of where Black Feather's men lick their wounds, the wagon train reaches the hills northeast of Cherry Creek. Long aware of Zeb's feelings for her, Sarah succumbs to the mountain man's gentle warmth. Under a starlit night, she finds solace in his strong embrace and deep kisses. Rebecca holds her mercurial and magnetic attraction for Reuben at arm's-length, refusing to forsake the notion of returning to England. Johannes remains morose, tormented that as Inga lay in his arms at Two Otter Creek, taking her last breath, she may not have heard his final whisper, "*I love you.*"

As Book Two draws to a close, the lives of the characters of the Threads West saga weave on the loom of an irrevocable future. The tragic future of the Indians is unfolding, bitter conflicts already igniting, and a gathering storm will soon pit brother against brother. Across the lands of uncommon cultures, dark, lost souls and hopeful spirits braid the tapestry that will become our shared past.

*An American Saga*

## BOOK THREE—*UNCOMPAHGRE, Where Water Turns Rock Red*

The courageous men and women of the saga confront the Rockies.

*Book Three—Uncompahgre, Where Water Turns Rock Red,* opens on May 27, 1855, the day Book Two concludes, in the high, undulating, grassy hills north of tiny Cherry Creek, later to become Denver. The Europeans are confronted by the spine of the Rockies just months before the ravages of winter descend on the Uncompahgre. To the east, long simmering enmities go unresolved, and a cauldron of differences beset the country—slavery, states' rights, economic parity, power and territory.

Zeb and Buck reluctantly pick their careful way down to the confluence of Cherry Creek and the South Platte to bring the unwelcome news of Mac's death to his brother Randy at Gart's Mercantile. Sarah relaxes in the late morning sun of the grass-covered slopes of the expansive South Platte Valley. The sharp, shimmering, white outline of the massive Rockies rises abruptly in unimaginable challenge. Sarah feels a stirring in her belly, *Jacob's spawn,* as she watches a mother squirrel shepherd two kits among the rocks. The kits romp and scamper until one, for no reason, attacks the other,

the surprising and violent onslaught halted only by the scolding chatter and intervention of their mother. Joined by Rebecca, Sarah does not grasp the omen. The two women discuss their futures, the magnificent power of the land and the choices that await Rebecca—return to England or journey with Sarah, Reuben and Johannes across the rugged peaks spread before them.

In an uncomfortable moment, Zeb relays the news of Mac's death to a shocked and somber Randy, delivering the dead brother's possessions, including his 1855 Colt ten gage shotgun, and his sure-footed feisty sorrel mare, Red. Curious, Sarah and Rebecca determine to ride into the settlement to get a feel for the people. Reuben and Johannes soon follow.

Still shunned by order of the Council, Eagle Talon and his four warrior friends remain morose. The birth of their first child growing ever closer, a worried Walks With Moon continues to withhold from Eagle Talon the full implications of the visions of Talks With Shadows.

Black Feather nurses Dot in her slow recovery from the almost mortal rattlesnake bite. The thieves and killers who remain are familiar and relatively loyal. He decides the band will journey up the Poudre, letting the cold, powerful rising waters of spring close the trail behind them at the Narrows. After they rest, recuperate and hunt, they'll push over Cameron Pass and pick their way into North Park, villains ever in search of their next victim. Dot has begun to emerge from her shell, but her fragile trust extends only to Black Feather and Johnson, his new second-in-command, who accords her respect and courtesy not offered by any of the other men.

The Mormon family, Joseph, Roberta and their young children, descend the western slope of the Wasatch, preparing to strike north to a homestead on the Bear River, the northern rim of Cache Valley.

The women browse in the mercantile, meeting Randy who recognizes them immediately from Zeb's description. With their goods purchased, they stroll out the door to take the brief tour of the fledgling town. They are accosted by Floyd Bummer and his gang, the settlements' two-bit, but dangerous ruffians. The men grab Sarah and Rebecca, seizing Rebecca's Sharps, and insist the women accompany them into the hills "for a ride." The redhead and brunette adamantly refuse. Reuben's commanding voice and the ominous hammer click of Johannes's Sharps carbine rescue them from the predicament. In a blur of action, Sarah escapes, and Rebecca is violently knocked to the wooden planks of the sidewalk by Floyd, whose wrist is shattered by a bullet from the pearl-handled Colt. Humiliated, vanquished, disarmed and told "to git" by Reuben and Johannes, Floyd clutches his bleeding wrist and snarls a promise of revenge, which Reuben nonchalantly dismisses.

The Sioux push eastward looking for their brothers. Unable to speak to one another, Eagle Talon and his four warrior friends are relegated to the dust at the tail of the moving village. Danger from enemy tribes and mounting signs of more white men prompt Flying Arrow to direct Eagle Talon to secretly ride near-guard on the flank, staying in a treed line bisected by a creek that Lucy, Israel and the mule are using for concealment. A sudden confrontation

between the unarmed elderly black couple and Eagle Talon threatens but quickly defuses when Eagle Talon lowers his drawn bow. Neither can understand the other, but a truce ensues. They share food, and Israel and Lucy enjoy their first taste of pemmican. The encounter links two cultures, one that has suffered centuries underfoot, and another about to experience the same.

Brought periodically by the stages out of Fort Laramie, mail has accumulated at the mercantile in Cherry Creek. There is a letter from Prussia for Reuben. Ludwig has died, and younger brother Erik has determined his future lies not with his incessantly quarreling brothers, but rather in America with Reuben. Two letters from England are for Rebecca, bearing both sad and promising tidings: one, the final letter from her mother, eloquently scrawled with a feather pen on the finest of linen paper. The second, later postmarked correspondence is from their solicitor. Elizabeth has passed, and the family finances remain in turmoil, but a £100,000 cash offer for the Spanish Land Grant Rebecca has traveled so far and arduously to dispose of has been received.

Her heart broken, her motivations and decisions conflicted, Rebecca seduces Reuben, who has returned to the wagon intent on proposing. Their lovemaking is violently tender and all-consuming but made more desperate by shared anguish and an unknown future. To Reuben's surprise, wishing to be alone, Rebecca insists he not spend the night with her in the wagon. Reuben leaves, his proposal never spoken, his heart sinking and his emotions jumbled.

The last of the wagons prepare to leave for separate

destinations and differing dreams. Reuben determines to strike south with Johannes in quest of additional hands for the ranch he hopes to build, and three hundred cows and thirty bulls. Their destination is two large cattle ranches south of the small, ravaged settlement of Pueblo where the previous Christmas most of the inhabitants had been massacred by Apache. But first, at Randy's unenthusiastic urging, he needs to meet a *vaquero* named Philippe Reyes, well known for his sense and expertise with cattle, particularly if he is rustling them.

Plans are laid. Sarah will drive the freight wagon she has "inherited" from Jacob, and depending on Rebecca's decisions, Zeb will drive the prairie schooner. Reuben, Johannes, the cattle and the wagons will meet up in twelve days at Fort Massachusetts, on the west side of La Veta Pass, ever closer to the wilds and promise of the Uncompahgre. In a stiff goodbye, still torn, Rebecca tells Reuben that she will either be at Fort Massachusetts or she won't, and that is how he will know her answer.

Philippe quickly agrees to accompany Reuben and Johannes. Heading south, the three men make one stop at the rundown Sampson Ranch. They are greeted by a drunken, bellicose patriarch leaning on the door frame of the sagging ranch house, brandishing a shotgun. Reuben explains the purpose of the visit is potentially to employ his sons, 15-year-old Jonathan and 16-year-old Michael. Despite his stupor, Sampson brusquely invites the men in, "except that Mexican." Reuben insists on all or none of them, silently strengthening the newly formed bond between he and Philippe.

The leaky ranch house is ramshackle. Barely enough food sizzles on the breakfast fire tended by Mrs. Sampson, the thin, haggard wife with a purple bruise on her cheek to feed two, let alone six. Both of the boys are offered to Reuben by their father, the young men bent over their plates and cowering as they are cuffed for imaginary disrespect. Reuben determines Jonathan is too young but decides the outfit needs a hand, and severely stuttering Michael needs rescuing. Their mother, ignoring the threatening stares of her husband, offers up her old horse for Michael to clinch the deal. As the four men ride south, young Michael brushes away tears.

Overlooking Cherry Creek, Sarah comforts a nauseous Rebecca next to the wagons. Mentioning her queasy feelings that have been arising most mornings of the previous week, Rebecca remains undecided as to the next leg of her travels. Familiar with the feelings and symptoms of pregnancy, Sarah perceptively connects the dots. An unbelieving Rebecca reluctantly faces the surprising reality.

Far to the south, Johannes, Reuben, Michael and Philippe stop for Philippe's midmorning ritual of stout, trailside *kaffee*. Michael shyly ambles off to relieve himself only to be confronted by a tightly coiled rattlesnake sunning on a rock. Two shots ring out as one, and the snake's head explodes in red mist and bloodied scales. Their guns drawn and smoke curling from the barrels, Reuben and the *vaquero* lock eyes, suddenly aware of their equal, lethal skills.

On the east side of the hogbacks separating the plains from the meadowed mouth of the Cache La Poudre River, Black Feather mounts up his men, knowing they need the rest, fresh deer meat and seclusion offered by the high country following the recent upheavals. Though not infected, Dot's leg is far from healed.

Several hundred miles to the southeast, the four men of Reuben's outfit follow the trail to the Dawson and Christiansen ranches. Christiansen can't spare cattle having just shipped some to the Army, but big-shouldered Dawson, gray-haired, jovial and shrewd, agrees to sell some, though is reluctant to sell the full three hundred cows and thirty bulls at the price Reuben wishes. To the astonishment of all, Reuben bets the big rancher that if he can eat one of the thick, Belgian shot glasses on the rancher's shelf, Dawson will sell them three hundred cows and thirty bulls at Reuben's price. Incredulous, Dawson agrees, his counter bet being fewer cows and bulls at a far higher price. As Reuben had seen Ludwig do whenever his father wanted a prize bull from an unwilling seller, a hammer, a cloth, a large pitcher of water, butter and a thick, red slab of freshly cut beef are laid out on the rocks. Dawson loses the bet but is delighted anyway. As a bonus, he throws in his best lead cow, bells and all.

The men and cattle head northwest, planning to skirt the western slope of the San Isabel Mountains, then curving back northeast to Fort Massachusetts to meet the wagons. Reuben is increasingly apprehensive that Rebecca won't be with Zeb and Sarah.

Thirty miles south of Pedro's fly-ridden corpse, the mutinous Snake and the blood-thirsty, soulless men who followed him attack a wagon driven by a settler couple. The man is killed, their old horse likewise. The wife—after his

men have their way with her—is finished off by a leering, morbidly demented Tex. Deadly intent in their ultimate purpose, Snake and his men head south to the Colorado River country, north of the Uncompahgre, to continue their pillaging.

Five thousand miles to the east, Erik's friend, Rudolf, drops him at Bremerhaven Harbor at the dock of the SS *Edinburgh,* the same ship Reuben sailed on eighteen months prior. Nervous but filled with excitement, Erik shoves one hand in his coat pocket and closes his fingers around the sheathed dagger that brother Helmon secretly slipped to him the night before he departed. *"Be safe little brother. Father would be proud,"* he had whispered in contrast to the stiff angry words that had come from Isaac.

As the herds move the last few dusty miles to the fort, Reuben's heart jumps when, through Mac's telescope, he sees Red, the spirited mare Randy had promised Rebecca if she was continuing west. Sparks of attraction fly as Sarah and Philippe exchange first glances. Rebecca tearfully breaks the news that she is with his child. Reuben sits heavily on a log in bewildered surprise, followed by elation.

With Zeb guiding, the wagons and cattle strike west, aiming for Wolf Creek Pass and a hoped-for shortcut between Red Mountain Pass to the south and the longer trek up the Animus, which would mandate trailing the herd over the Uncompahgre plateau near old Fort Uncompahgre and the Gunnison and Uncompahgre confluence. Quiet animosity kindles between Zeb and Philippe over Sarah's attentions. Rebecca looks on with increasing disapproval of her redheaded friend's inconsiderate dismissal of the older trapper's ongoing affection. Johannes struggles with cows and cow lingo.

Black Feather's band relaxes in the chilly spring sun above the Narrows, the rushing Poudre already rendering the downstream trail impassable. But as is their nature, they are getting antsy to move, seek, destroy and take.

Several hundred miles to the east, the band of Oglala moves slowly. Alerted by a forward scout, Tracks On Rock and Flying Eagle summon the braves, including the five warriors still in shame, to ride out ahead and view the senseless scene reported to them. Their ponies spread shoulder to shoulder on the ridge, the warriors are aghast at the carnage spread below in the grassy bowl. Sixty red and rotting skinned carcasses of their brothers the *tatanka*, meat intact but ruined, only the hides taken, are strewn about the valley of wasted death, an ominous foreshadowing of the oblivious hairy-faced ones, and their uncaring disregard for life and resource.

Stumbling upon an Army Cavalry patrol in dense cottonwood cover along the creek, Lucy and Israel are challenged by the patrol's leader, Captain Henderson. When the Captain demands his papers, Israel fearfully, but proudly, hands the officer the yellowed, dried and brittle copy of the Constitution he cut long ago from the *New York Times.* Captain Henderson, empathetic and in tacit agreement, blesses their westward progress, taking time to draw a detailed map of the safest route to the Uncompahgre, recommending following the Laramie River upstream, then through North Park, over Rabbit Ears Pass, down into the Yampa Valley, south to the White, then down to the

Colorado and finally to the Gunnison and Uncompahgre rivers.

After days of rest, solid food, fire and coffee, Black Feather's men propose they head over Cameron Pass in advance of Black Feather and the girl, who needs several more days of rest. With Black Feather's permission, Johnson agrees to lead them subject to strict orders by Black Feather to neither venture down to North Park nor to take any actions until he and Dot catch up. Though less worried now about being shot in the back, he is uneasy about Johnson. The memory of the gold they had taken from wagons the two of them had looted years ago, rises up. They had buried the treasure, south of the Yampa, agreeing never to reveal their shared secret to anyone.

Hundreds of miles southwest, the wagons and cattle have begun their long, slow assent to the Divide. Reuben makes a clumsy proposal of marriage to Rebecca, who, in typical fashion, but with a kiss, demands that he do far better if she is to take him seriously. Black Feather's men head west up the Poudre, and Dot begins to revive. Short, but complete, sentences occasionally escape her lips, and color is finally showing in her cheeks. The vacant look in her eyes has all but vanished.

In the ever-increasing altitude, and the change from juniper, jack pine and sage to aspen and fir, Rebecca finds herself drifting in and out of nausea and feelings of discomfort. Her anger toward Sarah at the redhead's treatment of Zeb and coquettish flirting with the *vaquero*, grows.

To the north, Black Feather and Dot saddle up, following

the tumbling, snowmelt currents of the Poudre toward Cameron Pass. Black Feather's uneasy suspicions are realized when he spots a dark shape in the unsettled snowfield of an avalanche. It is Johnson, still alive, but dying, buried to his chest, his body twisted and broken. Dot is shocked at the predicament of her only other friend. Johnson asks Black Feather to send the girl back down to the horses. The Texan pleas with him to dispatch him from his misery. But before Black Feather follows the Texan's wishes, Johnson admits what Black Feather had sensed, his recall of the gold down south of the Yampa from long ago. The dying man directs the renegade leader to dig down in the snow for his Colt and to give his half share to the girl for schooling. Surprised at himself as he speaks the words, Black Feather agrees, promising in return to likewise give his half to the girl. He gives Johnson a few final tastes of whiskey. Johnson peers up, his eyes glazed, and says, "*Been good riding with you, Samuel*" to a startled Black Feather. "*You talk in your sleep sometimes,*" Johnson explains. Mercy comes shortly after with a silent thrust of Black Feather's knife.

To the east, the Council lifts the shame weighing on Eagle Talon and his warrior friends. Scouts report finding the bodies of three Cheyenne who had simply been watering their horses, two shot in the back. The horses of the attackers were shod. Flying Arrow suggests, and the Council concurs, that The People must learn more of the hairy-faced ones. How many? When might they come? What are their intentions? The Council discusses sending Eagle Talon south to the land of the enemy Utes, where water turns rock red and where Zeb-Raih traps. If dispatched, his mission will be

to talk to the hairy-faced one, Roo-bin, with whom he has bonded as a spirit brother, and Zeb-Raih and learn all he can of the hairy-faced ones. Eagle Talon requests that he make his journey only after Walks With Moon gives birth. The Council concurs.

Near the summit of Wolf Creek Pass, under a high-country sun, most of the heavy snows of the mountain blizzard are gone, replaced by the scent of early summer sap emanating from firs and aspen. Reuben proposes again to Rebecca, fumbling the ring into the snow under her feet. They laugh, and she finally accepts. But disaster soon strikes when one of the wayward cows bolts from the herd and into the forest. In pursuit astride Bente, Johannes hears the panicked cow scream and bellow as Bente bolts into a small clearing. A grizzly rears up on its hind haunches, towering ten feet over the ripped and bleeding body of the cow. Bente rears and Johannes is flung to the dirt. The bear charges, snarling, saliva flying. Johannes's fall has wedged him between two aspen saplings, slightly protected from the enraged animal, but his arm is snagged, and it takes time to free his hand and draw his pistol. With the animal's foul breath hot on his face, Johannes gets off a single shot at the bear's head before his weapon is clawed from his hands. Further enraged, the beast sinks his teeth into one of Johannes's legs, but a shot rings out. The bear turns and rears. Reuben and Zeb rush the clearing, emptying their guns. Philippe arrives and unloads his musketoon. The charging grizzly's end comes from Zeb's Enfield. Zeb stitches the gaping wounds in Johannes's badly injured leg with a painfully thick antler dowel and thin strips of rawhide.

To the north, the shame now lifted, Eagle Talon is reluctant to worry Walks With Moon about the pending decision of the Council. Walks With Moon remains unwilling to share the full extent of Talks With Shadows's vision, but the two, deeply and always in love, agree that the name of their first offspring shall be Dream Dancer.

On the west slope of Wolf Creek Pass, the cows bunched on the narrow, steep trail, Zeb finds the north slopes of the shortcut to the Uncompahgre still blocked by crusty snows, forcing the descent down the west side into Little Medicine, the winter camp of the Mountain Ute, of Chief Guera Murah and his son, Ouray, Ouray's wife Black Mare, and their ever-present companion Chipeta, all of whom are known to and friendly with Zeb.

Reuben meets Ouray, and with Zeb interpreting, requests permission from the Ute to establish the ranch in their summer hunting grounds of the Uncompahgre. A trade is made. Rebecca and Black Mare meet, each instantly liking the other. A series of cascading suggestions and whirlwind decisions quickly result in the Utes offering to host an extremely rare wedding ceremony. The Ute decide the event will be conducted by the tribe *puwarat* and *bowa'gant* who have great *puah*. The tribe delightedly plans the wedding festivities to be held that very night to coincide with the last day of the Ute pow wow with the Unita-at and Yamparika Ute bands. Unsure of what is transpiring, Rebecca finds herself spirited away by Black Mare and Chipeta to the giggles and knowing glances of the other women. Rebecca is sponge washed and dressed in Black Mare's finest white

doeskin dress. The men of the tribe smudge Reuben with sage smoke and Ouray loans him a fringed and beaded ceremonial leather shirt and a cream-colored beaded belt. Evening approaches with meat roasting on spits, pemmican and other special foods being laid out on makeshift platforms, Indians swaying to the beat of drums and the flashes of the quartz rattles of the *Puwarat*. To the delighted amazement of both Reuben and the tribe, Rebecca brings the new world to the old by retrieving two fine goblets from one of her trunks. In a brief, but spectacular ceremony, the practices of the Ute people blend with the ancient Jewish tradition of hooked arms and shared wine glasses, shattered as part of the ceremony so that no one other than the bride and groom shall ever touch their lips to them.

To Zeb's discomfort, Sarah appears at the wedding with Philippe. When the *vaquero* bends his head in an obvious attempt to kiss the redhead, Zeb leaves a note in Reuben's saddlebag, saddles Buck in a hurt, silent fury and rigs the mules. Scattering cattle at a gallop in the darkness, the mountain man heads north toward the delta of the rivers and old Fort Uncompahgre, his ultimate destination one of his cabins on the flanks of the Red Mountains, and solace for his wounded heart.

Unaware of Zeb's departure, Reuben and his bride are directed by Ouray to the wedding tipi set up on the edge of a small, bubbling hot spring, the subchief and Black Mare nodding their heads knowingly.

Several days later, sixty miles to the northwest, Zeb and Buck pick their way like ghosts in the bright light of the moon through an edge of ridged timber several miles from the old, crumbling Fort Uncompahgre, abandoned and now inhabited only by travelers, drifters, bandits, outlaws and traders. Three large fires burn down by the crumbling remains of the fort.

Several days later, drawn by an impulse he can't explain, Zeb veers from the Uncompahgre River trail to the Red Mountains, instead following the early summer rush of Dallas Creek toward the snowclad Snaefel, pausing when he reaches the top of the ridge and the edge of a large aspen grove overlooking tree-ringed, benched meadows, bisected by the tumble of the creek. A vision creeps involuntarily into his consciousness. *They could grow a passel of hay here. That ridge would break the west wind.*

The vision paints a picture, a modest one and a half story log home, hand hewn, smoke curling from a rough stone chimney, jack leg fences and a two-wheeled track of a road winding up from the Uncompahgre, past the house to further down the meadow where a barn and loafing shed stand near a series of square and rectangular corrals. He sees the shapes of mottled cows dabbling the meadow, so real he can almost hear them bawling, their great, twisted horns glistening in the sun. Horses are tied to the hitching post in front of the home, swishing their tails lazily at flies, and the small forms of three children are playing. The paint brush of his mind colors two women coming from the house, stepping from the covered veranda along its front, lifting their hands above their eyes to shield their view from the sun, their gaze fixing in his direction. One of the women is short and heavy, her features dark skinned, the other petite, a red auburn sheen around her face where the sun reflects her hair.

*Threads West*
*An American Saga*

# The Saga Continues with Book Four, *Moccasin Track*

June 26, 1855

# *C*HOICE OF TRAILS

TWO HUNDRED NINETY-ONE MILES SOUTHWEST OF WHERE Lucy and Israel lay huddled close to a fire at the base of Rabbit Ears Pass, Rebecca, eyes closed, felt the warm press of Reuben's chest against her back, and the comforting drape of his thigh over the flare of her hip. The smell of sage and sulfur, of tanned leather and soft smoke, mingled with the scent of their bodies, spent in the afterglow of their loving.

Reuben was snoring gently, his chest and legs molded to the length of her under the buffalo robe that covered them, one hand gently covering her breast. She sighed languidly. *What a pleasant dream.*

Her eyes fluttered open. A few feet away, a finger of smoke rose in gray spirals from the embers in the lodge fire.

Suddenly, she was fully awake, eyes wide open. *My God. It wasn't a dream!* Pulling her left hand slowly from the robe, she stared at her finger and the reed of grass Reuben had woven into a ring as they had relaxed in the hot springs, her body still straddling his, both of them almost faint with the pleasure and heat of their coupling.

*Mrs. Rebecca Elizabeth Frank. Mrs. Rebecca Elizabeth Frank.* Her lips formed the words silently as her eyes roved the inside of the tipi, its textured, tan, hide walls surreal, but calming. Her lips curled in a smile as her gaze came to rest on the white doeskin wedding dress crumpled on top of Reuben's clothing.

Tucking her shoulders gently into his chest, she pressed his hand more firmly around her breast, her other hand reaching down to rest on the slight mound of her belly. *Where our child grows.*

Reuben stirred behind her. "Good morning, Mistress Marx..." Pausing, he laughed softly. "Mrs. Frank, my wife." His lips moved feather-like, his words a warm whisper of breath on her neck.

"Good morning, Mr. Frank." she sighed. "I woke just a short time ago. I thought I was dreaming." She pressed his hand against her breast again, "but I'm glad I'm not."

A thought struck her, and her body jerked.

"I just realized, Mr. Frank, that after months together from the time you were such a bore on the *Edinburgh*," she giggled, "this is the first full night we have ever spent together, in the same bed."

His lips trailing down the nape of her neck, Reuben chuckled into the smooth skin between her shoulder blades, "Never thought of that. You're right, Rebecca."

Her voice shy and husky, Rebecca whispered, "I... I love it when you take me, Reuben."

He laughed softly, into her hair. "I do believe, Mrs. Frank, that is you who took me."

Giggling, she raised his hand to her lips and kissed his

fingers. "You may be right, Reuben, and no apologies about it. I shall do so again." Her smile was hidden from him, but not her meaning. *And again, and again and again.*

"I don't know, Rebecca; a ranch is hard work. Building it from scratch, clawing a home out of an unknown wilderness will be a monumental task. We must get a roof overhead before winter, corrals for the animals, a fence around the homestead, figure out some way to get hay up and stored for winter feed, stock food for the winter, cut wood for the fire and the long cold months that will be coming." His tone was teasing. "It will be sunup to sundown and then some, until the snow flies.... Even then..." his voice trailed off, "we will be tired."

"Well then, my husband, I suggest you reserve some energy each day."

―――

A BOOT SCRAPED THE GRASS JUST OUTSIDE THE FLAP OF THE lodge. Reuben tensed, reaching for his pistol, then relaxed as someone cleared his throat outside the tipi, and Johannes's voice filtered through the skins. "Don't want to interrupt, but we need to talk. I have a note that was shoved in the flap of your saddlebag. You need to read it."

"What time is it?" Reuben sat up, rolling the hide off him, his eyes searching for his britches.

"The sun is halfway to noon. We all stirred a bit late this morning after the festivities last night."

*Such a serious tone.* "Who's the note from?"

There was a moment of silence from outside the tipi.

Reuben, standing, britches hurriedly pulled up, paused in the buttoning of his shirt.

Rebecca was sitting now, worry and puzzlement etched in her eyebrows, her fingers nervously kneading the edge of the robe she was clutching.

Reuben strode to her. Kneeling, he put one hand on each of her shoulders and bent his lips to hers in a short but tender kiss. Rising, Reuben took three rapid steps to the door of the lodge, quickly untied the flap and stepped outside, closing the flap and tying it behind him. Straightening, he turned to the tall Dane. Johannes's lips were tightly pressed, his eyes narrowed.

Turning abruptly, Johannes walked quickly toward the horses, his long-legged strides purposeful, despite his limp.

Reuben hurried after him keeping his eyes fixed on the back of his friend. Seventy-five yards from the tipi and halfway to the horses, Johannes wheeled back to him. The pale green leaves of the quaking aspen that rimmed the meadow shimmered in the cool morning breeze. As if hearing Reuben's unspoken question, he answered, "You just need to read it for yourself, Reuben." The lanky Dane's eyes fixed on his. He reached into his jacket pocket, withdrew a folded piece of paper and handed it to Reuben.

Squinting against the brightness of the midmorning sun, Reuben unfolded the paper. His hands shook, and he could feel Johannes's eyes on him as he read. The scroll was penciled, all capitalized, blocky, and awkward, distinctively darkened at various points in the print as the writer had obviously sharpened the pencil with a penknife.

*REUBEN*

*THIS AIN'T ANY KIND OF NOTICE, BUT I HAVE TO PICK UP AND GO. NEED ALONE TIME BACK ON THE MOUNTAIN. YOUR TRAIL SAVVY AND WOULDN'T BE NEEDIN' ME MUCH, ANYWAY. YOU GOT ONLY TWO CHOICES IN TRAILS. TALK TO OURAY BEFORE YOU CHOSE. HE HAD SCOUTS OUT TO CHECK ON THE SHORTCUT TRAIL OVER THAT MOUNTAIN JUST WEST OF HERE. MIGHT BE TOUGH GOING FOR THE WAGONS EVEN IF IT'S PASSABLE. IF IT AIN'T, THE OTHER TRAIL, LIKE WE TALKED BEFORE, HEADS NORTH AND DOWN TO THAT DELTA COUNTRY BY THE OLD FORT UNCOMPAHGRE. FIVE, MAYBE MORE DAYS IF YOU BACKTRACK THE ONLY OTHER WAY BACK TO WOLF CREEK, THE ANIMUS AND OVER RED MOUNTAIN PASS. THAT COUNTRY GETS PILES OF SNOWS AND MIGHT BE BLOCKED, TOO. THE DELTA TRAIL WILL BE ANOTHER 7 TO 10 DAYS. JUST FOLLOW THE UNCOMPAHGRE RIVER UPSTREAM FROM THERE. EAST BANK LIKELY BETTER FOR THE WAGONS, BUT CROSSINGS ONCE IN A WHILE ARE FOR SURE. RIVER WILL BE HIGH, SO PICK YOUR SPOTS. AS THE VALLEY NARROWS, KEEP YOUR EYES PEELED WEST. YOU'LL SEE WHERE DALLAS CREEK COMES IN. YOUR MAP SHOWS IT PLAIN. I RECKON YOU CAN FIND A CROSSING AND HEAD UPSTREAM TO FIND YOU A SPOT.*

*MIGHT BE WE CROSS PATHS SUM TIME UP THERE. MAYBE NOT. BUT SPIRIT WILL BE WITH YOU. GIVE MY GOODBYES TO THE REST. CONGRATULATIONS TO YOU AND THE MISSUS.*

*ZEBARRIAH TAYLOR*

Reuben slowly lowered the paper. Raising his eyes, he returned Johannes's stare, "It says..."

Johannes cut him off, "I know. I read it."

"Where...?"

Johannes finished the question for him. "Where and how did he go?"

"Philippe found his tracks headed north, Buck and the mules at a gallop. Disappeared into the trees over there," Johannes nodded with his chin. "I searched every saddlebag thinking maybe he left word. Found this in yours."

There was a long silence, the two men looking at one another. "I have Michael and Philippe out gathering cows, as you've already gleaned, and I've talked to Ouray. Seems his scouts say heavy snows up higher have caused snow slides— big ones. They've downed some trees, and at some point, the shortcut trail becomes impassable."

Breathing a long sigh, Reuben straightened his shoulders. "Well, we sure as hell don't want to backtrack up the pass. Based on what Ouray told you, the nearest shortcut is impassable and seems to me if Zeb was headed north down to the delta country, that's the way we ought to go. We don't have much choice in trails."

Johannes's eyes searched his face. "Going to be short one

hand, and I'm still not hundred percent." He gestured at his leg where the grizzly had mauled it.

Reuben shrugged. "It is what it is. We have fences and corrals to build, a barn to put up and a hell of a lot of work to do before the snow flies. Maybe we can pick up a hand around that old fort there at the junction of the Uncompahgre and the Gunnison."

"I agree, my Prussian friend." His eyes locked on Reuben's, his lips thin and compressed. "There may be no choice in trails, but trails always offer choices."

Turning away from Reuben, Johannes walked toward the horses, his limp more pronounced, calling out over his shoulder, "I've already saddled Lahn for you. I'll ride out and find Michael and Philippe, and make sure the damn cattle are bunched. You get the women moving."

Reuben stood for a moment watching the retreating back of his friend. *Trails always offer choices? What did he mean by that?*

June 27, 1855

# *N*ORTH PARK

TWO HUNDRED EIGHTY-ONE MILES NORTHEAST OF WHERE
Zeb and Buck rode south to the Red Mountains, clouds
scurried in shape-changing billows across a narrow window
of deep blue sky formed by the high, heavily treed ridges
surrounding Lucy, Israel and the mule.

The scent of pine, fir and spruce faded, then intensified,
before fading again, high altitude perfume driven by spurts
of waffling breeze flowing down the incline toward them
from the west.

Israel stopped and breathed in deeply, awed by the view.
*From the hands of God.*

"See them rocks?" he exclaimed, pointing at twin spires
of gray and brown stone that rose from the dense conifers at
the top of the mountain to the east.

"Israel, I ain't interested in no rocks. My knee is hurtin'
bad, and this ol' mule is wheezing like a broken fire bellows,
even without my fat self on her."

"Well, Lucy, first of all, you ain't fat, and if we go slow, she will be okay. Why don't you climb back on and ride for a while? We're way high up. Air's thin. But if that map that captain drew for us is halfway right, we're close to the top. Those spires? Might be the Rabbit Ears he told us about."

Israel held up the page of the map that depicted this leg of their journey for her to see, but she shook her head. Her lips were trembling, and her eyes watery. One of her hands rested for support on the gray shoulders of the old mule.

"I know that climb was god-awful tough and long, wife. But it will be easier going downhill."

Taking a step to her, he wrapped a thin arm around her shoulders and pressed his cheek against hers, "Should be warmer and less wind down low, too." He could see in her eyes when she looked up at him, her lips compressed, that she was trying to still her shaking.

"Let me help you on, Sally." He bent, lacing his long, dark bony fingers together as a step. Lucy's first attempts to lift her foot failed, and he had to lower his hands until she finally got one foot up. Pressing his palms around the side of her worn boot, Israel noticed there were tears where the leather had separated from the sole. *Her feet must be wet.*

"Okay, Lucy, you pull yourself with your arms on Sally's neck, and I'll ease your foot slow and sure till you get that other leg over."

Facing the mule, Lucy placed both worn hands on the animal's neck. Israel rose slowly, pushing with his legs, taking care not to put too much strain on his back as he lifted her. Gradually, after several wheezing attempts, she was astride the mule.

Resting for a moment, Israel leaned against her leg,

patting her thigh. "We'll go nice and slow, not work Sally too hard." He smiled, trying to make his voice enthusiastic. "We get us over that crest up ahead, and then we be on our way down to the bottom. Maybe, we'll go a little bit out of our ways.... Don't seem like far on the map, maybe a mile or less to that Northgate Canyon. I'll catch us some fish at the river, and we can have ourselves a big old supper, rest up before we head further. See if we can find those hot springs. Maybe spend a few days there and let you soak."

Lucy wagged her head side to side, her lips still a thin line, her teary eyes narrowed. The mule, looking at him reproachfully, with one ear forward and one ear back, whistled out a low bray.

"I don't wanna go out of our way, Israel. I just want to get where we be going. And I am praying we get off this mountain quick."

Israel sighed. "If ya gotta pray, pray for a gun. We'll be a whole lot safer and way less hungry."

Rubbing the mule's muzzle, Israel forced a smile. "That's right, Sally, you be due for some rest too."

Turning, he caught the lead rope, took a deep breath and began to walk in short, slow uphill steps west again.

June 27, 1855

# HEADIN' TOWARD THE PROMISE

FIFTY-TWO MILES NORTHWEST OF WHERE JOHNSON'S broken body lay buried in the avalanche, Black Feather tightened the reins on the black stallion's hackamore just enough to slow the animal's long-stride gait.

Looking over his shoulder, he called out to Dot, "What are you doing? Stay ten, no more than twenty, feet behind. Things can go wrong in a hurry."

The girl had been looking down at her hands swaying with the movement of her horse. She nodded, saying nothing, and dug her heels gently into the flanks of the mare. The horse sped up slightly.

Black Feather kept his eyes on her. *Been like this since we found Johnson all broke up in the avalanche. Almost like that day on the Poudre, when...* he swallowed, clenching his teeth, *when I killed her ma and pa.* Something turned over in his gut.

Cursing silently, he put full rein on the stallion, bringing the horse to a halt. The black shook his head defiantly. When Dot had closed the distance, he gestured for her to ride up beside him.

"I know it's been slow going down the back side of Cameron—snow and mud and slick, and stopping to work on that leg of yours." He pointed at the valley below them, "That would be what they call North Park, that big flat sage area. All sorts of water down there, the Grizzly, the Michigan, lots of others and the North Platte. You like to fish?"

Dot looked at him, her blue eyes vacant. She shook her head. *Need to settle her down again, check the snakebite, hunt up some deer meat.*

"Well, fishing can be fun," he said. "Trout are mighty tasty fried up in fat with a bit of flour, and wild scallions if you can find them." Her face remained impassive.

Swinging forward in the saddle, Black Feather raised his arm, pointing. "East is where Fox Ridge comes down near Northgate Canyon. Those big white mountains way out, the Indians call the Rawah." He swung his arm toward the center of the valley. "If you squint real hard, you'll see some old trapper cabins. No one had been there for a spell last time I was through. Them jagged mountains behind is called Zirkel." He rotated left, his finger pointing past the distant cabins. "Out there, on the other side of the Buffaloes, smaller creeks flow down toward the Yampa. There's a bunch of side canyons, good water and cover where we can hole up for a couple days. I can doctor that leg of yours. Water will be clearer high up. We can catch some fish. Maybe I can arrow a deer, too. How does that sound?"

The girl just stared at him, as if not seeing him. Turning away, Black Feather let out a long, involuntary exhale, hoping she didn't notice.

Resting his hands on the saddle pommel, he thought for a minute, the stallion impatiently shifting weight beneath him. "You liked Johnson, didn't you, Dot?"

The girl looked at him, surprise showing through the tears welling in her eyes. She nodded, biting her lip.

"Thought so. I miss him, like you do. That was a tough deal back up there in that snow slide." He paused. "Guess you ought to know..." Black Feather caught himself, "...before he died, he and I made a promise to each other, and to you." The corner of the girl's mouth twitched, and one of her eyebrows raised slightly between strands of dirty blonde hair. "And where we're heading is so I can keep that promise."

A look of curious interest flitted across the girl's dirty, smudged features.

"You follow me close. Give that mare her lead and let her pick her way along behind the black. We're gonna follow these contours heading northwest, staying in these trees as much as we can. We'd stand out like red flags down in that sage, easy to spot for miles."

He flicked the reins across the sides of the stallion's neck. "Let's go, then."

# CHAPTER

## 4

June 27, 1855

# $\mathcal{I}$N SPIRIT'S HANDS

AS BLACK FEATHER'S STALLION AND DOT'S MARE PICKED their way west through the scattered firs and pine along the south rim of North Park, four hundred miles to the east, Walks With Moon stood slowly from her squatted stance, leaning forward only slightly not to strain her rounded belly. Heat from the midday sun radiated off the slender tips of fescue and needlegrass stirred by a slight breeze whispered down the slopes of the shallow valley.

Stepping back a few paces, her hands on her hips, she cocked her head, surveying the bow length, thin, stout, green alder branches lashed at the top, their lower ends spread out like a toy tipi. Her eyes shifted to the buffalo hide stretched out three paces by four paces and then to the pile of coarse, semi-rotten wood stacked feet away. Brushing one forearm against her forehead to keep the trickles of sweat from her eyes, she squinted at the sun.

A tiny creek, its course marked by the occasional cottonwood and alder and clumps of red willows, murmurs through narrow banks amidst the drone of flies. *You cannot run, little creek. Soon, the sun of summer will consume you, and you will be but a sandy trail awaiting next year's spring.*

Twenty paces away, nearer the creek, she could hear the wet scrape of Turtle Dove's fleshing rock on skin as she industriously worked on another buffalo hide staked into the sandy soil. Scattered nearby were other women of the tribe, all in various stages of fleshing, softening and preparing hides. A few had already built or were building smudge domes like hers.

She returned her eyes to the smudge dome, shifting to the hide and then back again. *It should hold the weight.* Satisfied, she stepped to the small structure and gingerly knelt, again supporting her weight just before her knees touched the earth. She reached out to the woodpile, selected the smallest of twigs and began the makings of a fire under the apex of the lashed alder branches—a wad of dry grass as starter, a cone-shaped assembly of twigs, larger sticks nestled outside. So intent was Walks With Moon that she was unaware of Eagle Talon until his shadow fell across her arms.

"This will be a fine robe." His eyes roved over the hide and the carefully laid fuel for the drying fire. He surveyed the other women of the tribe scattered down the long, narrow meadow and turned back to Walks With Moon. "You've been hard at work, wife. You are ahead of almost all the other women, except perhaps Talks With Shadows." He chuckled. "But then, she is guided by unseen forces."

Walks With Moon smiled, despite herself. "You cannot deny that her vision has been accurate thus far." *What he really wishes is the full story of Talks With Shadows' premonitions.* Her mind drifted back to the scene in the tipi, she and Deer Tracks transfixed, Talks With Shadows' apparitional shadow bouncing and swaying on the walls of the tipi as the lodge fire glowed and flickered, the chanting in a strange voice. *How does the baby in your belly grow? ... Does he feel strong? ... Eagle Talon has bonded with a hairy-faced one... The future of The People is not bright.* Then, the memory of Talks With Shadows riding up to them in the long line moving east and north in search of buffalo rose up. She had stared at Eagle Talon before looking at her strangely. *"It is not yet time."*

She feigned a smile at Eagle Talon, pointing at the stone pestle laying on the flat grinding rock, drying remnants of meat still clinging to the slight concaves of its smooth surface. "I have a surprise for you," she said, sweeping one arm expansively at the other women. "We ground and smoked much of the meat yesterday. I had just a few dried chokecherries remaining from last fall. I've already mixed the grease into the meat. It has not yet set, but you will like the pemmican, husband. It is your favorite.

"And where might you have hidden this not quite ready pemmican?"

Walks With Moon looked down to hide her thoughts, knowing they would show on her face, *Food is always the best distraction for his preoccupation with the vision.* Pretending to busy herself again with the makings of the fire, she spoke. "It shall remain hidden till the sun rises tomorrow and the fat has set."

Eagle Talon grunted, trying to keep from smiling. "You are a tease."

Turning her head up at him over her shoulder, she giggled and patted her protruding belly, "Not always such a tease, my husband."

Eagle Talon laughed deeply. Several of the women glanced over at them. "Perhaps tonight," he said, "when the moon chases the sun from the sky. I shall hold you to those words, wife." Falling silent for a long moment, his expression suddenly pensive, he sank to a squatting position beside her, his tone serious. "Walks With Moon, there is something of which we must speak."

Walks With Moon felt an unpleasant quickening of her heart. She lifted her shoulders and straightened her back, sitting back on her calves.

Picking up one of the smaller sticks from her woodpile, Eagle Talon traced the tip of the wood aimlessly in the sandy loam. *He is thinking about how he will say what he needs to tell me.*

When his eyes returned to hers, they were soft and worried, "At the Council meeting several suns ago, when Brave Pony, Turtle Shield, Three Cougars, Pointed Lance and I were informed of the Council's decision to lift our shame, Flying Arrow bade me to remain after the others had left." He etched another furrow in the soil, his eyes avoiding hers.

"And?"

She did not mean for her question to sound sharp, her voice high pitched. He looked at her. "You know of the senseless killing of the sixty brothers by hairy-faced ones, and the stripping of their carcasses of hides, the meat left to rot," he said. "But several suns ago, one of our scouts found three Cheyenne braves, all with bullets in them, two shot in the back. They had only been watering their horses. The horses of their attackers had been shod."

His words left a hollow feeling in her chest. "*The People's future is not bright,*" Talks With Shadows had said. Walks With Moon willed her face to look passive and said nothing.

Again, the tip of Eagle Talon's stick began to move between the grass stems. He swallowed and began to speak, his voice measured and even, "The Council is deciding within a moon if I am to ride south to find my spirit brother, Roobin, and the tall one whose wrist you tickled as a child, Zeb Riah. They will tell me of the ways of the hairy-faced ones, what they want, how many there are and when they will come."

Her hand rose to her mouth, catching the soft exhale of her gasp in its fingertips. "But husband, Zeb Riah traps in the lands of the Ute where the water turns rock red. They are not friends of The People." Her mind reeling, she tried to calculate. "It might take you a moon to get there, another moon to find them if you can, and talk, and then another moon or more to come home. The village will be close to winter camp by then, far to the northwest and..." Her voice faltered, but before she could continue, Eagle Talon reached out a powerful hand and rested it on her shoulder, squeezing gently.

"I know, Walks With Moon. Our son will be arriving near that time." His smile was earnest. "This, I would not miss. I have so informed the council."

Walks With Moon sighed, a small portion of the tension

leaving her chest. "But when will you go?"

"Maybe after. I may face the onset of winter. I might not be able to come back until the rivers are running high with melted snow and the south sides of the hills are brown with early spring grass. Or they could send me at that time, in the season of spring, when the buds appear on the cottonwood trees. I would have to find the trail of the village, already on the move in search of the tatanka upon my return, or they may decide I should not go. It is the decision of the Council, and that is in Spirit's hands."

CHAPTER

*5*

July 27, 1855

# *F*ERVENT WISH

OURAY SAT CROSS-LEGGED, A FEW FEET FROM THE DYING embers of the lodge fire, midmorning sunlight sifting through the tipi's smoke hole and open-door flap, casting a comforting glow over everything within the lodge.

Outside the lodge, the shouts of children and murmur of voices sifted through the walls. Ouray could hear the sound of travoises being loaded and strapped down. The *Unita-at* were preparing to return to their lands near the salty lake. From beyond the encampment came the seldom heard sound of cattle bawling.

Next to him, Black Mare knelt on a shaggy, cinnamon-colored bear hide, her thighs settled back on her calves. The fringed hem of her supple leather dress was tucked demurely over her knees, the tips disappearing into the coarse fibers of the bear's brown fur. The bodice of the dress was cross-stitched and embroidered in trade beads of red, turquoise and blue, ascending the swell of her bosom.

Across the dying fire from Black Mare knelt Chipeta. Ouray watched her diligently rolling up three buffalo hides, tanned side in. After she set the large bundles aside, she rolled up the smaller mule deer and elk hides. *Added warmth on chilly nights,* he thought. Her slight, square shoulders tapered to a narrow waist that flared to a shapely curve where the leather stretched across her hips. She is not such a child anymore, he realized.

Turning to his wife, he flashed a broad smile and nodded his head in approval. "It is good that *la muchacha* straightens up our lodge. In a few suns, it will be time for the village to move higher into the canyons of the Gunnison and the great peaks of the *Uncompahgre.*"

His eyes drifted to Chipeta, intent on tying a rolled elk hide with a rawhide string. Turning his gaze back to his wife, his heart warmed at the site of her womanly figure. *We have great love,* he thought. *We need only a son.* Feeling the admiring rove of his eyes, she blushed. Ouray chuckled. "It is getting to be that time," he nodded his chin to the growing bundles of hides beside Chipeta. "when much heat can come from sources other than the pelts of our animal brothers."

Black Mare, her cheeks now a blushed bronze, glanced at Chipeta to see if the girl had overheard. Leaning closer to Ouray, she whispered, "My husband, should you be so forward in front of the child?" Her soft-spoken tone conveyed more appreciation than admonition.

Outside, the morning sun cast the dim shadow of a man in a broad-brimmed hat against the tipi walls. Recognizing the shape of the approaching visitor, Ouray rose, belching softly as he straightened up.

Ouray rubbed his stomach, grinning at the women, who hid their giggles behind raised hands. "Far too much to eat last night," he said. "slices of deer, slices of elk, and," he sighed contentedly, "that pemmican you made from last year's moose, Black Mare." He paused. "I ate so much of that, others complained there would be none left for them."

The visitor appeared in the open tipi flap, his body bent slightly forward to look inside. Over one forearm was draped Ouray's ceremonial beaded shirt and belt, both neatly folded.

"Ouray?"

Reuben's deep voice made Ouray think of a young bull elk full of prowess. Stepping toward the opening, Ouray gestured, inviting Reuben in. He smiled as the young man hesitated, removing his hat before stooping to enter the lodge. Straightening, he extended the shirt to Ouray.

Taking the shirt, Ouray draped it over his shield, then turned back to Reuben, who was rotating the brim of his hat in his hand. *Not nervous, but thoughtful.* He extended his arm and hand to the young man. Reuben moved as if to shake Ouray's hand, but remembering, instead clasped Ouray's forearm and elbow, as Ouray did to his, their arms moving in unison up, then down, in greeting.

"I come to say *adios* and *gracias.*" Reuben's eyes held his, then dropped with a smile to Black Mare and Chipeta. He nodded and bowed slightly. His eyes returned to Ouray's. "It was..." His voice trailed off.

"*Muy bonita,*" finished Ouray for the young man. "As was your new wife, Ray-bec-ka. Black Mare and Chipeta have discovered a way to polish the glass from her gourds."

Black Mare nodded excitedly, pride in her voice. "*Si!* We have put them in small pouches of buckskin, together with coarse sand. The drawstrings are drawn tight and the bags shaken hard. It will take time, but the glass grows smoother, losing its sharp edge." She held up a finger, the scabbing cut on its tip evident, and laughed. "We *comprende* quickly that the pieces of Ray-bec-ka's gourd are sharp, more so than even a man's blade."

"I am sure," Reuben said, "once smoothed, you will make *bueno* use of them. Perhaps, when the sun catches their sparkle, you will remember last night."

Black Mare's grin widened in agreement, "*Donde es* Ray-bec-ka?"

"I was not sure you would be in your lodge, and she did not want to intrude. She is down at the wagon, making final preparations to leave. Philippe, Johannes and the boy have gathered the cattle to begin the move north."

As Black Mare and Chipeta rose from where they were kneeling, Ouray regarded the young man thoughtfully. *Strength and command mixed with common sense—a good combination.* Black Mare cast a questioning glance at him, her face brightening as he nodded assent. "Let us go say *adios* to Ray-bec-ka," she said, waving Chipeta to accompany her.

The excited chatter of the two women receded from the lodge. Ouray reached out a hand and placed it firmly on Reuben's shoulder, looking intently into the young man's green eyes. *Verde, like the grass that grows in midsummer by the creek.*

"We will make good use of the cow," said Ouray. "It is a fine animal. The Noochew are pleased to have you on their lands." Unflinching, Reuben's eyes held his. "We know you will take good care of our land."

Though the young man's eyes were unwavering, a muscle in his cheek twitched, almost imperceptibly. "We will take care..." he paused, "of all lands now used by our friends, the Noochew."

Sifting Reuben's words in his mind, Ouray decided nothing further should be said on the subject. *It is merely the difficulty in communication.* "I shall instruct my people to leave a sign near where you build your lodge each time they move to and from Snaefel or follow the course of *Las Dallas.*"

The young man smiled but said nothing.

"Go with Spirit, Roo-bin. Prosper in the home of the Noochew. Have many children with Ray-bec-ka. From time to time, in the season of the warm moons, Ouray, Black Mare and Chipeta may visit your lodge, and you are welcome in ours."

"And you in ours, Ouray," Reuben responded warmly. Turning, he stooped low, disappearing through the lodge flap, his broad-brimmed hat in his hand, his steps headed toward the wagons.

---

THE MIDDAY SUN WAS SHINING DOWN ON REBECCA AS SHE sorted goods on the open rear gate of the wagon, repacking for the last leg of their push to the Uncompahgre, her mind whirling. *The note...Zeb...shorthanded...Sarah and Philippe...my very first day in this life as a married woman...the baby...the unknown.* Looking up from the clutter on the tailgate, she spotted Black Mare heading toward the wagon, the younger Chipeta beside her but respectfully walking a step behind.

Straightening up, Rebecca smiled at the approaching women and waved. Their bronzed faces softened, bright white teeth flashing in return.

"*Buenos dias,* Ray-bec-ka."

"*Buenos dias,* Black Mare. *Este dias es muy Bonita. Sí,* Chipeta?"

Black Mare giggled softly at Rebecca's Spanish, and Chipeta, a shy expression stealing across her face, merely said, "*Sí. Bien.*"

"Ouray tells us you and your husband are headed to *Las Dallas* to build your lodge," Black Mare said, "and grow your cattle." She raised her head to the sun, thinking. "*Diez,* maybe eleven suns traveling in these," she gestured to her side at the wagon.

Leaning over the open tailgate into the wagon, Rebecca retrieved the white doeskin wedding dress Black Mare had given her from the blanket in which she was about to wrap it. She draped the dress carefully over her forearm. "*Muchas gracias. Me gusta mucho.*"

Black Mare beamed. "It fits you well. You were *muy bonita* standing there in the firelight, the sparkle of the *puwarat* rattles dancing around the two of you. All could see the love in your eyes. The dress is for you to keep—a present."

Rebecca felt a tinge of heat rising in her cheeks. "Are you sure you wish me to keep this?"

Black Mare's eyes widened, and her smile faded. Rebecca

feared she had, without meaning to, said something wrong. Chipeta's eyebrows lifted. "You do not like the dress?"

She smiled broadly, clutching the dress to her breast. "I love the dress," she said quickly. "But it is so beautiful and so special. I would not want your heart broken if you were to part with it. But if you truly wish me to have it, I will cherish it, wear it only for the most special occasions. I would be honored," she finished, hoping she had undone any damage.

To her relief, she saw the expressions on both women's faces soften, the corners of their mouths turning upward. *Thank God.*

Black Mare gently pressed the dress even more tightly to Rebecca's chest. "It is yours, Ray-bec-ka. We have received the glass pieces, which will adorn other clothes. As this white doeskin carries memories for you," she pivoted, one hand sweeping around to encompass the village, "so will the shiny glass pieces remind us, and our people, of you and Roo-bin."

Leaning again over the tailgate, Rebecca laid the doeskin dress carefully back on the blanket. When she turned back to Black Mare, she noticed her staring at the heavy, green, cotton blouse she wore tucked into the waistband of her riding skirt. Her hand went instinctively to the curve of her belly. *Can she tell?* Black Mare's thoughtful but fleeting expression was answer enough. Black Mare turned to Chipeta and leaned down, speaking softly in the language of the Noochew. Chipeta's eyes widened. She nodded in return, and then spun around and began walking briskly back toward the village.

Black Mare turned back to Rebecca, her eyes earnest.

"Do you and Roo-bin hope to have children immediately? Have you thought about how many?"

Rebecca knew that despite herself, she had been caught off guard by Black Mare's inquiry. *Very strange... Should I tell her? She will one day find out.* She allowed a soft smile to play on her lips. Patting her tummy at the belt line, she said, "I am already with child."

Black Mare's eyebrows shot up, but her expression softened in the way only women would understand. Yet, there was something else. *Concern, perhaps? Worry? Envy?*

Black Mare was looking down at the ground, moving a pebble with the toe of her moccasin. "I am happy for you," she said. "You are so fortunate. I hope you have many, and I hope that they are born strong and healthy. Maybe even growing into warriors who raise cattle and always be friends with the Noochew."

When she raised her eyes, Rebecca was startled to see a teary film in them. Black Mare's lower lip quivered as she continued. "Ouray and I have been hoping for three winters to have a son," she sighed, "or even a daughter."

"Oh, Black Mare, it shall happen. I know it will." She reached out a hand and touched Black Mare's arm, giving it a gentle squeeze. "You shall have at least one fine, strong son," she said, trying to impart the right tone of enthusiasm and hope, "maybe many more!"

Tears escaped Black Mare's eyes. "An elder woman of the tribe, a birthing woman, says something is not quite right. I may never be with child. It pains me not to be able to give my husband his most fervent wish."

Rebecca wanted to console her, to reassure her, but

before she could offer words of hope, Black Mare turned away, embarrassed to have revealed so much. The sun, which had been shining so brightly only moments ago, slid behind a cloud, casting a shadow over Black Mare as she ambled back toward her lodge.

# 6

June 27, 1855

# ITALIANO

SWAYING WITH THE PITCH OF THE *EDINBURGH'S* FOREDECK, Erik surveyed the sea's angry gray swells as the bow of the ship plunged into them. White froth erupted from the tips of the waves as they rolled and roiled. Windblown, he hugged his violin case tightly, *I should've come up this morning as I planned when all one could see was a glassy blue sea. How quickly its mood changes.*

Disappointed, trying to shield the instrument's case from the fine mist and drops of salt spray erupting from the pitching bow, he turned, descending the narrow steps of the ladder to the main deck. He wrapped one hand around the instrument case, and with the other, clenched the rail to stabilize himself on the yaw of the stair treads as the *Edinburgh* plowed into the increasingly heavy seas.

Reaching the bottom of the stairway, he maintained his hold on the railing. Above the light gray smoke trailing from the ship's funnel and the swaying masts, patchy clouds scuttled across the sky as if hurrying back toward Europe. In the sheltered rise of the bridge, and protected from the direct assault of salty spray, the weather was almost pleasant. *I really don't want to go down in that hole again.... Perhaps to the stern, on the lee of whatever we are sailing into, tucked up against the superstructure in whatever warmth remains before the sun sinks below the horizon.*

Releasing his hold on the rail, he took two bold steps toward the stern of the ship. The sharp lurch of the main deck staggered him back an equal distance. He laughed to himself and then forged forward once again, his outstretched hand bracing along the superstructure for balance.

He rounded the starboard corner of the weather deck, leaned against the structure and angled his feet in front of him. *Relatively stable, good sun from the west. My hunch was correct. Far less wind and spray,* he chortled to himself, *relatively speaking.*

Closing his eyes, he let the pitch and roll of the vessel transport him back to the day he left and Isaac's raging temperament. Helmon's furtive expression of goodbye had been much different. He had whispered brotherly love and had made a gift of his dagger. Nervous, almost overwhelming excitement had clutched Erik with every clip-clop of horse's hooves on the road to Bremerhaven, and then down the cobbled streets to the *Edinburgh.* All shapes and sizes of folks speaking foreign languages had crowded the dock, young, old, men and women, families dragging wailing children, clutching the small ones tightly. *As if the whole world is headed to America.*

While aboard the ship, he'd been keeping mostly to himself, making a few friends– acquaintances rather, he corrected himself. His only real connection was with a young

man, slightly older than himself, seventeen or eighteen—
Andre Androfski. He was also a farm boy, though his family
in Poland focused on crops rather than cattle. Jewish, like
Erik, he was on his way to America to work for his
grandfather, who apparently owned a company that cut trees
for lumber somewhere in a place called New Hampshire.

Smaller than most of the young men on the ship, Erik had
endured periodic teasing, some of it mean-spirited. But he
had sidestepped any confrontations, coming close to drawing
his dagger only once, when two tow-headed, stocky ruffians
from Russia insisted on taking his violin case. "And what do
you suppose he's got in here?" they had bullied. Andre
intervened, and with the odds no longer quite in their favor,
the pair had backed down, *leaving to find someone else to
bully, no doubt.*

The wind, slung by the sea gods around the curved
corners of the weather deck, bounced off the overhangs and
abutments of the aft structure. His cheeks felt whipsawed
by it. He closed his eyes, and his whole body felt alive. The
sun, except when shadowed by a cloud, was warm, its heat
reflecting off the metal against which he had braced his back.
He loosened his grip on the violin case.

Opening his eyes, he glanced left, then right. A young,
blonde woman stood about ten paces away. She returned his
gaze. Short-statured, slender but well figured, she leaned
against the superstructure, as if mimicking his pose. Her lips
were pale but perfectly formed, her nose nicely carved, and
set between high cheekbones. Tucked under her long
tapering neck was a strong, petite and seductive chin. The
tapered black jacket she wore reached to the flowing curve

above her hips. Large gold buttons winked suggestively in the sunlight. The wind caused the pleated skirt she wore to ebb and flow against her ankles, revealing the shapes of her legs, first from one angle, then another. The curls at the tips of her long blonde hair, billowing in the wind, spilled in startling contrast over the shoulders of her black jacket.

Erik was stirred by a strange and unfamiliar current. He had seen her twice before, maybe three times, but always accompanied by a man and a woman he had assumed were her parents. The man was broad-shouldered, small-statured and wiry, with a darker complexion and wavy, dark brown hair. The woman, slightly taller, had blonde hair. Her features seemed remarkably similar to the young woman's. Erik had never ventured close enough to introduce himself, though she'd stirred his interest each time he'd seen her.

The ship bucked, and he almost lost his footing, nearly dropping the violin case. *I am making a fool of myself,* he thought as he regained his balance. She turned toward him, keeping her left shoulder tucked against the superstructure, her wide, blue eyes locked on his. Her eyes narrowed as her cheeks lifted in a soft smile. *Well, after that, there is nothing to lose.* Her gaze followed him as he moved slowly toward her. As the distance between them narrowed, her beauty grew. Reaching her, he leaned his right shoulder into the structure, angled out his feet and crossed a foot over one ankle, he hoped nonchalantly, though the damn violin case made everything awkward. She looked amused. The hint of a smile played on the corners of her slightly parted lips. She was teasing him. Her tongue moved across her upper lip. Once pale, now it shimmered.

Slightly frantic, Erik opened his mouth to speak. No sound came out. *Say something, you idiot.* "I am Erik," he blurted. *Oh, brilliant.* "I am from Prussia," he blurted again. Her smile widened, cheeks lifting upward. He could see a vein pulsing on the side of her neck. *That feeling again.*

"Alysia. Italiano."

"Do you speak Prussian?"

She shook her head.

"English?"

She again shook her head.

"Hebrew?"

Her eyebrows arched, and she giggled, her breeze-blown golden locks swaying side to side.

"French?"

"*Solo Italiano.*"

Erik sighed, loudly, but thankfully the fingers of the gusty winds hurled it somewhere out to sea. An image flashed in his mind. *The picnic, Reuben, Gretchen. So long ago.* He put down the violin and smiled.

Keeping his eyes locked on hers, *so blue,* he reached out and took her hand. Gently holding it, feeling only the slightest resistance in the bend of her wrist, he bowed, raised the back of her hand to his lips and kissed it. Her skin was as smooth as the bow of his violin.

A male voice, sharp, stern, authoritative, shattered the moment. "Alysia!"

*Annoying, intrusive, yet...*

She snatched her wrist from Erik's lips. They broke eye

contact. Twenty feet to port stood the short, dark-haired man Erik had seen her with previously. Behind the man, more muscular than Erik had noticed before, stood the blonde woman, hands on her hips, disapproval etched on her features.

"*Padre?*"

Alysia's voice, a high-pitched exclamation of surprise, revealed her embarrassment. The man said nothing, but narrowed his eyes, alternating his gaze from his daughter to Erik.

"*Cosa e' questo?*" he demanded, his lips set in a grim line, his voice as cold as the salt spray.

"*Venire. È tempo di cena.*"

She flashed a quick look at Erik, dipping her eyelids in a hidden gesture of goodbye. She walked quickly to her parents, her tapered jacket and pleated skirt swaying with the movement of the ship. Her parents turned abruptly, the three of them disappearing around the corner. Erik watched Alysia's father bend toward his daughter, speaking rapidly, the emphatic motion of his hands punctuating his words.

# CHAPTER

## 7

June 27, 1855

## ZION

As THE S.S. *EDINBURGH* PITCHED IN THE SWELLS OF THE Atlantic, and while Reuben stood reading Zeb's unexpected note, hundreds of miles northwest, Joseph rested one hand on the shoulder of his four-year-old son, Paul, wrapping his other arm around his wife's ample shoulders. "Roberta, we are truly blessed by the Lord." Their humble one-room cabin, with its rough-sawn walls, would at least provide protection. Clumps of green grass, where stubborn seeds had sprouted, were already springing from the sod roof. Behind them, a feast had been laid out on long wooden tables, meat roasted on spits and the skeleton of the barn had been raised.

His wife beamed up at him from the crook of his arm, her dowdy, round face split with a smile, eyes shining, her arms bouncing their two-year-old daughter.

John the Elder walked to them, weaving his way through the milling men and women, his eyes proudly surveying their first day's work. "We made significant progress," he said. "If we could have rounded up more men, I think we'd be done." He gestured toward the massive structure a hundred feet from them, two and one-half stories high, the barn's rafters and eaves framed in the traditional Dutch design. *A hawk's wings in a downward curl.* Sage and grass-covered hills, and an expansive meadow with green and red pockets of brush and willows were visible through the open studs and rough-sawed lumber, the smell of fresh-cut pine wafting over the scene. At the downstream edge of the meadow, the shallow hills dipped their toes in the slow current of the Bear River, which then wandered in curves through another vast meadow to the west. Two day's ride to the south, the rugged ridges of Porcupine Pass rose from the floor of Cache Valley, and still further loomed the sharp white peaks of the Wasatch Front.

John's medium build stood a foot shorter than Joseph's lanky height. "I'm sorry, brother Joseph," he said, his drooping salt-and-pepper mustache lifting in a smile. "We should have been done today. You're far to the north of Salt Lake, a fair distance to travel. Some of the men from the outlying farms didn't want to leave their families alone on account of the Ute. We will have the barn roof and siding up tomorrow, and the loft and doors also."

Smiling, Joseph glanced toward the tables laden with food. "I think everyone's focused on eating after a long day. We are honored to have you all as our guests." He turned toward the four stocky women who stood behind the tables, their hands folded demurely in front of their white aprons, light-colored sunbonnets shading their broad smiles. "And thank you, too, ladies, for helping Roberta prepare such a fine supper."

John smiled. "This is your farm, Joseph. Would you lead

us in prayer?" The men removed their hats, and everyone bowed their heads as Joseph gave thanks to God.

The four stocky matrons, with some assistance from other women, bustled back and forth from steaming cauldrons, and three fires crackling beneath spits skewering four hindquarters of mule deer, carrying trays of meat, pans of sourdough bread, pitchers of milk and boiled potatoes.

The aroma from the various dishes succulently mingled with the scent of fresh timber and the damp smell of river grass. The field Joseph had begun to plow smelled of freshly turned earth, and a breeze brought the scent of sage growing on the slopes around the meadow.

The elders, served first, chewed and nodded to one another. The men, their plates already heaping from generous portions they had doled out to themselves, spoke hurriedly between forkfuls. Happy chatter swelled from the tables as the women, deferring to the men, reached with outstretched arms, piling food first on the plates of their children, then on their own.

As dictated by tradition, the hosts and their children hung back. They would eat last. Joseph squeezed Roberta to him again as he studied the solid frame of the barn. *Before the sun rose today, that was but a patch of grass.* He sighed. *Zion indeed.* "It's quite something," he whispered, "and makes the place...well...official." He pondered their choice to settle there. "Do you ever think about those people from that other wagon train we met on the trail right before Fort Kearny? The folks headed to Cherry Creek?"

She looked up at him, her blue eyes blinking in surprise, her short dark hair bobbing up and down. "How odd you should mention that. Yes, I do, Joseph. Frequently, though I don't know why they made such an impression on me. That very tall blonde man with a thick accent who we spoke with seemed to be truly impressed by the reading of the elders that day. And that equally tall, pretty young blonde woman, they kept exchanging looks, and he walked away with her, though they were on opposite ends of the congregation during the service—very strange. And that beautiful, dark-haired slim woman with that rugged looking young man with the big brown hat over by the wagon, I don't think they ever stopped talking."

Joseph chuckled. "I watched them, too. I couldn't help but wonder if they were brother and sister, deeply in love or if they didn't like one another at all."

Roberta giggled. "I looked closely. None of them wore wedding rings. I wonder what has become of them?"

His hunger enticed by the smells, Joseph tore his gaze from the tables and stared down at her. "I have wondered myself from time to time...but the Lord has a plan for us all, Roberta, and I believe one day when God wills it, we shall find out, *as we shall of the Ute, the winter and the fertility of this heavy soil....* Now, let's join the others before those plates are scraped clean."

CHAPTER

*8*

July 1, 1855

# THE BAIT

"THOSE ARE SOME MOUNTAINS," EXCLAIMED JOHANNES, reining Bente in behind Lahn, and staring northwest at two soaring peaks. Wispy, ephemeral clouds clung like ground fog to the rocky faces below the pinnacles, the highest mountain rising to an odd canted angle at its top, both shimmering white with snow. The reflections and refractions of the early morning sun from the summits contrasted sharply with the forest green edge of their timberlines, and the deep, blue, sky dome above them.

Reuben pulled back on Lahn's reins, backing the palomino two steps until he was abreast of Johannes. He fumbled in his saddlebag, drawing out the map. Unfolding the heavy parchment, his eyes shifted from the map to the peaks and then back again.

"That bigger one with that odd slant-shaped angle at the top is Uncompahgre Peak. Scout noted here it's over fourteen thousand feet. The other one is Sheep Mountain, over thirteen thousand feet. And those," he said cranking his shoulder left and to the rear in the saddle and pointing, "poking with a reddish tinge on the south sides above those smaller peaks and trees are the Red Mountains. *Las Montanas De Rojas.*"

He grinned at Johannes, "Almost there!"

Then he sighed. "I wish we weren't going all this distance out of our way. Getting pretty near to the point where we can branch off this Lake Fork River we been trailing, and head westerly around the toe of those foothills below Sheep Mountain."

His brown cowboy hat swiveled right as he nodded with his chin to the northeast. "Big canyon up there according to the map, on either side of the Gunnison River. If we had more time, we'd take a little detour and see that country, but we're behind as it is. I hated going this far north."

Johannes looked at him, quiet for a moment, *frustrated.* Then he glanced back over his shoulder at the three red-tipped peaks poking above high tree lines. "There's no way to get from here direct to those Red Mountains, not with these wagons, maybe not even with horses by the looks of that snow up high. And, my Prussian friend, I can tell you, from watching men haul cannon and supply wagons back in Europe, sometimes sticking to a trail on fairly level land— or at least gently sloping—may be more kilometers, but is less time, less chance for an accident and far less strain on the teams and equipment."

Reuben nodded in reluctant agreement, carefully folding the map and returning it to the saddlebag. "It gets flatter the farther northwest we go before we turn downstream on the Uncompahgre. I'm just wondering if it's worth losing a day to see if there is anyone around Fort Uncompahgre...."

Johannes noticed his friend's mouth tighten above his square jaw, and his teeth clench. *Zeb leaving bothers him more than he's letting on.*

"...now that we're shorthanded," Reuben finished.

"Well," Johannes said, keeping his tone light, "Zeb was not overly enthusiastic about the cattle. In fact, other than one or two times when there was no choice, he went out of his way to avoid even having to look at them."

Reuben shook his head. "True enough, but he was our eyes and ears, letting the four of us concentrate on the cows." His gaze rose to the looming mass of Uncompahgre Peak, and he added glumly, "That's not a luxury we have anymore."

*Change the subject a bit.* "According to that map," Johannes said, diverting the subject away from Zeb, "that old fort has been mostly abandoned since 1844. Read somewhere it was started by a trader named Robidoux. I saw notes under it on the map, *Ute attack, then burned.*" He steadied Bente as he thought for a minute, watching Reuben. "Maybe we could leave the wagons half a day's horseback ride from the old fort. You and Philippe go up and take a quick look. We could get up there and back in an afternoon, faster if there's no one there at all." He patted his leg. "I've only been in the saddle for about three hours, but that's about all this leg can take so far. Me and the women will be fine, especially if we pick a good open area to hole up, so no one can sneak in on us."

Reuben stared at him without expression. "Maybe." He tugged his hat brim down hard and craned back around to look over his right shoulder. Johannes turned as well. The wagons were two hundred yards behind. Trailing the two rigs, Philippe and Michael were riding drag, weaving back and forth on opposite flanks of the cows, spurring on stragglers.

"Let's take a break," Reuben said, "get you off that horse and back in a wagon. You overdo it, and you won't be back in that saddle for a while."

Johannes nodded. "Good. I can likely do a few hours in the saddle this afternoon, too, if I am needed!"

---

MICHAEL EAGERLY TOOK THE CUP OF *KAFFÉ* PHILIPPE handed him, grabbing the handle with one hand, the other curling around the opposite edge of the tin cup. "Ouch! h-h-h, hot," he stammered out, shaking his left hand and spilling coffee on his knee.

Phillippe flashed him a smile and laughed. "*Sí, muy caliente, muchacho.*"

Taking care not to burn his lips, Michael brought the cup tentatively to his mouth *just for a small sip,* his eyes roving around the group clustered on the shady side of the prairie schooner. Reuben leaned against one of the wagon's wheels, the heel of one boot off the ground and resting on a spoke behind him, nursing his coffee, looking up toward the big mountains to the west of them, and then more northerly out from the wagons, *thinking about something.* Rebecca was sitting uncomfortably on a rock near the fire, looking pale and dabbing at her neck with a handkerchief. Sarah was kneeling in some sparse grass near the fire placing small sticks of sage on the embers around the coffee pot, and Johannes was sitting on the open tailgate of the wagon, his back propped against one edge of the wagon box, running his hands and outstretched thumbs up and down the leg the bear had mauled.

Staring down at the dark, steaming brew in the tin cup, Michael felt a pang. *Miss my mama, but I like these people, especially the Mexican. And I sure like working those cows.* Philippe was kneeling by the fire, he and Sarah sharing occasional smiles across the flames. Sensing his stare, Philippe turned toward him, catching his eye and winking.

Straightening up from the wagon wheel, Reuben walked to Rebecca, bent down and kissed her cheek, saying something in a low tone Michael couldn't make out. The brunette smiled weakly back at him, shaking her head, *very pretty.*

There was a commotion halfway down the mass of cattle that were milling behind the wagons searching out the tender young shoots of early summer green grass. Two cows bolted in a lumbering lope into the scattered trees to the west, their mottled brown and white rumps and full, twisted horns disappearing quickly in the timber.

"Damn," growled Reuben disgustedly, flipping the coffee in an arc from his cup angrily. "I'll go out there and round them up."

Michael half raised his hand, "I will go, go, get th-th them."

Johannes stopped rubbing his leg, Phillipe flashed him an approving look, and Reuben stared at him for a moment and then nodded. "Okay, Michael. Thanks. Just move 'em back down with the rest of the herd and wait for us if we're not already out there." Reuben turned toward Johannes, his face shadowed by his broad-brimmed hat, "I like that idea of yours, Johannes." The Dane nodded and resumed rubbing his leg.

Swinging into the saddle, Michael dug his heels gently into the old mare, *mama's horse,* and the mare stretched out in an easy lope headed toward the timber where the two longhorns had vanished.

The sunshine in the pines was mottled with shadows, the sound of the mare's hooves muted by the scattered coverings of the previous fall's needles. The scent of pine sap floated on the gentle breeze from the west. Michael slowed the horse looking ahead up the gentle slope to where the timber became denser. *No sign of them. Better look for tracks.*

Bent forward and to the side of the saddle, he located, then carefully followed, the prints of the two strays. He didn't see the two riders, motionless, concealed in the shadows, hidden behind a tight grouping of pine trees, but he heard the hooves of their horses as they leaped toward him from fifty feet away. Startled, he straightened up, hesitating for a panicked moment and then reached for the pistol in his belt. It was too late. They were on either side of him, boxing in the mare. The tall, thin man covered him with an Enfield rifle and the other, medium height but powerfully built, had hold of his reins on the opposite side.

"I wouldn't pull that pistol, Chub," snarled the rider with the Enfield.

Michael's hands felt clammy, and his throat constricted, making it difficult to swallow. Fear boiled in his chest, and his heart was pounding.

Without taking his eyes off him, the tall man's lips split into a thin, malicious, triumphant grin. "That's right smart of you, Chub. What ya think, Floyd?"

The shorter man's eyes were narrowed and vicious, his lips curled in a nasty leer, "I think I always knew we'd meet up with that cocky son of a bitch with the pearl-handled Colt again." One side of his face lifted, stretching the leer in an ugly half grin, "And we have an unfinished date with those women."

The tall man ran his tongue hungrily over his lips, "Yep. We surely do. I like the redhead."

The man called Floyd had drawn his pistol. *Oh gawd, they gonna shoot me right here. Mama!*

Suddenly, without warning, the barrel of the pistol flashed as Floyd viciously backhanded him with the barrel across his forehead. Splitting pain erupted over his eyes, the trees spun, there was a burst of light, then darkness and then hazy light again. He almost toppled off the rear of the horse, but Floyd reached out, grabbing one arm before he could slump backward. Michael felt himself being pulled to lean forward, unable to think, his skull pounding. The other man moved his horse closer, holding him so he couldn't lay over the saddle horn. *Tying my hands—to pommel—rawhide.*

"Good thing you caught him, Floyd. Would a taken both of us to lift him back on that horse."

The other man chortled. "What we gonna do now?"

The voices sounded strange and distant as if far off in a tunnel. Michael leaned far forward, his wrists tied to the pommel keeping him in the saddle, and vomited down the old mare's withers.

Floyd laughed meanly, "Keep doing that, you might lose some of that weight." He looked at the other man. "I think we'd be fools, the two of us against those three men, particularly that kid with the Colt. But...," he reached out and grabbed Michael's hair, tipping his face up, *blurry, can't see them,* then letting go with a savage downward push to the back of his head, "...I think we got us some bait. Let's get him back to the rest of the boys. We can stay in these trees past where that timber comes out in a point up ahead, hightail it around the toe of the hill and be out across the flats before they see us." He cackled a dark-spirited laugh that echoed in Michael's semi-consciousness. "And we will leave a trail a blind man could follow, right back to the rest of the gang."

*9*

July 1, 1855

# $O$LD SCORES

REUBEN WAS ANNOYED. *LOSING MORE TIME.* HE GLANCED up into the timber looking for Michael, and then at the wagons already moving slowly ahead, followed fifty yards back by Queen, the lead cow, bell jingling, most of the other cows plodding behind.

"Where the hell is he?" Philippe asked, riding alongside him, his face serious.

*He has a bad feeling too.*

Pulling one of the onyx-handled Colts from his belt, Reuben watched Philippe dig his spurs into Diablo's flanks, the big horse surging forward without hesitation. They disappeared at a fast lope, weaving through the tree trunks.

Reuben jerked Lahn's muzzle from the grass. Sighing, he patted the palomino on the neck, "Sorry boy." Taking one last look up through the trees, he cantered out toward one stray, slow-moving cow, got behind her and clicked the animal into a fast, waddling walk toward the dust at the tail end of the herd.

There was a whistle from the trees. Fifty yards in the

timber, Philippe waved him over. Reuben kicked Lahn into a fast trot. Philippe wheeled his big black stallion around and headed back into the shadows.

When Reuben caught up to him, he was off Diablo, holding the reins, and kneeling, his fingers playing lightly over impressions in the matted pine duff. He stood up; his face expressionless, but his eyes dark. He pointed. "These are the tracks of the cows." He swung his arm, and these, here, *el muchacho.*" He paused. "And these, *dos caballeros.* "

Leaning over, he picked up a handful of pine needles, rubbing them in his forefinger, and held them up to Reuben. "Blood," he said grimly.

Anger and apprehension boiled in Reuben's gut. "Looks to me like they were shod hooves," he said.

"*Sí.* "

"Well, not Indians, and we know Michael's alive but likely hurt."

The *vaquero* nodded.

"Stay here, Philippe. I'm gonna ride down to the wagons, let them know what's going on, go over the map with Johannes and pick a spot they can hole up. Then, I'll be back up, and you and I will follow these tracks."

Philippe pulled a pistol from his belt, spun the cylinder and checked the loads. His eyes, what Reuben could see under the wide brim of his sombrero, were glittering slits, his lips set in a tight, thin, grim line.

"*Sí,* señor Reuben. We will make things right."

Back at the wagon, Sarah and Rebecca greeted Reuben's news with disbelief, their mouths slack and eyes wide. Johannes' jaw clenched; his eyebrows buried in a steep downward curve above his blue eyes. "Sarah, check the loads in those two Sharps and bring that shotgun and my Saber up here, would you? Check the load in your derringer too."

Reuben handed Johannes the map, watching him trace the route. They quickly agreed on the general area the wagons would stop and the likely first sizable open expanse.

"What about the cows?" Johannes asked, glancing through the open rear of the wagon canvas at the now milling herd.

"I don't think you'll be much more than a couple miles up. Most of them will follow the wagon and old Queen. If there's any stragglers, they won't go far. This grass will hold 'em, and we'll do a sweep when we get back."

---

PHILIPPE WATCHED REUBEN APPROACH; THE BIG PALOM-ino given his lead by the young Prussian. The horse nimbly angled between trunks, his gold body standing out against the brown bark of the trees, his flaxen tail flashing in the dappled shards of sunlight that filtered through the conifer canopy.

The young Prussian reined Lahn in hard as he reached Philippe.

"*Señor* Reuben, I will follow the tracks. You stay close behind. You will be our eyes."

Reuben nodded, drawing his Sharps from the scabbard, checking the load, then bobbing his head once when he was ready.

Philippe loosened Diablo's reins, trusting the horse to

pick his way through the trees and leaned down low over the saddle, his chin below the pommel, eyes riveted to the ground. *They are leaving a trail that a child could follow. This is not an accident.* Shifting slightly in the saddle, he felt the reassuring press of the two Colts against his belly. Diablo was moving at a fast walk. Philippe kept his eyes roving out in front of the horse's neck, and then again back to the near ground by the stallion's forelegs.

Soon, they were out of the timber and into flat country with the slightest roll to its contours, dotted here and there by trees, Philippe enjoying the lazy warm wind in his face, the deep tracks of the riders, three of them, clearly visible ahead in clumps of upturned sod and the bent and broken grasses that trailed northwest.

Philippe straightened, in a half lope now. He glanced quickly behind at Reuben, who spurred Lahn until they were abreast of one another, ten feet between them. Still in a slow lope, Philippe reached down and drew his musketoon from the belly scabbard. He rested the butt of the rifle on his right thigh, bore pointed skyward, his eyes searching far ahead looking for movement. The horses' shadows, cast ahead of them by the high sun, moved in synchronized rhythm, their front haunches melding into the heat shimmers. *As eager as we are,* Philippe smiled. *We're coming, muchacho. We're coming.*

———

AFTER MIDDAY, FAR AHEAD, THE MEN COULD SEE THE RAG-ged outlines of structures, the tracks they were following leading straight toward the buildings. Reuben fought to control the simmering white anger that had been building as they galloped north. *It must be Fort Uncompahgre. Don't want to stumble into any surprises.*

They reined up about a mile from the structures, Reuben digging in the pocket of his jacket for Mac's telescope, *Damn, left it with Johannes.*

He noticed Philippe watching him intently. As if reading his mind, the *vaquero* said quietly, "No matter, *señor* Reuben. We will see all there is to see when we get there."

His arms feeling encumbered, Reuben slipped from the saddle, removed his jacket and lashed it with the rawhide ties behind the cantle to the saddlebags.

He mounted back up, speaking in low tones to Philippe. "We will ride in slow. Get off, tie up the horses a hundred or hundred fifty yards out and leave the rifles." He patted the Colt. "Inside there, these will be better."

Philippe nodded, and they began a lazy lope toward the structures.

Reuben examined each part of the old trading post as they approached. It was fenced in, stockade style, uneven, unmilled knotty poles creating gaps, wider where the stockade had been burned, the black outer charcoal skin of the posts stark reminders of a deadly past.

Through the uneven gaps in the stockade fence, low rambling log structures were visible, some with roofs caved in, others partially burned. There was a depressing, foreboding feel about the place. Reuben could tell by the purse of his lips that Philippe felt it too.

Tying off the horses out of pistol range, they dug in their

saddlebags for additional cartridges, stuffed them in their pockets and began a deliberate walk toward the entrance to the stockade, scanning for any telltale signs of movement. One side of the gateless stockade entry was half burned, the other side tilting inward at a steep angle. Driven by the wind or pulled partially over by Indian ponies, Reuben couldn't tell.

Without speaking, each of them chose a side of the entrance and hugging the end posts, walked through one step at a time, pausing, looking, searching, their hands dangling inches from the grips of their Colts. The tracks of the three horses disappeared into the compound. There was a building to the right, part of its front wall burned out, that appeared to have been a kitchen in decades past. The building to their left, the side nearest them, was mostly collapsed, a broken roof hanging over the remnants of the wall, like the front of a broad-brimmed hat pulled low over a wrinkled forehead. Through the collapsed wall, they saw the rotted and brittle remnants of old hides scattered on the dirt floor. They eased around the corner and stopped.

The courtyard stretched two hundred fifty feet in front of them to a long low building, mostly intact. Another building, logs sunken but in place, was to the right. In the far corners were dilapidated horse corrals, and sheep or chicken pens. To the left was an open-faced building, several rusted blacksmith tools still hanging on spikes, and another building beyond, mostly burned down.

"Took you long enough."

They froze at the voice. Reuben crouched slightly forward.

Three men walked out from behind the far wall of the old blacksmith shop, two of them medium build carrying 1840s vintage muskets, the third, short, thin, wiry with a mean, swarthy face, a pistol in his belt and one hand stretched behind him, fingers wrapped in the collar of the stumbling boy he was dragging behind him.

*Michael—and one of Black Feather's men!*

From the building to the right of them, a door opened. Four men emerged, one heavyset, almost bald with round, pudgy cheeks, the other medium but powerfully built. Reuben took it all in, one quick and dangerous detail after another. *Floyd Bummer from Cherry Creek,* he realized. The third man, Floyd's sidekick, had been slow to drop his musketoon back in Cherry Creek until Reuben had turned the still smoking barrel of his Colt toward his chest just ten paces away. *But where are the other two?*

The seven men stopped about fifteen paces away, spread out across the debris-strewn central open expanse. Three more outlaws appeared suddenly from the small building next to the blacksmith cabin, two with pistols in their belts and the third carrying a musketoon like Philippe's.

The thin, swarthy-faced man leered at Reuben, his eyes mere slits beneath a filthy, beaded headband, "Ahh...*muchacho con la perla pistola,* we meet again. Time to settle old scores, *sí?*"

At his feet, the battered boy raised himself to his hands and knees, blood streaming from his nose and split lips, his face pale. He craned his head sideways to look at Reuben and Philippe, one eye swollen shut, one good eye beseeching.

"I hear you know Floyd here, too. This is for him." The

outlaw raised a leg, and viciously heeled Michael in the back, driving his chest back into the dirt. The men behind the outlaw laughed and slowly spread out. The tall one held a musket. One had a round face with wild eyes and tow-headed hair spilling from beneath a battered hat. He curled back his lips, the disgusting tip of his tongue bulging through the gap in his front teeth.

Seething anger rose in Reuben. He forced it down. *Think.* He could sense Philippe's slow sidestep away, spacing out their adversaries' targets, and getting an angle. Without looking, he knew the vaquero's hands were hovering around the grips of the twin onyx-handled Colts snugged crosswise in his belt. *Ten to two. Unless they get lucky, we might catch some lead, but we can take them.*

As if reading his mind, the leer on the outlaw's face tormenting Michael twisted with a mocking, vicious curl of his lips. Shadowed by the remnants of the log structures in front of them, more men drifted out. A barrel glinted in a roofless window aperture to the left of the gathering group of desperados.

*Eleven...twelve, thirteen, fourteen. It's a trap!*

"So, you *men*," the leader spat the word contemptuously, "gonna let this poor boy suffer?" He kicked Michael again. The young man groaned and coughed, doubling up. Lethal energy radiated from Philippe twenty feet to his right. *Easy, vaquero, easy. Make a mistake now, and all three of us will be dead.*

One eye on the desperado, Reuben's gaze swept the band, picking targets, prioritizing the most dangerous first.

"That's right, *pistolero*," the thin man's voice was

sarcastic and taunting, "thirteen to two."

*He doesn't think I've seen the man with the rifle in the cabin.*

"Three," Johannes' calm voice rang out sharply from behind him, twenty feet to his left. He willed his gaze not to slide from the ragged line of killers in front of them. From the corner of his eyes, he saw a muzzle swing up and into position. *Mac's shotgun! That'll equalize things a bit.*

"Three?" The bandits shared a menacing chuckle. "A tall blonde gimp will make little difference." The swarthy man, never taking his eyes off Reuben, leaned to the side and spit, grinning malevolently. "So, your women in the wagons are now alone?"

"That's right, Snake..." spat Floyd, picking up on the taunt, "all by them pretty selves."

Reuben's gut twisted, but he kept his face stony, eyes unblinking. *Rebecca and Sarah, alone! Two of the Bummer band not in sight.*

Getting no visible response from Reuben, Snake's mouth curled. He shifted his moccasin, pressing Michael's head into the dirt. "We ain't used knives on the youngster yet," he hissed. "Been saving that. Figured you'd want to see."

The man with the wild eyes laughed, drew a long silver blade from its wide sheath and took a step toward Snake and the boy.

"No, Tex. We just want to play with him first, not kill him...yet. José!" a short, slight man with a dirty, bent sombrero and a filthy serape flashed a mostly toothless smile. Smirking, he ambled slowly toward Snake and the boy, his bony knees poking through the holes in his brown leggings. He reached down and drew a stiletto from his boot.

Slit eyes still fixed balefully on Reuben, Snake ground Michael's head into the dirt. The boy groaned and gagged, struggling to breathe. Floyd looked on.

Reuben's mind was racing. *First, Floyd. Snake will be a little off balance. Then Snake. Hit the ground, roll, then the man in the window. Johannes will go for the nearest to him with a shotgun. Hopefully, Philippe doesn't pick the same targets. No time for wasted bullets.*

José reached Snake and Michael, his saunter animated now. He knelt, grabbed one of Michael's thrashing ankles and anchored the boy's leg to the ground with his own. He grinned up at Reuben, the black gaps in his teeth as vacant as his eyes and twirled the stiletto in his raised hand like a baton. With a flick of his wrist, he caught the knife by its handle, glinting blade pointing downward. He lifted his arm, poised for a downward thrust.

Reuben's gun hand moved. He could feel the deadly aura of Philippe in motion to his right. To his left, his peripheral vision caught the rising barrel of the shotgun. The outlaws' hands descended in a blur to the handles of their pistols.

A deep-throated boom echoed from behind—the loud report of an Enfield rifle, then a pause—no longer than the split second between life and death. Snake's motley band made the mistake of raising their gaze, searching for the source of the shot. In that moment, a bullet whizzed within feet of Reuben's head, parting the air. Then, a sudden thwack of bullet meeting flesh. A gaping red hole appeared between José's eyes. A mist of skull and brains sprayed out the back of his head onto the clothes of the outlaws standing behind him.

They stared at the gore, and at the lifeless body in front of them. Then a deadly bedlam erupted.

The Colt bucked in Reuben's hands. Floyd's eyes widened in disbelief. He dropped his pistol, both hands flying to his throat, blood spurting between his fingers. As he toppled over, Snake spun and ran to the rear, gun hand stretched behind him, bullets flying wildly. Flame came from a muzzle blast in the window. Heat and force seared Reuben's left arm, the force of the bullet spinning him around. The Colt came alive in his hand again, and a gurgling scream erupted from the glassless aperture. An outlaw toppled over the sill, arms dangling almost to the dirt. The shotgun roared to Reuben's left, again and then a third time. A blast blew a bandit backward. He flew through the air, hands and feet outstretched, his chest a red gaping hole where the full load of buckshot caught him.

Another man's legs crumpled, and he fell heavily to the dirt, screaming, clutching his torn thighs. Raising his hands to his eyes, a third staggered backward, forward, then side to side, blind. Floyd's tall, thin accomplice, who had ineffectively discharged, then dropped his musketoon, had his pistol out, straight-armed, pointing at Johannes. The Enfield roared again. He clutched his chest, sinking to his knees and pitched forward, face first in the dirt. In the courtyard to Reuben's right, Philippe's Colts were blasting. One outlaw, then a second and a third, buckled, spinning and falling in crumpled heaps.

The remaining killers ran toward a gap in the back of the stockade, its charcoaled edges marking the only escape and out of shotgun range. Johannes limped hurriedly over to the cover of an open threshold in one of the buildings, his .44 caliber Army Colt drawn. Philippe walked calmly after the fleeing bandits, his two black-onyx Colts in front of him like the fangs of a striking rattlesnake, their silver barrels sparkling in the sun.

Reuben's shirt was wet with blood. The courtyard seemed to turn in front of him, the debris-littered ground seesawing up and down. Michael tried to push himself up. Fighting to keep his balance, Reuben staggered toward him. He sank to his knees beside the battered boy, pushing him down. "Stay down, Michael. Stay down." Seconds later, Philippe stood beside him, a bloody crease in his outer left calf oozing blood. The Colt in his left hand barked twice, and the outlaws wounded by the shotgun blast ceased their writhing.

Led by Snake, most of the cowardly survivors of his band had reached the gap in the far wall of the stockade. Pausing to turn, they fired wild shots back toward Reuben, Philippe and Michael, the bullets kicking up ineffective explosions of dust as one by one, panic-stricken, they slipped through the break in the posts. Johannes braced his Army Colt against the splintered jamb of the doorway where he stood. The pistol barked once, and a fleeing outlaw clutched his leg. Limping, he dragged his wounded limb through the gap in the stockade, following the others like the last rat leaving a sinking ship.

A figure burst from the window of the building closest to the old corrals, somersaulted as he hit the ground and then jumped, his hands grasping the top of the stockade fence. He pulled himself up, the toes of his boots desperately seeking purchase on the knotty wood.

The fort spun around Reuben, and the Colt in his hand felt almost too heavy to hold. He waved the barrel weakly toward the fugitive straddling the stockade fence. Philippe spun, both barrels rising, but before he could fire, the Enfield boomed again in the distance, and the man, ready to drop to the other side of the fence, was knocked violently forward, the .52 caliber slug hitting square in the back. The force smashed his head forward into the top of the stockade, his body falling to the inside of the fence, one ankle lodged in the gaps between two uprights, his torso dangling grotesquely in its death twitches.

Reuben struggled to think through the fog. *It's over. We're alive, but where are the other two of the Bummer gang?* Johannes reached them, half hopping, half running as he favored his damaged leg. Kneeling down beside Reuben, he barked at Philippe, "You tend to Michael. I'll take care of Reuben."

Philippe dropped to his knees by the bloody boy, untying the kerchief from around his neck as he bent over Michael's trembling body.

Reuben heard Johannes's voice through a thickening haze, "Lay down, Reuben. We need to get a tourniquet on that arm. Don't think it hit the bone, but you lost a lot of blood." Johannes eased him onto his uninjured side. Stripping his belt from his pants, he wrapped it around Reuben's arm four times just below the shoulder, one edge in the armpit. He tightened each wrap of the thick leather and cinched the buckle.

Philippe turned Michael onto his back and wiped the

blood off his face, one hand gingerly pressing on either side of the boy's heaving chest. He smoothed his fingers along each side of his jaw. "Easy, *muchacho*, easy. You're going to be *muy bien*. You'll have a headache. I am fairly certain your jaw's dislocated, maybe broken, and at least one rib is cracked. But you are a tough *hombre*." Michael's lips parted in a weak smile as a frothy pink foam wheezed from the corner of his mouth.

Quickly cutting Reuben's sleeve lengthwise up to the tourniquet, Johannes glanced sideways at Philippe. "Who do you think...?" His words died in his throat as a long shadow fell across them. Philippe twisted, reaching for pistols, his eyes wide, mouth open. Johannes turned, looking up over his shoulder.

"Well, I'll be damned—Zebarriah Taylor. I should've known, with that Enfield."

The tall mountain man chuckled. "Figured you greenhorns might get lost without me, and comin' back cut the tracks of them three horses, and then the stallion and Lahn on top of that trail and knew something was up. When I seen what was happening, I didn't want to miss the party, so I hunkered down out there about two hundred and fifty yards."

He pointed out through the opening at the front of the stockade. "That there log next to the dead cottonwood was a perfect rest. Weren't much more than shooting ducks in a barrel."

He paused, one hand stroking the dangling side of his mustache where it disappeared into the gray stubble of his jaw staring at Michael, and then Reuben's arm. "I'll go out and gather up those horses and see if I can find some plantain for poultices."

He reached up, drawing the rawhide cord of a bulging bladder bag from around his neck. Leaning over slightly, he dropped it on the ground by Johannes. "Filled that up with water on the way in. With the blood they've lost, they're gonna need it."

He turned, Enfield cradled in one arm, and walked back to the front of the stockade, whistling for Buck.

July 1, 1855

# OF HORSES AND

# FISH

TURNING TO LUCY AND THE MULE, ISRAEL GESTURED DIS-
gustedly at the roiling brown waters of Oak Creek swirling
over submerged rocks. The current tugged at grassy banks,
clutching partially submerged tree limbs and rushed over
snags in a tumultuous downstream froth toward the Yampa.

Israel waved at the snow-covered peaks surrounding the
valley. "It's no wonder these lower creeks are a muddy mess.
The sun here carries the heat of a forging iron." He grimaced
in the direction of Lucy and Sally. They both stared at him,
the mule's ears flicking forward and back. Lucy shook her
head, the hint of a smile on her pudgy lips.

"That's right, husband. Me and the mule is relyin' on our
guide. That would be you. With all the newspapers you read,
ya oughta know these things." Shaking her head with
exaggerated motion, she breathed a pronounced sigh. "And
I'm hungry," she teased. "Now, what you going to do 'bout
that, mister guide?"

"Well, we ain't gonna catch no fish in this soupy mess. Fast as that water is, doubt the worms will sink. We'll just wind up losing one of our last fishhooks."

Raising his hand to shield the sun from his eyes, he looked out to the foothills at the southeast edge of the valley. Their gradual contours curled downhill toward them, punctuated by dense stands of mountain mahogany, occasional clusters of conifers and stands of white-trunked quaking aspen. The green of the cone-shaped junipers had a bluish tinge from coming berries. "We only got two choices: keep on heading west and be hungry or spend a little time following this creek upstream till the water settles out. Still going to be high, but I bet it's clearer a mile or two higher."

"You be the guide, Israel," said Lucy, her approval of the second course of action evident in the bob of her head. She threw him a sharp look, adding, "Just so long as I don't have to get off dis mule."

⸻

HOLDING UP HIS HAND, BLACK FEATHER MOTIONED THE girl to rein up behind him. Standing in the stirrups, he peered down the trail to where it fell curving to the southwest below the summit of Rabbit Ears Pass. The broad, green expanse of the Yampa Valley stretched out behind and far below the tapering western ridges of the pass, the Yampa River cut through the valley. The river's course, a silver ribbon dissecting the green, ran straighter close to the foot of the pass. Down the valley, it snaked slowly back and forth in a broad, braided floodplain as the width of the flow spread

out.

Two small red squirrels made rapid taps on the bark of the hem-fir towering over the horses. Worried, they raced up and down the tree trunk, stopping to peer at the invaders, chattering indignantly at Black Feather and the girl.

Twisting slightly in the saddle, Black Feather spoke to Dot in low tones, "Ain't a whole lot of people in these parts, but any of them there is, if they're coming over this mountain, will be on this trail. Don't have much choice coming up the other side but I think we will drift off the trail to the south, follow them contours around those low ridges out there and work our way down to the valley. Bit steeper and slow going, but safer."

He stood in the stirrups again looking far down the valley. "If we're going to do some fishin', it ain't gonna be the Yampa. You can tell from here that river ain't done with snowmelt just yet. There's a creek they call Oak Creek that comes into the Yampa from the south a few miles out from the toe of the pass. A smaller creek feeds it. Think that one's called Service Creek."

He settled back down in his stirrups. "I reckon we'll cut the corner of where it hooks up with the Yampa, and just strike straight across the valley to a few miles upstream where that other creek comes in. Might be clear enough up there for them trout to see a worm."

Leaning forward, Dot gently patted the mare's neck. Looking up at him, she bobbed her head.

"Let's go then." Glancing up at the sun, the renegade did some quick, mental calculations. *Shouldn't be much if any snow still lingering on the south-facing hillsides. We ought to be upstream on the creek by midafternoon. Catch some fish and have us a supper. We're down to the last of the deer meat, and might have a week, maybe more, left of flour, fat and coffee.*

———— ··· ————

LUCY LEANED AS THE MULE'S SWAYBACK ROLLED WITH each step, watching Israel lead Sally. His thin legs moved slowly, and she could see the crisscrossed stitching where she had repaired his leggings. He planted each foot with care, correcting his occasional stumble as one foot or the other brushed a hidden rock or branch buried unseen in the grass. Watching her husband, she tried to work the stiffness out of her upper back by lifting one shoulder, then the other. *We be plumb crazy.*

The sun baked down, radiating off the grasses and the damp meadows along the valley floor, their intermittent pale and dark green expanses broken by lines of willows and alders. Outposts of white, yellow and violet wildflowers dotted the meadows. Occasional, small stands of cottonwoods stretched out to the foothills, defining the southern edges of the valley. Dense scraggly looking brush, as tall as the mule, covered the north and west slopes of the higher ground. *Ain't seen no trees like that before.* Above the roll of the lower foothills, the slopes rose gradually, then more steeply, forming plateaus and ridges, ending in the steep mountainsides. Large stands of dark conifers pocketed the slopes, interspersed by strips of shimmering pale green leaves and white trunks of quaking aspen hugging some unseen rivulet flowing down from the peaks. *My Lord. You done made some beautiful places*, Lucy chortled, *but we still be crazy.*

Stopping, Israel grabbed the tail of his shirt, raising it from his pants to wipe the sweat from his forehead as he turned to her. "It's like a wet oven down in these meadows." He swiped his face. "And Lordy, the bugs!"

Looking down at him from her perch atop the mule, and suppressing her smile, she kept her voice level, "You be the guide, Israel."

Israel laughed. "You say that one more time, woman, and I'm getting on the mule, and you'll be getting down here and pullin' her up this creek." There was a moment's silence as they both envisioned the impossible. They broke into laughter.

Israel raised a long arm, stretching out a bony finger, "See where them willows come down to the creek on the right side? Likely a smaller creek. Don't matter if it's high, and it likely will be if it's clear. I think that might be our spot if we can find a break in the willows to poke the pole through and get a line into the water."

---

CAREFULLY ASSESSING THEIR POSITION IN ALL DIRECTIONS, Black Feather was satisfied with where he had chosen to stop. Tied off in a patch of alder and virtually invisible, the two horses nickered quietly. The gold and red stems from the copse of willows growing along the banks of the small creek shielded them from view.

He stripped a few strands of hemp from a short length of rope and tied them to a stiff, green, tapered alder branch. Cursing with each failed attempt, he finally tied a hook to the end of the line dangling from the makeshift fishing pole.

"Hold this and stay here," he said, handing the rod to Dot. "Don't move that tip or it will get all tangled in this brush, and we only got two hooks." *That was all there was in that bastard Pedro's pockets.*

Some distance from the spongy, late spring soils that extended fifty or more feet from the creek, the ground rose slightly. A few hardy Queen Anne's lace plants grew in the drier soil. Picking his way up the rise, Black Feather paused when he spotted two large rocks. He pried the larger of the two loose, then the smaller. Once loosened, he rolled them over, chuckling at the thick nightcrawlers beneath. Stunned by the sudden light, the worms tried vainly to slink to safety. He picked up two of the writhing creatures and walked down to Dot, placing one in a cupped rock shaded by red willow. Tearing the other worm in two, he impaled its upper half carefully on the barb.

Bending down to the girl, he pointed out a break in the growth along the bank. "You just creep over there. Careful you don't make no noise because them fish can feel vibrations. Not too close to the bank or they'll scatter. Stick the pole out over the edge of the bank and drop that worm in the water. See what happens."

He grinned, watching her steal slowly toward the creek holding the rod extended, carefully negotiating its tip between the willow branches. A soft afternoon breeze stirred the air. She dipped the pole toward the water and the current dimpled when the worm encountered the surface. Almost instantly, a wake erupted from the undercut bank five feet away on the opposite side of the stream, followed by a golden green flash.

"Fish. Fish!" cried Dot, her face animated as she looked at him and pointing.

Black Feather laughed, "Don't be talking about it. Lift that pole tip, get that hook set in its mouth. Then, ease back here through them willows. I'll take it off, and we will catch us some more."

The girl jerked the pole tip up, and the water exploded as the hapless fish danced and jumped in futile attempts at escape. Lifting the wiggling, twisting trout from the waters, she backed up several steps until she could swing the pole around, dropping the flopping fish at the toe of Black Feather's muddy moccasins. A wide smile creased her face, her eyes rounded and excited.

Looking down to hide his expression, Black Feather smiled inwardly. *Horses and fish.*

He backed the hook out of the trout's jaw and held it up for Dot to see. "Whenever you see coloring like this, it would be a brook trout. They like these higher-up creeks. See that gold on the belly, white fin edges and that green gold on the sides with the colored speckles? Only fish quite like it. Good pink meat, too."

Sticking his pinky down the wiggling fish's mouth, he bent its head backward until there was a soft pop of its spine breaking. He held it up. "Eight, maybe nine inches. We ought to be able to catch ten or twenty. Good for a couple of meals." He watched her, surprised by the girl's enthusiastic nods, one small hand pointing at the other half of the worm in the shaded concave rock.

"You want me to bait it for you again? I'll do that. Just do the same thing you did before. When they stop biting here, we'll walk upstream till we find another break in the willows. You fish. I'll keep a lookout."

Grinning, Dot turned, holding the rod in one hand and the end of the line just above the hook in the other. She took a few, not so delicate, bouncing steps back to the creek.

*Best spirits she's been in in weeks.*

Dot was backing up again, the end of the pole twitching and bobbing with another splashing fish, larger than the first. The trout dangled over the rushing current, his tail slapping back and forth in the air as if waving a terrified goodbye to its watery home.

Again, swinging the rod toward Black Feather, a smile spread from one thin cheek to the other. She pointed and said, "Fish!"

Laughing, Black Feather gently clapped her on the shoulder, "Yep, another fish—bigger. But I ain't takin' him off the hook. You caught him. You get the hook out."

Dot's eyebrows shot up, her widening eyes moving from Black Feather's face to the fish on the ground. Stooping, she closed one small hand around the trout, withdrawing it quickly, staring at the slimy wetness covering her fingertips and palm, and then up at Black Feather. Her nose wrinkled.

Hiding his laugh, Black Feather knelt down beside her, picking up the fish. "First, stick a finger down its mouth. Then, bend the head toward its back till you hear that little pop. Hear that?"

The girl nodded, her eyes fixed on the fish all but lost in Black Feather's hand.

"Breaks its neck. Kills it. Much easier taking the hook out and less chances of sticking yourself." He handed the limp brookie back to the girl, who took it gingerly, her nose wrinkling again.

"So, that hook is shaped like this...." Black Feather crimped his pinky in the shape of a J. "That sharp point goes up through the jaw. Easier if you back it out of the jaw rather than tugging on it."

Bent over the fish, Dot worked at the metal protruding from the slight hook in the tip of the trout's upper jaw.

"See that little hook bump on the jaw? That's a male. Can tell by that reddish on the belly, too. That other one," he pointed at the first fish, "dull colors. That's female. Probably be eggs in her when we clean it."

Squatting, focused on the fish in her hands and working the hook out, the girl cast a quick sideways look at the first fish and nodded imperceptibly.

The hook extracted, she pointed at the remaining worm on the shaded rock.

"I'll set bait this one last time for you. Watch how I do it. From here on in, if you're fishin', you're stickin' the worm." *She needs to learn these things. Might save her bacon sometime.*

The hook again baited, Dot was beginning to walk back to the gap in the willows when Black Feather's peripheral vision caught movement. He drew his Colt from his belt, hunched down and peered through the dense willow branch.

The calf of a leg flashed through the riparian cover, and then the foreleg of a horse, *or mule?* The shape disappeared from the narrow window of sight so quickly that he couldn't be sure. In a half-crouch, he moved the short distance to Dot, who was focused on a brook trout making darting passes at the bait.

Startled, she jerked when he placed one hand gently over her mouth. "We got company," he whispered. "You hunker down right here, as low as you can get. Just keep the pole over the water. Don't worry none about the fish. There's plenty of them. And don't move till I come back for you, even if you hear a gunshot."

Dot's mouth parted slightly, her lips trembling, her eyebrows creased in worry.

"I'll be fine. Remember, don't move. Don't stand up." Black Feather backed away from her, opened and quickly spun the cylinder of his Colt, checking the loads. Hunched over, moving from one dense clump of willows to the next, he began his stalk.

July 1, 1855

# Answer to a Prayer

LUCY WATCHED ISRAEL PEER THROUGH THE WILLOWS AT the glistening surface of the smaller creek, just upstream from where it tumbled into the larger one. Wavy patterns of light and dark drifted across rounded rocks, playing in patterns on the golden creek bottom.

"Like I figured, just as fast up here," he said to her, smiling, "but less water, and a lot clearer. Let's find us a break in this creek cover and get ourselves some dinner."

Lucy began to return his smile, but her expression froze. Fifteen paces away, a tall, angular figure, his muscled, bronzed arms exposed, a sweat-stained leather vest covering his torso, stepped from the brush. She took in the man's sharp, high-cheek-boned face, the white scar above one lip, the grim steady eyes, their menacing look and the pistol pointed at Israel's back. Lucy sucked in her breath, her heart pounding. Israel stopped talking midsentence. *He's watching my eyes. He knows somethin's behind him.*

Israel turned slowly.

COCKING THE HAMMER OF THE COLT, BLACK FEATHER rose and took one step from the cover. A thin, dark-skinned man, gray hair curled over the collar of a threadbare shirt, had his back to him, speaking to a heavyset, equally dark-skinned woman astride a long-faced, gray-whiskered mule. The woman's salt-and-pepper hair was partially tucked into a gray bandana knotted over her forehead.

Black Feather's eyes roved over them. *Can't see no weapons and they ain't spring chickens.* The man turned to him, slowly, one hand dangling limply to one side the other holding the lead rope of the mule, his eyes wide and startled. The craggy lines of his face disappeared into the short, curly silver of his beard. His gaze scanned Black Feather, then froze at the sight of the gun muzzle pointed at his chest.

Wagging the barrel of the pistol, Black Feather commanded, "Drop whatever guns you have real gentle, left hand, just your thumb and forefinger."

"We ain't got no guns. Got us an old knife," came the baritone reply with a strange, slow, thick accent.

*Darkies! Awful far west for them.* A memory of his mother, Sunray, telling him of the black-skinned slaves kept by the Osage and other tribes of the Five Nations, flashed across his mind. A sudden realization struck him. *They're on the run just like us.*

"You slaves?"

The man's face tightened, and his lips compressed. He

straightened, throwing his shoulders back. "We be free. I'm Israel. This here's my wife, Lucy, and that's our mule."

Black Feather rose from his crouched stance, regarding Israel and then the woman on the mule. The corners of her lips were turned down, and her cheeks quivered.

His eyes shifted back to Israel, who returned his stare steadily and unflinching. "What are you doing way out here?"

"Fishin'."

Despite himself, Black Feather chuckled. "You're on the run, ain't you?" The woman's frightened eyes flicked down to the back of her husband's head and then returned to Black Feather.

"If you mean we're far away from where we used to be, you'd be right. But free men don't run. They just do what they gots to do to stay free."

Black Feather straightened up, uncocking the Colt and lowering the muzzle. *Won't shove it back in my belt just yet.*

"My name is Black Feather," he paused, observing them for any flicker of recognition. There was none. "Got a girl traveling with me—my niece. She's back behind me. We're fishin', too."

The old negro's eyes widened, then scrunched again, a slight smile playing on his lips.

"Guess we got something in common."

Shoving the pistol back in his belt, Black Feather spoke on impulse, "Well, seein' as how you're just fishin' and we're just fishin' and don't seem like neither of us has anything the other wants, why don't you just pick a spot here, and get some fish. I'll just build one small fire, save you folks the trouble and we can have ourselves a fish supper."

He glanced over his shoulder. "That sun's going to be down in two or three hours. No sense crossing this meadow in the dark, fighting bogs and willows. Tomorrow morning, we can go our separate ways."

He began to turn away, surprised by his own words. He snapped his shoulders back, throwing a hard look at Israel. "Ain't real smart being out here, middle of nowhere, with your wife and no gun. That mule couldn't outrun a two-legged coyote."

The old man sighed, "Yup, we know. Ain't had much of a choice."

———

A BLAZE OF ORANGE EDGED THE TREE LINES AND RIMMED the snowcapped peaks to the west of them. The final fire of the day, the waning afterglow of sunset, was being pushed from a cloudless sky by the creeping indigo of night. Black Feather had a small fire crackling on the rise just a pistol shot from the creek. His cast iron skillet, fat melting in the dark bottom of the pan, perched on two flat rocks to the side of the fire.

He turned to Dot. "That's a nice mess of fish, Dot. You're a natural." He peered out into the gathering dusk. "We might have company. Some old folks—darkies. Think you'll like them. These trees and brush ought to shelter this flame from just about anywhere but the creek. They'll see it. They can come on in or not, as they please."

ISRAEL STOPPED HIS CAREFUL PLOD TOWARD THE DIM flicker of the small fire. The swarthy man with killer's eyes, who called himself Black Feather, knelt on one knee by the flames occasionally shaking a cast iron frypan and checking a pot to the side of the coals. Flickering shadows of fire played up and down his bare arms, and imparted an amber glow to his long black, stringy hair. His face was cast in shadow. A few feet from him, a small skinny girl with scraggly light hair sat gazing into the flames, both knees drawn to her chest, her thin arms wrapped around them, her shoulders hunched.

Behind him, the mule blew softly. Raising one hand and cupping it around the corner of his mouth, Israel called out, "It be Lucy and Israel. We got some fish."

The girl raised her chin. Black Feather, whose hand had flashed to the pistol protruding from his belt, now relaxed. He turned his attention back to the frypan, throwing a sideways glance in their direction.

"Come on into the fire then. We got some fish too. Just getting ready to fry 'em up. You can tie that mule off with the horses in them alders behind us, about fifty feet other side of the fire. Got a tether line posted twixt that pine and fir tree."

Leading Sally up to the edge of the firelight, Israel helped Lucy slowly dismount, holding her for a minute as she steadied herself, her bad knee buckling. Black Feather was watching them, and the girl's eyes were fixed on them too, though she barely lifted her head from the top of her knees.

Helping Lucy over to the fire, he spotted a small log just outside the ring of light and dragged it closer so she could have a seat. She lowered herself to the log clumsily, sighing when she was finally settled. "We sure appreciate you sharing your fire, Mr. Black Feather." Turning her head toward the girl, she smiled broadly. "Ain't you pretty? What your name?"

The girl began rocking back and forth, her arms still wound around her knees, her eyes fixed on Lucy six feet across the fire from her. "Dorothy..." Israel watched her eyes flash to Black Feather, who had stopped moving the pan and was staring at her, obviously surprised. "I mean, Dot."

Lucy's eyebrows burrowed momentarily, her eyes darting to Israel, then back to the girl. Lucy beamed a broad smile, her rounded cheeks picking up the glow of the flames, her teeth white in the half night and against her skin. "I surely like that name—one of my favorites. One of my sisters had a baby girl named Dorothy. Had a boy, too, named Abraham...." Her voice trailed off, and Israel wished she weren't quite so chatty. "But we ain't heard from them in years. Don't know where dey is."

Lucy craned her jaw forward, cocking her head side to side several times, staring at Dot. "Lordy, Miss Dorothy, your hair could use a combing." Lucy flashed another wide smile and laughed, one meaty hand patting the ground next to the log, "Come on over here chile and sit beside Lucy. Let me get you straightened up a bit, if that be okay with your uncle."

She paused, glancing quickly at Black Feather, whose eyes

were darting from Lucy to Dot and then back again. Israel noticed the raised eyebrows, the mouth slightly agape, the frying pan momentarily forgotten.

The girl looked at the man, her glance eager but questioning in the firelight. Israel couldn't quite make out who they were to each other, wasn't quite sure if the man was to be trusted. She sure ain't his niece.

Black Feather nodded, half smiling. "If Lucy wants to help you gussy up, might as well let her."

*Lucy always had a way about her.*

Rising, the girl took the few steps to the log and sat down near Lucy, who raised her round face toward Israel. "What you standing there looking at, husband? Go tie off that mule and bring me back a bandana and my comb out them parfleches."

Swirling her head toward Black Feather, she waved one pudgy hand at the fire. "Mr. Black Feather, could you hand me that pot you're fixin' to make coffee in? Just need a little a that water."

Israel worried that Lucy might have overstepped. Already arched under the unkempt black hair that concealed his swarthy face, the man's eyebrows raised higher. The man stared at Lucy and then, without leaving his position, extended a leg forward, leaned over and stretched out a long arm, placing the small pot next to Lucy's side.

"Okay, Miss Dorothy, turn around a little bit, dear, facin' me. That's right." Lucy's thick hands were moving Dorothy's hair, brushing it back with stubby fingers from the girl's forehead and ears. She cupped her palms around the sides of the girl's chin, moving her young face one way, then the other. "You be a very pretty girl, Miss Dorothy. Let's get you fixed up."

Israel, less uneasy, tied off Sally as far down the tether line from the horses as he could, returning with one of Lucy's bandanas and her comb.

"Here you be, Lucy."

Without looking up at him, she reached out one hand. Placing the comb on her lap, she rolled up one end of the bandana, dipping it in the water, and began to wipe the girl's face beginning at her forehead, along her hairline, dipping the bandana every so often. The girl's eyes were closed, the slightest of smiles on her lips.

*Enjoying the touch,* Israel could see. *Ain't no woman nowhere that doesn't like gittin' prettied up.*

Dot's face clean, her skin glowing in the firelight from the rub of the wetted cloth, Lucy tilted the girl's face up just a bit with two thick fingers under her chin and began to comb her hair gently.

Black Feather, Israel noticed, was staring at them, transfixed. Israel laughed, "We got six fish."

Black Feather looked away from the women, up at Israel standing near him. "We got eight. Not as many as we wanted, but it was Dot's first time fishin'. She did good. Should be plenty for the four of us. When I get that water back, I'll brew us up some coffee."

Trout soon sizzled in the frypan over a fire down to embers, just the occasional stubborn flame flaring from the coals. The smell of coffee wafted from the pot, which rocked back and forth in an exuberant boil.

Israel sat cross-legged several feet from the fire. He

watched Black Feather sprinkle some flour and crushed sage leaf on the fish, turning them often with his knife. Raising his eyes up to Israel, his voice quiet, he said, "Ain't sure I ever seen the girl that pleased and friendly." Lucy was just finishing combing the girl's hair, which had a shine to it now, and a slight wave where it fell just above her shoulder. "Your wife, Lucy's, awful good with young 'uns. Dot's taken to her like a bee to honey."

The man grew silent, staring into the coals. *Thinking about sumthin'.*

"And, I'm obliged...." he said suddenly. Moving the pan off the fire onto the two flat rocks, Black Feather rose, pushing on one knee, then strode into the darkness toward the horses. He returned in less than a minute, a Colt pistol with a polished wood grip and blued barrel dangling loosely at the end of one hand. Israel leaned away when he knelt down close. Holding the weapon up to the firelight, the man opened the cylinder and spun it, checking the cartridges. Poised, Israel watched Black Feather straighten and reach his hand in his right pocket, his fingers digging for something. He withdrew four cartridges, bouncing them in his palm.

"Put out your hand." The command held no meanness to it. Israel did so, and he dropped the cartridges in it, handing the Colt to Israel, grip first.

Lowering his head to hide his surprise, Israel turned the Colt one way then the other, one hand on the grip and the other on the barrel. *Why's he showing me this?*

He started to hand the pistol back to Black Feather, "Sure is a nice gun."

Black Feather stared at the Colt in Israel's outstretched hand. "What the hell you givin' that back to me for? It's yours. Least I can do, your wife being so kind to Dot. The Texan it belonged to would've agreed. It's an Army Colt .44 caliber. I only got them ten bullets."

He tipped his head back toward the frypan, turned to the fire and leaned over peeking at the coffee. "Supper's 'bout done,"

Along the dark creek, the chirp of crickets gave a backdrop to the sounds of the current, and a long, lonely howl echoed somewhere in the ridges above them, answered by another. *Coyotes*, Israel guessed. He'd heard of the wild dogs. Blinking back a tear, Israel raised his eyes to the stars, countless, glittering, full of promise and mystery. *An answer to a prayer. Thank you, Lord.*

July 5, 1855

# THE HOMESTEAD

TWO HUNDRED EIGHTY-TWO MILES SOUTH OF WHERE Israel polished his new Colt with one of Lucy's bandanas, the freight wagon cutting new tracks along the river in front of Rebecca and Sarah took a savage bounce. Its right rear wheel lifted off the ground, then fell with a creaking thud as it cleared a large rock, the left rear corner of the wagon doing the same seconds later.

*Poor Michael. That can't have been good for his ribs.* Rebecca tightened the lines, slowing the prairie schooner to a crawl, searching for another way across the shallow ravine pockmarked by boulders and oversized rocks. There was none. Even slowed, both sides of the prairie schooner lifted precariously, falling with savage rattles as the wagons in front had done, A stabbing pain shot through her belly and she winced, immediately feeling Sarah's hand on her arm.

"Are you all right, Rebecca?"

Lifting her chin, Rebecca shook her dark windblown locks, straightening her back, her shoulders forward. "I am fine, Sarah," she tersely replied. Subsequent rocks brought additional pangs but clenching her teeth, she made no sound, keeping her expression stoic.

"Rebecca..."

*I am not in the mood for conversation.* She felt Sarah's hand lightly on her arm again. "Rebecca, I just want to tell you that I'm glad you didn't listen to me back there in those flats when we were waiting for Reuben and Philippe. You were right to shoot."

Keeping her eyes to the front on the rock-strewn, grassy bank that hugged the rushing current of the Uncompahgre River to the right, she focused on keeping the prairie schooner wheels in the fresh tracks being made by Johannes in the freight wagon. She replied curtly, "There was no choice. It was obvious those two men riding in with guns drawn were not coming for a cup of tea."

"Did you... Did you feel bad? Like the way you felt back at Two Otters Creek?"

Surprised by Sarah's question, Rebecca turned quickly, staring into the redhead's wide blue eyes. Turning her attention back to the rear of the freight wagon, she shook her head slightly. "Just a tinge when I saw him fall from his horse, but that disappeared when Reuben told me he was one of those four monsters who took my rifle and tried to kidnap us back in Cherry Creek."

"Oh." There was a note of surprise in Sarah's voice. "I see."

"In fact, Sarah, the only thing that I'm sorry about in retrospect is that I did not shoot them both out of the saddle." Her friend's head snapped up. In front of them, the freight wagon jostled viciously again, and Rebecca braced herself.

"These mountains and this valley are just amazing," Sarah said, "I've never seen such peaks nor so many of them. I—"

Rebecca snapped a glare at her. *Small talk. Unbelievable.* Sarah stopped midsentence.

Shifting her eyes quickly back to the team and the track, Rebecca cut off any attempt by the redhead to finish her sentence, "Are you happy that Zeb is back?" she asked.

Again, her friend's pale, freckled face glanced at her quickly and then away, her fingers playing nervously in her lap, "Well, of course. Why would you ask?"

"Because, in my opinion, you haven't shown it."

Out of the corner of her eye, she could see Sarah's delicate fingers stop their nervous play with one another. She clasped her hands, the knuckles white where they protruded between the intertwining of her fingers.

———

REUBEN GAVE LAHN HIS HEAD AS THEY APPROACHED THE groaning, swaying prairie schooner. Reaching behind him with his one good arm, he untied the rawhide that held his jacket and then, cursing to himself, managed to drape the jacket over both shoulders, obscuring the red stain that had seeped through Rebecca's careful bandaging. He slowed Lahn to match the crawl of the wagon and drew abreast. Sitting on either side of the seat, Sarah and Rebecca both stared ahead, jaws set and lips pursed.

*Friction over something.* Seeing him, Rebecca's lips spread in a subdued smile, "Reuben! How is your arm?"

"Doing fine as long as I keep it in the sling."

She glanced over quickly to where his wrist and hand extended beyond the inside edge of the jacket, cast her eyes quickly up at him and then back to the team. She obviously didn't believe him.

"Zeb just told me that the creek coming down from the west, this side of the Snaefel Peaks, is Dallas Creek.

"It's getting too late to cross the river, even though the current has started to recede," he said, gesturing at the red rocks that extended on either side of the turbulent flow, several feet above the surface of the water. "And we've only got three or four hours until sunset. But I'm going to go up that drainage a mile or so and see what it looks like. Would you like to come with me, Mrs. Frank?"

His wife's eyes blinked, obviously intrigued. Then, her shoulders lowered, her lips pursing in disappointment. "I would love to come with you, Reuben, but all this bucking and bouncing has left me a bit unsettled.... I am not sure clambering up on Red and riding several miles back and forth in this rough country would be prudent."

Her eyes locked with his, and she smiled radiantly, shifting the lines to one hand and holding the other up to Reuben. He leaned toward her in the saddle, bent over and, clasping her hand to his mouth, kissed it.

"Unfortunately, I shall have to wait to see it until tomorrow from the seat of this wagon," she said, flashing another quick warm smile. "I am quite anxious to view this place that will be home. *Our home.* But you go ahead, Mr. Frank. Scout for us." She giggled slightly. "I know that you can barely wait to ride up there and see the place for yourself, alive and real, not just lines on a map."

Reuben straightened back up in the saddle. "Then I'll get going."

"Reuben," Rebecca's voice was stern, "be careful. Remember that arm might start bleeding again if you are foolish, and please be back to the fire by dark."

*Start bleeding? I'm glad she can't see under this jacket.*

Sarah looked over at him. "Yes, Reuben. Be careful,"

As he lifted the reins to steer Lahn away from the wagon, he could see Rebecca's jaw muscles tensing as the redhead spoke. *Yes, friction over something.*

———

REUBEN REINED IN LAHN HALFWAY UP THE TIMBERED RIDge in a small grove of aspens. To the southwest, the Snaefel poked its line of sharp white peaks into the brilliant, blue belly of the sky. Behind him, he could hear the plaintive, muted bawl of the cattle, still several miles distant but amplified by the wide canyon he had ascended. Occasionally, a faint hoot and holler of the drivers echoed eerily between the smooth bark of the aspens.

The subdued roar of a creek, guarded by willows and alders, rushed with the snowmelt through the broad meadow tucked under the ridge. Wild irises poked lavender blossoms above the emerald green expanse while nearly hidden in the almost knee-high grass, the yellow, red and white blossoms of other early wildflowers unfurled. Further below him, the silver serpentine thread of the Uncompahgre River coursed its way north through an ever-widening fertile valley framed on all sides by the jagged peaks of the San Juans and the Uncompahgre.

To the south, at the toe of three stately iron-red peaks, their flanks embracing the steep faces of El Diente and the Wetterhorn, and another looming cone-shaped peak behind them, the valley tapered to a narrow end.

From his vantage, he could see the ground rise to two benches, the higher one dotted by conifers at its upper end, its grass appearing shorter than the lower. *Several perfect sites for the homestead.* A north-south ridge ran unevenly above the bench meadows, a natural windbreak. He craned around in the saddle, north, then south and east, cursing softly as his arm twisted in the sling. *Hell of a view, too. The Red Mountains, The Snaefels, the valley and the San Juans.* Lahn tipped his muzzle up several times, the hackamore squeaking.

The leaves of the aspens around Reuben fluttered, stirred by a touch of wind, their supple branches imparting a welcome. The palomino shook his head, whinnying, and Reuben leaned forward, patting the horse's neck. "I feel it too, Lahn. We're home."

Reuben relaxed into the saddle, putting aside the list of monumental tasks to accomplish in the few short months before the first snows. Savoring the energy and promise of the place, he sighed, his long exhale caught by the breeze and curled to the sky. *We're here, father. I so wish you could see it.*

CHAPTER

*13*

July 7, 1855

# $\mathscr{N}$OTCHING LOGS

SWEAT SHINED ON LAHN'S WITHERS WHEN THEY REACHED
the top of the rise that leveled out into the expansive meadow
of the second bench. Reuben wheeled the palomino around
in the shade of a small stand of fir trees to face back toward
the wagons.

From his vantage, he could see the entirety of the lower
meadow, and the wagons settled by the red-hued line of
willows along the creek. The distant figures of Sarah and
Rebecca seemed to be nursing the fire, its thin gray smoke
trailing, then twisting into gentle spirals as the westward
wind lifted it above the lee side of the wagon tops. A quarter
mile south, at the far end of the meadow, the cattle were
clustered, their heads lowered in the high, green grass. Bente
and Diablo stood shoulder to shoulder facing opposite
directions, Johannes and Philippe leaning on their pommels
talking. Every so often, one of them would point in one
direction or another. *Figuring out the lay of the land.*

He turned at the sound of an approaching horse in an easy
lope. Zeb reined in Buck next to Lahn, the two horses

shaking their heads at one another and then gently touching muzzles.

Zeb said nothing, taking in the scene as Reuben was. Reaching into his buckskin jacket, he withdrew his tobacco pouch and began building a smoke, looking up from the rolling paper to watch as a golden eagle cast its shadow on the grasses in front of them, its aileron feathers tipping up and down in its fixed-wing spiral.

Still working on his smoke, he glanced sideways at Reuben, then refocused his attention on the cigarette taking shape between his fingers. "Rode almost a full circle about two miles out, most all directions from the wagons. Just making sure there ain't been no one else."

Sticking the rolled cigarette in his mouth, he twirled his fingers as he withdrew it from between his lips. "Weren't nothing but last year's tracks, all Ute, and all Ouray's band."

The cigarette lit, he drew deeply on it, tipping his head back and exhaling, still gazing out over the meadow and the valley beyond. His tone calm, and his voice low, he asked, "So what's your plan, Reuben?"

Reuben studied his profile. The thin double scars from the grizzly bear, which ran from his ear to his stubbled chin, were more noticeable in the shade of the trees. His brow was furrowed, his eyebrows more silver than when they had met back in St. Louis, and his eyes squinted as he pondered the valley. *He is driving at something.*

"Was just thinking about that, Zeb. That fracas up there at the fort set us back. Lost at least two days getting everyone patched up, going up the Uncompahgre took longer than I figured, and it took us more than half of today just to ease the wagons up to the bench."

Zeb nodded, his eyes now fixed on the distant figures of Sarah and Rebecca and the thin curls of smoke from the fire. "This far out, and this high up, most things take longer than ya figure."

Reuben grunted. "My arm won't be good for much for at least a week. Probably a couple of weeks till I have full use of it. Johannes's leg's improving every day, but still not a hundred percent. Michael will likely be able to sit a horse in a few days, but with his ribs, he will be limited for the next couple of weeks at least."

Taking another draw on the cigarette, Zeb chuckled, his eyes still fixed on the two women at the fire. "I'm not sure Michael had it any better in the back of that freight wagon bouncing over those rocks than he would've up on that old gray mare of his." He lifted the cigarette to his lips again, inhaling, and turned to Reuben, his green eyes intent.

"And could have been way worse. Anybody else driving that freight wagon across the river this morning but Johannes, and you likely would've lost that rig and all your tools and building supplies." He was silent for a moment and then added, "And we're all alive. Things could've turned out different in that run-in with them renegades."

"You're right, Zeb, all counts. Never gave any thought to the fact that those two wagons are likely the first wagons ever up the Uncompahgre, and sure as hell the first two wagons to ever be up on that bench." Reuben lifted his right hand to his chin and rubbed his jawline. "I think the first thing we ought to do is get up a small corral in case we have to separate cows that need doctoring. Might save a few of them, and I'm certain it will save us time trying to find any that we've helped once we get them back in the herd."

Zeb raised two fingers to his lips and wetting them with his tongue, put out the cigarette, placing the half-smoked butt carefully back into his tobacco pouch. "Well...," he said slowly, "Much as you might not like to, better losing a few critters than losing any of your outfit."

The comment was confusing. *Somebody planning on leaving?*

"Losing any of the outfit?"

"As in people dying." Zeb's voice was terse.

"I don't think anyone's in any danger of dying. Michael's the worst hurt. He'll pull through just fine."

"That ain't what I meant, Reuben. This here is somewhere around the first or beginning of the second week of July. I don't much keep track. But the first couple weeks of September, them nice green meadows down there could be under four feet of snow—six, eight feet in drifts. I've seen it happen. More likely, that'll be mid to late October, but you never know. And no matter when the snow comes, night temperatures will start freezing up water just two months from now, give or take. Come November, things will start getting life and death. You can't take care of them cows if you can't take care of yourself. I have seen that list of things that you want to get done. Might be a right fine list. I ain't no farmer, and you know what I think of them cows."

Reuben chuckled. "Yes, I'm well aware."

Zeb raised one hand to his mustache, slowly stroking it with long fingers, thinking. "If I was you, I'd give everybody a day off tomorrow. Let folks just relax and start healing up.

And I'll take you up to my main cabin in the notch, show you how the logs are put together and the way I put that roof on, hung the doors and chinked her up. Might be good for you to see how that fireplace is built, too. These logs go up entirely different than frame houses down in the big city. You don't build one wall at a time and stand it up. Each wall comes up with the other, log by log."

"That'll just put us back another day, Zeb."

The mountain man looked at him sharply. "Nope. It'll put you ahead weeks. No sense notching logs till you know how to do it. You can do what you want, son, and I reckon you will, but if it was me given everyone's condition, two women pregnant, four men hurt and first snow just two months out, I'd take that list of yours and put it in order of things that are just surviving. You have all next season, if you make it, to do those grand things you're thinking about putting the ranch together...." He paused, "You're a cow man. You can only brand one calf at a time. You know that. So, might be best if you set your sights on the most important calf."

Sifting Zeb's words in his mind, Reuben knew the mountain man was right. His gut turned. He hadn't been thinking about things that way at all.

Sensing he had Reuben's attention, Zeb continued, "What size place ya thinking of putting up for living quarters?"

I was thinking maybe forty or fifty feet long, about half that wide, two or three rooms down most on the ground level, just a portion two-story."

Zeb looked at him strangely. "Think I seen something like that—recently, in fact." He leaned back, reaching a hand into the lower pocket of his buckskin jacket, drawing out a penknife, which he opened and began carving back the nails on one hand. "You're not going to have time to build anything like that, son. You'll be lucky to get up a twenty-by-thirty, single-story."

Reuben clenched his teeth. "That's not going to be enough space. There are six of us, two of them women. There would be no privacy for anyone."

Focusing on his nails, Zeb chuckled. "If you and Rebecca want some privacy, you can use one of my cabins till she's too far along to ride or bring a blanket out. Go a quarter-mile from those wagons, and you'll have all the privacy you need."

He looked at Reuben, a broad smile spreading under his mustache. "Just don't spread that blanket down by the creek. Them mosquitoes can be distracting."

Reuben couldn't help but laugh.

"No, Reuben. I'd figure on getting something up that will keep you dry and warm, that you can cook in, and folks can spread their bedroll out and sleep comfortably. You overshoot, and you won't get it done. And those cows gotta eat this winter, don't they?"

Reuben nodded.

"Well, don't know much about them and don't care to, but they got to eat twenty or thirty pounds of feed a day as big as they are."

Reuben jerked with surprise. "Good guess, Zeb. Twenty-eight to thirty-two pounds a day, actually."

"And where are they gonna find that grub under four feet of snow at twenty below in January?" Zeb asked quietly.

"Twenty below?"

"Might be thirty below, but it ain't often going to get to zero, even in the daylight." His penknife paused, poised on a nail. "So, that means you have to store a whole lot of hay out of these meadows. Then, you're going to have to cover it somehow so it don't get wet and iced."

*And moldy* thought Reuben.

"And ain't them cows gonna have calves?"

"Yes. Dawson, the rancher I bought them from said he couldn't be sure, but thought most were carrying calves and had been bred in May." *That means March calves.* He gulped. "What's the weather like in March?"

Zeb kept his head bent over his nails, but his eyes popped up sideways to Reuben. "All depends. Might be on your way to spring, but there's still plenty of weather. Fact, some years we get the most snow in March and April, though it's warmer. But sometimes that just means that wet snow freezes up. A horse can't hardly stand on the level much less a sidehill." He shook his head slowly, his voice somber. "Fact is, you're going to lose a bunch of them cows and calves over those three or four months. You ain't gonna be full ready."

Reuben knew the worry showed on his face.

"There ain't nothing you can't get done, son, if you got the time and the guts to do it. You have the guts, for sure. But if you don't do things right smart, in right smart order, you ain't gonna have the time. I'd get that place up first, and maybe along with it some kinda shed even if it's open on one face with a single slant roof where you get all that stuff out of the wagons under cover mostly, and protected, and have that wagon space available, too. Besides, you need that freight wagon to haul the timber for the house and the shed. It's one of them chicken and egg things. Once you know you got them licked, you'll have to focus all your time on putting up that feed."

Reuben's mind raced, grappling with this new, irrefutable perspective, "But we have no time to build a barn, not even a hay barn."

"No, but I might be able to show you how to build a big fir bough cover. Won't be perfect, but it'll be a damn sight better than nothing. We figure right, we can do it so you can get hay out and that cover will stay in place." Zeb was stroking his mustache again, "Maybe lash the front corners to trees but let the backside just settle as you take the hay out front. I'll pitch in and help, Reuben, but I have to get ready for winter too. So, it ain't gonna be every day or all the time."

Reuben's mind was a blur. "Now, you have me worried about supplies."

"You got plenty if you go easy on the flour. How much a man eats depends on how warm and comfortable he is after working. Colder you are, the more food you need. Water's not a problem—just melt snow. I know it's like killing money, but one or two of them cows ought to keep everybody well fed no matter how long the winter winds up being. And...," he turned to Reuben with a grin, "you get things under control, and I'll take you hunting. That's sumthin' you gotta learn, and I don't 'spect there was a lot of elk hunting back there in Prussia."

Reuben shook his head.

"You ever eat elk?"

Reuben shook his head again.

"Well, you'll likely love it. Good leather, too, and you can make all sorts of things or tools from the antlers. Hunting them is fun though they are a pile of work once you get one down. Problem is..." His eyes flicked up from his nails, "once you eat elk, you might never go back to one of them cows."

Zeb closed the pocketknife, shoving it back in his pocket, and unwrapped the reins from the pommel. "I'm headed up to the cabin first thing in the morning, right after daybreak. We'll be up there by midmorning. I'm staying for a night or two, but once you know the trail, you can find your way back here no problem before dark." He paused, waiting.

"I'll be saddling up with you, Zeb." Reuben reached out a hand to the mountain man's shoulder, "Thanks for getting my mind right."

Zeb nodded. "Well, we're neighbors now. Let's go down and see what those women whipped up for supper."

# *14*

July 8, 1855

# $\mathcal{T}$RAIL OF QUARTZ

THE SOUND OF THE DULL ROAR OF THE CREEK RUSHING TO its rendezvous with the Uncompahgre, stones rumbling against one another as the current tumbled them, lent sensuous texture to Rebecca and Reuben's lovemaking, the calls of songbirds—thrushes and meadowlarks, tanagers and robins—the backdrop to their primal rhythm.

As the sounds of daybreak sifted through the canvas of the prairie schooner, the faint light of dawn filtered into the wagon. Rebecca's thighs quivered, and her body pulsed with their loving. Reuben's hand sent currents through her with each soft stroke of her breast, and the gentle twirl of her nipples.

Squirming slightly, she wiggled her bottom tightly to his groin, driving more deeply his still rigid girth. Reuben, his touch feather-light, traced down her chest and stomach, his fingertips coming to rest in the fertile valley between her hips. With his warm palm against her skin, his fingers pressed slightly on the smooth flesh where her hips flared. His hips bucked forward, and she spasmed, yet again, groaning softly, "Oh my God, Reuben." Her hand descended to the top of his, pressing his palm more firmly to the slight rounding where their child grew. Encircling her shoulders, Reuben's right arm tightened, molding her back against his chest. Steadying her shudders, his lips tenderly played on the nape of her neck where he had brushed her hair back.

"I have so missed that," she gasped in a whisper.

She raised his hand to her lips, ran her tongue across his knuckles and kissed his wrist.

Reuben's breath was warm on her ear. "It was nice of Sarah," he said, "to volunteer to stay in the freight wagon last night."

Rebecca had her doubts. *Just an attempt to get back in good graces.*

She felt him begin to withdraw gently. She reached behind them, digging her fingers into his buttocks and curved her leg over his knee.

"I must go, Rebecca—as much as I would love to simply stay deep inside you all morning."

"Why?" she teased, tightening her grip on his leg.

"Zeb and I are saddling up at daybreak, which is just about now. Heading up to his main cabin, that place he calls 'the notch' up on Red Mountain. I'm getting a lesson on log cabin building."

"You mean our home, Reuben."

"No, Rebecca. A real house will have to come later. We'll have a roof and a door to keep out the weather, and a fireplace, but a *real* home will have to wait."

Her mood faded at the discouraged tone in his voice.

"This winter will be spent in a cabin, likely just one room

for all of us," he continued. "It was not in our plan, and not what you are expecting, but Zeb and I talked yesterday afternoon, and he made sense." He was silent for a moment. "In fact, Zeb opened my eyes to reality. I've been tripping over the present, thinking only about the future; irrigation, ditches, fences, corrals, barns, water storage reservoirs..." His voice trailed off.

Rebecca's heart fluttered. "What's changed, Reuben?"

"Nothing. That's the point. I didn't realize it. Winter is coming, maybe even a *brutal* winter. We can't stop the weather; we can only prepare for it."

Rebecca loosened the grip on his leg. She clasped his hand, tightly this time, and raised it to her lips, murmuring against the rough skin behind his knuckles, "I want to go with you this morning. I can be ready in fifteen minutes if you would just throw the saddle on Red for me."

She could feel Reuben's head lift, his words like a penetrating stare. "I thought you weren't feeling well. Are you..."?

She cut him off. "Yes, I'm sure, Reuben. I would love to see the Red Mountains, Zeb's cabin, everything he's done up there. Have you forgotten how much help I can be?" *She was pregnant, but she wasn't useless.* She moved his hand, pressing it against her belly, "It might help all of us." She paused. "I'll bring my map. Maybe Zeb can have a quick look at it up there. Father's land is supposed to be somewhere in those mountains, maybe even *that* mountain. Maybe Zeb will recognize the general location."

Reuben pulled slowly away. He kissed her between her shoulder blades, "I've learned not to argue with you, Mrs.

Frank. Red will be saddled."

——••——

Z EB URGED B UCK INTO THE RIVER FOLLOWED BY L AHN
and Red.

The three horses plunged across the haystacks of the
river current, rushing and milky brown, wide arcs of spray
erupting with each lunge of their front quarters. On the east
bank of the river, they paused, the horses shaking violently,
spray flying in shimmering droplets from their soaked hair.
South of Uncompahgre Peak, the first golden ring of sun
peeked through the steep, vee-shaped gaps of the lesser
peaks of the Uncompahgre range.

Zeb looked at Reuben and Rebecca, letting his eyes linger
on the woman. "Everybody all set? Come summer...," he
pointed to the river, "that crossing is barely a riffle, six
inches, maybe a foot deep."

Rebecca blinked. "Zeb, this *is* summer. It's July!"

"Up here," he teased the brunette, "summer comes late
and leaves early." He turned and, with a slight lift of the
reins, clicked to his horse. "Let's go, Buck. We're heading
home." The tobiano moved out with a long-legged stride. *No
doubt,* Zeb thought, *he knows exactly where we're headed.*

——••——

T HE OLD, NARROW TRAIL ROSE GRADUALLY AT FIRST ON THE
shallow alluvial shelves that spilled down to the river from
the toe of the steeper slopes. They rode the faint contours

ascending from the scrub above the river bottom, through small pockets of aspen, and crossing several small but fast-moving drainages. Zeb knew this trail like the back of his hand—how the tree cover changed to coniferous forest as they rode higher, the firs, and spruce growing taller, denser, their trunks thicker.

Every so often, he turned to look over his shoulder, checking on Reuben and Rebecca, particularly Rebecca. There was nothing he could've said about her coming along. A man's wife was a man's wife. She was moving comfortably in the saddle as Red climbed the trail. Every so often, her eyes narrowed when the sorrel slipped or his hooves came down hard. Reuben seemed uneasy, his sling pressed tight against his chest, glancing left and right, or southwest toward the steep-walled gap where the Uncompahgre exited the mountains and began its run toward its junction with the Gunnison.

The trail changed from sidehill to a series of benches and shelves, the trees broken by red walls and ledges, the soil under the horse's hooves the same reddish color. Here and there, when the filters of sunlight hit the red rock, there were sparkles in the rock faces, sometimes whole bands of sparkles.

From thirty feet behind, Rebecca called out, "Zeb, can we take a two-minute break? I just want to stretch my legs."

Zeb pressed his knees to Buck, and the tobiano stopped. "Sure." *Should've told her she ought not to come.* "Edge of that meadow might be a good place."

Rebecca rode a few feet closer, to where a small clearing was lit by the morning sun and dismounted. Currents of warm air wafted up from the valley floor, carrying the sun's heat with them.

Behind him, he heard the creak of Reuben's saddle leather. "How much longer, Zeb?" he asked.

Zeb raised a hand and stroked his mustache. "Not much, Reuben. Half an hour—maybe more. Depends on whether we have to backtrack. There's some bogs and slimy areas coming up."

Shifting in his saddle, Zeb looked up the trail. Without turning around again, he said, "You can make it to that river crossing coming down from the cabin in maybe an hour and a half if you don't dee-daddle. If you poke around, more. Faster going uphill than down. On the steep, gotta watch out for these muddy areas. He pointed to the ground where the red soil glistened with moisture. That clay is slick."

"I love these rocks, Zeb," Rebecca called out from twenty paces away. She was standing at the toe of a red ledge, running her hand along its rough surface above her head, her fingers touching the line of glitter shining in the sunlight. Zeb watched her bend down, pick up several stones and walk back to the horses, putting them in her saddlebag. She mounted smoothly and smiled at the men. "Thank you so much, Zeb. That was perfect."

Zeb turned, gave a slight twitch to the reins, and Buck eagerly stepped out. *Putting rocks in her saddlebags?*

---

REBECCA DREW IN HER BREATH AS THEY RODE BETWEEN the straight trunks of hem-firs circling the small clearing where the cabin, and some sort of pen, sat. Long horizontal poles over heavy log bucks, one tipping precariously, created a sort of jackleg enclosure. *His corral.* The chinked walls of the cabin, a low-slung structure perhaps sixteen by twenty feet, were weathered but substantial. The large hewn logs at the base of the cabin were well fitted, the walls rising with smaller logs until they disappeared under the sloped cover of the roof. The lighter-colored chink appeared to be a mixture of grass and dried mud. Lodgepole pine rafters strung out unevenly below the edge of the roof over a small front stoop by the door. The roof seemed to be a mixture of mud and grass, and she realized with a start there was no glass in the windows, but rather, shutters formed of smaller tree boughs fastened from the inside of the cabin. There were horizontal slits in each of the shutters, *firing slits*! The door was heavy and sturdy, built of thick, rough-sawn planks. There were four hinges, all doubled up leather hide strips, their ends nailed to the frame and, most likely, the inside edge of the door.

Rebecca watched Zeb dismount, swinging one long leg over Buck's head, then wrapping the reins loosely around the pommel. "Go get yourself some grass, boy," he said, patting the paint on the rump. Rebecca could not bring herself to move.

---

ZEB WAS SURPRISED TO SEE NEITHER REBECCA NOR REUBEN had yet dismounted. Reuben was staring at the cabin, as was Rebecca, her mouth open. "Oh my, Zeb. What a pretty place, so much care and attention. It's obvious you built this with love." She raised one hand slightly in the direction of the cabin.

Reuben swung himself off the saddle, wrapping Lahn's reins twice around a rail of the jack leg. "I'm impressed, Zeb. Didn't quite picture it this way. It's a hell of a spot."

Zeb grunted. "It serves its purpose. It's the largest of the four I have scattered around. Gets the best sun on this southwest face, and the creek has better fish." He held Red while Rebecca dismounted, tying off the sorrel next to Lahn. "Come on in."

Once inside, Rebecca and Reuben stood in the center of the cabin, their eyes roving the interior, their heads swiveling left and right.

Zeb watched Reuben paying attention to every detail, the rope lashings that let the shutters swing, the river stone fireplace that rose on one wall, the cross brace logs that ran from the top of one log wall to the other every four feet, spiked into every other lodgepole rafter for stability and to prevent losing the roof to the wind. His friend took off his hat, laid it, crown down, on the plank table and walked along one of the walls, running his finger along the chink line, peering at it.

Rebecca seemed drawn by the fireplace. She stooped over, looking at the fireplace aperture and the stone hearth. She bent her head and craned her neck upward, looking into the flue. Rebecca stood, her fingertips brushing several stones in a slow horizontal swipe of her hand.

She turned to Zeb, her eyes shining. "It is simply wonderful, Zeb. Such a good job."

"Don't know about wonderful, Miss Rebecca, but it's warm and dry, and there's nights coming..." He flicked his eyes to Reuben, who had turned to him, "where that's mighty important. Rueben, you might want to look close at how them logs are notched and fitted at the corners."

He smiled at them. "I know enough that when you throw a big party like this..." his hand swept the two of them, "the host's supposed to have some fixins. I'll go out and get some jerky and pemmican from my saddlebags. We'll have a bite. Then, I got a bunch to show you." He directed his gaze to Reuben. "I bet you got a pencil and pad in that saddlebag of yours."

He laughed, not surprised when Reuben nodded. "Better fetch them," he said. "Them pages is going to be mighty full once we get done."

---

THE SUN WAS HALFWAY THROUGH ITS DOWNWARD ARC TO-ward the Snaefel as Red and Lahn picked their way back down the trail. In the lead, Reuben was silent, and Rebecca could tell he was thinking hard about all they had seen and learned.

Cooled at higher elevations, the afternoon air currents whispered gently downslope. The trail was leading, now in the opposite direction, through the higher grassy plateaus, rimmed by red rock glowing and pulsing with the lower angle of the sun. Stands of trees gathered in clusters wherever unseen springs bubbled to the surface. Here and there, tall, dark outcroppings of stone sparkled as the sunlight caught the lighter stones embedded in their faces.

*The trail of quartz,* thought Rebecca, excitedly recalling the scene as they had departed the cabin. Zeb had been standing on the stoop as she dug in the saddlebag for her father's map. "I don't think you've seen this, Zeb. It's my father's map of our land out here somewhere. I think it's somewhere near, though I've learned that's a relative term in these mountains."

She handed it to him, asking, "Would you mind taking a quick look? Maybe you can tell its general location. The map is nowhere near as finely drawn or detailed as Reuben's."

The mountain man had hesitated, then reached out and slowly unfolded the parchment. His jaw muscles seemed to slacken, and his eyes widened as he studied the map and looked over her head toward the southwest, then back to the map again. He stepped off the stoop, down onto the ground beside her. He leaned over, his long arm extended, and pointed toward the reddish cut between the mountains to the southwest, just a few miles from the cabin site.

"I do believe, Miss Rebecca," he said thoughtfully, "though the Utes would disagree, your land lies up there this side of where the Uncompahgre cuts its gorge, a bit above where she mouths into the main valley. And by the looks of it, comes several miles this way or the other. Can't rightly be sure till I am up there on those contours. But by memory, I don't think they are drawn quite right." A thrill of excitement pulsed through her, head to toe.

She had tried to subdue it, but she was sure Zeb heard it in her tone and saw it in her face. "Thank you, Zeb. Thank you. Perhaps one of these days, when things are more set up at the ranch, we could all take a ride up there. I would love to see and stand on it."

But Zeb had only nodded, noncommittal. *Why was he so reserved?*

Despite the mountain man's peculiar reticence, she felt a sensual quickening in her body at the memory of finally knowing where her father's map led. Further coaxed by the glow of the rocks and lazy wave of the meadow grasses, a current began to pulse in her loins. "Reuben," she called out to her husband, a horse length in front of her. "Wait for me."

Reuben reined in Lahn, and she slipped Red next to the palomino, slightly off the narrow trail and uphill. She leaned over and kissed him.

His green eyes wrinkled in a smile. "And what's that for, Mrs. Frank?"

Returning the smile, she batted her eyes coquettishly. She leaned back, patting the rolled-up blanket behind her saddle, "See this?"

Reuben nodded; his eyebrows raised.

She leaned forward, pointing over Lahn's ears to a sunlit meadow, a column of red rock its guardian on the south end. "See that?"

Reuben nodded, a hungry smile beginning to spread above his square jaw.

Rebecca bent her arm, fingers pointed upward, all of them closed with the exception of her forefinger, and beckoned three times.

CHAPTER

*15*

July 8, 1855

# THE GOODBYE

TWO THOUSAND SEVENTY-FOUR MILES EAST OF THE WAG-ons lurching upstream on the Uncompahgre, Erik paused as he stepped to the wharf from the timbered drawbridge leading from the Castle Garden immigration buildings. *America!* The wharf and carriage-lined South Street beyond were a blur of motion; people of all shapes, sizes and complexions, some finely dressed, others in clothing not much more than tatters, some with porters wheezing behind them carrying large, ornate trunks, others with aged duffel bags slung over their shoulders, all in their own individual hurries to their separate destinations. Dozens of languages sifted in various tones and pitches through the hot, muggy air.

His eyes roving the mulling throngs, he spotted her golden hair first. Alysia was flanked by her parents, walking briskly toward the line of carriages, several porters behind them carting their luggage. She seemed to be peering back over one shoulder, then the other, and then she saw him, her smile apparent even at that distance. She raised one hand in his direction, a gesture Erik returned with a grin. Seeing her wave, her father looked behind him, saw Erik and reached down, grabbing her arm. Without breaking stride, he leaned over and spoke to her. She didn't look back again except to cast one brief, furtive glance as three men loaded their luggage into a waiting, closed carriage. Then she was gone.

Erik sighed. *I wonder where they are bound.* He sighed again. *Not that it matters.* He hailed a returning porter preoccupied with finding the next immigrant whose luggage he would carry to the street for five cents per item. The man had a thick accent Erik couldn't place. Barely stopping, without a word, he swung an outstretched arm, vaguely indicating a milling group of people over by the street.

Hefting the duffel over one shoulder and grabbing the violin case with the opposite hand, Erik made his way to where a ragged line of twenty or more immigrants, single, or in small groups or families, stood waiting, their luggage to the side and behind them. A man in a red vest, sweat staining his armpits where his shirt ballooned at his shoulders, was pointing in turn to each of the people waiting, and then gesturing at one carriage or another as the rigs rolled up and halted. A black, open surrey stopped several carriages down, and Erik was pointed in its direction. The driver, short and stocky with light brown hair, was dressed in a shirt with cut off sleeves that clung to him with humidity and sweat.

He jumped from the surrey, walked rapidly around its rear and hefted Erik's duffel as if it was weightless, tossing it five feet to rest on the opposite side of the passenger seat. He reached for Erik's violin case, but Erik drew back, making sure to smile as he did so. "Thank you. I can take this."

The man nodded, motioning for Erik to get into the passenger seat in the rear of the buggy. When Erik was seated, the man sprang into the driver's bench and turned, "Welcome to America, young man. Where to?"

"157th Street off Kingsbridge Road, please."

The driver's eyebrows raised. "You know how far that is from here?"

"No, I don't, but it is what it is. *Reuben's saying.* And that's where I need to go."

The driver shrugged, and half smiled. Turning, he raised the lines and laid them across the backs of the two older gray geldings that leaned forward into their traces.

The surrey bounced and clattered on the cobblestones. Occasionally, the hard pavement would end in a long expanse of dirt or gravel. *So many people—going so many places. So many buildings.* A current of nervous anticipation coursed through Erik, *like when I was approaching the Edinburgh back in Bremerhaven.*

The first part of the ride was through a seamy section of the city; crudely dressed people, street urchins playing and screaming in the street, the signs on the shops mostly weathered and in need of paint. They turned on Broadway, and the buildings grew higher, many of them newer brick or stone. Storefronts with the latest fashions and large glass windows lined the sidewalks. Women in fine dresses and men with top hats and suits scurried from one mysterious destination to the next.

Then, the city transitioned again to less imposing, lower buildings, very few over two stories. There were trees here and there, and the walls of the structures were separated by several feet of space rather than connected. The feel of neighborhoods began to change, brightened by the green of occasional small yards, the blocks becoming clearly more residential with larger separations between the homes.

The carriage turned off the Kingsbridge Road onto 157th Street. Here, there were larger lawns, well-kept masonry homes set back five to ten meters from the street edge, and high, spreading, fully leafed oak and elm trees on both sides of the narrow, gravel street surface.

The driver tightened up on the lines, and the horses came to a halt in front of a two-story brick home with large stone ledgers under tall, arched windows, their panes separated by bright, white, painted mullions. Erik had barely alighted when a voice behind him boomed. "Erik!" And then in Prussian, "At long last we meet."

Straightening up from the violin case he had laid down to catch the duffel the driver was about to throw from the seat, Erik turned, smiling at the man leaning on a cane and standing on the porch of the home. *He looks so much like father.* "Uncle Hermann!" he called out, waving.

The driver paid, the surrey on its way down 157th Street and the duffel once again slung over one shoulder, Erik made his way to the house, laboring up the steps with the weight on his back, aware his uncle was watching.

*My father's brother!* Uncle Hermann held the door for him as Erik shifted his stance to get the duffel through the opening. Inside, his eyes immediately caught the subdued oil paintings of Villmar and the farm that adorned the walls and the portrait of Uncle Hermann and Ludwig standing with their arms over each other's shoulders on the banks of the Lahn. That painting hung in a scrolled gold frame over a brick fireplace with a heavy, dark-stained, oak mantel.

Erik rested the violin case upright against the wall inside the front door and then hitched his shoulders, moving the weight of the duffel forward, its straps sliding down his arm and catching his cupped hand, the weight of it pulling his shoulder down toward the floor. He caught his uncle scanning him head to toe, slight creases of concern in the corners of his eyes, not quite a full smile playing on his lips.

"Come my boy. You're the only nephew this old man has never met. Tell me about the farm and your brothers...," there was a catch in his voice, "and my brother's passing."

Erik followed Uncle Hermann into the study and sat in an overstuffed chair. The elderly soldier limped a few feet to a bookcase, opening the cabinet doors in the center. Leaning his cane against a shelf bulging with books, he turned, two snifters in one hand and an ornate glass decanter in the other. "Do you drink brandy?"

Erik shook his head, "No uncle, except a sip on the High Holy Days, and once in a while at a wedding or bar-mitzvah."

Uncle Hermann laughed. "Today is far more than a bar-mitzvah or a wedding. Today is the day a third of our family has come to America, and the first day that uncle and youngest nephew have met." He poured both snifters full handing Erik one. He leaned over, grabbed his cane and then eased himself down in the other overstuffed chair.

"Mae, who takes care of the house and does my cooking and cleaning and lately, as my leg has deteriorated," he lightly slapped one hand on his thigh, "helps me get around.

She is cooking us a fine supper. You are actually here two days early, you know. Fortunately, she went shopping yesterday."

Leaning forward with the snifter, he held it out to Erik. Hesitating for a moment, Erik realized his uncle wanted to toast. He too leaned forward, the glass of the two snifters meeting gently in a dull chime. Erik told his uncle of the farm, Ludwig's quiet death, Helmon, and Isaac, not mentioning their constant bickering or their treatment of him.

"And of your voyage on the *Edinburgh*? It's the same ship Reuben took, you know. He was accompanied by a tall, blonde man, military, probably an officer, from one of the Scandinavian countries—a fine fellow. I was pleased he had met such an able traveling companion."

Erik realized uncomfortably that his uncle was again studying him, his hands, legs and his shoulders. Uncle Hermann's eyes were keen, fixed on his as Erik briefly relayed the voyage, the young man from Poland, the narrowly averted altercation with the two Russian ruffians and then shyly, his meeting Alysia and the intervention by her parents.

Uncle Hermann grinned. "Ah! Italian women." His eyes rose to somewhere on the wall above Erik's head, *remembering*, and then dropped, intersecting with Erik's again. "Very fiery. And you never want to get on the bad side of their papa." He smiled like a man speaking from experience.

A voice echoed from somewhere else in the house, "Herr Frank, supper is ready. Come get it while it's hot."

A DELICIOUS SUPPER CONSUMED- BOILED POTATOES, PER-
fectly baked ham, red cabbage and creamy cucumber salad
and ginger crumb cake for dessert- Uncle Hermann grew
quiet, leaning back in his chair. He looked healthy, but gaunt
under the gaslight dining room chandelier.

"Come, nephew. Let us retire to the study again and talk
more."

Reclined once again in the overstuffed chair, Erik
delighted in the smell of old books and cherry tobacco as his
uncle stuffed the bowl of a pipe, regarding him with a steady,
probing look over the bowl he was lighting.

The pipe lit; his uncle leaned forward. "So, you wish to
venture west and be with your brother?"

He smiled slightly at Erik's unhesitating enthusiastic,
"Yes!"

Quiet and thoughtful, he settled back in his chair, puffing
on his pipe. "It is a very rigorous life, not at all like the farm,
and the land is not at all like Villmar. Where you are going
nothing is level. There are heavy winters with snow higher
than your head, frigid cold, steep mountains, no law and
Indians, some of them unfriendly, to say the least." He
tapped the pipe, paying studious attention to the bowl as it
thumped against the ash box.

He finally looked up again. "It is a perilous and
unforgiving place that you wish to go." His voice was quiet.
"There are thieves, killers and men without conscience.
Though I thought it a possibility before, I am now convinced

that this country is headed for an internal war over the slavery issue. Violence has increased in the west half of the Kansas territories, and enmity has only grown since the 1854 Kansas-Nebraska Act passed. This will not be the gentle pasturing of cattle on the lush green fields of Villmar and, as I told your brother, you will have to fight to keep what is yours."

*He thinks I am too young and weak.* "Uncle, I'm aware of all this. I have read a number of books on America. I've read every story I could find in every newspaper I could get my hands on. I know it is nothing like Villmar. I know America is nothing like Prussia." He smiled, "That is why I'm here."

Uncle Hermann's face was somber, "You are far younger than Reuben. You are...," he hesitated, "not built quite the same as he is. You will be traveling without a companion such as his friend Johannes." His jaw tightened, "I say this not to hurt your feelings, nephew, but your violin case will give others a predisposition towards you, whether merited or not. Are you sure you would not like to stay here? There's plenty of room in the house. There are many things to do in the city. There are musicians like yourself who enjoy books and music. There is no limit to the opportunities."

Stunned, Erik leaned forward, dropping his eyes to his boots, thinking. *Like Isaac and Helman. Like the immigrant officers at Castle Garden who asked me why I was in a different line than my parents and questioned my age three times looking incredulous when I answered his question about my destination.*

Looking up, he willed his voice to be as deep and as sure

as possible. "I am aware, Uncle, that there is little or no culture where I'm headed, that I will be leaving that behind when I leave the cities and cross the Mississippi. I will think about your advice on the violin case." Pausing, he looked directly back into his uncle's eyes, "But I am going to Cherry Creek and the Uncompahgre to help Reuben build our ranch."

Uncle Hermann was impassive, knocking more ash from his pipe into the ash bowl. There was a soft smile on his face. "You are your father's son. It is important that you understand your limitations, nephew. There is much you can do to help Reuben, but there will be some things you can't. You will have to listen to your older brother and not take on certain matters, certain dangers, until you are ready." He sighed. "If I was not so old, and my leg now so weak, I would go with you. I would prefer my last breath to be of mountain air, and my last sight, my family and a place with no people, rushing rivers and mountains that reach the sky."

His lower lip trembled just slightly, and then his face grew stern, and he leaned forward, his eyes boring into Erik's, "Your greatest asset, Erik, is your head. Promise me that you always use it before you act...," he paused, "no matter what you may believe others think of you and regardless of your wish to prove something to them or to yourself. Make me this promise."

Surprised, Erik returned his uncle's stare. *He understands.* "I promise, Uncle."

Uncle Hermann leaned back in the chair, "In that case, I have not been out of this house for several months. I crave a trip. Tomorrow, we will take my buggy down to Booraem's

Mercantile. I shall introduce you to Wallace, who happened to be my sergeant and carried me off the battlefield the day I was wounded. A good deal of Ludwig's money is still here. Reuben only took part. We decided he would let me know, and I would get it to him when needed. I will give you some of that for traveling expenses. Keep it well hidden. Some we will use tomorrow to get you properly outfitted, the right clothes, and boots, a hat, a .52 caliber Sharps rifle, which I will instruct you how to use, a good knife, and perhaps a pistol of some sort.

However, you must always keep the pistol concealed. In the American West, I've read, and been told by our scout and others, that a pistol on your hip or tucked in your belt can sometimes invite trouble you don't anticipate. I am tired. I must get my leg up; I've been on it quite a while today. Tomorrow will be a big day that I'm very much looking forward to."

He rose, as did Erik. Taking a step toward him, the old soldier threw his arms around him and hugged him tightly. Erik could hear his voice rumbling in his chest.

"It is unlikely," his uncle said slowly, "that I shall live much longer. I am older than Ludwig, you know. I will have a letter for you to give to Reuben. Make sure it reaches him. I am leaving the house to Mae for her many years of loyal service. The letter will have instructions on what to do with the rest of my things back here in New York and banking information on the rest of Ludwig's funds, and mine. I made rough, smaller copies of the scout's maps, which I will give to and review with you. Then, we will get you booked on the trains to Chicago and finally St. Louis, and spend a few days together until you leave, talking and taking a few hours each day where I will show you some sights of the city."

Erik felt a building constriction in his chest as he listened to his uncle's words. His eyes felt watery, and he was glad his uncle could not see them.

Hermann patted him on the back, "And then, my boy, you will be on your way, this old man happy in his heart that he has met all of his brother's sons, and we shall say our first and last goodbye."

July 10, 1855

# ECHOES IN THE ASPEN

THE THUMP OF CANNONS, CRACK OF RIFLES, AND CRIES OF men both enraged and in agony swirled in the dust and smoke. Below, on the sandstone and clay cobbled toe of a steep rise dotted with junipers, a line of supply wagons had halted their advance. Johannes watched soldiers leaping from the wagons, scrambling to find cover behind wagon tongues and wheels. One lone officer galloped up and down the line shouting indecipherable orders.

Aware of the battle raging over the next ridge ahead of their column, and on the left flank of Johannes's heavy platoon, the men below were unaware of the fifty riders on the rugged low rise above them. They expected conflict to boil their way from the north, down the trail on which they had stopped, not from above.

Raising his saber, the uniformed sergeant beside him, Johannes twisted in his saddle and turned to the men and horses spread to either side and massed behind him. Slashing the saber forward, sunlight glinting on the deadly steel, he shouted, "For the United States! Charge!"

Digging his spurs into Bente, the bay mare raised slightly on her front hooves, then barreled over the edge of the ridge. Behind them, Johannes heard the shouts of his men and the pounding hooves of their mounts. An ancient Danish battle cry erupted from his lips. The faces of the enemy turned upward, aghast at the image of death hurtling down the slope toward them.

Johannes woke with a start, sweating, sitting up quickly, his forehead colliding with a strut underneath the freight wagon. He sank back down, one hand pressed to his throbbing head. *How many times have I laughed at Reuben for doing that? What a dream.* Lying still for a minute until the pounding in his skull receded, he rolled out from under the wagon. He stood staring at the wagon cover, remembering the dream in vivid detail, the feeling of righteous might, the adrenaline of conflict and the thrill of command. Even now, he could feel the lethal saber in his hand flashing forward.

"You okay, viking?" The Prussian's eyes lifted to the red welt beneath Johannes's hairline.

His reverie broken, he turned to Reuben, who chuckled.

Not fully disengaged from the scenes of battle that had swirled in his mind just minutes prior, Johannes half nodded. His eyes surveyed the mottled shapes of cattle grazing contentedly far out at the edge of the bench meadow, the Red Mountains towering behind, Philippe mounted, standing guard on the herd. *Damn cattle.*

Reuben's eyebrows furled over narrowed eyes, "You

sure?"

Johannes feigned a smile. "Yes. After all the times you splintered your cranium on the underside of the wagon, I was just trying to see what it felt like."

Reuben's eyebrows lifted partially, and his eyes lost some of their narrowing, but there was a reservation in his smile.

Johannes picked up his Sharps carbine that had been securely lodged between the wheel and box of the wagon. He lifted his nose. "Smells like bacon. I'm going to get some breakfast, then ride out and spell Philippe. I hear Michael's ribs are to the point it doesn't hurt him to breathe anymore, and he's going to spend half a day in the saddle today, anyway. When he spells me, I'll take a short ride to the aspen grove up the ridge from the cattle to get a better view of the valley to the south. Then, I'll be down to help you and Philippe unload the freight wagon and cover it all."

Reuben raised his eyes to the sun. "Four hours give or take till noon, I'd say. Michael's planning on saddling up shortly before then. Philippe and I...," he nodded his chin at his sling, "or half of me, should have that log platform ready. Keep everything we unload off the ground till we get a proper storage structure built."

"See you in a few hours then," Johannes said, turning to walk toward the prairie schooner where Rebecca was mixing sourdough batter in a large tin bowl. Sarah squatted at the fire, shaking a cast iron skillet sizzling with bacon.

<hr />

NEAR THE HERD, JOHANNES DISMOUNTED IN KNEE-HIGH

grass. He had his eye on a longhorn cow with a slight limp in her left hindquarter. Taking a step, his foot slipped, an audible squish under the sole of his boot, the foul odor of fresh cow manure rising from the grass. He stopped, looking down at the fibrous pile of green oozing over the instep and toe of his boot, the outer surface of the cow pie baked dark brown by the blaze of the sun. The longhorn craned her head toward him, shook her twisted horns, bawled once, then ambled off, her apparent limp cured.

Johannes stood looking after her, shaking the dung from his boot, hands on his hips. *Damn cows.*

Several hours later, lost in introspection, he didn't hear Michael until the boy was almost to him. "G-g-good m-morning, Johannes." The boy's round face was all smiles, his eyes roving the grazing longhorns. The purple bruises and deep cuts on his face and around his jawline were visible but healing.

"Good to see you back in the saddle again, Michael."

"Th-th-thank you for, c-c-coming to, to help me, Johannes."

Johannes returned his smile. "No thanks needed. You would've done the same for us."

The boy's head bobbed up and down. "Y-yes!"

"Well, you got the cows, Michael. They're in far better hands than mine...." Johannes threw a backhanded wave at the herd. "Look at the grins on their faces."

Michael laughed, delighted at the compliment.

"I am going to head up that hill into those aspens, then back to help Philippe and Reuben. You'll be all right?"

Michael nodded vigorously, the broad smile never leaving his face.

THE ASPEN GROVE CLIMBED THE NORTHEAST SLOPE, THE trees' pale green leaves shimmering from a southwest breeze. Sifting rays of sunlight moved brightly across the white bark and black gnarls of the tree trunks, then faded. Scatterings of younger quakies, four to eight feet high, kept company in tight clusters, protected by their older, taller companions. At the top of the ridge, the family of aspen tapered into the scattered cover of fir and pine spilling down the opposite slope.

Johannes reined in Bente at the transition line between aspen and the conifers. The highest snowcapped points of the *El Diente* and Wetterhorn to the south and west, and the Snaefel, shone like bright snowcapped beacons against the green of their flanks and the endless blue of the sky.

Sounds filtered up through the aspens. Johannes stiffened and looked back down into the linear blur of white trunks. The sounds grew louder, sounds he knew well— marching boots, muttered conversations, the breeches of rifles tapping against belts, exposed bayonet handles protruding from their sheaths. The noise drifted through the light-barked trees and the thin, high country air. He caught glimpses of a partially unfurled flag moving, ghostlike, in the alleys between the rise of the aspen trunks, its colors unclear.

Then, up through the trees erupted the loud, raucous bawling of cows protesting as Michael moved them from one part of the meadow to the next.

Johannes blinked, realizing with a surprised jerk that he

had been gripping his pistol. Bente's head craned sideways; one eye rolled back toward him, her ears up.

Johannes sighed, relaxing back into the saddle, and shoved the half-drawn Colt roughly back into his belt. *I must be going crazy.* He gazed back down through the stand of aspens, eyes carefully searching. *I know I heard it.* He massaged his ears, rubbed his eyes and looked once more, but there was nothing, just the amused flutter of leaves and dabbles of sunlight flashing on white bark, as if winking to him at the wraith of his mind.

# CHAPTER

## *17*

July 18, 1855

# *N*O WAY HOME

STANDING IN THE LOBBY OF THE ST. LOUIS HOTEL, ERIK reached over and picked up the small brass bell on the front desk and rang it twice. A clerk hurried through the ajar opening of a door and greeted him with a smile. "What can I do for you, young man?"

"Good morning. Would you happen to know where a place called The Livery is located?"

The clerk nodded, reaching under the counter, its surface rimmed on both sides with a scrolled cherry wood, polished to a dull sheen. Three feet of polished marble countertop separated them. Pulling out a piece of paper and a sharpened pencil, he smiled at Erik. "It is not far—an easy walk. I will draw you a map. The hotel is at Fourth and Walnut. The Livery is on Fourth by the river."

Forty-five minutes later, Erik stood looking down Fourth Street, a dusty side street compared to the main thoroughfares. Rough looking characters lounged at various points down the street. At the end of the street, where it tapered off, flowed the Mississippi. Black smoke belched from the twin funnels of a riverboat headed upstream, its paddlewheel propelling the craft through the blue chop.

Erik took a deep breath, comforted by the .41 caliber Philadelphia Derringer snugged securely in his boot holster. He touched the pocket of the light canvas jacket he carried over one arm, making sure Helmon's dagger was securely hidden.

He walked down the center of the street, avoiding the uneven boardwalks where the rough characters lounged, some leaning against upright columns supporting porticos, others in doorways. He studied the men, taking care not to let his stare linger too long on any of them. Some wore coonskin caps; belts dangled from their waists with strings of something that looked like hair. Then, the thought struck him. *Scalps!* Every man carried a long gun of some type. He recognized several Sharps like his, and one that looked like an Enfield as Uncle Hermann had described the rifle to him and a number he didn't recognize. Some had pistols in their belts, usually ball and cap, and fringed knife scabbards hung low off their waistbands. Further down the street, out on the river, the single side paddle riverboat had been joined by another that chugged along in its wake, their side paddle wheels glistening in an uneven cadence, the second riverboat having a single stack which, like the first, belched steam and smoke.

At the end of the alley were makeshift corrals, some with oxen, others with mules or horses. Most looked well-tended. A sizable low building of aged wood sat to the side of the corrals. Wind gusted off the river, swirled and danced along the street, the whirling edges of the dust devils dissipating as they made contact with the building.

Making his way toward the sign that said, "Livery Stable," Erik paused at the doorway underneath the signage and peered in. There were open stalls at the front of the building and just inside the door, blacksmiths were industriously shaving horses' hooves and fitting shoes. Broad-shouldered Morgan and quarter horses, bred to pull and haul, whinnied in the stalls. Past the stalls was a table of sorts made from a door set atop some hay bales. Empty wooden water barrels served as seats. A man with thin features, *but likely on the tall side,* sat on one. His neatly trimmed hair hung slightly over his ears and down to the collar of his red plaid cotton shirt. Stacked behind him on the far wall were barrels and crates marked sugar, flour and molasses. Pulled partially into another large door was a wagon with two men industriously working on a wagon wheel they had pulled from one of its axles. They were dipping portions of the wheel in a large low barrel filled with water, then removing the wheel, pounding on its metal rim with mallets. Standing back, they cocked their heads one way, then the other, surveying their work. Erik took a deep breath and walked, with a stride he hoped looked purposeful, up to the makeshift desk.

The man was engrossed in making quick marks with a pencil on the top sheet of a stack of papers. He turned each page upside down next to the original stack, and then repeated the process.

Swallowing, Erik said, "Excuse me. Are you, John?"

The man looked up, thin brown eyebrows raised, lips pursed in an annoyed line underneath the thick, brown, well-trimmed mustache that curved above his lips and ended halfway to his chin.

"We don't need any help." The man's voice was of medium tone but authoritative, his words rendered with finality. He looked back down at his papers and continued his work.

"I'm not here looking for work. I'm here to buy passage on your next wagon train to Cherry Creek."

The man stopped writing and lifted his head from the papers. He eyed Erik silently for a few moments, then leaned back on the barrel and put down his pencil. His eyes were hard, his face expressionless. "You are, are you?"

Erik nodded, a slight flush rising.

"And you're traveling without your parents?" There was a note of incredulity in the man's tone.

*And again.* Erik stifled a sigh. Jutting out his chin and squaring his shoulders, he replied firmly. "Both my parents are dead. I am heading west to join family already out there."

The man's lips moved in a slight smirk. "You are, are you?" Do you have a wagon?"

"No."

"Can you drive a wagon?"

"Yes."

The man stood, appearing slightly off balance. Looking into Erik's eyes, he said, "Give me your hands." He grabbed Erik's hands, twisting the palms upward, then releasing them with a mutter of disgust and sat back down again.

"How old did you say you are?"

"I didn't. I am fifteen."

"Fifteen?" The man's eyebrows dropped over his eyes,

and his jaw tightened. "Well, maybe you are, and maybe you aren't, but you can't walk to Cherry Creek. I don't have any horses to spare, and I doubt you could handle a prairie schooner. Besides, a whole wagon for one youngster is a waste...." After a moment, he added, "and I just sold my last one."

Dismissing Erik, the man returned to his paperwork. Heat coursed through Erik, anger boiling in his chest. *What's to lose.* "I am indeed fifteen," he said. "I can, indeed, drive a wagon and have done so my whole life. I grew up on a farm, and while I make no claim of being an American frontiersman, I know my way around the land and around animals, and I need to get to Cherry Creek."

Erik's firm and resolute tone caught the man's attention. He leaned back on the barrel, arms crossed in front of his chest, eyes boring into Erik's, and said, "You know, when you walked in here and started speaking, your eyes were green. Now, I'd say they're almost gray. Only seen that one time before."

A long silence ensued while he studied Erik's eyes, his eyebrows raising as he reached some realization. He leaned forward slightly, "Where you going after Cherry Creek?"

"The Uncompahgre."

The man's eyebrows lifted further. "What did you say your last name was?"

"I didn't. You didn't bother to ask."

The man's lips spread in a partial smile, "You have a brother?"

"Four."

"Would, by chance, one of them be named Reuben?"

Erik blinked. "Yes."

The man slapped both hands on the table. A loud thump echoed through the building. Several horses shifted in their stalls, and the two men working on the wagon wheel stopped and looked over. The man rose, walked around the table with a pronounced limp and stopped a foot from Erik, towering over him. "And your last name is Frank."

As Erik nodded, a broad smile spread over the man's face. He stuck out his hand, which Erik took, and shook firmly. "Yes, I'm John."

"So, you are Reuben Frank's brother? I'll be damned and go to hell. If you have his guts, son, you'll do well. That brother of yours is hell on wheels. Mac, the previous wagon master, made him assistant wagon master in the first several weeks. I heard he took over the train and got 'em to Cherry Creek after Mac was killed in an Indian attack."

He gestured with his hand down one leg. "They had to leave me at Fort Kearny to get doctored up. And the day I got this, your brother saved my life and likely a whole bunch more. We were outnumbered more than two to one, head-to-head with a bunch of cutthroats, bloodthirsty no good sons of bitches led by one of the meanest renegades in the West. Didn't look all too good, and I likely kicked it off cocking the hammer of my Enfield...." He shook his head. "But I'm pretty sure it would've blown up anyway."

Erik was spellbound. The man not only knew his brother; he had gone west with him!

"Your brother got off that big blonde horse of his, pretending he had to stretch his legs. We all believed him, and the outlaws thought he was loco. But he was just gittin' set up. When the shootin' started, that pearl-handled Colt of his knocked five of them out of the saddle and took out a sixth when they were on the run. Happened in the blink of an eye. Still ain't seen nothing like it."

He stopped talking, a frown clouding his forehead as he seemed to think of something. "Do you know where the Uncompahgre is, how far it is from Cherry Creek? What kinda country ya gotta go through to get there?"

Erik shook his head. "I only know, according to the map I have, that it is southwest of Cherry Creek."

A laugh rumbled in the man's chest. He rested his hand on Erik's shoulder. "Son, that's an understatement. It's the wildest part of a wild territory. Pretty sure if Reuben and that Danish cavalry officer he was traveling with, Johannes, and them women with them, if they didn't go back to England or wherever they were from, they're likely just getting there about now. There ain't no transportation over there. There's only a few white men know the country well. Depending upon what route you take, you will have to contend with outlaws, Ute, Apache and maybe Sioux if you go the northern way—or if you're real unlucky, all them. Few men, except the best of the mountain men and trappers, travel those trails alone." His eyes scanned Erik head to toe. "I'm not being mean—just real. And I don't want to see no brother of Reuben Frank get killed and scalped, and that's exactly where you'll be if you try to go by yourself."

Erik thought hard, *his mind jumbled. Reuben, pearl-handle Colt, women, killed six men. Killed six men? I never thought about the last leg of the journey—just assumed carriages or wagons, people going back and forth.*

"You mean there's no one at all that goes back and forth?"

John shook his head slowly. "No, there ain't. But at some point, there might be. One thing for sure, there ain't no one going to the Uncompahgre from St. Louis. Your best bet getting over them mountains is to get yourself to Cherry Creek. Wait there, keep your eyes and ears open, your nose to the wind and latch onto the first honest outfit headed in that direction. Maybe get you over the mountains at least as far as the Gunnison or the Colorado. You'll most likely have built up enough skills and smarts between the wagon train to Cherry Creek, and that jump over the Rockies, to make it the last five or ten days on your own."

He thought for a minute. "In the meantime, Randy—who was Mac's brother and owns the Mercantile—he's my boss, and he has a hell of a time keeping good help. Good man, big red-bearded Irishman who doesn't take any guff. He'd likely let you spread your bedroll in the back of the store and be pleased to have Reuben Frank's brother working for him for a spell. And anyone who comes to Cherry Creek will sure as hell go to the mercantile, so you'll have a leg up on who's going where."

"But I thought you had no wagons left, no horse to spare and you said it was far too long to walk."

John grinned at him. "Well, I might just find a horse for Reuben's brother, and there is a young couple, no children, bought the last prairie schooner I had. They have kinfolk out there near Cherry Creek, so they are traveling lighter than most. They bought the wagon, but they were scraping to come up with the fees. Bet if you paid their fee for them, and they knew you had a horse, so they had some privacy when they needed, being fairly recent newlyweds and all, they'd agree to carry your supplies and your luggage if it ain't too much. Probably let you use the wagon for shelter when weather comes in, as it sure as hell will from time to time."

Erik's mind flew over this new scenario. *A young couple, luggage, just two duffles, one with a violin case in it!*

"The fee is two hundred dollars, by the way, and the horse I got in mind for you will be ten dollars. Normally charge five dollars for a horse, but this one's a particular good one, the kind you're gonna need when it comes time to go over those mountains and find your brother."

Erik looked up at John. *What's to lose?* He stuck out his hand and shook John's firmly. "Talk to that couple, John. I would appreciate it. What you outlined is fine."

He reached in his pocket, pulling out fifteen twenty-dollar gold coins, counted out ten, and then another, slapping them on the table.

Ignoring the money, John threw some final questions at him. "You got a rifle, pistol, everything else you're going to need? There ain't no stores on the trail and there ain't no turning back when we start. The train can't wait for stragglers, especially unprepared folks who cause trouble."

Erik nodded solemnly. "I do, and I believe I am fully prepared."

John grinned, slapping him on the shoulder. Erik staggered a half step.

"Well, brother of Reuben Frank, you come by tomorrow afternoon, and I'll let you know what those folks say. I'll have that horse down here for you to take a look at. Give you a feel for what size tree you'll need for that saddle too, especially since he has a big back and you got thin hips. We'll see what I can rustle up for you in the way of tack."

Erik's head had not stopped spinning. *Reuben—killed six men—women.*

John looked at him closely. "But remember this, Erik. Once you get to Cherry Creek, you might have to wait a long, long time to get further. Right now, there's no way home."

# CHAPTER
## *18*

July 18, 1855

# $\mathscr{S}$IGNS

REUBEN LEANED BACK, WATCHING THE FLICKERING FLAMES of the small cook fire cast their shadows on the schooner's box and canvas cover. It felt good to stretch after an arduous day of cutting, hauling and positioning logs. Overhead, the wispy threads of mare's tail clouds were fading from fiery pink to gray against the darkening sky. To the west, their cousins stretched more feathery ends to the Snaefel and beyond, cloud tips still glowing crimson orange from the angled rays of the hidden sun.

Reuben listened to the dull scrape of Philippe's fork gather the remnants of supper from his tin plate. Sarah's empty plate sat on the grass in front of her. She was sipping a cup of coffee, both hands clasped around her enamelware cup, staring silently into the fire. Rebecca sat next to him on the log, one of three makeshift benches they had arranged around the fire. Johannes held his plate in both hands, bent forward, his forearms resting on his thighs, half his food still remaining. Occasionally, his head turned toward the dying color of the clouds to the west.

"I think I'll have another helping of that sourdough," Rebecca whispered to Reuben. "Not just eating for one, you know." Reuben kissed her on the cheek, his eyes circling the fire again as Rebecca rose, stepped to the fire and stooped down by one of the cast iron skillets sitting to the side of the flames on two large flat rocks. *No one's very talkative tonight.* He patted his belly, "I'm full! Great supper, Sarah and Rebecca. Thank you."

Rebecca turned over her shoulder as she lifted a piece of sourdough to her plate and smiled at him. Sarah didn't acknowledge the compliment, her eyes still fixed on the fire.

Philippe stood, "*Sí, la señorita y la senora are muy bueno en la cocina.*" His teeth flashed white in the gathering dusk. "I will ride out, and Michael can come in for supper...." He laughed. "It is not easy to get that boy to leave those cows."

Johannes stood also, and as Philippe had done, put his plate, still half full, next to the rocks of the fire ring. "Philippe, I'll take the first watch tonight. I'll let Michael know to come in. You can relieve me whenever you wish. Wouldn't mind staying out all night, if you want to get some sleep."

Reuben couldn't see Philippe's expression in the descending gloom of the evening, but by the quick movement of his head, he knew the *vaquero* was surprised.

"*Sí, señor* Johannes. I could use some rest. I will be out to spell you, or join you, as you wish, around midnight." Philippe turned, walking toward the rear of the wagon where they stored their bedrolls during the days.

Saying nothing more, Johannes strode off into the darkness, and a short time later, Reuben could hear the beat of Bente's hooves heading out to the herd. He peered out into the gathering darkness. *Johannes has not been himself at all for the last ten days. Maybe hit his head harder than he thought that morning under the wagon?*

Reuben looked beyond the vague shape of the tongue of the prairie schooner at the large, dark mass of stacked logs. Next to them were the barely discernable linear lines of other logs forming a rectangle, one on top of the other, two high. To the side of the infant structure, the dark shape of the freight wagon could be made out, the ends of logs sticking far beyond its rear etched slightly against the lighter grass of the meadow behind them.

---

JOHANNES LEANED FORWARD ON THE POMMEL OF HIS saddle, only vaguely aware of the longhorns milling in front of him. Night had come on, but no moon had risen. The wings of a nighthawk thrummed above his head and down toward the river, a coyote called to its mate. One memory after another flooded his mind.

*...A misty day on the border of Alsace, the one hundred sixty men in his company behind him in columns of fours, the snap of the king of Denmark flags and the colors of his command giving texture to the silent mist that hung in the air. Sergeant Helgerjen rode up beside him, announcing them to the two men in the road. "We are First Company, Fourth Battalion, His Majesty, the King of Denmark's Heavy Dragoons."*

*...the cavalry patrol from Fort Laramie riding into the*

*wagon train on the South Platte cutoff trail toward Cherry
Creek. Cantering up to the patrol commander, who had held
up his hand, "Hooooah."*

*...the voice of his sergeant yelling in a thick Irish accent.
"Troop halt!" Twenty-four pairs of curious eyes had fallen
on him from the two by two column as he reined in Bente,
Johannes and the mare facing the commander and his horse
diagonally. He wore captain's bars and threw Johannes a lazy
salute.*

*"I would be Master Sergeant O'Malley. This is Captain
Henderson. We are C Squad, F Troop, United States Army,
Second Cavalry." The Master Sergeant had rubbed his nose
with the back of his hand, then blew one nostril out over the
side of the horse pressing the other tightly.*

*The captain had looked at Johannes, "and you are...?"*

*Annoyed at the sloppy salute, he had hesitated, but just
briefly and then had thought, what the hell. "I am Captain
Johannes Svensen, former commander of First Company,
Heavy Dragoons in service of his majesty, the king of
Denmark."*

A cow bawled on the far side of the herd and, for a
moment, the flood of memories slowed. Johannes took in a
deep breath of the cooling night air wafting down valley from
the Uncompahgre. He remembered how saying those words
had lifted his spirits, how he had relished the jut of his chin
and the squaring of his shoulders.

*He executed a perfect salute, and Captain Henderson's
eyes widened in surprise. He, too, had straightened in the
saddle, squaring his shoulders and returning the salute, this
time as one professional to another. "You are a mighty long*

*way from home, Captain Svensen."*

"*This is my home now—America, and an honor for it to be so.*"

*...The knowing smile on Wallace's face, clerk at Booreams Mercantile in New York, and Uncle Hermann's former sergeant, as he had asked him to point out their selection of sabers, Sharps carbines, and Army Colt pistols.* Johannes chuckled to himself. *And a campaign hat instead of a cowboy hat like Reuben's.*

Then, the dream, slightly more than a week ago, was followed by the mysterious ghostly sounds echoing of a nonexistent army on the march in the aspens. Permutations of the dream had recurred several times since then, as if destiny were calling.

What is it Reuben says? *There are no coincidences—a succession of signs.* Johannes shook his head, clearing it, listening to sounds of the cattle and the creek, turning the memories over in his mind. He straightened in the saddle, taking another deep breath of the night air. In front of him, several hundred yards away, Reuben could hear Philippe softly singing in Spanish to the cows. He gently touched his heels to Bente's flanks and moved slowly through the longhorns toward the song.

---

WHEN THE VOICE CAME OUT OF THE DARKNESS, "Mississippi," Philippe stopped crooning his Spanish lullaby mid-stanza. A minute later, Johannes reined in Bente next to him, his tall profile and light hair reflecting what pale light there was.

Philippe chuckled. "You do know, *señor* Johannes, that this word is almost as difficult for me to say as it is for the Indians."

The Dane laughed. "Michael has problems with it, too."

Philippe hesitated for a moment then, realizing the comment was not intended to slight the stuttering boy. "Yes, but *señor* Johannes, I only slightly mispronounce the word. *El muchacho* takes a week to say it."

Philippe laughed with him this time, no unkindness intended.

"You plan on sticking around, Philippe?"

The query, coming in the dark, caught Philippe off guard. *It's good he cannot see my face.* "*Sí,*" he answered. "I signed on to ride for the brand and build the ranch."

His eyes roved the dark, jagged edges of the mountains that pressed against a mass of glittering stars. "I like this country. *Muy bonita.*" The sounds of the gunfire, flashes from pistol barrels and bullets slicing the air at the old fort welled up in his mind. "And, I trust Reuben when the odds are *muy malo,*" he paused, "*Y me gusta la senorita, pero quién sabe.*"

Out of the dark silence, Johannes finally replied, "Good."

There was another long silence. Then the Dane spoke again. "I am going to head in and see if there's any coffee left in that kettle. I'll join you soon."

As rider and horse turned toward the wagons, Johannes tossed a lighthearted comment over his shoulder, "Wouldn't want to miss any of that singing."

Philippe smiled at the fading figure of Johannes and his

mare heading back to the wagons. He leaned on his saddle horn, watching them until they were no longer distinguishable in the darkness. *Do I plan on sticking around?* This question did not come out of darkness. *There is a reason he wishes to know.*

# CHAPTER

## *19*

July 19, 1855

# TWO TRAILS
# DIVERGED

JOHANNES DISMOUNTED, LASHING THE REINS AROUND THE wheel of the freight wagon, not wanting to disturb those sleeping both in, and under, the schooner. Leaning against the saddle for a moment, he patted Bente's neck, thinking about the brief conversation he had had that afternoon as Zeb was mounting up on Buck to head back to the notch cabin.

The mountain man had stared down, his expression questioning when Johannes walked to Buck and rested one of his hands on the pommel of the tobiano's saddle. Looking up into the trapper's steady green eyes he had asked simply, "Zeb, you ever regret not doing anything in your life?"

At the question, Zeb's eyebrows had raised under his coonskin hat. He looked off in the distance toward his cabin, one hand absent-mindedly stroking his mustache. His voice had been slow and thoughtful. "Don't think there's anyone that doesn't ever regret something. Question is, how many regrets you have, how big they are and how long you let 'em last."

Johannes blinked at the older man's words.

"It ain't like you get do-overs, Johannes. Some folks like this...," he swept his arm around the valley, "others not so much."

He had picked up Bente's reins but made no motion to move out. "The way I see it, son, depends what you want to be around. Follow your heart, captain...." His voice had dropped an octave, punctuating the word, "Pretty damn simple, really. You either want to be with cows or soldiers."

He had looked back out at the Wetterhorn, then down at Johannes, his expression understanding. "Tell Reuben I'll be down tomorrow, a couple of hours after daybreak with that other block, tackle and pulley. They're might heavy for Buck to move more than one at a time on that slick trail." The paint craned his neck toward Johannes and blew once, bobbing his muzzle up and down.

Lost in thought, Johannes walked to the faded glow of coals in the fire ring, not realizing that Sarah was now sitting huddled on one of the log benches.

"Sarah, what are you doing? It's halfway to daybreak."

"I couldn't sleep, Johannes." The redhead's voice was a quavering whisper. "I gave Reuben and Rebecca the wagon tonight, and the ground is lumpy under the freight wagon."

Her breathing was ratcheted, and Johannes realized she was crying. He walked over and sat down next to her, moving one long leg to the side and shifting his position to bring them closer. Putting his hand on her shoulder, he asked softly, already knowing the answer, "What's wrong?"

"I don't know what to do, Johannes. This is so, so different from my dream to own a seamstress shop. Rebecca is very cold to me. I fear I'm losing her friendship. I'm torn between Zeb and Philippe, and I carry that towheaded rapist's child. Maybe I should just leave."

Johannes reached toward the fire, a slight warmth rising from the dying embers. He picked up the coffee pot, sloshing it around. *Half full and still warm.* He slowly filled a cup, buying time to think.

"Not too sure leaving is an option, at least right now. No real way to get anywhere from here..." He paused, making his tone as empathetic as possible, "And it's a fairly long trip out of here to any place with people, Fort Laramie, Salt Lake, Santa Fe, Cherry Creek. Leaving too soon wouldn't be a good choice for you." *Especially pregnant by that towheaded swine, Jacob.*

She seemed to nod in the faint light. "I know. I was quite uncomfortable the last day or two bumping over those rocks, and I think Rebecca was in pain several times."

"You and Rebecca will need each other. There's just the two of you women. You share...," he searched for the words, "the same condition." You won't lose her friendship. You're just going through a temporary misunderstanding. But...," he could tell she raised her head slightly, "you do need to make a decision. Even if that decision is neither of them." She nodded again. "It's not fair to anyone, including you, if you don't."

"Oh, Johannes." Her voice choked. "I have thought about it. I truly have. Zeb is stable, kind, knowing and gentle. Philippe is exciting and attractive and worldly."

*She has been thinking about this.* He was quiet—
wondering. *How can a woman endure such a thing? Such a
soldier, she is.* He sipped the lukewarm coffee, draining the
cup. Maybe some humor would help.

"There is a fourth alternative."

"Yes?" she asked.

"Next time a priest comes down the valley, he could
anoint you as a nun."

She giggled through her tears, the shape of her hand
rising to her mouth to stifle the sound. "Johannes, I do love
your sense of humor." She patted her stomach. "I think it a
bit too late for that."

Johannes chuckled, "Likely so."

She rose. "Thank you. You have no idea how helpful it
was simply to have someone to talk to and make me laugh. I
think I can sleep now."

Johannes stared into the embers. *You do need to make a
decision. He could have been talking to himself.*

He swished the coffee in the kettle once and poured
himself a second cup. Taking another sip, he craned his head
upward to the glowing blanket of light spreading across the
night sky—the Milky Way. He swiveled his head and looked
up valley in the direction of the Gunnison and Colorado, and
above that, the North Star.

He smiled into the dying glow of the coals. *Thank you,
Sarah. Feel better already.*

————

THE NEXT MORNING, TWO MORE LOGS WERE ADDED TO

each wall of the nascent cabin. They used Zeb's recommended sequence and combination of block, tackle, pulleys, the team of horses detached from the prairie schooner and long log skid ramps, hewn flatter on one side, temporarily spiked into the last log in each wall on which the next log was rolled and dragged into position. Zeb and Johannes stood together watching Philippe and Reuben, now minus his sling, cinch a heavy rope around one end of one of the timbers cantilevered from the rear of the freight wagon, fastening the other end to the trailing drag harness Zeb had shown them how to rig.

"When do you think it'll be ready for a roof, Zeb?"

The weathered man's eye shifted from the walls taking shape to Reuben and Philippe. "If the weather pretty much holds, these walls ought to be up in seven, maybe eight days."

"And the roof?"

Zeb turned to him. "With me, Philippe and Reuben working on it, and the boy watching the cows, we can probably get the roof framed up in maybe four days. No more than five."

Johannes began to ask another question, but Zeb answered him before he posed it. "The actual roof, the sod, goes pretty quick if the women are cutting the sod and the three of us form a chain to get it up and in place. Maybe a week, maybe more."

The log the team of horses was pulling fell from the wagon with a heavy, bouncing thud. Zeb cupped his hands and shouted to Reuben and Philippe. "Drag it over here. The east side, put it at the foot of the ramps. I'll hook up the tackle, and we'll get another one in place."

THEY HAD NOTCHED THE FIFTH COURSE OF LOGS ON EACH corner. The sixth log, the first of the next new course of timbers, was in position at the bottom of the ramps on the west wall. Two ropes stretched back to the sets of block, tackle and pulleys, wrapping around either end of the log just inside the rise of the ramp timbers. Reuben felt an excited satisfaction. Rebecca, Sarah and the four men stood just off one corner, admiring the work.

"What do you think, Zeb?" Reuben asked, without taking his eyes off the structure that had appeared in just three long days.

Zeb took off his coonskin hat, running his long fingers through his thick, sweaty, graying hair. Snugging down the cap again, he said, "We're making good time. Them notches in all those corners are a bit rough. But no matter. Just be some more chinking."

"Is there a way to tighten them up?"

"There is, but every hour you spend making it look pretty is an hour you don't have a roof. You ain't putting it up to impress anyone, and the chink will fill the daylight. More important, it'll be windproof and watertight. Philippe, when you're up there with that adze and hatchet, angle the blade more. That'll take some of the steep out of the sides of the notch, and that round bottom of the top log will set down lower with not so much gap."

The *vaquero* nodded.

"Supper's about ready," said Rebecca. Her face was

pinched and drawn behind her smile, and she had one hand unconsciously on her belly.

"If you have enough for dinner, I think I'll stay the night. You womenfolk cook way better than this old trapper."

Smiling, both women turned, heading back to the fire and the smell of stew and sourdough biscuits.

Zeb turned to Reuben. "In fact, I think I'll stay down till these walls are up. You boys will know enough by then to get your shed up and...," he nodded with his chin at the tarps and *gutta perchas* covering the pile sitting off the ground on six logs spaced about eighteen inches apart, "...and get all that stuff protected. The shed'll go faster, being smaller and only three walls. Somebody can ride up and get me, and I'll come down and we'll get both of these roofs on."

Zeb's eyes moved from the piled logs to the few timbers not yet pulled from the freight wagon and then to Reuben. "Reuben, you're gonna need five- to six-inch logs for them cross braces that run from top wall to top wall. They go every four feet like up at my place, and you're gonna need a number of smaller logs than you got here for rafters—four or five inches. There's a pretty good stand of lodgepole higher up and over the ridge. Probably has all you need plus some. Them rafters ought to be two feet apart so you can figure what you need, and multiply by two for either side of the roof." Zeb was pointing at the placements. The mountain man slid his thumb and forefinger slowly down his mustache, thinking. "And then we'll have to have one big tree, thirty-four feet, straight, eight to ten inches across. If you can't find one, or more likely if you can't move it, I'll show you how to cut it so you got a strong joint overlapping. That cut's different than the splice we been usin' in these long walls. We'll put ourselves in an upright post in the center of the cabin right under the joint. Rest its bottom on some big flat rock, so it doesn't sink. That'll work just fine."

Sarah called from the fire, "We didn't cook all this food to have it go cold."

The four men exchanged glances, and Philippe and Zeb turned, heading back to the fire.

Johannes reached out a hand, closing it around Reuben's arm. "Reuben, why don't you and I talk for a few minutes."

Reuben felt a tug of anxious premonition.

"What is it, Johannes? Your leg okay? Seems to be doing fine. You barely have a limp, though I noticed lifting those logs you're still favoring the good leg."

The Dane's face was somber, concerned, with creases of stress around his eyes, which didn't ease Reuben's anxiety.

"No Reuben. It's not my leg....," he paused, his jaw tight, one cheek quivering slightly. "You remember that talk we had the morning after you got married and I found that note from Zeb?"

Reuben's stomach turned queasy. "Yes."

"You said there is no choice of trails, and I said that might be so, but trails always have choices."

Reuben swallowed and nodded.

Johannes took a step toward him, reaching out one hand, putting it on Reuben's shoulder and squeezing with a firm, steady pressure. His startling blue eyes bored into Reuben's, his eyebrows tight and earnest, "You're my best friend, Prussian. In many ways, the only true friend I've ever had and that will never change."

Reuben felt his heart sinking.

"I promised to come to the ranch with you. That's done. We've been through much together. And I have a feeling we will be through much more shoulder to shoulder. But...," his mouth compressed and, to Reuben's surprise, the corner of the Dane's upper lip trembled slightly, "I've come to a fork in my trail, Reuben. Our trails are diverging. Fate is tugging at my heart. My destiny is as a soldier, not as a rancher. I've talked to Zeb. Though I didn't ask him directly, he's perceptive enough to know what I was driving at, and he assures me that you, Philippe and him, even with Michael mostly handling the cows, can get this place put together and ready for winter without me. And though it's one less set of hands, I've never scythed hay in my life, so you won't be missing much."

He smiled slightly. "You'll be less one rifle, and one horseman, but you also have one less mouth to feed and one less body taking up space. It's going to be a crowded winter in that cabin."

Reuben stood, unsure of what to say, a mixture of tumbled feelings and heavy thoughts running through his mind, all laced with a tangible, palpable feeling of sudden loss. "Johannes... I..."

Johannes squeezed his shoulder harder and shook his head. "I've made my decision, Reuben. I have to follow the calling. Your destiny lies here; mine lies elsewhere. Though I believe they are meant to interweave again, and they shall."

Reuben took a deep breath, exhaling slowly. "When are you leaving?"

"I'm going to help you finish the walls of the cabin. And

then I'll be on my way. If Zeb is correct, that'll be about a week."

"And where are you heading?" Reuben heard the catch in his own voice.

"Fort Laramie. Going to look up that Captain Henderson we met on the way to Cherry Creek. See if he wants to enlist a Danish rogue in the United States Cavalry. Maybe I can talk him into being an officer..." A forced smile played on Johannes's lips, "but if not, I'll settle for corporal."

"Have you let the others know?"

"I think Zeb knows. I think he's known for a while, maybe before I did. I'll tell the others, each one in my own way. They are all my friends."

Numb, Reuben stuck out his hand, his voice low, "Well then, I guess it will soon be farewell."

Johannes stepped to him, wrapped his long arms around him, and hugged him.

Reuben, the handshake quickly forgotten, hugged the Dane back, both men in a firm, long-lasting clasp, Reuben blinking back the filmy moisture he could suddenly feel in his eyes.

CHAPTER

*20*

August 3, 1855

# THE BLACK ROCK

BLACK FEATHER THREW DOWN THE SHOVEL WITH THE splintered handle in disgust, the sharp gray edges of the old break matching his mood. Sinking heavily to the sandy clay and broken shale hillside, he took care not to encounter a prickly pear. Dot squatted near him, both of them in the shade of a cluster of scrub oak trees.

"I don't know.... I could swear me and Johnson buried that loot." He corrected himself quickly, "Stuff we bought, on this hillside right about here." He shook his head, squinting angrily at the hillside around them pockmarked with their diggings. "It wasn't too deep, neither, maybe a foot. Been here a damn week. And it took us twice as long to get here as I figured when that snake-bit leg of yours blew up."

He swiveled his head toward her. She was looking at him, her eyes wide, neither a smile nor frown on her face. He tried to subdue his frustration. The dry, hot breeze coming out of the west swayed Dot's sun-lightened hair across her shoulders in golden highlights. His anger slightly dissipated.

"That darky woman did quite a job on you. I think your hair looks better now than when she combed it."

Dot's eyes wrinkled, and the corners of her lips turned up in a partial smile.

"And I see you been cleaning your face every night at whatever water's around."

The girl nodded, her smile getting wider.

"Well, it was plumb fortunate we ran into them darkies. Nice people. Though I don't know if they're going to make it wherever they're goin'."

Dot's face fell, a worried frown appearing on her forehead.

He fell silent looking over the long rolling hills and ridges, punctuated by steep draws where drainages trickled down. Sage, bitterbrush, mountain mahogany and scrub oak dotted the countryside. His eyes traced the trail down on Good Spring Creek, a half-mile below to the west as he tried to remember.

*That drainage there, the second one south. I know that's where Johnson and I were holed up when them two wagons rolled by. Then, we eased down to the bottom, used the toe of that second hill for cover and took them from behind, right there.*

His eyes fixed on a curve in the trail where the creek chewed away at the bank. *Picked that spot because they couldn't maneuver. Then, we dragged the bodies up the next drainage and left 'em in that secondary creek coming down from the south. Ransacked the wagons and found that gold, jewelry and fancy silverware in that false box they had under the floorboard on the linesman side of the driver's seat.*

*Stuffed it all in them two gray metal boxes that had their papers in them.*

Even now, Black Feather could see the documents blowing out of the boxes when they first opened them, then drifting forlornly with the wind, important testaments to people they had never known—folks with families and lives of their own. He clenched his jaw. *Can't fix that now.* He looked over at Dot, whose eyes were fixed on a hawk soaring close to the ground on the opposite slope, its wings dipping and tipping as it hunted for lunch. *Find them boxes, and what we did will all be for some good.*

"I wish I had that goddamn map. Took me and Johnson an hour to draw it—down to detail, and then made a copy on the backs of one of them papers in the boxes, one for him and one for me. Made that pact that neither of us would ever come back here without the other unless..." the image of the twisted body of his friend, buried in snow, pink blood frothing from his lips, flashed through his mind, "...unless one of us bought it."

He turned to the girl. "Did you see any piece of paper anywhere? I didn't drop something when I was emptying out his saddlebags before I slit...I let his horse go?" He watched her eyes to see if she had caught his slip. She hadn't.

She shook her head, slowly, her tiny voice all but lost in the breeze. "No papers."

Black Feather stared at her. "You know you're talking a lot more since that night with those darkies."

She nodded her head, a full smile spreading her cheeks. She leaned over to one side and dug in the frayed pocket of her pants, pulling something out. She held her hand out, a glittering piece of obsidian, black, with angled swirls in several facets, was cupped in her palm.

Black Feather glanced at the small black rock. "Oh yeah, that was in the saddlebag. You liked it right off."

She nodded her head vigorously.

"I don't know why the hell he carried a rock in his saddlebag. It's rare enough it didn't get there by accident."

The girl stood, Black Feather's eyes trailing down her figure. *She is starting to get some curve in them hips.* She pointed back uphill toward the ridgeline.

"We been diggin' in this damn hillside...," He thrust out the heel of one boot scattering rock shale and pebbles, "for a week. Good thing we found that old broken shovel out behind that caved-down cabin we stayed in that one night. Otherwise, we both would've been diggin' with flat stones like you have been."

Dot's pointing grew more insistent, raising her forearm and bringing it level again, forefinger extended. Black Feather shook his head and lay back on one elbow.

She stamped her foot, frustrated, still moving her forearm up and down in an exaggerated point to some location above them. Her lips trembled, and with an effort, she said, "There."

Black Feather looked up in surprise. "What did you just say?"

Her lips moved, and again after several attempts, she said, "There."

Black Feather rose, took the two steps downhill to where he had hurled the shovel and turned to her. "Well, we've dug up most of this hill. No reason we shouldn't dig up the rest.

Show me." He followed her up the hillside diagonal across the contours. She was almost running, and sweat was dripping below his headband, stinging his eyes as he tried to keep up. She stopped and pointed down just below the ridgeline toward something that shone with a muted dull shine twenty paces away.

Black Feather walked briskly past her, and then it was her turn to hurry to keep up.

He stopped, looking down.

"Son of a bitch, Obsidian."

He turned to Dot, "Let me see...." But she already had her hand outstretched, the black rock in her fingers.

Black Feather grabbed it, bent down and held it up to the other chunks of obsidian protruding here and there in the small, concentrated area. It seemed to have the same markings and sheen. *Maybe all obsidian does.*

Looking closer, just below the freckles of exposed obsidian, Black Feather saw two rounded stones the size of his fist. They seemed out of place on a hillside covered with jagged-edged rocks, large and small. The round stones appeared to have been pushed into the porous, coarse soil.

Then he remembered. *Johnson insisted on walking all the way back down to the creek bottom to find some markers only we could recognize.*

The drainage was narrower and steeper toward its head. Black Feather looked down at the tiny stream in the bottom, his excitement growing. "That's it. That's where Johnson walked down the hill to get them two rocks."

He pointed them out to Dot. "See how they're round and everything around them ain't? You're one smart girl."

The girl looked at the rocks and him and nodded, her face beaming.

"Stand back. Don't want to hit you with any dirt that's gonna be flyin'."

Black Feather dropped to his knees, scooping soil behind him with the busted shovel, three or four inches of cover spraying and rolling down the hillside behind them with each draw of the shovel. Halfway through his fourth swipe, the shovel blade hit something with a metallic click. He dug at some small rocks, then dropped the shovel and scraped away sand and pebbles with his fingers until the square corner of a rusty metal box poked up from the excavation.

Dot knelt down beside him, her little hands digging in the hole with his.

He lifted out the first box, then the second, both about a foot square and five inches deep.

Black Feather brushed the soil and stones back into the hole, smoothing it with his palm, creating a level area. "We lost the key up here somewhere." Hefting one of the boxes onto the level, he pried it open with his knife, and as the lid sprung back, the sun glinted, winked and sparkled on the gold coins, jewelry and silver pieces inside. He guessed it to weigh *ten or twelve pounds.* He hefted the other up. *About the same.* He handed the unopened container up to Dot, whose eyes were fixed on the glitter radiating from the open box.

"That's right. That's your surprise from me and Johnson. It's all yours, girl. When this is all spent, you'll be readin', writin' and doin' numbers as well as anyone."

Dot knelt, putting her hand in the box, picking up a

bracelet and turning it on her wrist, then dropping that gold piece and plucking a silver coin, holding it between her thumb and forefinger moving it to reflect in the sunlight.

"I'll carry this open one, so nothing gets lost. You think you can carry that other one out in front of you?"

She nodded.

"Well, let's go, then."

Dot stuck out her arm again. "Shovel."

Black Feather stopped in his tracks, whirling. "Did you say, shovel?"

She bobbed her head.

"Well, I'll be damned. Good thought. Doubt anyone's been up here since Johnson and I set foot, 'cept maybe some Ute ponies, but no sense drawing attention."

He reached down, grabbing the shovel halfway between its broken edge and its blade. "We'll dump it someplace where someone else can find it. Maybe it'll bring them luck too."

An hour later, they were saddled up.

"See," Black Feather said, patting the saddlebags on The Black. "Them boxes fit perfect. That's why we chose them." He glanced up at the sun. "Got a couple hours till we lose daylight. We'll get some miles under us, head north and hole up near a creek. You can do some fishing. Still got some good slabs from that mule deer I killed two weeks ago, but we're running low on salt. We'll have us a nice meal and talk about where you're going to get learned up."

Dot smiled widely.

He fixed his eyes on hers. "We got a long ways to go, and this ain't very friendly country. Keep your eyes open and keep that mare right on The Black's tail."

## *21*

August 3, 1855

# *S*ACRIFICE

THE DAY DAWNED STILL AND SULTRY, THE SUN ABOVE THE rolling hills southeast of them already angry with heat. Mosquitos droned around their heads, dodging the swipe of their hands, and flies buzzed around the horses.

Black Feather turned to Dot, "Go ahead and mount up. I'm gonna fix this fire so don't look like anyone's been here and we'll keep pointed north. Damn..." He slapped a mosquito on the back of his neck, "We ought to reach the White River by noon without pushing, even in this hot glare."

Black Feather looked quickly up at the sun and then down again, wiping his forehead above his headband with the back of his wrist. *About eight, I figure.* He brought his hand down, glistening with the sweat from under his hairline. *Forgot how hot this country is in the summer.*

It was late morning when the trail bent, and a long meadow spread before them. Ahead of them a few hundred yards, shallow gray and yellow shale and sandstone ledges protruded from the base of the toe of the hill. Ten paces from the hill and Good Spring Creek, the ledges formed small, shallow but , shaded caves.

He twisted back in the saddle to Dot, about to tell her that they would hole up in the shadows under those overhangs and have a few chunks of salted venison for lunch when he heard a noise high on the hillside—a rock rolling down, maybe, on their side of the creek.

Keeping his hand down to avoid any unnecessary movement, he held it out from his left leg, keeping it saddle-level, palm toward the girl in warning. He reined in The Black quietly. She did the same with the mare.

Black Feather searched the hillside. *That rock didn't roll by itself—too big.* His eyes probed the ridgeline where spindly, sharp, twisted limbs of mountain mahogany and scrub oak intersected with the skyline. His gaze slowly traveled down its length, and then clicked back above one thick bush where the top two feet of an Indian's lance pointed toward the sky. The dense brush proved good cover. He turned carefully back to Dot and slowly raised one forefinger to his lips, tipping a single finger up toward the hill.

She blinked, grew pale and swallowed. Her head rose, her gaze following where he had pointed. She couldn't hear his thoughts, but she could sense them.

*We'll just hold firm here, not move a muscle, not make a sound. Chances are they'll drop down over the other side or pass us by—never notice. Too far for a pistol and I don't want to move to draw that musketoon from the scabbard.*

He kept his eyes fixed on the lance and a small gap in the ridgeline brush, maybe twenty feet wide, not far from the danger on the rim. Every few seconds, only moving his eyes, he scanned left and right to see a bit farther.

The black stallion swished his tail at the flies. Black Feather froze.... The lance began to move and, by its upward and downward motion, he knew the Indian was mounted, not on foot, and heading toward the short break in the dense, high brush. The forelegs of a brown and white spotted mustang entered the opening. Then, its rider appeared with bare bronzed legs hugging the side of the saddleless horse and upper body exposed to the sun above his loincloth—a Ute brave. *Yamparika. Not good.* Then, another spotted horse. This brave wore a leather vest above his loincloth, no lance, but held a bow. Then, a third and a fourth with an older-style musket perched on his thigh, and finally a fifth, the last warrior riding a red sorrel that looked more quarter horse than mustang. *Probably stole in some raid.*

The first three Indians crossed the little gap in the brush and disappeared again. The fourth was about to do so and the last warrior, riding the stolen pony, was more than halfway across the short opening. *They ain't gonna see us!*

Flies buzzed around the stallion. Behind him, he heard Dot's mare stomp a foot. The slight soft sound of the jingle of the metal rings on her hackamore rose above the buzzing. The fifth brave, on the verge of disappearing behind the brush, glanced down at them, froze for an instant and then cried out a warning.

"Shit. They seen us," he shouted at Dot. "Ride hard for them rocks. Follow me!" The ground was a blur, the screams of the Yamparika growing louder behind him, the black stallion and the mustang racing for the cover of the ledges still sixty yards away.

He glanced back over his left shoulder at Dot. She was just a few strides behind, the white of her mustang's eyes mirroring the girl's fear, the mare's neck stretched out like the stallion's, the girl's small frame low over the pony's withers, her chest brushing the mustang's wild mane, Dot's chalk-white face and wide eyes fixed on the protection toward which they galloped.

Arrows hissed through the air, falling short. A rifle blasted, kicking up a small explosion of dust ahead of their horses. *They'll get a better bead with the next rounds.*

He drew the Colt from his belt and, extending his right arm rearward, fired twice. Another shot rang out. The mustang screamed and stumbled, trying to keep her footing, then pitched forward, throwing her young rider onto the sandy soil of the creek bottom.

Hauling back on the reins, Black Feather wheeled the stallion in a spray of sand and dirt. The girl was on her hands and knees shaking her head, stunned. Leaping from the saddle, he shoved the pistol in his belt and gathered her from the waist, folding her in his arm like a rolled blanket. A hiss flew through the air, and his right leg buckled. Searing, numbing pain shot up his thigh to his hip, the shaft of the arrow quivering as he tried to keep his feet, its tip protruding from the other side of his leg.

"Son of a bitch!" He cursed in pain and rage, panicking the stallion. The animal wrenched his head and reared, ripping the reins from Black Feather's hands.

Stumbling through the last few feet of the creek, Dot still under his arm, the smooth soles of his boot slipping on the slick wet creek stones, he tried to hobble up the bank.

Dragging his leg, Black Feather drew his pistol from his belt again, this time backhanded with his left hand. The Indians were closer now, and he could see them clearly, one waving a tomahawk above his head, two with arrows notched in their bows, the fourth with the musket held high. The brave with a lance held his deadly projectile at the ready. War cries rent the air.

He slipped and stumbled, trying to get up the bank, his pierced leg without the strength to either propel or haul his body the two feet from the creek bottom to the grass. Lunging up the bank with his good leg, he dropped on both knees to the grass, releasing Dot. Pain shot from his wounded leg up his hip and side. Swiveling backward, he fired a shot from the Colt. The lead Indian's horse, coming at full gallop just fifty yards out, squealed a terrible death cry. The horse fell forward, pitching its rider off its upended back, the dust and confusion slowing the other four braves. One of them dismounted at a near-run to help the fallen rider.

Black Feather staggered to his feet, hauling Dot up by her arm, hopping the final three paces to the welcoming shadow of the ledges, pulling the girl with him, half throwing, half shoving her into the protection of the small cave.

He turned to fire again, but the force of an arrow meeting flesh staggered him backward. A wooden shaft protruded from his chest, just below his left shoulder. His pistol fell from his grasp, his arm numb, useless. He groaned in anger, the pain dropping him to his knees. He reached desperately for the Colt with his right hand, an arrow embedding itself just inches from his outstretched arm. He fired the Colt without lifting the butt of its grip from the ground. He hit the brave who had leaped from his horse to help his friend. The warrior cried out, sinking on one knee, both hands clutching his opposite thigh.

*That evens things out, you bastard.*

He pinned his gaze on the overhanging ledge and the protection it offered Dot. Her small white figure stood out in the sunless space. *Got to crawl. It's the girl they want.*

Using his right elbow to pull, and left leg to push, he willed himself to move despite the excruciating pain. An arrow nicked the top of the ledge just over his head. Pieces of stone raining down on his shoulder, the shaft rattled along the small ceiling of the overhang. It hit the far wall and broke in half, falling in pieces next to Dot. She screamed, holding out one hand toward him, half offering him assistance, half begging for his help. Under cover and in the shadows now, Black Feather rolled to his right side in front of the girl.

"Stop your screaming," he shouted, peering out of the darkness into the glare. "Get as low as you can behind that rock. Stay right behind me!"

The girl shrieked again, her cry of terror echoing hollowly in the rock.

"Dot! That ain't helpin'. It will just get them all riled up."

The four braves drifted out of pistol range and regrouped. Cursing, Black Feather tugged cartridges from his belt, slamming four into the empty cylinders, then laying out six on the rough surface of the little cave.

The brave whose horse had been shot out from under him had leaped on the back of the mustang ridden by the wounded Indian the others had dragged back by his arms.

He was rolling from side to side on his back, his knee in the air, clutching his thigh. His leg was blood red below his hands all the way down to his exposed buttocks. His loincloth lay flat on the ground below him. *Good, you son of a bitch. Hope that bullet went right through the middle of your bone.*

The Indian ponies were milling, two braves notching new arrows in their bows, the warrior with a lance repositioning his grip, the warrior with the musket reloading. Behind Black Feather, Dot's shrieks subsided to terrified whimpers. He looked down at the protruding arrow. *Might have nicked the bone.* The blood oozed in pulsing spurts from its tip. *Gonna have to push it out. Can't pull it.* A warm, wet, stickiness flowed down his shoulder under his vest. Blood pooled on the porous stone underneath him.

He blinked. The outlines of the Indians blurred, their shapes fuzzy and unclear. He tried to focus. *I can get one of them as they are coming in; they got to slow a little for the creek. Only ten paces might get a bullet in two of them. But that'll still leave one.* He looked over his right shoulder at Dot. The fleeting thought of killing her to spare her from the life he knew she'd have if they took her raced across his mind. He clenched his jaw, his thoughts traveling back through time, back to boyhood. *No, not like the old mare. It ain't gonna be that way.* Lowering his head to the top of his right arm, he closed his eyes to clear his vision, jerking it up again as he heard the war cries.

The Indian mustangs had hurtled half the distance to the shadowed shelter where Dot and Black Feather hid. The barrel of the Colt wobbled at the blurred outlines charging them. He fired. The right shoulder of the Indian with the musket was thrown backward. He screamed, dropping the rifle but staying on his horse and in the attack. Darkness crept into the distortion of Black Feather's vision. *Can't let them take her. Can't let them take her,* promised Johnson.

Then, there was another rider.

*Another damn injun. No, it ain't.*

The Colt weighed heavy in his grip. Slowed from by the loss of blood, Black Feather's mind struggled to comprehend what his eyes were seeing. On a gray mare at full gallop, the rider was but thirty yards from the flank of the Indians. Tall and blond, the man sat upright and forward in the saddle, sunlight wavering above his head on something gripped in his outstretched hand. *A saber!* The man entering the fray shouted a battle cry in a tongue Black Feather had never heard. The Indians, galloping toward Black Feather and Dot, turned their heads. Realizing the danger, the braves tried to wheel their horses around to meet the sudden threat from the side.

Redirecting the aim of their bows, they turned their ponies with legs pressed tight against the ribs of the confused horses. Only the warrior with the lance, his free hand still holding the guide ropes tied around his paint's muzzle, was able to fully turn his mount. With his lance ready, he confronted head-on the tall man galloping toward him and the swirling dust behind. Sunlight glinted on the blade as it arced in its swing. The warrior's lance was knocked to the side, the deadly steel running straight and true through his neck, front to back. The force of the blonde man's charge knocked the warrior from his horse. The front quarters of the gray mare barreled into another mustang, its rider suddenly headless.

One Indian galloped out and turned, drawing his bow. The man pulled a Colt from his belt, calmly raised the pistol and fired, his target dropping his bow, and slumping forward, the warrior's arms dangling lifelessly over his horse's neck. Wielding a tomahawk, the last brave screamed and charged. He too toppled from his horse, felled by the Colt.

Black Feather struggled to keep his head up, his fingers on the grip of his pistol, his forefinger on the trigger—and then, *blackness...*

Black Feather forced his eyes open. He had been propped up, his back against the rock Dot had taken cover behind. She was sitting by his shoulder, sobbing. The tall blonde man who had ridden like a badger into a nest of rattlesnakes was kneeling next to Black Feather's wounded leg, the arrow through his shoulder already removed.

Black Feather weakly raised his right hand, wiping his lips to rid them of their salty taste. When he drew his hand from his mouth, pink blood frothed over his lower forearm and wrist. He tried to focus his eyes on the man's blurry image.

"I know you."

The man raised his head. "My name is Johannes. I ride with the man with the pearl-handled Colt."

Black Feather felt a jerk go through his body. "That wagon train." His tongue felt too large for his mouth. "You were the son of a bitch out to the side with the rifle."

The man looked up again. "I was," he said, finishing, with

more force than necessary, the knot on the tourniquet he had tied below Black Feather's groin and above the quivering arrow in his thigh.

Black Feather gritted his teeth, biting into his lip. His right hand searched for his Colt, but he didn't have the strength to turn his head to look for it.

"I have your pistol, Black Feather." The man leaned back on his haunches looking directly into Black Feather's eyes. "I was up on the ridge opposite the Ute, headed north to Fort Laramie. Saw the whole thing. Couldn't get here any quicker."

The man's piercing blue eyes turned to the girl who was hunched into a ball, her chin below her knees, her hands over her head, whimpering. His gaze returned to Black Feather. "I saw you trying to protect the girl, shielding her with your body, turning back your horse when hers went down, and then lying here half dead between her and them...." His hand waved at the corpses on the other side of the stream. "Whatever else you've done in this life, your sacrifice is the only reason she still lives."

Black Feather let the back of his head slowly sink against the stone. He closed his eyes, focusing on moving his lips and forming words. "Take her—with you. Find black stallion...saddlebags...her money...school."

The words took all his strength.

The man's blurred image was like a ghost. Black Feather felt as if he were floating. He heard a voice, the accent thick.

"I can't fix you up. Don't have the skills. I can't move you, or you're a goner for sure."

Keeping his head resting against the stone, Black Feather

fluttered open his eyes, clicking them downward to the blurry face in front of him. "Take her. Leave me be. Put...pistol in my hand. A round...in every cylinder."

The man reached down. Picking up Black Feather's Colt, he leaned over and gathered up the shells Black Feather had prepared on the stone floor of the tiny space. He spun the cylinder, sliding a round into the one empty chamber. He set the pistol across Black Feathers hips, below his belt.

Black Feather weakly turned his head to Dot, "You—go with him. Good man."

Dot lifted her head, reaching both small hands out and grabbing Black Feather's right arm.

"No. I'll be fine," he whispered, hoarsely. "Go with him. I...will...catch up."

Then, there was only darkness.

August 3, 1855

# OCCASIN TRACK

INSIDE THEIR TIPI, FIVE HUNDRED SIX MILES EAST OF where Black Feather lay pierced by Yamparika arrows, Eagle Talon studied Walks With Moon's smile as she handed a gourd filled with pemmican to him. With his fingers, he lifted a large bite to his mouth. His wife, pestle in hand, was intent on grinding chokecherries and jerked meat, but the wind pressing in on the hide walls of the tipi made her nervous as the leather scraped against the lodge poles in gust-driven bulges, portending a coming storm.

"I am glad, husband, that Flying Arrow and Tracks On Rock decided to stop our travels early today and pitch the lodges."

Chewing, his fingers clutching a second bite, Eagle Talon grunted his agreement. At the sound of Three Cougar's voice outside the drawn tipi flap, his hand stopped halfway to his mouth. "Eagle Talon, the Council wishes to see you."

Walks With Moon, her face drawn and eyes rounded and anxious, stopped grinding and lifted her shoulders from the bowl, the bone pestle still in her hand.

Eagle Talon swallowed and spoke. "When would they like to see me, Three Cougars?"

"Now."

Walks With Moon sat back on her calves, one hand on the leather stretched tight over the distinct roundness of her belly. Scraping the pemmican from his fingers back into the gourd, Eagle Talon lowered his head and set his meal down.

"Tell the Council I am coming."

There was no response from Three Cougars, just a sudden strong gust of wind that made the tipi sway, the lodge poles squealing in protest where they were lashed together at the smoke hole.

Eagle Talon knelt, leaned over and rested one hand on Walks With Moon's knee. "I shall return shortly, my wife, and finish this fine meal."

Walks With Moon bit her lower lip. A tear zigzagged its way over the angular rise of her cheekbone and then trickled down the side of her face.

Reaching out, Eagle Talon tenderly brushed the wet, salty track with his thumb. Walks With Moon's eyes followed him as he rose and exited their lodge, fighting to lash the wind-drawn edges of the tipi flap closed behind him.

———

WHEN EAGLE TALON REACHED THE COUNCIL LODGE, Three Cougars already stood holding the unfastened flap open. His friend peeled it back against the wind, remaining outside and securing it tightly after Eagle Talon stepped into the lodge.

A small fire burned in the fire ring beneath the smoke hole. The gray, boiling clouds sweeping in from the west had already obscured the sun, and there was only half-light in the lodge. The Council sat cross-legged, Flying Arrow and Tracks On Rock together, nearest the flames, the lesser chiefs spreading out from them in their usual hierarchal order.

Eagle Talon's eyes quickly surveyed the group. *The look of twilight.*

Flying Arrow was gazing at him intently, as were the rest of the Council members, except for Tracks On Rock who stared morosely into the fire.

There was a protracted silence during which Flying Arrow's assessing stare never left Eagle Talon. Finally, the chief spoke. "The Council has discussed what we talked of one moon ago. The decision of the Council is that you will go to the lands of our enemy, the Ute, where water turns rock red and find the hairy-faced one with whom you bonded and Zeb-Raih." He paused, casting a quick sideways glance at Tracks On Rock whose eyes remained fixed on the fire. "Because his daughter Walks With Moon is your wife, Tracks On Rock has not participated in the Council's decision."

*When?*

Sensing Eagle Talon's question, Flying Arrow continued, "You will go early in the season of the Moon of the Thunderstorms, when the snow is off the warm slopes of the hills, but before there are buds on the cottonwood trees."

The eyes of the entire Council were fixed on him, some of the members nodding their heads. Tracks On Rock raised his head from the fire, joining the group's collective, penetrating stare. "This will allow you to be at the side of Walks With Moon when she gives you your first child," *my son,* "and to spend time with her in winter camp."

Flying Arrow straightened the bony stoop of his shoulders and lifted his chin, his cheek muscles tensing, his eyes narrowing slightly. "You are to find out all you can about the hairy-faced ones. How many are there? When are they coming? Where are they heading? What do they want? And what do they think of The People and our lands? You may take one brave with you, but...," he paused, "only if they wish to accompany you. Think hard about this, Eagle Talon. Four eyes see in more directions than two, but the moccasin of a lone warrior leaves only a single track."

Reaching out a long thin arm, Flying Arrow grasped a small stick with bony fingers and added it to the fire. "When you return, The People will be east in the Season of the Warm Moon, searching for our brothers. The prairie grasses may have already turned brown, and the nights will have begun to lose their heat. You are to find our sign, catch up with the village and issue your report to the Council immediately upon your return. The men of the tribe will hunt for you. Walks With Moon shall have hides to flesh, and your lodge shall have meat."

*If I return.*

Several of the Council members turned to one another speaking in hushed tones as the first splats of rain collided dully with the lodge walls. *A fitting day for news such as this.*

"I said, that is all, Eagle Talon."

Eagle Talon felt himself jerk slightly. *I missed his words.*

Flying Arrow raised his voice, "Three Cougars." In response, the lodge flap opened, Three Cougars straining to keep his grasp on the wind-whipped leather edges of the tipi's door. As Eagle Talon bent to exit, Flying Arrow spoke once more, his voice deep, *and concerned.* "The People are relying on you. *Wakan Tanka* shall be with you."

His lips thin and tight, Three Cougars shot a furtive look at Eagle Talon, and hurriedly closed the lodge flap. Large drops of rain, a vanguard of more to come, splattered against Eagle Talon's head and shoulders.

*Who should I ask to go with me? Or should I ask no one? What shall I tell Walks With Moon?*

August 3, 1855

# $\mathscr{S}$ADDLEBAGS

BENTE STOOD PATIENTLY ON THE OTHER SIDE OF THE creek, the swish of her tail brooming flies from her rump, reins wrapped twice around the saddle horn. Johannes scanned the ridges carefully, cautiously examining either end of the meadow beyond where the corpses of the Indians lay in crumpled heaps.

He turned to the sobbing girl behind him. She was staring into the shadows of the small cave. One of Black Feather's boots peeked just beyond the edge of sunlight and shadow. He took a step to her, and leaned down, speaking softly, "There's nothing we can do here. We can't move him, and we can't stay." *Doubt he has hours left.* "We've left him some food and water. Might take weeks for him to mend up enough to sit a horse or travel."

The girl shook her head violently and sank to her knees, shoulders slumped forward, strings of hair falling from her neck around her hand-covered face like a blonde frame of grief.

Johannes knelt, putting a hand gently on one heaving

shoulder. She recoiled, twisting away from his attempted empathetic touch. He sighed. "I know it's a tough thing, leaving your... friend." *I wonder.* "What's your name?" he asked softly. No response. Just ratcheting sobs. "Well, Black Feather entrusted you to me. That makes your safety my responsibility. And we can't stay here. Those Indians may not have been alone. The gunfire and commotion may have been heard. We have to leave."

The shaking of her body stilled somewhat; her gulps of air diminished. She sat back on her calves and turned her tear-streaked face to his, fingers frantically brushing her cheeks. *So young.*

"If...when he gets better, I'm sure he'll be along. I'm headed to Fort Laramie. That will get you to a safe spot, and there will be folks and other women.... They can look after you until...he comes by."

The girl's head swiveled to the dirty, cracked leather boot, dull brown with mud and sand intruding into the sunlight, and then back at Johannes, the full rounding of her red-streaked eyes less pronounced. Johannes held out his hand. "I'll help you get across the creek. It's fast, and this bank's a steep drop-off. Did you have a horse?"

The tears had slowed their cascade, but now they welled again, the corners of her mouth drooping still lower. She raised one arm limply and pointed. Sixty yards or more out, close to the other side of the creek, lay a saddled gray mare, a swarm of flies above the carcass already like the dark boils of clouds gathering for rain.

"Why don't we cross the creek and gather up that saddle of yours. Where was that big black horse he was riding?

Killed also?"

She stared at him, cheeks quivering, shook her head and pointed upstream.

"So, as far as you know, that horse didn't get hit?" She just stared at him, the deep, sudden intakes of her breath like a sad bass to the music of the stream.

"Well, let's get that saddle in case we find Black Feather's horse. I'll figure out how to rig it somehow on my horse. Fort Laramie is more than a week's ride. Two horses would be far better than one." *Get her involved. Distract her.* "So, what you think of that plan? There's two of us—two votes."

Her eyes flickered momentarily. She turned her head back slowly to the ledge and the boot. Johannes rose, reaching out one hand, "Take my hand. I'll help you up, and we'll get across this creek together. Once we cross the creek, I'll lift you up in the saddle on my horse. Her name is Bente."

They crossed the creek; Johannes's firm grip on her wrist saved her from falling several times. When they reached the opposite bank, she collapsed to her knees, shaking her head, her sobbing rebirthed.

Johannes squatted next to her again trying to keep his voice soft and level, "I can't leave you alone. Your friend said I should take you with me. You heard him, didn't you?"

The girl's head moved slightly in her hands.

I'll walk Bente for a while, and you can ride. A thought struck him. "You can keep a lookout for Black Feather's horse. You will be high up in the saddle. Likely better to spot him than me on the ground."

The girl's face lifted from her still cupped hands, watery eyes looking into his. Johannes stood. Leaning forward, he wrapped his hands around the curve of her waist above her hips, his thumb and fingers almost touching, and lifted her into the saddle. *So small, so thin, so young.* Bente tipped her head back at him, quizzically. He handed her the reins, which she held deftly. *Knows how to ride.* "Just hold them loose. She'll follow me." The girl's cheeks glistened where the sunlight sifted between strands of blonde hair. "You keep a sharp lookout now."

He clicked softly to the mare and began walking. Bente hesitated, then followed. Johannes glanced back once as they neared the upstream edge of the meadow. The girl was twisted in the saddle, one thin arm and small hand outstretched back toward the rocks, lips quivering and tears dripping from her chin.

A QUARTER MILE UPSTREAM, JOHANNES SPOTTED BLACK Feather's horse. The big black stallion was on their side of the creek, standing where the narrow meadow grasses brushed against the dense mountain mahogany at the bottom slope of the hill. The saddle had slipped three-quarters of the way off the stallion's belly, and it appeared a dangling stirrup was snagged on something at ground level that Johannes couldn't make out.

He stopped, Bente's muzzle nuzzling his neck lightly from the rear.

"What's your name?" he asked the girl.

He turned into the silence. The girl was staring at him, her lips trembling, a tear welling from one eye. "Well, my name is Johannes—Johannes Svenson. Do you think my words sound odd?"

The girl nodded slightly.

"That's because I'm from a place far away, across the ocean, a country called Denmark." She heard him but remained expressionless.

"You see any sign of that horse?"

She looked up, her head turning left to right and then she froze as she spotted the black horse one hundred fifty yards ahead. Her eyes widened, and she raised one arm. Johannes turned, pretending to be surprised. "That's a good job! I knew you'd spot him before I did. Let's go round him up. What do you think?"

The girl nodded. The quivering had left her lips.

As they neared the horse, the stallion shifted his weight nervously and shook his head. He tried to back, but the stirrup had slipped over a thick extended fork of a log embedded in the soil. The horse whinnied, straining against the snagged stirrup, then snorted, his eyes rolling white.

"Stay there, Bente," Johannes said softly. He stretched out one arm walking slowly toward the stallion. It shook its head violently, the metal joints of the hackamore jingling, and tried to rear but the trapped stirrup wouldn't allow it. The saddle slipped, further agitating the animal.

Johannes stopped, studying the nervous horse. *I could get a lariat around him, but that will just spook him more—and he's big.*

The girl moved past him, walking toward the quivering

stallion, her hand outstretched. The big black horse ceased shaking, brown eyes fixed on her as she slowly advanced toward him. She stopped an arm's length away, her hand held out, palm up. The stallion blew, then tentatively poked his muzzle toward her hand, withdrawing, then again. She took a half step closer. The horse pulled back slightly and then extended his neck, coarse red tongue flicking from its mouth licking her fingers.

*Well, I'll be damned.*

The girl crouched down, slowly gathering the reins trailing in the grass in one hand, and then rose, her other hand still outstretched. She turned and looked expectantly at Johannes as if to say: What are you waiting for?

Johannes moved gingerly toward the horse, which pulled back against the tight grip of the reins in the girl's hand and then relaxed as Johannes reached the saddle and began to shift it upward, freeing the stirrup from the thick crooked hook of the log. "I'll lead him out toward Bente, then undo that cinch and get it right-side up. That ought to settle him down a bit."

Bente and the stallion were separated by several feet, neck to neck, their heads turned, each appraising the other. Johannes removed the saddlebags. *Heavy. Wonder what's in there. Didn't he say money? No time to check now. Have to get out of this area.* Then, he slipped off the saddle, straightening the awry saddle blanket across the stallion's back. The saddle re-cinched and straightened, and the saddlebags again tied off and dropped behind the saddle, Johannes turned to the girl. "Let me help you back up in that saddle of that mare. I'll ride the black." The girl gave him a quick look, took two steps to the side of Bente and hopped, getting one foot in the stirrup, then fluidly swung her other leg over the mare's back, easing into the saddle trough.

Johannes chuckled. "Guess you don't need any help." He turned to the stallion and with the reins bunched in one hand gripping the pommel, lifted one foot into the stirrup and paused, letting the horse get used to him. The animal scatted sideways a few feet, but he had a tight hold around the saddle horn.

"Easy, boy, easy." he whispered. He straightened his leg slowly, lifting himself. The stallion shook and then quieted. Johannes swung his other leg over slowly, gritting his teeth at the dull pain, making sure he settled into the saddle gently. He slipped just the balls of his boots onto the stirrup plates. The horse pranced sideways. Johannes held the reins firmly but not too tight. The stallion stopped his dance of protest, and Johannes leaned forward, patting him on the neck, "You and I are going to get along just fine, Blackie," he said in a low voice. He straightened, shifting his shoulders back at the girl. "Ready?"

She nodded.

THEY FORDED THE WHITE RIVER AN HOUR LATER. Johannes was impressed by the girl's handling of the mare and the way Bente responded to her urgings as they crossed the swift, turbulent current, spray erupting in arcs, each drop shimmering in the early afternoon sun. High on the rising terrain on the north side of the river, they paused, letting the horses catch their breath.

Johannes jerked in surprise as he spotted distant figures below them and to the east on the opposite side of the river. Squinting through the lazy wave of the pine boughs, he tried to make them out. *One walking, one riding—not Indians. And that horse is stocky. Maybe a mule?*

He pointed through the pine needles, "See those folks way out there?" He turned to the girl. To his surprise, her face seemed animated, and she ran the fingers of one hand through the flow of her hair as if she was combing it.

"Well, they probably saw us, but that doesn't matter much. I think these horses are rested. You ready to ride?"

The girl's stare remained fixed on the distant figures. Filmy again, her eyes looked somehow wistful. Her stare shifted to him, then back to the far-off people. She took a deep breath and nodded once.

———

"THIS LOOKS LIKE A GOOD SPOT TO SPEND THE NIGHT." A small mountain stream bubbled through a tiny meadow that sloped off steeply on their backtrack. A thin band of aspen trickled down the hillside following the course of the creek. The scent of pine and fir hung in the air, squirrels chattered angrily, and somewhere in the broken timber, a thrush crooned its evening song.

"It's early enough we have time to set up camp, make a fire and check out what's in these saddlebags before dark." An alarmed look spread across the girl's features, and she pressed her lips together.

Pretending not to notice her angst, Johannes dismounted, wrapping the ends of the stallion's reins three times around the gray, skeletal remains of a downed pine tree.

He untied the rawhide ties on one of the saddlebags, lifting the flap and began to pull out a gray metal box. Suddenly, the girl was next to him. He turned toward her, the box in his hands, and she grabbed it, taking three steps back, then sinking heavily to the pine duff, both of her arms wrapped around the box clutched to her chest. With shoulders forward, she cradled the gray metal.

Johannes stood dumbfounded. *What is this?* "Do you know what's in them? Are they yours?"

The girl said nothing but began to rock backward and forward, holding the box tightly.

*Don't push it.* Johannes walked around the rear of the stallion, careful to give its hooves a wide berth, opened the opposite saddlebag and lifted another gray box, identical to the first, from the well-worn leather.

The girl appeared beside him again, grabbing the second box. She returned quickly to a sitting position in the pine duff, next to where the first box lay.

He walked to her and knelt. "Let's see what's in them."

Keeping one arm wrapped around the box pressed to her chest, she reached out her other hand and laid it protectively on the lid of the first box.

"Just want to see what's in it," he said, his voice soft.

She withdrew her hand slightly, and Johannes carefully pried open the lid,

Coins, gold and silver, and strands of jewelry reflected dully in the light of the fading day.

She put one small hand on top of the contents, her face upturned, her lips pursed, her eyebrows down in a slight frown.

"Same thing in the other box?"

Her chin moved slowly up and down.

"And is this yours?"

She nodded again.

"Where'd you get it?"

The girl looked at him, pressing her hand more firmly against the treasure.

"What's it for?"

The girl said nothing, just stared at him. Johannes leaned back into the heel of his boot; its toe dug in the soil behind him, shifting his gaze between her and the gold and silver over which she had spread her fingers.

"Well, if it's yours, it's yours." *Likely came from people that outlaw robbed and killed.* "Let's close them up and put them back in the saddlebags."

The girl's cheek muscles relaxed, and the thin line of her lips softened.

Twenty minutes later, dusk descending more rapidly, the scent of coffee curled in steam from the kettle. The fire burned low but bright. Bente and the stallion were tied to a tether line fifty feet away, their muzzles deep in grass. A cloud bank far to the west glowed with a dying crimson, its feathery edge a bright gold. The evening star, Venus, blazed and the creamy white upper half of a crescent moon emerged above a jagged tree line to the east.

"You like that pemmican?" Johannes asked, leaning against the curve of his saddle.

The girl chewed without acknowledging his words, her eyes riveted on the flames. Johannes leaned further into the saddle. "I have an extra blanket. You can roll that up and use it as a bedroll." Her eyes flicked to him, then back to the fire.

THE SWELLS OF THE TREE-COVERED FOOTHILLS OF THE Laramie Mountains loomed behind them and west over their left shoulders. In front of them and to the east, the undulating roll of the tall grass prairie stretched endlessly, broken only by a distant line of cottonwoods escorting the lazy southeastern flow of the Platte River.

They rode silently, Johannes puzzling over the child enigma riding with him. *She hasn't said three words in ten days and all of those in the last twenty-four hours. The only things I know is that her name is Dorothy. She was riding with that renegade, and she won't take her eyes off those two gray boxes.*

He jerked suddenly, straightening in the saddle as an image from back in the mercantile in Cherry Creek many months prior sifted into his memory.

*Reuben and Randy discussing cattle, me standing back surveying the store, that poster on the wall, and then Randy's words as he handed me a copy, his thick arm extended over the counter stretching the paper toward me, "The Army figures it was the Black Feather bunch." The Irishman's gaze had shifted momentarily to Reuben's Colt. "You boys met them bloodthirsty bastards. Here. Take it. You never know;*

*though, she's likely dead or worse."*

*He had taken the poster from Randy, studying it, thinking she was very young, and then had folded the heavy paper, shoving it in his jacket pocket.*

He reined in the stallion and twisted in the saddle back toward the girl. "Let's give the horses a rest. Need to stretch my leg. You probably noticed I have a slight limp. Had an unfortunate encounter with a grizzly bear."

The girl straightened, looking furtively around her.

He laughed. "Nowhere near here."

Johannes dismounted, walked around the rear of both horses, loosened the strap on a saddlebag draped behind Bente's saddle and reached his hand in. Rummaging through its packed contents, his fingers touched a tightly folded piece of heavy paper.

To distract her, he pointed to the northeast, "We're not far from Fort Laramie, I don't think. But I bet you see it before I do just like you did with the horse."

Her eyes rose to the horizon, and he slipped the folded paper from the saddlebag, cinched down the flap and walked back to the opposite side of the stallion, using the big horse's body to conceal the poster as he unfolded it.

*MISSING – DOROTHY ANNE EBERLYN – Age 14. Family Murdered In The Poudre, March, 1855. Kinfolk In Independence, Missouri WILL PAY $100.00 REWARD For Information.*

Johannes's eyes flicked from the faded poster with a rough drawing of a young woman to the girl's profile, then back again. *I'll be damned. I do believe it's her.*

# CHAPTER 24

August 3, 1855

# PATCHED

ALONG THE SOUTH BANK OF THE WHITE RIVER, DROWSY from the heat of early afternoon and the humidity from the sodden soils and high grasses still wet from recent runoff, Lucy, half asleep, swayed to the gait of the mule. Hills rose dark-green with conifers on either side of the valley. The air was still except for the sounds of the river current, the drone of flies and the deep-throated grunts of frogs. Israel walked ahead of the mule in boots soaked nearly through. Lucy's cotton dress, still damp from crossing the White several hours previously, clung to her knees and thighs. Occasionally, she reached down, lifting the material from her skin, moving it up and down to dry.

Israel plodded through the saturated meadow; the tail end of the lead rope coiled loosely in one hand. "Ain't that two riders?" he asked.

At the sound of her husband's voice, Lucy opened her drooping eyelids. Israel was pointing far downriver where the water curved to the southwest.

Squinting in the glare, Lucy raised one hand, shielding her

eyes from the sun. "Sure enough, but they way far away."

"Well, that may be so, Lucy, but if we can see them, they can see us, though they be headed north, so they ain't likely lookin' this way."

"Israel. Can't tell this far, but ain't that a big black horse like that Mr. Black Feather was riding?"

Israel stopped walking, raising one hand to his forehead as she had, and stooped slightly forward as if to close the distance. "I do believe you be right. Tall fellow on it too, seems like. And that rider behind him, much smaller. Can't tell if it's man or woman."

"Or that chile Dorothy, I didn't know they were comin' this direction. He was pretty close-mouthed 'bout what they was doing and where they was going."

Israel spoke over his shoulder, keeping his eyes ahead, every second or third step raising his head toward the distant riders. "Well, glad to see that they is okay if that be them. Never have figured out exactly what they was to one another, even with all the talking about it you and I done." His free hand rose to scratch the gray, curly stubble that rose up his cheek to his ear. "She was mighty sweet...though didn't say more than a word or two. Ain't his niece, on that we surely did agree."

"Yep, husband, and she been through sumthin' bad. Wasn't quite right. You think he ever bothered her, Israel?"

Israel shook his head, still glancing at the two horses high above the river, mere specs disappearing into the trees. "No. There was mean in that man, and cold, but there was sumthin' else, too—some connection between the two. Can't put my finger on it."

The riders out of sight, Lucy lowered her hand. "Well, likely we never will get that figured exact." The growl in her belly distracted her. "So, what about food? I could do with some of that smoked deer meat that took you five hundred bullets to get for us." She pressed her lips hard together to stifle the teasing laugh bubbling in her chest.

Israel stopped and snapped his head back, one hand suspended in the air, his initial sharp look relaxing into a grin when he saw the expression on her face. "You always exaggerate, woman. That fawn took just three shots. Though, if I hadn't wasted three shots the day before figuring out how to work that pistol, might surely have been taken a hundred more."

No longer able to suppress her laughter, Lucy slapped her thigh. Sally jerked, turning her head, one ear forward, one ear back and blowing. "Might a had to do with the fact you had your eyes closed the first time you pulled the trigger. You were ten steps from that tree and missed it altogether."

Israel drew himself up. "I'll have you know, woman, that was the very first time I ever fired a gun. I didn't know what all was going to happen. It took me the next two shots to figure out how to line up that front sight with the back one." He jutted his chin proudly. "And then I hit the tree both times."

Lucy felt cool tears of laughter rolling down her cheeks. "Well, given the tree was two feet wide, and you was almost huggin' it...," she gasped for breath, "and you was careful to never tell me which of them knots you was shootin' for, though you didn't hit neither one of them."

Israel joined her laughter. "You got a point. Wasn't much better with that po' deer."

"Oh, Israel you ain't foolin' no one. The fawn was twenty feet away, and the mama was twice that. You just picked what you could hit. And now we only got four bullets left."

Israel sighed. "All true." He laughed again, shook his head, and turned, giving a gentle jerk to the lead rope.

"ISRAEL, I DONE ASKED TWICE. AIN'T WE GONNA STOP AND eat? What's the name of this creek?"

Ignoring what he knew would be the reproachful stare of Lucy and the mule, Israel dropped the lead rope and fumbled in his pocket for the worn, folded map the Army captain had drawn. He looked up and down the creek, scanning the low, rolling hills covered with mountain mahogany, twisted scrub oak and bitterbrush that framed the narrow valley.

"Don't rightly know. The captain didn't put no name on the map. I'm sure we're on the right one. First, decent size creek split to the south we came to. If this map's right, it'll bring us to the Colorado River a couple of days from now."

"Well, husband, after you almost drowned yourself, me and poor Sally in that water we crossed this morning, and what that captain said about that Colorado, you best be thinking long and hard how we're going to get across that river." She squinted her eyes in that concerned way she had.

"We'll find us a place," he said, hoping his voice sounded confident. He'd been wondering the same thing. "Might have to go along for a spell, though."

They rounded a bend in the creek where it careened around the toe of a steep-sided, brush-covered hill and stopped short. *Bodies! Dead horses.* He exchanged a quick glance with Lucy. His hand went to the pistol in his belt, jerking on it twice, the cylinder catching against the belt on the first tug and the raised front sight catching the edge of the leather on the second. *Gotta get smoother with that.*

His eyes fixed on the scene in front of them. His face just partially turned toward her, he whispered, "Keep your eyes peeled, Lucy, and sing out if you see anything moving."

"Be careful, Israel," her voice quavered.

Moving slowly just a few steps at a time before pausing, his eyes roving the landscape of the little valley, they reached the first body, an Indian, his head appearing to be mostly severed from his neck. *A sword?* A brown and white spotted horse lay near his corpse, its brisket red with blood oozing from a bullet hole, flies covering the wound, muzzle and eyes.

Several shadows floated across the ground. Israel looked up. Three turkey vultures, black wings spread wide, trailing aileron feathers translucent in the sunlight, were circling above the grisly scene.

Without turning, he said in a low voice, "Looks like they is all Indians."

He took another step, stopping suddenly at the anxious sound of Lucy's voice behind him, "Israel, what's that on the other side of the creek under them rocks?"

His eyes traveled the direction of her outstretched arm. In the shadow of an overhanging ledge surrounded by bitterbrush, sage and several scraggly scrub oaks protruded some type of unnatural shape. *Man's boot?* Leading the mule toward the rocks, Israel dropped the lead rope at the edge of the creek. "Wait here," he said.

Trying to keep the pistol pointed at the gap between the rock ledge and the ground underneath, he slipped and splashed his way across the creek. Raising one leg high, he struggled up the eroded edge of the opposite bank. "Who's in there?"

*No answer.*

His hand, and the pistol in it, shook. Taking two steps, he called out again, "I know you be in there. Answer up. I got me a gun."

The gurgle of the creek and the buzz of insects were the only response. Across the meadow, a slight breeze had sprung up, carrying with it the scratch of scrub oak and the stench of death.

Dropping to both knees a few feet from the shadowed ledge, he leaned forward, one hand on the rocky soil supporting his upper body, and the other outstretched with the pistol. He eased his head under the rock, letting his eyes adjust from the bright sunlight to the darkness. "Lucy!" he shouted, his voice echoing in the tiny cavern, "it's that Black Feather man."

Israel crawled a few feet farther, wincing each time his knee made contact with the hard rock floor of the shallow cave. With his eyes fixated on the thin scar that ran up one side of the man's face, he reached out the tips of his trembling fingers and placed them on the man's neck. *A pulse!*

"Lucy, he's hurt real bad but still alive."

Israel scanned the shadowed, dark features, then pulled

back out into the open. "This bank on this side's too steep for you and the mule. If you can, lean over and grab that guide rope. Go on down the creek. Find a place where the bank's easier and then come on back here. This man needs your doctoring. I'll look around, see what I can find for some poultice."

Israel leaned under the ledge again and held his hand out to Black Feather's mouth, the skin of his palm sensing the faint movement of air from the wounded man's shallow breathing. He peered closely at the shoulder wound, and then at the thigh. *Ain't clean holes. Must've been arrows.* His eyes roved the interior of the space noticing the pemmican and bladder bag tucked in the rock near his left side coming to rest on two arrows, thin shafts a dull red, their fletching torn and matted with congealed blood.

He heard Lucy wheezing behind him. "I found us a spot. My Lord, Israel, he don't look good."

"Somebody started to doctor him, looks like." He pointed at the arrows, food and water. "But looks like they left off. Lucy, I'll grab hold of his head and shoulders, so they don't thump on this rock and don't drag. If you can grab hold of his boots up by the ankles, between the two of us, we can move him out of here a little bit at a time and get him in the light, so you can see better."

---

LUCY SCRAPED THE SMALL PEBBLES AND ROCKS FROM beneath her knees and then leaned over Black Feather's now sunlit, prostrate form. "Israel, take his knife out of that sheath and cut away that shirt up there round his shoulder and then his pants all the way down the thigh. Can't see nuthin' with that bloody cloth in the way. Then, go fetch me some sage and see if you can find some plantain growing along the creek."

"I'll get you one of my shirts, too. You can use it for bandages."

Lucy looked up and over her shoulder at Israel kneeling behind her. "What are you thinking? You only got three shirts, and one of them is mostly tattered."

Israel stared back at her; his eyes intent but firm. "And he gave me a gun."

Lucy shook her head, "And while you're at it, get my sewing stuff. Bring it all. I gotta find that heaviest thread." She studied the pale, waxy sheen of Black Feather's bronze skin, "But I got a feeling it ain't going to matter. He's lost lots of blood, and that one below his shoulder must have nicked the top of a lung."

Israel began to rise, and she reached behind her, tugging at his shirt, "Where's the chile, Israel? If that was Mr. Black Feather's horse we seen a bit ago, then somebody else be ridin' it, and the girl's with him."

"Been thinking the same, Lucy. But I'm pretty sure it ain't no Indian." Israel rose, gently pulling her hand from his shirt. "Ain't nothing we can do about that now. Let's tend to him. We'll ponder what happened after."

Bending over, Israel slipped Black Feather's knife from its sheath, cutting away the pants leg and then his shirt from his sternum to the back of his shoulder, peeling back the blood-soaked cloth. "Let me fetch that shirt, an' your needle and thread. Then I'll go look for the poultice fixin's you need. Unless you need my help when you doctor him, I'll take a look-see if there's anything useful on them Indians for us. Can't do them no good anymore."

"Israel, start me a little fire too, not too close, but where I can reach it and bring our pan. Fill it with some creek water for me and put it next to the fire. First thing, I'll boil one of them sleeves, then clean these wounds off so I can see what I'm doin'."

———————

THE PURPLE HUE OF FADING DAY COLORED THE EDGE OF the sky where it touched the rim of the hill to the west above the creek. Lucy slumped back, wiping one thick forearm across her forehead. A small fire, just a few short sticks burning at a time, crackled a few feet away from her, the odor of the burning wood a thankful mask to the smell of decomposing flesh carried by the shifting breeze. The ebb and flow of amber firelight reflected on Black Feather's skin on either side of the bandages Lucy had fashioned from Israel's shirt, bulges in the cloth marking poultices resting against his roughly sutured wounds.

"Israel, raise his head again. I gotta get some more water down him."

Lucy spread Black Feather's lips with her thumb and forefinger, carefully dripping water from the tin cup onto his teeth. His larynx moved as he swallowed. He coughed and moaned. She exchanged a quick look with Israel,

"First sound he's made. Lordy."

Lucy dribbled some more water between his lips, and he swallowed again, choking slightly. His eyelids fluttered open and then closed, his voice a coarse whisper, "Girl."

Her eyes shifted quickly to Israel then back to Black Feather. "She be okay."

The man's head nodded faintly in the cushion of Israel's hands.

ISRAEL JERKED AWAKE, HIS BACK LEANED AGAINST A ROCK, one hand around the pistol in his lap, Black Feather's pistol on the ground beside him. He rubbed his eyes with the back of his hands blinking at the shadows playing hide and seek between the scrub on the hillside and sunlight shimmering on the swift current of the creek.

Lucy was already awake and had coaxed the small fire back to life from the last embers of the night. She had Black Feather's head raised in one arm and was alternately dipping the tin cup filled with water to his lips and trying to get him to chew and swallow small strips of smoked venison from a cut of meat she had placed on a rock to her side.

"How is he?"

Lucy raised her eyes to Israel, then cast them quickly back toward the head cradled in her hand. She shook her head twice. Feigning a smile, she crooned softly, "Now, Mr. Black Feather, that's real good. You have to eat another little strip of this." The man chewed slowly, gagging slightly as he swallowed.

Israel rose and moved to her, dropping down and

whispering in her ear, "There's no way he can move. And ain't no way for us to move him."

Black Feather's eyes fluttered, and he breathed words in short, broken, staggered breaths. "Back in the rocks...gun...knife...water...food." His chest rose as he tried to take a deeper breath, exhaling, "Leave...me...be."

Lucy started to speak, "We can't..."

Israel reached out a hand, squeezed her shoulder and shook his head. Her voice died off.

Israel leaned close to Black Feather's ear. "You just nod your head if I get what you want right. You want to go back under the rock in the shade. We'll make it comfortable as we can. Leave you with your gun, your knife, some water and some food."

The pale, swarthy face in Lucy's arm nodded weakly.

---

ISRAEL LOOKED BACK WHEN THEY REACHED THE downstream edge of the meadow where the creek curled to the east.

Lucy's voice came from atop the mule, "I don't feel good at all about just leaving him, Israel."

Dropping the lead rope, Israel walked back and stood beside her, reaching out one hand, clasping hers and squeezing. "We did right by him, woman. You patched him as good as anybody could. It was his wish to be left. Made him as comfortable as we could. He has what was left before, some of that deer, that pemmican we took off one of them Indians and two of them bladder bags filled with water, though don't much think he'll last long enough to drink even part of it." Lucy's lower lip was shaking, and tears wove tracks down her cheeks.

He squeezed her hand again. "Now, we got ourselves a musket and a little bit of ball and powder, a tomahawk, and a knife off them dead warriors." He sighed. "That man we don't know again provided for us in some mysterious way."

Lucy choked back a sob, "What about that lil' girl, that po' lil' chile, Israel?"

Israel looked down scuffing at the meadow grass with the toe of his boot and then raised his eyes to hers. "We'll likely never know, Lucy. But hopefully the good Lord will watch after her..."

He turned and looked across the meadow, nodding with his chin, "And him too."

# CHAPTER

## *25*

August 14, 1855

# *A*WAKENING

ONE HUNDRED EIGHTY-THREE MILES NORTHEAST FROM where Reuben and Philippe struggled to unload the last of the ceiling rafter logs from the freight wagon, Dot watched Johannes throw a small stick on the fire and settle back against his saddle. The stallion stood nearest the fire, his black coat shining in the flickering light.

The indigo of night had chased the thin blue hue of crimson dusk from the sky over the Laramies. As she finished her meal of pemmican stuffed between two halves of stale sourdough biscuits, she watched the tall man with blonde hair and blue eyes like hers finish his meal across the fire.

She took one finger, then another, sticking them in her mouth, licking the last morsels of food from her callused skin before withdrawing them from her lips and wiping her hands on her pants.

"I want to thank you for telling me your name, Dorothy," the man said.

She looked up from her fingers, and half smiled at him,

bobbing her head slightly. *Nice voice. I like his accent.*

"So, how long were you and your friend riding together?"

*My friend? Kind to me. Killer of Ma and Pa.* She raised one eyebrow and lowered the other to let him know she was thinking about the question. *March, April, May, June, July, August.* She held up two hands, one with five fingers spread and outstretched and the other with just her forefinger raised.

"Six months?"

*He asked as if he knew that.* Dot nodded her head and smiled. She could see the surprise on his face at her smile, and she looked down quickly, her fingers tracing a rip in her pant leg above the knee.

His voice, with its strangely pleasant pronunciation, came from the other side of the fire again. "You know how to read or write?"

*He is going to think I am stupid.* She shook her head, still pretending to be engaged by the tear in the pants fabric.

"Has anybody ever told you, when you smile, you're a very pretty girl?"

Startled, her head snapped up. She hoped the strands of hair hanging down the sides of her face and reddish glow of the fire masked the heat she felt in her cheeks. She tightened her lips and looked down quickly again, as if studying her fingers.

"Did you have enough to eat? That was the last of our biscuits. It's a good thing we will be reaching the fort tomorrow."

She watched his gaze look out in the distance to the jagged outlines and silhouetted rock outcroppings of the

Laramies. He tilted his head as if looking to the north at the larger peak rising above all the others. *Such a square jaw.*

He smiled softly at her and lifted the hand resting on his bent knee. He pointed away from the mountains and the afterglow of the setting sun. "That tree line that we've been paralleling to the east is the Platte River. The Indians call it the flat water." He swung one arm in the firelight and pointed at the dark mass of the higher peak northwest of them.

"And that's the mountain white men call Laramie Peak. The tallest in this range, and only mountain in the whole Laramie Range over ten thousand feet, it's my understanding. Fort Laramie is east by northeast of that. It's kind of the marker for the fort. I've never seen it, but I understand it's built where the Laramie River runs into the Platte, out in the flats, but not too far from these mountains."

She stared at him, then looked east toward the dark and distant tree line, finally turning her gaze north to where Laramie Peak was etched against a starlit sky, its rocky, pointed pinnacle painted with the soft silver light of the crescent moon emerging from the far rim of the horizon.

His eyes moved to hers in the firelight. "I hear they have the best hospital for hundreds of miles at that fort, teachers, and I would imagine lots of people and chil— young men and women like yourself, who live at the fort or are passing through on wagon trains."

School? The thought brought a flicker of hope. She fixed her eyes on the strong lines of his cheekbones augmented by the low dance of the flames, trying to will a word to spring from her lips. "Learn," she heard her voice say.

His eyebrows lifted, but his gaze dropped down to his hand. He pretended to be picking dirt from beneath a nail. "Yes. That's right. Reading, writing, arithmetic, history. I think you'll like school and I bet you do very well at it."

She could feel herself beaming and raised her arm, pointing just beyond the firelight to the black stallion, his coat silver in the moonlight.

"The saddlebags?"

She nodded.

"So, the gold and silver in the boxes, you're going to use to go to school?"

She stared at him, waiting for a reaction. *Approval, disapproval—something.*

He grinned. "I hope you get the best education there is." She smiled in response. Their eyes met and held until she felt overcome by her shyness and looked down.

He craned his face skyward. "Roll yourself up in that blanket. Don't get too close to the fire, in case one of the sticks pops, and there's a spark. Tomorrow, we'll ride into Fort Laramie, get you checked out by the doctor and see how we can settle you down with school and such."

Delighted, Dot clapped her hands. But the sound triggered the memory of gunfire, and a jolt of fear grabbed her. She felt a clutch in her chest at the sudden image of a boot poking out from beneath the shaded ledge. "Black Feather?" The sound of her voice surprised her.

The tall man's eyebrows shot up, and he again busied himself with his forefinger.

*He's thinking.*

He looked up, trying to smile convincingly. "When he gets better, I'm sure he'll be along."

Dot felt some of the tension leave her jaw. *What about you?* She raised a hand, pointing her finger at him across the fire.

He stared at her, raised his hand and tapped his chest with his fingers. "You mean me? Where am I going to be?"

She nodded slowly, her eyes holding his. *Cheek feels warm again. Must be the fire.*

"I'll be at the fort. I plan to join the Army." He sighed, raising his eyes to the stars. "I used to be in the Army a long time ago in that place I told you I was from—Denmark."

She kept her eyes fixed on him, and he cleared his throat, suddenly intent on ensuring his Sharps was in close reach. "Now, roll yourself up in that blanket and get some sleep. We have a big day tomorrow. Lots of exciting things will be happening."

She sank down on the blanket she had already laid out, pulled it over one shoulder and then rolled away from him, unaware that he was watching her thin form and the curve of her hip where the wool was pulled tightly around it.

———

BENEATH THE TREE LINE IN THE DISTANCE, DENSE GROUND mist clung to the serpentine meander of the Platte. Visible above the cottonwoods was a rim of a bright pink horizon, transitioning in bands of red, gray and purples into pale blue. The first yellow edge of the sun erupted over the horizon in golden flame, piercing the palleted edge of daybreak. The ground mist ebbed and flowed as if trying to hide from the sun, shifting sideways, rising then falling, luminescent, changing from a silver-gray to light-gray, and then to silver-white as the sun rose.

Several miles to the north, the shrouded river bottom merged with low, rolling hills dotted with clusters of pine and juniper and punctuated with sharp ridges ending abruptly in chalky, beige cliffs and rock formations, their highest points glowing with the first kiss of sunlight.

Dot sat up, facing the breaking day, and lifted the blanket over her shoulders against the cool dew of dawn. The twinges of dull cramps that seemed to come monthly since the spring sporadically pulsed in her belly. She stretched, feeling the awakening of the day, its promise and something more. Drawing her legs to her chest, she wrapped her arms around her shins and rested her chin on her knees, slowly rocking herself back and forth with her toes. She glanced across the remnant gray ashes of the previous evening's fire to see if the tall man who called himself Johannes was stirring.

Sensing her stare, the man lifted his head from his saddle pillow, contemplating her with a sideways glance. She lowered her head, resting the side of her face on her knees, returning his gaze.

He cleared his throat and rose. "We best make some coffee, break camp and saddle up. Today's the big day!" He threw a grin at her and then leaned down to lift his saddle from the ground.

# CHAPTER
## *26*

August 14, 1855

# *F*ORT LARAMIE

JOHANNES REINED IN BENTE AS HE CRESTED THE LONG, low, low ridge, and Dot rode up beside him. He leaned over toward her, reached out one long arm and pointed northeast.

"See those buildings way out there down in the hook of the river and the white tops of those wagons?"

She raised in her stirrups, one hand to her forehead, then sank back to her saddle with an animated expression.

Relieved, Johannes grinned at her, "Let's go present ourselves to civilization!"

An hour later, the scattered buildings of Fort Laramie loomed ahead of them, a quarter of a mile distant, nestled in an oxbow of the Platte. *No stockade or wall!* The nearest building, a small, single-story wood and adobe structure set higher on a slight rise, was the Post Hospital he assumed. Beyond that rose a long, narrow rectangular, two-story building. *Likely the enlisted men's barracks.*

Stretching south from the barracks to the north was a low-slung building that seemed to be bustling with activity. Across a gap of golden grass to its south rose a large two-story white frame structure. *One is probably the Sutler and Post Store, the other one the headquarters.* Further south were three other one-story buildings, *likely officers' quarters.* Additional buildings were situated to the east toward the river on the opposite side of an open parade ground of sorts. Much smaller log, frame and adobe structures were scattered with no particular pattern east and north. A large American flag, its red, white and blue bright against the green of the river tree line and the beige tones of the buildings, fluttered from a high flagpole to the south side of the central parade ground. Johannes estimated the entire complex to be approximately five to six hundred feet wide and seven or eight hundred feet long, the outpost arranged and built in an imperfect rectangle.

Between them and the fort, and stretching out to the north, were a significant number of small clusters of tipis, six to more than twenty in each grouping. Some of the forms looked familiar. *Like the tipis back in Cherry Creek. Those must be Arapaho.* The fort was busy with blue uniforms, both infantry and mounted. Two groups of wagons, one on the other side of the Platte, stretched for approximately one-eighth of a mile in a long line. The other already across the river was forming up to move out, its lead wagons pointed northwest. People and soldiers on foot and horseback in groups of two or three moved to and from the wagon trains or the other buildings of the fort, most of the traffic centered around the low building on the northwest corner of the sprawling compound.

As Johannes and Dot rode abreast of the wagons in final preparation to continue west, men and women smiled and waved at them. Johannes twisted back in his saddle toward the girl. "I think that little wood and adobe building—the first one on top of that rise—is likely the Post Hospital. Let's start there. I bet it's been a long time since you saw a doctor."

Dot shot him an anxious glance.

INSIDE THE BUILDING, LIGHT-COLORED STUCCO WALLS provided a cheerful backdrop to the bustle of several staff, one nurse in white linen smocks tied behind her waist and two men, one uniformed, one in a white smock. The men moved with an assertive lift to their steps.

A plump, gray-haired woman with spectacles manned a small, heavy oak desk just feet from inside the entrance. Johannes watched the woman assess them as they took several steps toward the desk, her eyes flicking back and forth several times between he and Dot until they reached her.

The woman peered at Johannes, her voice friendly, but crisp and authoritative. "May I have your name, please?"

"I am Johannes Svensen, and this young woman goes by the name of Dorothy." Dot looked up at him and smiled.

"I take it you are her older brother, then?" The woman's eyes moved between them again, lingering on their similar physical characteristics: blue eyes, blonde hair and thin stature.

Johannes chuckled. "No. We are not brother and sister...." The woman's eyebrows raised, and she started to speak.

"No, we're not married." Johannes answered the question before she formed it. "I'm bringing Dorothy here to the fort because a friend of hers asked me to. She doesn't seem to have any family. It's been some time since she has seen a doctor, and I thought it might be wise for one of the doctors or nurses to examine her. She's been on the trail for many months, though she came under my charge just ten days ago."

The woman pursed her lips and pushed her spectacles back on the bridge of her nose. Her focus shifted to the girl. "Well, Dorothy, what is your last name?" Dot looked down at the floor, her mouth curled unhappily.

The woman's eyes rose quickly to Johannes, then back to Dot. "Do you know where your parents are, Dorothy? Do you have any brothers or sisters?"

Johannes couldn't see Dot's face, just blonde hair hanging forward over her cheeks from her bowed head, but he noticed the wet splatter of a tear just beyond the toe of one of her boots. "She doesn't talk much. I don't think her parents are still living. I have to talk to Captain Henderson about several things...." At the mention of the Captain's name, one eyebrow rose above the top rim of the woman's spectacles, "And I have some other news concerning Dorothy that I'll share with him," he added.

The matronly woman started to speak, her tone not cold, but definitely imperious. *She's obviously used to running the show.* Resting one hand on Dorothy's shoulder, Johannes cut the woman off politely. Dorothy seemed to relax under his touch.

"If you would be so kind as to have a nurse or doctor tend to her," he asked, "I will speak to Captain Henderson. Perhaps I will then have additional information for you."

The woman's mouth opened, closed, opened again, then shut, her lips pressed firmly together, her ample cheeks twitching, her eyes narrowed. "Very well, Mr. Svensen. I look forward to your return, so I can complete this paperwork."

Ignoring the two of them, she half rose from her chair, twisting her body to shout down the single corridor. "Nurse Margaret, we have a young lady here for you to look at when you have a moment." The head of the young nurse poked from one of two doors along the short hall, long dark hair falling from a thin, pretty face underneath a white linen hospital duty cap. Her eyes caught Johannes's and then fixed on Dorothy. "I will be there when I'm done stitching up Sam's arm. It will be just a few minutes."

"Where...?" began Johannes.

Without looking up, the matron finished and curtly answered his question for him. "Headquarters is the white, frame two-story building past the enlisted men's barracks. The first you come to, past the Sutler's store, opposite the flag on the parade ground. It's called Old Bedlam." She continued to scribble furiously on her papers, raising her eyes to Dot without moving her head, but studiously ignoring Johannes.

"Dot, I'll be back for you shortly. You'll be fine," he reassured her.

Back in the sunlight, Johannes stopped, looking down the rutted, gravelly road toward the headquarters. He peeled the campaign hat from his head, slapping it against his leg until dust no longer exploded from the crown. He bent, slapping and brushing his pants and sleeves with his hands, opened his trousers and tucked in his gray cotton shirt. He straightened, took a deep breath, and exhaled slowly. *The worst he can say is no.* He chuckled to himself. *Or, private, go clean the latrines.*

## *27*

August 14, 1855

# *O*NE, BOTH, OR NONE

ACROSS THE SMALL LODGE FIRE FROM COUGAR WOMAN, Black Mare knelt on a mule deer hide. Curls of sage, sweetgrass and cedar smoke rose in dark tendrils from four smudge pots placed equidistant from the fire ring. Pine sticks smoldered in the fire, the smell of pine mingling with the fragrance from the smudge pots. Gray wisps disappeared through the lodge's smoke hole like dancing spirits.

Cougar Woman, the elder, knelt on the hide of a mountain lion, her heavyset frame draped in a loose-fitting leather dress, one shoulder fashioned of heavy-grained but finely-tanned buffalo hide, the other of smooth deer hide. Black Mare admired her wide belt, the delicate beadwork of red, white and gray, the four animal tails hanging from it, two striped raccoon tails and two black-tipped coyote tails. An elaborate, zig-zag bead pattern adorned the bodice of her dress, the fringed leather sleeves of the garment hanging just below her elbows. Twin loops of heavy necklace, nuggets of turquoise spacing long and curved silver bear claws, fell from her neck to just above the sagging swell of her bosom.

Black Mare watched the older woman, the wizened leather of her face, her closed eyes. Cougar Woman's lips moved in a song the sound of which was hidden from Black Mare, her full, sun-wrinkled cheeks framed by silver pigtails streaked with stubborn tinges of black.

The older woman opened her eyes and stared at Black Mare before asking, "This is now your second monthly moon that has not come?"

Black Mare let her gaze fall to her knees where the tuck of leather hemmed her dress. "Yes."

"How do you feel, Black Mare?"

"I feel different, somehow."

"Stand for me, Black Mare."

Black Mare stood, her arms hanging loosely to her side, her heart beating rapidly. She watched the difficulty with which Cougar Woman rose, how she supported her movement first with her hands on the grass floor of the tipi before raising her upper torso, both hands pressing against her knees. The older woman walked slowly around the lodge fire, her short, heavy legs spread to support her body, which rolled sideways with each step.

Black Mare felt her hands first touch the back of her head, then trace down her neck to her shoulders. Her hands lingered there, thumbs pressed against the top of Black Mare's spine, her thick, strong fingers crooked with age, draped over Black Mare's shoulders, her fingertips pressed firmly into the depression under her collar bone. Cougar Woman's hands continued their travels down the side of

Black Mare's ribs and then forward to her stomach, thumbs touching at the belly button, fingers pointed down, meaty palms pressed against Black Mare's abdomen. From anyone else, the touch would have been intrusive, unwelcome.

"Face me," she told Black Mare.

Black Mare turned, looking down at the elderly medicine woman.

"Show me your tongue."

Black Mare stuck out her tongue and the old woman smoothed along its edge lightly with her thumb and forefinger, then raised both hands, gently spreading Black Mare's eyelids, peering up at them, the irises of her brown eyes circled with blue rings of age. She stepped back and nodded. "Yes, Black Mare. What you have been feeling is true."

*I never said what I was feeling.*

"You are with child."

Black Mare could not keep her elation to herself. She smiled down at Cougar Woman. "Then, Spirit has finally blessed us."

The old woman did not return Black Mare's smile. She gestured impassively to Black Mare to kneel again by the lodge fire. She turned, waddling to the other side of the waning glow of pine embers, lowering her knees carefully with a soft groan to the cougar pelt.

When she was settled, she picked up a stick of sage, its long light-green and gray-blue leaves bright in the dim light of the tipi. Black Mare watched her backhand the sage over the fire, and then at each smudge pot, brushing the air, sage and cedar scent toward Black Mare. The older woman reached to her other side and picked up a thin aspen branch the length of one of Ouray's arrows. She held it over the lodge fire and bowed it, its arch pointed at Black Mare. The thin strip of wood bent and cracked but did not break. Her eyes raised under heavy lids, she returned the stick to her side. Black Mare felt uneasy under her glare, her jubilation replaced by anxious trepidation.

Black Mare stared back at Cougar Woman, the sounds of the village outside the tipi, the shouts of children, guttural talk of the braves and singsong chatter of the other women fading away until there was just the two of them, a palpable energy springing on an invisible thread of silence from one to the other, and back again across the coals, the smoke from the smudge pots seeming to pulse rather than curl.

Black Mare watched as Cougar Woman closed her eyes and swayed back and forth, then side to side, her motion surprisingly supple, as the movement of her namesake might have been. Her eyes snapped open, and Black Mare felt the strange connection break.

Cougar Woman spoke slowly, her voice as deep as a man's and scratchy with years. "Yes, you have been blessed, Black Mare. You and I have talked in the past as you have with several of the other older women of the tribe. We believed it was unlikely that you would have a child but..."

Black Mare felt penetrated by the older woman's gaze.

"I forewarned you that should you be blessed, the blessing may be short-lived." Her eyes didn't waver, nor did she blink. "You may lose the child." She leaned over and picked up two short pieces of pine no bigger than a point of a lance and laid them carefully on the tiny fire. Immediately, their flame shot higher, then quickly died, burning blue at its base, tinged with a thin flickering, yellow-gold.

Her eyes, steady and searching, returned to Black Mare. "If you do not lose the child, the child may lose its mother...or Ouray may lose his wife and his child. But of this, I am certain, Black Mare, one, or both of you will not survive. There is something inside of you that is not turned quite right. Your child may not be able to emerge into daylight, or if he does, the damage to you will be great."

Black Mare blinked, the foreboding premonition bringing more questions than answers. "Did you say he?"

The old, leathery face across the fire nodded. "I believe you carry Ouray's son."

Cougar Woman's leathery cheeks softened, and her lips pressed together. "You may do as you wish, Black Mare, but to inform Ouray too soon that you are with child may not be wise. There will be ample time for that. A moon or two at least should pass so he will not be disappointed if your son decides to leave you early. You must be very careful. Have Chipeta lift anything heavy for you. Ride only the gentlest of Ouray's horses. Eat what your son tells you he needs, but do not overeat. Additional weight will not be helpful to either you or him."

She fell silent. Black Mare felt the tremble in her fingers. Her mind was a jumble of thoughts. *One or both of us will not survive? Ouray may be left with no one. But Chipeta? A son? Our most fervent wish, but with a price.*

Cougar Woman tilted her head back slowly, her eyes rising until she appeared to be gazing at the blue of the sky through the smoke hole, the creased folds of her neck skin stretched tight by the upper lift of her chin. She dropped her eyes back to Black Mare.

"If the time comes, Black Mare, I will be with you. I will not hide the truth from you now or then. I will summon all the *puah* that I can. You will not be able to go out into the grasses in the shade of the trees as do the other women to give birth. It must be in your lodge, protected, poultices, dressings and boiling water prepared and ready. Even then, it will likely not be enough."

She leaned over, throwing another short pine stick on the fire and contemplated the flame. She stared, unblinking, at Black Mare. "If you lift heavy objects, if you carry the water skins full, or move large rocks when you pitch your lodge or ride the more spirited of Ouray's mustangs, then it is likely your son will never be born...."

Her eyes softened.

"But you shall live."

August 14, 1855

# *G*OLDEN LATITUDE

TWO UNIFORMED SOLDIERS, DARK-BLUE TUNICS WITH corporal stripes on their shoulders over blue-gray trousers, stood at parade rest on either side of the closed, double wooden doors of Old Bedlam. The butts of their rifles rested on the ground, the muzzles of each with a fixed fourteen-inch bayonet, canted at stiff angles from their bodies. They watched him approach, just their eyes moving. As he neared the door, both of them in unison took one step sideways toward each other, blocking the entrance.

"Your name and business," asked the taller of the two in a firm but flat tone. Johannes drew himself up and saluted smartly, enjoying the look of surprise on both their faces. "Would you tell Captain Henderson that Captain Johannes Svenson of His Majesty's Heavy of the King of Denmark is here to pay his respects."

The two soldiers turned slightly toward each other, caught themselves and hurriedly looked forward again, just their eyes roving Johannes's trail-worn clothing and the curls of hair spilling from beneath the battered campaign hat.

Neither their curiosity or disbelief surprised him.

The taller corporal clicked his heels together and turned smartly. "Follow me." He opened one door for Johannes, followed him inside, then took the lead. He stopped when they reached a hallway off the central room in which several more sentries stood at attention, their rifles held at port, without bayonets.

His escort raised his arm, all four fingers pressed rigidly together. He gestured down a hallway. "This way... Captain." He reached the last door on the left. Standing stiffly, the corporal knocked loudly three times. "Captain Henderson. There is a Captain John..." he paused.

Johannes smiled at him. "Johannes Svensen."

The corporal's chin dipped once. "John Svensen. Claims he's a captain in some cavalry somewhere and wishes to speak with you."

Behind the door, Johannes heard a chair scrape, then the quick, heavy click of military boot heels on a wooden floor. The door swung open, Captain Henderson smiling at him. He drew himself up in a formal salute, which Johannes returned. The corporal's eyes moved from one to the other, his incredulity transparent.

"That will be all, corporal. Thank you. Come in, Captain Svensen."

Captain Henderson waved his arm toward his desk, which was angled between two glass windows on either wall of the small corner room. One window framed the parade ground and the flag, the other Laramie Peak and the lesser mountains of the Laramie range miles to the southwest. Maps and two ceremonial swords crowded the walls. An

American flag, its pole almost touching the ceiling, stood in the corner between the windows behind the desk.

Captain Henderson extended his hand. His handshake was firm and warm. "I've thought about you a time or two, Captain Svensen. My men still talk about you riding up and the perfect execution of that salute. Even Sergeant O'Malley was impressed." Captain Henderson chuckled, "And very little impresses that Irishman, except a pretty woman, a fight and a bottle of whiskey."

Johannes smiled. "It would seem that first sergeants are the same in any army."

Captain Henderson grinned. "Indeed." He gestured at the chair in front of his small, but cumbrous oak desk. Its surface shone with a polished luster, dark grains accenting a deep golden tone. Seated, Captain Henderson leaned forward, his elbows on the desk surface, his eyes intent. "If I remember correctly, you and your friends in that wagon train were headed to Cherry Creek and then southwest down to the Uncompahgre. That seems to be an increasingly popular destination."

"Why is that?" asked Johannes, curious.

"After we ran into you, we happened to cross paths with an older negro couple with a mule along a small tributary of the main stem of the Laramie. I'm quite sure they are runaway slaves. They were headed to the Uncompahgre, also. In fact, I drew them a map," said the Captain, his expression implacable, his body still leaning forward, his blue uniform taut against his shoulders.

*The Captain is probing.* Johannes measured his answer. "Any man or woman who seeks freedom is a noble and wise soul. I take it you did not arrest them?"

Captain Henderson's upper body relaxed, and he leaned back slightly. "They had their papers in order," he chuckled, "an old crinkled copy of the Constitution cut out of the New York Times. It was wrapped in some cloth. Almost fell apart in my fingers." His eyes remained fixed on Johannes's face. *Gauging my reaction.*

"We are all Americans. I think I would've done the same thing myself, captain."

Captain Henderson's face broke into a broad smile, and he leaned back in his chair. Still watching Johannes, he said softly. "There are many who would disagree with that statement, Captain Svensen."

"Then, they are wrong," Johannes said firmly.

Captain Henderson's eyes blinked in unison with the slight nod of his chin. "So, what brings you to Fort Laramie and to my office? Your timing is excellent. I leave for patrol with a heavy squad day after tomorrow. Captain Flemming and thirty troops are escorting that wagon train forming up this side of the river to Salt Lake. Likely that neither of us will be back for a month." He slid open the single drawer of his desk, reached in and took out a cigar. Holding it up, he asked, "Care for one?"

"No, thank you. I'm here for two reasons. The first is that on the way here from the Uncompahgre I happened across an attack, I believe by Northern Utes, on a man and a young girl. The man was Black Feather."

Captain Henderson's hand paused, the cigar halfway to his mouth. He leaned forward. "Black Feather? The renegade outlaw?"

"Yes. I pulled two arrows out of him. I would be surprised if he is not already dead. He had a young girl with him, blonde hair, blue eyes, thin, fourteen or fifteen years old. He asked me, as best he could, to take her with me."

Captain Henderson's eyes grew wide. He lowered the cigar.

"I escorted her to the Fort. She's at the Post Hospital now. I thought it wise for a nurse or doctor to take a look at her."

Johannes pulled the poster from his shirt pocket, slowly unfolding it. He slipped it across the desk to Captain Henderson. "I am almost certain that she is Dorothy Eberlyn, the girl in this poster, though I didn't realize it until several days ago."

Captain Henderson grabbed the paper, glancing at it only briefly before asking, "Are you sure?"

"I'm not sure, but I am as certain as I can be. Is there any way to get word from the post to the family who is mentioned in there?"

Captain Henderson set the paper down, his eyes suddenly dark and somber. "Her kinsfolk were on a wagon train that came through here about three months ago. Late May, I believe. They had intended to stay at the fort and get an escort south, so they could follow the tracks that Dorothy and her parents must've taken down to the ranch they were starting on the Saint Vrain River north of Cherry Creek."

He picked the cigar back up and fixed his gaze on it. "The Eberylns had three wagons loaded with furniture and all their possessions. So excited and grateful." He gazed out the window for a moment. "Shortly after arriving late June this year, their kinsfolk died of cholera. Must've contracted it along the trail. Matter of fact, a full third of that wagon train died of cholera. Worst outbreak we've had since '52." There was a grim line in the press of his lips. "We burned the wagons about three miles south of here with the bodies and possessions in them."

Momentarily stunned, Johannes could only look at the captain. His long silence was not broken until he asked, "Well, she has no relatives, then?" He thought it better not to mention the gray boxes.

Captain Henderson shook his head. "None that we know of. Her entire immediate family and their hired hands were slaughtered down there in the Poudre by Black Feather. God only knows what he's done to the girl."

Johannes returned his look. "For some strange reason, I don't think he did anything with the girl other than protect her."

He told Captain Henderson the story of Black Feather saving the girl's life during the Indian attack, using his body to shield hers. By the end of the story, the cavalry man's jaw was slack. "Well, I'll be damned."

Johannes chuckled. "I say that myself, often."

Captain Henderson settled all the way back in his chair, rubbing his chin. "There's a decent school here at the Fort. The Army does not allow enlisted men to wed. A number, though not many, of the officers, sergeants and corporals are married with children. Several families don't have a bundle of children. In fact, one or two lost a young daughter for one reason or another over the last several years. I would be surprised if we can't find her a fine home with solid foster parents. Certainly better than shipping her back east to an orphanage or giving her to a Mormon family on one of those trains headed to Salt Lake. Nice enough people, but strange customs."

A memory from Fort Kearny flashed across Johannes's mind. *Twenty-two wagons. Three families.* "That would be a fine idea if it could be arranged, Captain. I assume there's a bank of some sort at the fort?"

Captain Henderson smiled. "Hardly a bank, but the Sutler's Post is a solid building. He has a safe, and we reinforced one interior room of the place with iron. Folks store their valuables, and it's administered by the Sutler, who is completely trustworthy."

Johannes nodded. "Well, I'd like to make a deposit on her behalf. She can use it for clothes and anything else she may need, and later, perhaps for some more advanced education."

Captain Henderson's eyebrows rose again. "That's right kind of you."

Johannes smiled. "It's not really mine, but I was entrusted with it and told to use it for a good cause. I think Dorothy's future is a good cause."

Captain Henderson bit off the end of his cigar and lit it. He took a long draw and blew smoke at the ceiling. "Now, what was the second matter?"

Johannes stared directly into his eyes. "I have always been a soldier. I enjoy a fight for what is right. I am drawn to the comradeship of fellow men in arms. The sounds and smells of battle are in my blood. It was our meeting back there at the wagon train that really began to bring it into focus. That focus has become sharper over the last months."

Johannes straightened his shoulders. "I would like to enlist in the United States Cavalry. And if you happen to need a decorated officer with a fair degree of experience in command and battle, so much the better."

Captain Henderson's shoulders sprung forward from the chair back. He slapped the desk and grinned at Johannes. "That was exactly the second matter for which I was hoping. In fact, with the rising enmities between north and south, and our discussion here convincing me of which side you would choose should hostilities break out, and I fear they will, we're shorthanded. As you are aware, it is three to four months to get official word back and forth from the east. Officers are few and far between, and those of us with the rank of captain and above out here on the frontier have certain latitude. I think we can muster you into the regiment tomorrow...."

He chuckled, his eyes roving the length of Johannes. "Assuming we can find a pair of trousers long enough to fit you." He took another puff of the cigar, exhaled smoke with a pleased air and opened his desk drawer again, rummaging in it. When his hand reappeared, it had twin, gold embroidered shoulder patches.

*Lieutenants' bars!*

He pushed them across the desk to Johannes.

"Pay is thirty-six dollars a month, First Lieutenant Svensen. As an officer, you must provide your own horses— no more than two—repay the army for your uniform, and supply your own weapons above standard issue. The next three buildings east are married officers' quarters. Upstairs here at the Bedlam House are quarters for the single NCOs and officers. I think there's several empty rooms up there. Those bars," he sighed, "belonged to a Lieutenant Grattan."

The flicker of surprise and recognition that Johannes felt flash across his eyes did not go unnoticed.

"Yes, the same, brash lieutenant, actually Brevet Lieutenant Grattan, who was killed along with twenty-nine men in an unfortunate and avoidable incident with the Brule Sioux last year...."

He paused, his eyes boring into Johannes's. "There will be a month of training, primarily relating to the duties, regulations and code of an officer in the United States Army and this regiment. You will also be familiarized with the 1851 Treaty with the Apache, Sioux and Cheyenne signed right here at the Fort. I am going to waive your field training. It would surprise me, Lieutenant Svensen, particularly after your account of the Black Feather incident, if you are not already adept in the use of that Army Colt in your belt, that Sharps Carbine that was sticking out of your scabbard when we met and the saber, the end of which was visible from your bedroll behind your saddle."

Johannes was impressed. "I compliment you, Captain Henderson, on your memory and your attention to detail."

The captain twirled the cigar in his finger, studying its glowing tip. "It is the duty of an officer to pay attention to detail and to remember. Otherwise, men die. Do you know much about Fort Laramie or its history, lieutenant?"

Johannes shook his head. "Other than its location is strategic, and more than fifty thousand pioneers have streamed through here on their way west, I honestly know very little."

Captain Henderson tapped the cigar in the brass ashtray on the side of the desk, "Well then, since this post is your new home, I will begin your training. It is usually garrisoned by three companies of the United States Army, 2nd Dragoon Regiment. As the sergeant informed you back at the wagon train, the new terminology, rather than dragoons, is cavalry.

"It began in 1834 as a trading post founded by two fur traders, William Sublette and Robert Campbell. Wouldn't surprise me to see some parts around this country named for them eventually. The original fort was a few buildings surrounded by a wooden stockade with two firing parapets—known as Fort William. No army, just traders, trappers, the Arapaho and Cheyenne."

He took a long drag on the cigar, raised his face toward the ceiling and tried to blow smoke rings, which fractured, losing their shape shortly after leaving his lips. He chuckled wryly. "Been trying to learn to blow smoke rings for a decade. Might not be a skill this old warhorse is ever going to master. Sublette and Campbell sold Fort William to another trading outfit, Fontanelle, Fitzpatrick and Company. Then, in 1836, they sold to the American Fur Company. Most folks around here call them the Rocky Mountain Outfit. They had to fix up the post around 1841 because of some competition from a man named Lancaster Lupton."

He took another puff of the cigar, trying to blow a smoke ring with unsatisfactory results and shook his head. "The stockade was falling down, so they decided to rebuild the whole place. Put $10,000 into the effort. Had thick brick adobe walls that surrounded a central courtyard. That's the structure down the south end of the parade ground. They called it Fort John.

"The politicians back East decided with folks streaming West and gold in California, maybe they oughta appropriate funds for a series of forts manned by a special regiment to be mustered out West. Keep the trails open, have reliable points of supply and repair and provide security and at least some law. So, in 1849, the Army purchased Fort John for $4,000 and the first garrison, called the Regiment of Mounted Rifles, took it over. At that time, it was the only permanent trading post, way station and army garrison for the eight-hundred-mile span between Fort Kearny to the east, and Fort Bridger way to the southwest on the other side of the divide."

The captain leaned forward, his hands clasped in front of his jaw, his forefinger and second finger holding the cigar. "This is a mighty important spot, lieutenant. It's the crossroads of the West." He looked sharply at Johannes. "Actually, more than a hundred thousand souls have streamed through here heading West. We're the anchor for the Oregon Trail, the California Trail, the Mormon Trail, and several stage routes, although the stages are intermittent.

"Can't remember a day between May and mid-September of any year there's not at least one wagon train resupplying. In June, it can sometimes be four or five. There can be well over three hundred pilgrims roaming through the place. Only resupply store and United States Post Office for hundreds of miles in any direction. And, though small, it has the best Post Hospital, other than Fort Kearney, perhaps west of the Mississippi. There's plans to expand it in the coming years."

There was a note of pride in his voice. He pressed his lips together, thinking.

"There's getting to be more folks all the time. We are all they have, and they depend on us. The quartermaster is located in the largest building on the east side." He bent down over the desk, scribbling a note and signing his name. "Give him this. Take what you need. When I come back from patrol, lieutenant, the next patrol from Fort Laramie will be under your command. Sergeant O' Malley will have your enlistment papers ready in the morning."

"I gladly accept this field commission, Captain Henderson. Thank you for your confidence and the opportunity."

Captain Henderson snorted. "Confidence is earned over the long-term, lieutenant. And opportunities are only what you make of them." He rose, snapping a salute. Johannes did likewise.

His new commanding officer smiled slightly, "And, lieutenant?"

"Yes, sir?"

"Get a haircut."

Johannes stood at attention, clicked his heels, turning with brisk, trained precision and walked from Captain Henderson's office suppressing a smile.

September 5, 1855

# $\mathscr{S}$TAKING CLAIMS

THE WARM, DRY DAY HAD TRANSFORMED INTO AN evening tinged with the chill of coming autumn. Low, guttural brays of cows sifted through the cobalt night, its eastern sky aglow with the crescent moon, still unseen as it ascended the opposite flank of the Uncompahgre, backlighting the sharp, rugged peaks of the range with its lunar sheen.

Sarah and Philippe sat across the campfire from Reuben and Rebecca on makeshift log benches. Reuben felt his wife's thigh stiff where it pressed against his, and in that stiffness, he sensed her deep disapproval. The redhead and the vaquero shared the log but were separated by a foot or more. *Intentional*, Reuben supposed, *for show*. Periodically, one or the other spoke, their voices one level above a whisper. Invariably the recipient of the communication nodded and smiled, Sarah looking furtively around the fire, paying particular attention to Rebecca.

Reuben watched Michael standing just inside the ring of firelight, his head bent over a plate held just below his chin, his fork rapidly spooning food into his mouth. The utensil scraped dully on the tin, and when he looked up, the firelight accentuated the roundness of his cheeks. He smacked his lips, "M- Miss S-S-Sarah, M-Miss Rebecca that was w-w-was really g-g-good. Is ther-there enough f-f-for s-s-seconds?"

Reuben laughed. "I believe that will be thirds, Michael."

The young man's eyebrows raised above his pudgy cheeks, a perplexed look on his face. "I-I already h-had s-s-seconds?"

Rebecca chimed in. "You did, indeed, Michael. But that is just fine. You have as much as you want. There's plenty left and two or three squares of pan bread, too."

The boy rubbed the roundness of his belly, "I'll just h-h-have a little. G-G-Gotta g-g-get back out to the the c-cows, anyway."

Philippe, his body slightly tilted toward Sarah, who had leaned toward him, speaking, smiled at Michael. "Keep eating like that, muchacho, and you'll need to herd those cows on foot to work it off. No *caballero*."

Sarah giggled. Reuben could feel Rebecca bristle next to him and knew she was glaring at Philippe and Sarah. *Time to diffuse this powder keg.*

"Philippe..."

The vaquero's head snapped up.

"Those roof rafters aren't fully cured but should be dry enough. I think with the cut out of the windows and doors over the last several days and getting that ridgepole, and vertical support post in place between the gable ends today, we are ready to start the roof on the cabin."

Philippe nodded agreement.

Reuben waved his hand toward the dark mass of cabin structure, its ridgepole an opaque line against the sky like a bridge between the stars. "Your notches show a growing expertise. There's almost no daylight in the last two courses of logs in the corners."

The vaquero's teeth flashed a smile.

"If Michael will help us for a couple of hours each day when we need him..."

The boy stopped eating, his fork raised half the short distance from the plate to his mouth.

"I think we can get the shed walls up in three days, certainly not more than four. Far simpler than the cabin, and now we've had some practice."

"Sí, *señor* Reuben, I agree. But perhaps we should take a few days off from building and get some hay cut. *Las ultimas os noches* have required a jacket. And I'm sure you've seen the turning colors of the leaves, the *amarilla* y *roja* beginning to show. The tall grass is going to seed, losing moisture. If we do not cut it soon, it will lose much of its protein for the cows."

Michael gulped the forkful that had hung suspended and put his fork down on his half-full plate, listening.

Reuben remembered Zeb's words back in July. *"That ain't what I meant, Reuben.... The first couple weeks of September, them nice green meadows down there could be under four feet of snow; six, eight feet in drifts. I've seen it happen.... You can't take care of them cows if you can't take care of yourself.... Fact is, you're going to lose a bunch of them cows and calves over those three or four months. You ain't gonna be full ready.... Much as you might like not to, better losing a few critters than losing any of your outfit."*

Reuben sighed. Leaning forward between his knees, he picked up his plate, half rose and stretching his arm out and set the plate next to the circle of rocks around the glowing edges of the fire. His hand moved to Rebecca's knee. She laid her hand over his. The gesture both pleased and surprised him.

"Everything you say is true Philippe, but I think first we must ensure that we, the tools and our goods, have cover. Zeb told me the first snow can come anytime in September. There was a heavy frost two nights ago. Probably the same tonight. Once we get the roof on the cabin and the shed, we can wait a spell on the fireplace. Sarah and Rebecca can start gathering stones and sand for the mortar while we are cutting hay."

Philippe stared at him for a moment, then shrugged. Sarah said nothing. Reuben could feel the questions in everyone's eyes. Out in the darkness, several cows bawled. *Yes, cows. I'm sure you disagree, too.*

"Zeb is likely busy up there at his cabin getting set for winter, also. We should give him a few days' warning that we'll be ready for the roofs, so he can figure it into his plans. But one of us is going to have to go up there and let him know."

Rebecca squeezed his hand. "I'll go, Reuben," she said. "I know the trail."

Reuben turned. Their eyes met. *So in love with her.* He shook his head. "Thank you, Rebecca, I'm sure you could, but I don't want you riding alone, and I'm not sure it's a good idea the way you've been feeling."

The softness left her cheeks, and her eyes narrowed. "Reuben, I am perfectly—"

Philippe's voice cut her off, "I will go up and get *señor* Zeb."

Next to him, Sarah stiffened. She stared at the vaquero, who kept his gaze focused on Reuben.

Reuben quickly weighed the pros and cons of Philippe's surprise suggestion. "Okay, Philippe. In the morning, Rebecca or I will take you down to the river. We can point out where the trail begins. You'll have no problem from there. Michael and I will get the logs sorted for the shed, maybe even get the first course in place. It will give us a head start for when you get back. Then, we'll have to go like hell to be ready for Zeb when he comes down."

——————

ZEB CONTEMPLATED THE COLD ASHES FROM THE PREVIOUS evening's fire, the powdery remnants heaped in an uneven, gray-white pile below the grate in the fireplace. Shifting in his chair, he stared down at the wrinkled paper lying before him on the planks of the table, its edges yellow from months on the shelf above his bed.

He rubbed his face with both hands and ran his fingers through his hair, his eyes again falling to the paper, its white space swallowing the few words it had taken him several hours to write:

*DEAREST SARAH*
*MAYBE I MISS COMPREHENDED THAT*

*EVENING WE TOOK OUR WALK BACK THERE ON THEM HILLS NORTHEAST OF CHERRY CREEK. FELT SOMETHING IN THE WAY YOU HELD MY HAND, LEANED INTO ME, AND RETURNED MY KISS.*

The old chair creaked in protest as Zeb leaned back, stretching his long legs under the table, pen knife absent-mindedly whittling on the pencil tip, which needed no sharpening. He gazed out the front window, its shutters thrown open to welcome the midmorning air, the heavy planks of the door several feet farther down the wall also partially ajar. Not taking his back from the chair, he reached out a long arm, slipped two fingers through the handle of the tin coffee cup and raised it to his lips, his eyes fixed on the gold of turning aspen leaves that fringed fir boughs on either side of the trail leading back down to the valley.

He sipped the coffee, puckering his lips at the cold, bitter liquid and set the cup back down with disgust, several drops exploding from its edge, protesting its collision with the rough-sawn tabletop. He leaned forward, trying to focus on the letter, then picked it up in one hand, studying it. Shaking his head, he crumpled it. "Stupid. She ain't never gonna read it anyway," he grumbled to the knotty logs in the cabin wall. He tossed the wad of paper disgustedly toward the fireplace. It bounced and rolled across the hearth, not quite making it to the edge of feathery ash deeper in the aperture.

The corner of his eye caught a movement out the window. He glanced quickly at the Enfield, loaded and leaning on the inside of the front door frame, and the Colt, grip toward him, laying on the table. More movement, hidden by the gentle flutter of the aspen leaves, unclear in the lazy wave of fir and spruce needles. His hand closed around the pistol grip, and he rose, careful to lift the chair behind him, so it didn't scrape on the rough-plank floor.

Keeping his form from the window, he moved to the opening, one shoulder leaning against the logs that separated the door and window frames, one eye peering around the edge of the window frame. A wide round hat, the forelegs and then the rump of a black stallion appeared in blinks through the trees coming up the trail to the cabin.

*That damn Mexican—probably looking for trouble.*

He took a step toward the door, shoved the pistol in his belt and picked up the Enfield, cocking the hammer and checking the load. He stood several feet back from the door, moving slightly to keep the vaquero in sight through the crack between the door edge and the jamb. He waited as Philippe approached the cabin.

The Mexican reined in Diablo twenty-five feet from the front door and leaned forward, his forearms crossed and resting on the saddle horn. "*Señor* Zeb, it is Philippe."

Zeb didn't move, gauging the distance between Philippe's hands and the handles of the twin, black onyx Colts wedged in the vaquero's belt. *I can swing the rifle faster than he can reach them pistols.*

He stepped back another foot, swung the door wide and walked cautiously out on the cabin's narrow covered porch, the Enfield cradled at an angle in his left arm, the bunched, fringed leather of his shirt at the elbow concealing his hand firmly around the grip and forefinger stretched out across the trigger guard of the rifle. "Morning, Philippe."

Other than his eyes, the vaquero was motionless. He scanned Zeb quickly, his assessment lingering briefly at the pistol in his belt and pausing longer where Zeb's right hand disappeared in the leather-clad crook of the elbow supporting the forestock of the Enfield.

Philippe smiled, his teeth white against the shadowed brown of his skin under the sombrero brim. "*Buenos dias, señor* Zeb. The trail up here is quite spectacular. *Muy bonita.*" His chin moved once, pointing at the cabin. "*La casa* is well-built. Very impressive. My compliments."

The two men studied each other warily, neither of them moving. Zeb noticed the vaquero was careful not to move his forearms from where they rested on the saddle horn.

The Mexican spoke first. "I unfortunately have no time for kaffee...." His teeth flashed again under the light-gray felt brim.

Zeb kept his voice level and low. "Don't think any was offered."

Philippe chuckled, but the skin around his jaw tightened. "I come *para tres* reasons. *Primero,* I wished to see the trail and the cabin Reuben and Rebecca have spoken so much about. *Segundo,* to tell you that Reuben says we will need you for the cabin and shed roofs in perhaps *tres o cuatro dias.* The logs are cut, and we are beginning to raise them for the shed *este dia.* The ridge beam and support post are in place on the cabin. All the rafters were cut a month ago and have been curing in the sun."

"What's the third reason?"

"*La mujer pelirroja, señorita* Sarah."

Zeb clenched his jaw, heat rising up the back of his neck. "And?"

The vaquero straightened in his saddle, keeping his hands on the saddle horn. Behind the leather sleeve, Zeb's finger stole to the trigger of the Enfield.

"What are your intentions, *señor* Zeb, *para la señorita?*"

The image of the crumpled letter laying in a wadded ball at the edge of the remnants of the fire flitted through Zeb's mind. "Don't rightly know. What are yours?"

Philippe grinned. *"La señorita es muy bonita."* He shrugged. *"Pero,* she is pregnant. I am not sure I am a family man." Philippe's eyes glittered through the shade of his hat.

*Mocking me?* The heat that had been spreading up Zeb's neck inflamed his jaws. He kept his silence, letting the squeaky chirps of chipmunks, the stuttering chatter of a far-off squirrel in the conifers and the brusque bark of magpies somewhere behind the cabin, calm him." "Well, I ain't never been a family man. But I don't think I'd mind."

The brim of the sombrero bounced slightly up and down in assent and understanding.

The vaquero raised his hands to shoulder height, palms out to Zeb, then lowered them slowly to the reins wrapped once around the pommel. The two men stared at one another. "It seems we have both stated the extent of our interest." Philippe paused, one hand brushing a mosquito from his ear. *"Me gusto, señor Reuben, mucho.* He needs both of us for different reasons."

Diablo shifted his weight impatiently, the stallion's muzzle flicking lightly several times. "May I suggest, *señor* Zeb, that each of us can try to stake those claims how we see fit, but we pledge not to confront one another. *Señorita* Sarah can make her decision and whatever that is, one or the other of us will abide by it."

*Makes sense, except...* "So long as she ain't treated bad, might work."

The two men's eyes bored into one another. Philippe nodded; the corners of his mouth curled upward in a slight smirk.

"Tell Reuben I'll be down three nights from tonight. I'll stay till them roofs are on."

The vaquero nodded again and sliding the reins sideways, clicked to Diablo. The sleek black horse began to turn.

"And Philippe..." The Mexican turned partially back in the saddle. "If she ain't treated right, all bets are off."

The smirk on the vaquero's aristocratic face exploded into a wide grin. "*Comprende.*" He straightened into his stiff-backed riding posture, his heels digging slightly into Diablo's flanks. "Diablo, *vamonos.*"

September 16, 1855

# *T*EMPORARY TRUCE

THE FREIGHT WAGON MOANED AND CREAKED AS IT bumped the trail down along Dallas Creek to the Uncompahgre River. The early afternoon sun had begun its descent toward its resting place beyond the Snaefel. An unblemished sky, bright and so clear that its height and depth were endless, stretched its blue dome over the ranges of the Uncompahgre, Ouray and San Juan. The upwards thrusts of their massive stone faces, dark-green conifer ridges and trails of aspens, shone iridescent gold in the angled sunlight. Bands of aspen color wound down draws, along tumbling creeks and bunched around unseen springs in protective clusters against the surrounding armies of fir, spruce and lodgepole pine.

Sarah swayed and jolted with the wagon, one hand stabilizing Rebecca's Sharps and the Enfield Zeb had lent her for the afternoon. The rifles leaned upright, butts resting on the floor beneath the wagon seat, their forestocks and barrels cushioned from the seat's wooden edge by a blanket folded twice. In Sarah's lap, tucked against her thighs by the pronounced rounding of her belly, was a Colt pistol, also on short-term loan from Zeb.

Sarah breathed in, holding her breath, immersing herself in the kaleidoscope of colors that surrounded them, her exhaled breath warming the crisp air that wafted around her. She could hear the steps of Rebecca's horse, Red, tied to the wagon behind them.

She flashed a glance at the brunette. Rebecca was deftly playing the harness lines, trying to keep the wagon wheels in the trail that was beginning to show wear from their traffic to and from the river, and Zeb's coming and goings from his cabin.

She watched Rebecca apprehensively before deciding to speak. "The men didn't know quite what to think when you told them that if we were going to be their rock pickers, they better smooth the road to the river." *Was it worth the try?* She waited for what she thought would be a cold-toned response or stony silence.

To Sarah's surprise, without taking her eyes from the trail, Rebecca chuckled. "Yes," she added, "I'm not sure which of them looked more astonished...." She smiled widely. "I thought that line about even the Egyptian slaves who built the pyramids had level ground and good roads was quite effective."

Relieved, Sarah joined in her laughter, "Well, it was the least they could do. It only took the four of them half a day with some pole levers to roll the biggest rocks out of the way and fill in the holes." She looked ahead of the horses down the trail to where the Uncompahgre twisted like a silver ribbon between dull red banks. "It was actually quite an improvement. Not that it's smooth but far better than our first trip down, and distinctly better than the first time we drove the wagons up in July.

"The men presumed, of course, we were going to get the rocks out of the creek behind the wagons. You and I have been carrying the water from that creek for suppers, dishes and coffee several times a day. I'm not sure any of them have been through those willows for the last two months."

Rebecca smiled, her look playfully wicked. "The expression on Reuben's face when we showed him how soft the banks were, and explained to him that even though we were simply two pregnant women in the middle of nowhere who know nothing, that once the wagon was loaded with rocks, not to mention there were no rocks of the size they wished in that creek—they would be spending each and every day digging out the wheels and hooking up six horses to drag us the two hundred feet back to the cabin."

Sarah nodded, remembering the scene. "Well, one good thing that came out of it was Zeb finding that clay deposit on the other side. Odd stuff, reddish with the gray streaks, it was so dense and heavy, I think you could almost make pottery of it."

"Yes, he was quite excited. Said they could use it for both the chinking and to strengthen the mortar between the fireplace stone."

"Rebecca, if they're not going to start the fireplace until after they cut hay, what if it's not completed before the snow comes?" She adjusted her hold on the rifles as the wagon bounced along the faint trail. "To hear Zeb and Reuben talk, soon, we will have to shovel our way out the cabin door."

"I think they're relatively confident they can get the fireplace done, but that R.R. Finch & Sons cast-iron cookstove that I thought Reuben was crazy to purchase back there in Fort Kearney, and that infernal flue pipe that we always had to keep on top of everything else all the way out here, so it wouldn't get bent..." Rebecca shook her head. "It turns out his lists have been wise. He's planning to put that stove in for the primary heat source until the fireplace is complete. And it will double for cooking, which is what he originally intended. He told me next spring they will build counters when they put the wood floor in and raise it up. It only sits thirty inches or so above the ground. Compact little devil."

Sarah had her doubts. "You think that little stove—it can't be more than two by two by three, not including that bread tray in front of what must be the oven—will heat the whole house?"

Rebecca burst out laughing, "Ah yes, that expansive mansion, all six hundred square feet of it, Zeb seems to think it will work just fine in the interim."

There was a brief silence. Rebecca snorted, grinning, her eyes fixed ahead of the team. "Yes, and they were almost wringing their hands with advice, as if we simple women didn't have brains and common sense." She stole a look at Sarah and then her eyes shifted quickly back to the trail, her left hand pulling slightly on the lines. "Nothing over eight inches or under five. If it's too heavy, don't pick it up."

Thrilled that their second trip to pick stone for the fireplace was not the frigid, silent repeat of their first two days, Sarah picked up on the cadence. "Don't drop the rocks in the wagon bed. It could splinter the wood."

Rebecca laughed, "Spread the weight evenly, so there's not too much strain on the axle.... Don't pick up rocks that look like they're layered. The fire could split them."

Sarah slapped her thigh. "The black rocks have iron. They're too heavy, and don't overload the wagon. Too much strain on the horses and you could break a wheel."

Infected by Sarah's laughter, Rebecca looked up briefly to the blue expanse above them and shouted, "And load the wagon from the back," Sarah chimed in halfway through the shout, their two voices echoing out to the shallow canyon walls on either side of them, the horses of the team glancing behind them perplexed at the ruckus. Behind them, losing his patience with being forced to follow behind the wagon, Red snorted.

Calm, level and tinged with a stern overtone, Rebecca's voice broke the moments of silence that ensued. "Sarah, it's good to laugh with you again. But you know that I remain quite upset over what I perceive to be your treatment of Zeb and your seeming inability to decide between he and Philippe, thereby keeping both men flopping like fish on a line waiting to be reeled in or released."

Sarah looked out to the Wetterhorn and the *El Diente*, the eastern faces of those grand peaks shadowed by the sun's descent, their tops patched with white, the sunlit southwest and western flanks pulsing with the brilliant palette of fall.

The two women exchanged a momentary look. Sarah sighed. *She's right.*

Rebecca continued, "I know this is a confusing time. The two of us the only women, at least the only white women for who knows how many scores, perhaps hundreds, of miles. Both of us pregnant and far along, especially you..."

Sarah watched Rebecca's gaze fall to the stretched fabric of the cotton dress curving over her rounded belly before she continued speaking, "But I'm not much behind you. I worry not only for Philippe and Zeb, each of whom are good men in their own way, though quite different, but for you, and for our little group. There are too few of us to be torn apart by friction born of rivalry and indecision."

The trail blurred as Sarah's eyes filled with emotion. She reached up, wiping the trickle of a telltale tear from one eye before it could reach her cheek. *Yours is not a rapist's bastard.* "I know, Rebecca. I talked about it briefly with Johannes before he left." Her voice cracked. "I miss him."

"As do I," Rebecca said, her voice heavy with sadness. "And I know Reuben misses him immensely also."

Sarah felt another tear about to escape the corner of her eye. "I was down at the creek just behind the wagons yesterday. I took my mirror, which is still miraculously mostly intact except for one edge, and Inga's silver brush."

Rebecca flashed a glance at her.

"I spent an hour brushing my hair thinking of all we've been through. Poor Inga. Johannes's grief. Mac, Philippe, Zeb, you and I. Even those Sioux warriors who came to our aid at Two Otters Creek, and that nice boy, Michael." She glanced at Rebecca's profile and breathed in deeply. "I hate the distance that has come between us, Rebecca. You're my best friend. I want you to know, I am yours."

"Given that, at the current moment, we are each other's only friends of the same gender, I understand and agree."

The brunette chuckled softly, and without sarcasm. "I think you know how I feel, Sarah. I realize that I cannot manipulate or shame you into making a decision you're not ready to make, whatever your reasons may be...." Rebecca's lips compressed, "So, I am declaring a temporary truce between us." She shot a quick look at Sarah, her eyes narrowed. "And, we shall see what decisions you make."

Sarah started to speak, but Rebecca shook her head. "No, I don't want to talk about it. Let's enjoy the day, and this incredible country God has created, which, it would appear is solely for us, given the lack of others."

She turned, casting a concerned look at Sarah, her brown eyes full and earnest. "Just know that I'm here for you. I will always give you my opinion," she chortled, "though we know there will be times you won't much like it."

Sarah sniffled. *I wish I had remembered a handkerchief.*

———

THE WAGON, GROANING IN PROTEST, WAS ON THE FINAL descent to the Uncompahgre, the river's clear current hurried but no longer rushing as it had been six weeks before. The river's dull red and rocky banks accented and offset the aqua blue waters as they sifted and rolled over a bed of golden, black and red stones.

Sarah's eyes followed Rebecca's outstretched arm as she quickly pointed. "Look, Sarah. See just downstream of where the trail goes across the river, where the current curves out and away from this bank? That looks like a sand deposit there. Probably where the water slowed as it receded. I think we can get the wagon close to that, fill those four pails halfway full, and together, lift them into the wagon."

Thinking of the men's admonitions, Sarah felt laughter boil up from her chest. "*And load them from the rear, don't forget,*" she mimicked.

Rebecca laughed, nodding as she shifted the lines to one hand. She pointed again, "It appears that there's a number of the right size rocks around that sand too—most of them out of the water. We'll set one rifle on each rear wheel just in case...." She glanced quickly at Sarah's bulging belly. "It's a little easier for me to bend, so I'll pick the rocks up, hand them to you and you can put them in the wagon."

In unison, their voices chimed out, "*But don't drop them because they could splinter the wagon bed.*" The two women roared with laughter.

September 16, 1855

# THE RIVER'S WHISPER

REBECCA WATCHED SARAH LEAN AGAINST ONE REAR corner of the freight wagon, patting her forehead and face with the hem of her dress, her pantaloons a creamy white billow below the uplifted material. Rebecca cocked her head to one side, her hands on her hips, surveying the wagon bed through the open tailgate.

"I think that will do it for today. The rocks spread out that way, one deep, side to side, ought to stop any shifting of the weight going up the trail even though they are smooth and mostly round. And those sand pails set across the bed at the upper ends of the rock layer should keep the stones from rolling forward."

The redhead lowered her dress, her cheeks flushed, one hand resting on her protruding belly. "Good. For small as they are, those rocks are heavy," she looked down at her hands, "and rough. I'm glad Zeb gave us those buckskin gloves. The few times I took them off to rearrange a rock, I either scraped my skin or grew an immediate callus. That was a great idea you had to push them from the rear with that limb and save us from having to get in and out of the wagon."

"Yes, a good idea indeed," Rebecca replied, waving her arm with an exaggerated, grandiose flourish at the valley and the mountain ranges. "What would the neighbors have thought of two fat, pregnant ladies clambering for hours up and down a ladder into the back of a wagon?"

Sarah giggled. "Yes, very unseemly. We might've ruined our reputations."

Rebecca cast a last look at the wagon bed and its contents. Satisfied, she raised the tailgate, latching one side. "Sarah, can you get your side?" Rebecca turned, shielding her eyes from the ever lower western sun as she peered up the trail toward the fledgling ranch.

"Sarah, why don't you take the wagon and get started. I'm going to saddle up Red, if you'll help me lift the saddle and slip it over, but I want to spend ten or fifteen minutes here alone. I really haven't had any alone time since we rattled our way up that trail two months ago."

The suggestion seemed to concern her friend. Sarah's eyebrows rose. She craned her neck back over her shoulder and Rebecca could see her chin lift as her eyes followed the trail from the mouth of Dallas Creek, where it emptied in a rush into the Uncompahgre, further up to where the tracks disappeared under the brow of a rise.

Sarah turned back to her, her face still flushed, an anxious look in her eyes.

"You can do it easily, Sarah," she reassured her. "You're

good with those lines. Just stay in the tracks we made coming down here the last two excursions and take your time. I'll be along quickly. In fact, I'll likely catch up with you before you're halfway back home." *The first time I've said that in that way—back home.*

Sarah shook her head, her eyebrows curled in a frown underneath her sunbonnet, "Reuben's not going to be happy. You told him you were just tying off Red to the wagon to give her some exercise since the horses have been tethered to that monstrously long line Philippe and Reuben ran."

Rebecca grinned back at her. "Well, that's the truth. I just forgot to add the part that I was going to ride her back."

Sarah pursed her lips worriedly. "I knew you had something like that in mind when you asked me to help load your saddle and close up that tailgate so quickly. And I saw you glance over where the men were working to make sure they didn't see."

"That makes you my partner in crime. I shall tell Reuben it was all your idea."

The redhead stared back at her blankly for a moment and then began laughing. "You shall do no such thing."

———

REBECCA FINISHED TIGHTENING THE CINCH ON RED'S saddle, wrapped the reins three times around the pommel, then grabbed the lead rope and led the mare to where a large cottonwood trunk with a thick crooked branch lay wedged at the edge of a cluster of high-water rocks. The branch's bark had been mostly peeled away by the greedy fingers of a fast current fed by snowmelt. She tied off the sorrel and watched the rear of the freight wagon disappear up the trail, its creaks and groans barely audible above the sound of the river and the gentle breeze that had begun to drift downvalley from the north. She walked gingerly down to where the sandy cove met the edge of the river and lowered herself carefully to the sand, the Sharps across her lap, the heavy hem of her light-blue cotton dress tucked beneath her legs.

She was alone in a vast empty space, at the edge of civilization, almost six thousand miles from the expansive city she had called home. *Just eighteen months ago.* She furrowed her brow at the thought.

Above the river's whisper where it caressed the red rock shore, she heard the distant screech of a golden eagle calling to its mate, the impressive birds circling, their wings motionless except for their tips. She watched their dark bodies gather height from the updraft of valley breeze, and the rising current of heat from the sunbaked western face of the mountains that rose across the river. Upstream, a coyote called. Another answered, and yet a third joined the wild chorus. Downriver, the water disappeared in shimmers of angled sun. On both banks, reddish rock that had been submerged just weeks ago, framed the flow where it disappeared into grasses now more gold than green. A fall flurry of red, orange and yellow willows, alders and cottonwoods marked the coming winter. The west-tilting sun behind her warmed her back and blazed the mountains rising abruptly in front of her in an explosion of orange and gold, the turning aspens vivid between dark green bands of conifers. The afternoon sky above the rocky peaks had just begun to fade from brilliant to diffused blue.

The vastness, the emptiness, the sheer space, enveloped her. The promise of life and season in transition stirred a feeling of excitement. She rested her hand on her belly, determined not to let the occasional painful twinge interfere with the moment and the movement of the life she felt within her. *Our baby.* She struggled with a wave of feeling, suddenly overwhelmed. *I'm going to be a mother.* She looked up and down the valley, then raised her head to the peaks towering above her to the east. The golden eagles were but distant specs, still circling, higher and higher. *No doctors, no medicines, no midwives.* Her heart fluttered. She clenched her jaw. *We shall be fine.*

She tried to remember her home in London—her bedroom, the cobblestone street lined by stately row houses and her mother. She closed her eyes, lifting her face to the cooling air, amazed to find that the memory of crowds, city noise and fine linens was distant, fuzzy, unreal, as if only a dream, never a reality.

Her eyes burned with moisture, and her cheek twitched. She looked above and whispered to the sky. "I miss you, Mother. I so hope that you can see what I am seeing, feel what I am feeling. Your last letter to me, so true and wise."

She wiped below her eyes with the bent knuckle of her forefinger, and reached in the pocket of her dress, her fingers closing around the small, faceted piece of quartz she carried with her since that day she had found it riding up to Zeb's cabin.

She drew it out, the stone refracting in the sunlight pouring over her shoulder and held it up to the sky. "See,

Mother—quartz. Father was not crazy. I know where our land is, and quartz could mean gold."

She returned the quartz to her pocket, making sure the stone was safely lodged. She inhaled deeply. *So dry, so clear, so untouched.* Her mind drifted back to the day she had stepped into the London carriage in all her finery. Adam's concerned and earnest brown eyes, his aboriginal features solemn, his deep baritone voice thick with the accent of his native land. *"It will be a different life, mistress, but you shall prosper. The power of the land and the man will hold you."* And her response, *"I assure you, Adam, I'll be back in London, my goals accomplished, by the late fall."*

She chuckled to herself. *You were right about that too, Father. Adam does have a gift for seeing the future.*

She remembered the evening, *it seemed like years ago,* back on the Nemhaw River, the wagon train forging west across the plains, still thinking she would return to London, her thoughts as the sun had set, in the middle of nowhere. *"I have myself, my friends, and my God."* She smiled to herself, one hand resting on her belly. *"And now my husband and my child."*

Rebecca rose slowly from the sand, with effort, using the Sharps to assist. She brushed the riverbed sand from her dress, walked to Red and slipped the rifle into its scabbard. She turned the horse so she could mount from the uphill side and carefully lifted herself into the saddle.

She wheeled the mare toward the trail, pausing for one last look up, then down, the river, and out to the southeast where autumn was spilling from the peaks in a jagged, colorful cascade. She flicked the reins, gently dug her heels into Red's flank and smiled.

"Okay Red, home we go. Perhaps you can explain all this to Reuben for me."

September 16, 1855

# *T*HE LIEUTENANT AND THE SCHOOL GIRL

JOHANNES WAS AWAKENED LONG BEFORE SUNRISE BY THE whinnies of horses, creak of supply wagons and the trudging cadence of marching infantry that assaulted the windows of his quarters in the second story of the Old Bedlam Fort Laramie Headquarters. He stared out of the window of his quarters at the burgeoning day, fastening the last button on the crisp, dark-blue tunic and wondering at the overnight explosion of military activity all around the Fort.

He gave a tug to the hem of his jacket, settling the new material over his shoulders and buckled his cartridge belt around his midriff, saber dangling off his left hip, holstered Army Colt snugged into his right side.

Johannes descended the stairs two at a time, his Sharps carbine in one hand, fitting his hat over neatly trimmed blonde hair with the other. The lower level of the building bustled with uniforms. Through the ajar double doors into a side room, Johannes glimpsed two officers. One was Major

Woodruff, the Fort Commandant, and the other a general huddled with several other junior officers, all of them bent over a large table covered with maps. Johannes blinked. *A general?*

Johannes paused on the landing outside the door in front of the sentries, surveying the frenetic motion around on the fort. Spotting his lieutenant forty yards away, Sergeant O'Reilly barked, "Ten-hut!" to the thirty cavalrymen standing behind him in columns of two beside their horses as Johannes strode toward them.

Drawing his beefy shoulders back, his legs locked, back ramrod stiff, the sergeant raised one rigid hand in salute, each of his motions executed simultaneously by the men. Behind the platoon, the American flag curled in lazy furls against a sky so bright and blue that it caused Johannes to squint under the brim of his hat as he neared the patrol. *First command in the United States Army.* The men watched their new lieutenant approach, eyes shaded by the broad-brimmed dark-blue hats they wore, the crossed sword insignia of the United States Dragoons in the forecrowns.

A small group of five women were gathered too, fifty yards distant, standing in the dusty gravel of the road running the length of the west side of the fort. Some of the women held the hands of young children. A few carried infants and toddlers in the crooks of their arms. One stood slightly apart from the others, childless, slight and thin of build, in a burgundy dress and a burgundy hat atop golden hair shimmering in the bright sun.

The weight of the saber dangling from Johannes's left hip offset the tug on his opposite side from the Army Colt .44

lodged in the new, black-flapped leather holster, still stiff despite his oiling it. But the saber felt balanced. *Just right.* He halted four feet from the sergeant who still stood at attention, his right hand drawn to his forehead, the troopers behind him doing the same.

Johannes drew himself up, clicked his heels and snapped a return salute, "At ease, Sergeant O'Reilly."

"At ease," the sergeant thundered, never taking his eyes from Johannes. In unison, thirty hands dropped, boots that had been stiffly together side-stepped and thirty pairs of hands dropped to clasp behind thirty waists. *Well drilled.*

"Do you have our orders, sergeant?"

Sergeant O'Reilly pressed his lips together. "No, lieutenant, Captain Henderson wished to deliver them personally to you. He will be along shortly." The sergeant dropped his baritone, Irish brogue to just above a whisper. "It is customary at this post, sir, to allow the married men a few wee moments to say goodbye to the women and children before the patrol moves out." He gestured with his chin toward the group Johannes had noticed on his walk toward the patrol.

The sergeant began to turn his head to communicate to the soldiers behind him, but at Johannes's voice, his eyes snapped forward again. "Not yet, sergeant. It is a custom in my command that I inspect the troops prior to their mounting up."

The sergeant's eyebrows shot toward the shiny bill of his cap, and the black strap forward under his chin tightened along with the muscles in his cheeks. "I beg your pardon, lieutenant. Inspection?"

Johannes looked down on the stocky Irishman, a foot shorter than he, but said nothing, letting his eyes convey the message.

Sergeant O'Reilly blinked. "Very well, sir," he said, his acquiescence gruff and grudging. He drew himself to attention again, his thumbs aligned with the seams of his trousers, and snapped his chin over his shoulder. "Troop. Ten-hut! Prepare for inspection."

There was the low murmuring of a few voices, and several heads turned toward the troopers next to them.

Johannes stepped to the side so that he wasn't shielded from his command by the sergeant. "Men, I am First Lieutenant Johannes Svensen." Several eyebrows shot upward. Eyes widened. *My accent.* "Over time, we will get to know one another."

He paused, looking down the two lines of soldiers. Memories rose. Pioneers lined up in the cottonwoods along the creek in the Missouri woods, he and Mac walking down the ragged row of untrained men with an assortment of meager weapons, the galloping hooves of the horse carrying Rebecca with her Sharps, the men muttering with doubt and laughter at the beautiful, primly dressed brunette as she slipped off her saddle, rifle in hand.

His eyes worked their way down the line, taking in each and every cavalryman. "We come from different places," he said. "We have different experiences, and from time to time, we may have different ideas. But we all share a common country, and...," he lifted one arm pointing at the flag, "a common flag and a common uniform."

A number of the wide-brimmed hats bobbed slightly in

agreement. Some of the soldiers wore surprised looks. Two appeared disinterested. Johannes made a mental note of them. *One tall and lanky. One medium height, stocky.*

"I have a friend," he continued, a vision of Reuben's green eyes sifting through his mind, "a rancher. He has a saying. If you work for the ranch, you ride for the brand." He raised his hand again to the flag. "That, gentleman, is our brand. I will make a pact with all of you here, now and forever so long as we ride together." Every eye focused on him. "I will always ride to your front. What I ask, in return, is that you follow."

Several soldiers smiled. All but two nodded. *One lanky. One stocky.*

"Lieutenant," came Captain Henderson's voice from behind him. Johannes stiffened, came to attention, clicked his heels and turned smartly, snapping a salute returned by the captain.

Captain Henderson took a step toward him, their faces just a foot apart, his gaze fixed on Johannes, his voice lowered. "That, lieutenant, might be the best first address by a new officer I have heard in more than two decades of soldiering."

"Yes, sir."

"I understand your orientation training went exceptionally well." He waved one hand at the infantry and cavalry crowding the parade ground, "Been quite a bit of commotion since this morning, as I'm sure you have noticed. General Harney and six hundred men from Fort Kearny attacked Little Thunder's Brule Sioux one hundred fifty miles south at Ash Hollow twelve days ago. Killed eighty-six

hostiles and took seventy women and children prisoners."
The captain shook his head, his eyebrows dipped in a frown.
*He did not agree with that action.* "They are leaving one
hundred fifty men here to bolster the garrison. The rest of
his command is moving out for Fort Pierre up on the
Missouri. It was the Grattan incident that precipitated this
most recent so-called battle...." His lips pursed.

"You and I will have a discussion when you return
concerning the 1851 Treaty signed here at the Fort with the
Cheyenne, Arapahoe and the Sioux."

*He means that we are not keeping our end of the bargain.*

Captain Henderson opened his mouth to say something
more, glanced to the side of Johannes at the patrol and the
sergeant and thought better of it. He reached beneath the
lapel of his dark-blue tunic withdrawing an envelope, sealed
and bearing the regimental stamp. "These are your orders,
Lieutenant Svensen. The major had originally wished you to
patrol east along the Oregon Trail, then south on the South
Platte cutoff where we first met, then down to Cherry Creek,
and then back up the front range to the Laramie River before
turning back to the fort."

*But?*

"However, we have received communiqués concerning
unrest beginning to brew in the Salt Lake area and slightly
north in the Utah Territory. It seems there is a certain sect
of Mormons who believe they are not part of the United
States, but rather their own separate country and territory.
You will note in the orders the suggested route of the patrol,
though you are free to make any changes as circumstances or
situations develop. The general requested I brief him on your

mission. He prefers strongly that you do your best to avoid any confrontations with the Mormons. He and the major are far more interested in whatever intelligence you may gather. You are, of course, free to act in your defense or that of your men and it goes without saying that if you encounter hostiles, such as the Yamparika or Brule Sioux, that you take any actions you deem appropriate. Your mission is to show the flag and remind those Utah folks that the United States Army has a long reach. Your next patrol, although I fear that will not be until spring with winter on its way, will be what was originally intended, to Cherry Creek."

"Yes, sir. Understood."

Captain Henderson nodded curtly, began to swing away, then pivoted back to Johannes. "One more thing, lieutenant. I assume Sergeant O'Reilly told you about our custom of allowing the men a few minutes of goodbye with their family?"

"Yes, sir, he did."

"Well, when you're done with your pre-mounted inspection, lieutenant, which, by the way, I like; perhaps the regiment should adopt it as a custom; there is somebody in that group of women who would like to say goodbye to you."

Johannes had difficulty hiding the look of astonishment on his face. Captain Henderson laughed aloud and, behind him, Johannes could feel the curious stare of thirty pairs of eyes.

Captain Henderson drew himself up and snapped a salute. Johannes did likewise in return. "Good luck, lieutenant," the captain said as he wheeled, walking briskly back toward the headquarters building.

JOHANNES EXCHANGED A FEW WORDS WITH EACH AND every trooper as he made his inspection, adroitly appraising each based on his previous experience and command. He returned to Sergeant O'Reilly. "All right, sergeant, let the men say their goodbyes."

The sergeant nodded and spun. Facing the troops, he barked, "All right, married corporals and sergeants, time to bid your lassies and wee ones farewell. You have five minutes. Be smart about it."

Four of the cavalrymen handed their reins to the soldier one side or the other of them, all of them walking hurriedly toward the women and children. The small figure with blonde hair, who had been standing apart, began walking toward Johannes. Perplexed, he strode to meet her. They met halfway between the twin columns of horses and the Old Bedlam building.

The young woman wore a form-fitting, light-burgundy calico dress that fell in a pleated flare from the slim of her hips to below her knees. A half-moon collar curved upward, well above the rise of petite breasts, her fair skin white and smooth where exposed by the cut of the collar. A burgundy hat was perched at an angle over long, blonde locks that turned to spiraling curls below her ears and fell in a sunlit sheen over her shoulders.

He drew up in front of her. She raised her eyes to his. *Blue, so blue.* "Dorothy?"

Her lips parted in a dazzling smile, and she nodded her

head.

Johannes struggled to hide his surprise. *She's put some weight on... truly a beautiful young girl...so young.* "I thought," he stammered, "I thought..." Annoyed at himself, he took a deep breath. "I have been training. I had heard that you had gone East."

She shook her head, raised one arm and pointed at a tall corporal with two young children under his arms, another clinging to his leg and his wife pressed into him, her hands curled in the lapels of his tunic. "McAllister's."

Johannes's eyes snapped back to Dorothy. "You are living with Corporal McAllister and his wife?"

She nodded, her lips moist and glistening in the sun, mouthing the word, "Yes."

Johannes stooped forward, decreasing their height differential. "You look very pretty, all cleaned up, and you've gained some weight."

To his surprise, she replied. "Yes. Better." *Speaking more.*

"Well, Miss Dorothy, you are very kind to come see me and the corporal off."

The girl dropped her head shyly.

"And school? Are you in school?"

She raised her face to him, beaming and said, "Yes." *Not quite a woman's voice, but almost.*

"I have to get back to my soldiers. We should be back in a month, give or take a few days. Perhaps, if you wouldn't mind, I could come down to the school and sit in on a few classes. I'll sit in the back. No one would ever have to know I was there."

She giggled, nodding.

Johannes straightened up and stuck out his right hand, palm up. "Do you know the way a proper soldier says goodbye to a beautiful schoolgirl who spends her time to see him off?"

Dorothy shook her head, wide eyes fixed on his.

"Put your hand in mine."

She hesitated only briefly and then raised her pale hand and placed it in his palm.

Johannes clicked his heels and bent, raising her wrist briefly to his lips and then let it down, straightening up and smiling.

Her lips were parted, her face scarlet.

"Goodbye, Dorothy." Johannes turned and walked back to the patrol standing by their horses, awaiting the order to mount up.

# CHAPTER

## 33

September 16, 1855

# EGACY

WALKS WITH MOON STOOD ANKLE DEEP IN LAPRELE Creek, its shallow flow clear and lazy with the parch of late summer. A small stand of cottonwoods cast intermittent shadows over the water, the slow wave of their leaves a mottle of summer green and autumn gold. Above her, the brilliant blue of a cloudless sky flickered through the gentle seesaw of branches. The crisp scent of the changing season permeated the dry air clinging to the creek's cool, refreshing waters.

Pulling up the leather of her dress to mid-thigh and holding the fringed hem with one hand, she squatted slightly, bending forward carefully, cupping water with her free hand. She splashed several handfuls on both upper thighs, already glistening from the slow escape of amniotic fluid. *Just as Turtle Dove told me I should expect.*

She straightened slowly and took one step toward the bank, stopping, taking in a deep breath as a painful spasm wracked her belly. She placed both hands lightly under her belly and the weight of their son. She breathed deeply again, her eyes closed, face upturned toward the sun. The spasm ceased, the pain dissipating. She resumed her careful walk in small steps to the bank, stepping out, then pausing to catch her breath and still the nervous butterflies in her chest.

Her eyes searched the trunks of the cottonwoods, lingering on one with two medium-diameter branches bursting from its trunk in a vee above the ground at the level of her chest. With feet spread wide, she made her way to the tree through the high, green grass tinged with golden seed. Reaching up, she wrapped one hand around one limb and her other around the second, testing their strength and allowing herself to hang, knees bent, legs spread far apart. She released the limbs and sank to her knees. Taking the knife Eagle Talon had fashioned for her from the base of an elk antler, she began to cut the grass in a circle within arm's reach, piling the cuttings high, then spreading them evenly, centered below the vee of the cottonwood limbs. She leaned back on her calves surveying the round, mown area and nest of grass, testing its softness with her hand. *This is where you shall drop, my child, and be blessed by Wakan Tanka with the sight of your first sun.*

Leaning forward, one hand against the coarse bark of the cottonwood for support, she rose. She could see the scattering of tipis southeast of the grove, an arrow-flight distant. Three days ride to the southwest loomed the broad, cone-shaped mass of Laramie Peak. *We are within seven or eight suns of winter camp!*

Another spasm clutched the middle of her body. She breathed again as the older women of the tribe had advised, one hand on the tremors at her middle, the other softly fingering the beaded necklace her mother, Tree Dove, had worn when birthing Walks With Moon. The sharp stabbing pain receded and the tremor, deep in her core, stopped as before.

*Time to drink my chokecherry potion and tell Eagle Talon his son has grown impatient with the darkness.* She turned, gazing at the cottonwood she had chosen for the birthplace, smiled and whispered to the tree, "You and I will do fine, you and I and the grasses, and the creek and our son." She looked up into the sky. *All one connected.* She recalled the stories she had been told by the elder women of the tribe, the *midewiwin,* and her friends who had already given birth, the memories stilling the butterflies that seemed to be brushing their wings against her heart.

EAGLE TALON TESTED THE BLADE OF THE KNIFE WITH HIS thumb, then held the weapon at arm's length, cutting edge facing him, centered in front of his eyes, carefully comparing the angle of each honed side of the steel. *A few more draws across the sharpening stone.* His gaze drifted to the tree line of Laprele Creek, the green leaves tinged with a yellow cast, and here and there a burst of bright yellow in the cottonwoods where a tree limb was dying, its leaves preparing to fall ahead of the rest.

Beyond the tree line to the northwest rose abrupt buttes and, ever higher, rolling grassy hills, golden brown with the ending of summer, stretching upward toward the headwaters of the South Fork of the Powder River, and the tribe's winter camp. He bent forward, his elbows resting on his knees, the sharpening stone held in one hand above his crossed ankles, the knife in the other.

The pleasant warmth of the sun playing on his bare shoulders after the morning frost was intercepted by Walk with Moon's shadow as she walked toward him, her feet oddly spaced, her step slow, her hand on the great roundness of her belly, which stretched the leather taut across her hips.

She smiled at him. "It is time, husband. Your son, our legacy, wishes to not miss the season of *canwapegi wi* and to meet his father." The corners of her mouth twitched, her cheek muscles tightening. She pressed her eyes closed, her body swaying slightly.

Eagle Talon hurriedly cast the knife and sharpening stone to the side, scrambling to his feet, stepping toward her and placing his hands gently but firmly on her shoulders. "Walks With Moon? Do you mean, now? Now is the time?"

She smiled up at him, one small hand rising, her palm resting on his cheek. "I wanted to be sure, Eagle Talon. This is my first...."

"Of many," Eagle Talon smiled down at her.

She bit her lip. "That, Eagle Talon, will be decided by *Wakan Tanka.* Now, please go to tell Turtle Dove."

September 16, 1855

# *A*IN'T NO WAY

"ISRAEL, I'M COLD. GOT CHILLED TO THE BONE LAST NIGHT waking up to that frost falling off the gutta-percha. That's the second night in four days." Lucy's voice traveled up to Israel from atop the mule where she perched, plaintive and worried.

Israel flicked his eyes toward the sun. *Three, maybe four hours till dark.* "We'll be fine, Lucy...." He glanced briefly over his shoulder at her and then quickly forward again as he stumbled over a rock. "I think we be in that Uncompahgre country we first saw on that map back in that old lady's place in the Nebraska Territory. I checked the map that Captain drew. I'm almost sure this here river we're heading up is the Uncompahgre."

Lucy's words, aimed like a dart at the back of his head, came again, slightly louder and a bit shriller. "I don't much care if this be the Atlantic Ocean, Israel. Where we're headed, them mountains gets higher and higher. Except for them bad looking folks we skirted way around down there in the ruins of that old trading post or whatever it was, we ain't seen another soul since we patched up po' Mr. Black Feather. What makes you think there's anybody up here? And if there ain't, how we gonna get over them mountains? There ain't no way. They monstrous tall and rough."

Israel looked up from the round, rough reddish rocks that edged the colorful lines of willows and alders they were hugging on their way upstream. Upvalley and all around them loomed masses of rock and timber, striped and punctuated with fall colors. Upstream in the distance, the gray-brown faces of two exposed peaks, their upper reaches spotted with patches of white, seemed to warn them away. *They do look impassable. And snow!*

He stopped, twisting slowly around to Lucy. Her eyes were narrowed above the bulge of her heavy cheeks and clenched jaws. Her thick, pink lower lip stuck out stubbornly from her chin "Lucy, I done showed you the map ten times, at least. I know we're in the right spot where we always planned to come," he paused, "or where the good Lord told us to go for some unknown reason."

Lucy's eyes narrowed further, and her lower lip began to tremble. "I know all that, Israel, but it won't do us a lick of good if there ain't no one else here or if there is, they be slavers or not likin' our type. Then, what we gonna do? Turn around and go all the way back? Where? I know you done seen that snow up there. And I know you was shivering just like me them last several nights. We be way high up. I think winter's just about here."

Israel rubbed his curly, silver-gray beard with the underside of his fingers. "I know there's people somewhere ahead of us...."

Lucy interrupted him. "What makes you so sure?"

Israel pointed twenty feet toward the river. "See them little indentations here and there where they ain't been totally washed out? Dem's wagon tracks. Been seeing them often over the last two days, and they be going that way," he lifted his hand, pointing up the river, "and they ain't come out." *And then there's them unshod pony prints. Don't figure I'll mention them.*

Lucy shook her head. "How do you know we ain't missed the tracks that come out or who them wagons belong to? We might be in worse fixins' if we find them than if we don't."

Israel stared at his wife. "I know they ain't come out. I've been keeping a keen eye. I'll be honest with you, woman. We spent too many years lovin' one another for me to be anything but truthful. You's right 'bout everything else you say. And I don't know if these wagons went somewhere and kept on going. These tracks look like they're couple months old."

Lucy listened attentively.

"But I know this. We be where we set out for, not even knowin' at first, more than a year ago. We come a long, hard way and plenty of times we almost didn't make it. For some reason, the good Lord told us to come here and helped us do it. Maybe we're in a pickle; maybe we ain't. But we need to see what's at the end of this trail. Nuthin' ever happens without no reason, and we'll deal with what comes when it comes."

Lucy ran the back of her wrist across one eye. Raising her head, she gazed over his head at the valley rising in front of them. "All right, Israel. There's sense in what you say. And this surely is the most beautiful place I've ever seen. Never even knew there was a piece of earth like this." Her eyes lowered to his. "As long as we're together, there ain't no prettier place if this be end of this trail."

Israel dropped the lead rope and shuffled between the rocks to her side. He gently took hold of her nearest hand and pulled it to his mouth, kissing the meaty rise of flesh behind her knuckles, then looked up at her. "Love you, Lucy. Always have, since the very first."

She turned her hand and squeezed his. "Me likewise, Israel."

LUCY'S ANXIETY SIMMERED. OVER SALLY'S TWITCHING gray ears and the salt and pepper rear of Israel's head; rough, sharp, jagged peaks rose ever higher, more imposing and wilder as they plodded toward an unknown rendezvous.

"Lucy, look at that," excitement laced Israel's voice. He had stopped, leaning forward, looking down in front of him and toward a sandy cove along the river just downstream of where a creek tumbled into the Uncompahgre from someplace higher.

"What is it, Israel?"

He pointed. "See them wagon tracks? They was made today—maybe even this afternoon. You see them prints? They was driving that wagon, and they be way too small to be a man's boot, less its chillun'. Two women, looks like to me. And see over there? They must a had some bucket or pail and scraped through the sand, filling it up." His voice grew more animated. "And look at them holes where there used to be rocks, but ain't no more."

He turned to her, and their eyes met, both of them in unison, saying, "Fireplace."

Lucy smiled at him. "Well, that answers one question. There is other folks here and if all this sign was made just this afternoon, then they ain't too far away."

Israel nodded enthusiastically, "Yep, and if they be building a fireplace, they aim on stayin' wherever they is. We'll just follow those tracks." He looked up and to the west where a quarter of the sun had already settled behind high, far-off, shadowed peaks. His gaze dropped to the near toe of a hill sloping toward the creek just ahead of them. "My bet is they went up that creek somewhere toward where the sun's sinking."

Lucy bobbed her head, not wanting to undermine his excitement. "But that leaves the rest of the questions, husband. Who are they and if we find them, what are they gonna be thinkin' about us?"

Israel's head snapped toward her, gray eyebrows low over his eyes, his lips a tight pensive line. He studied her for a moment, then turned his gaze back to the creek, two fingers rubbing his forehead above his eyebrow. When his eyes narrowed back to hers, they were calm and steady. His teeth flashed in a brief, reserved smile against the dark skin under the silver-gray hair that fell over the sides of his lips to his chin, "Well, woman, last time I checked, only one way to find out."

THE SOFT BREEZE OF AFTERNOON METAMORPHOSED INTO an insistent wind after the sun set. The howl of strong gusts swept downvalley from the west, drowning out the intermittent gurgle of the creek. Mountain's peaks towered mysterious and dark, silhouetted against a star-studded sky that had lost its day glow. As Lucy and Israel ascended the faint trail up Dallas Creek, the luminescence of the coming crescent moon, silver above the ridge lines, cast muted light across the waving meadow grasses and golden creek willows.

Israel stopped, turning back to Lucy's hunched and shivering figure on the mule. "Lucy, hear them cows? Keep Sally quiet. We didn't walk all this way as freemen to have no trouble now."

"I'll, sure enough, keep her quiet, Israel."

*Lucy heard them, too.*

A slow quarter mile later, he peered intently into the meadows up the creek next to its willow line, staring at the faint flicker of a campfire and near that, the dim beckoning glow of oil lamps in the shape of an elongated dome. *Looks like the canvas top of a wagon.*

Lucy's whisper hissed through the darkness. "What do you think we should do? I'm hungry and cold. Do you think it's safe?"

Israel shuffled back to her and spoke slowly and quietly, thinking as he formed the words. "Well, this is the edge of the country. We sure are a long way from Oklahoma. This ain't no plantation, and I'm betting all that grows here is hay. You can hear them cattle. It's going to be getting even colder soon, and these thin clothes of ours ain't going to be much help these frost nights and winter coming on. We're about outta food. I lost my last fishhook yesterday, and after missin' that rabbit, I only got three shells left in that pistol. I don't see as we have much choice. We have to take our chances."

Lucy laid one hand lightly on Israel's forearm. Her fingers were trembling. "You're my man, Israel. I'll do what you think."

Looking at the halo of lights a quarter mile or so out, she spoke in a low voice through chattering teeth, a tinge of doubt edged in the hope of her tone, "Maybe folks this far out will be happy to have company."

"Well, let me do the talking, woman. And if there's any sign of trouble, we'll just back our way out of there somehow. He squeezed her arm and smiled grimly at her through the darkness. "One thing I'll tell you; we'll freeze to death and starve before we are slaves again."

September 16, 1855

# ℰMANCIPATION

REUBEN POPPED THE LAST SLIVER OF PAN BREAD FROM HIS plate into his mouth, his eyes never leaving Rebecca's firelit profile as she chatted with Sarah. He watched his wife offer the pan with the remaining squares of bread to Philippe.

He let his gaze linger on the weighty bulge in her belly, accentuated as she bent partially forward, the pan extended. *Can't believe I will be a father.* He chuckled. "You two ladies did your usual exceptional job on supper."

Rebecca and Sarah's faces turned toward him, a broad smile on each.

Philippe's grin flashed across the glow of the coals. "*Sí, señor,* Reuben. *La mujeres* might make the best pan bread *al norte de Mexico.*"

Zeb sat on the third log bench, Michael standing behind him in his usual position at the edge of the firelight. "Have to agree," said the mountain man between bites, his long legs stretched out toward the flames.

Reuben's gaze bounced around the fire, observing each of their little band, musing. *Sarah and Rebecca seem to be getting along again. Still tension between Zeb and Philippe but tamped down.* He watched the redhead. She appeared to be careful not to flaunt any extra attention toward either Zeb or Philippe. *I hope it holds. Otherwise, that cabin's going to be mighty small.*

Reuben leaned forward, one arm outstretched, to toss his plate next to the fire ring. He froze at the sound of a voice coming from the darkness behind him. Dropping the plate, he whirled and stood. The Colt sprang from holster to hand. Out of the corner of his eye, he saw Zeb reach for his Sharps and Philippe already standing, firelight reflecting from the twin barrels of both pistols.

"Who's there?" Reuben barked, his eyes trying to penetrate the opaque night. He sensed both Zeb and Philippe, one to either side of him, easing from the light cast by the fire.

Reuben cocked the hammer of the Colt. "I say again, who's there?"

A baritone voice answered, "We don't mean no harm. Been traveling quite a spell. Just me, my wife, Lucy, and our old mule."

The voice was laced with a thick, peculiar accent. It took Rueben a moment to place it. *The docks in New York. The Porters.*

"Where you coming from?"

The hesitation out in the darkness was palpable.

"Answer me. Where you traveling from?"

"We figure we've traveled a thousand miles, maybe more. Started more than a year ago. Originally from the No-Name Territories. Some folks call 'em the Indian Territories, and some call it Oklahoma."

Reuben had only heard of that part of the country in passing conversations. "Well, don't know much about that place, but a year and a thousand miles is a long time and a long way. Ease into the light, nice and slow. Keep your hands up where we can see them. Whoever is with you, do the same."

Out in the darkness, there was the blow of a mule, and then the voice again. "Come on, Sally. They don't mean you no harm. Lucy, do as the man asked."

Thirty seconds later, a medium height man, thread bare, patched clothes hanging from his thin frame, topped by a face etched with age under short, curly, salt-and-pepper hair and silver-gray face whiskers, came into shadowy view. Behind him plodded the dark shape of a mule, its ears flicking back and forth, its head up. Astride the mule was an older, heavyset woman, her squat figure hunched and shivering, cloaked only in a thin, worn, cotton dress. Tight short curls of gray hair poked from beneath a faded blue bandana.

Philippe stepped back into the firelight to Reuben's left. Zeb did the same on his right. The old man had his hands up, about shoulder height. The woman held her thick arms partially extended from her body. The man glanced from Reuben to Zeb, and then to Philippe. *Apprehensive...and defiant.*

Watching the man's gaze shift past his shoulder, Reuben threw a quick glance behind him. Sarah was crouched behind the log bench, her red hair reflecting the flames. Rebecca knelt to her side, her Sharps held at port. Michael knelt down behind the log Zeb had used for a seat, his plate still in his hand, his mouth slack and eyes wide.

Reuben straightened up. "Come in a little closer."

The man walked slowly toward him, lead rope in his raised right hand. At five paces, Reuben called out, "That's far enough."

Zeb walked toward the man from Reuben's right, the Enfield leveled. From his other side, he heard Philippe's voice. "*Señor*, please take that pistol from your belt, *por favor*, left hand, just your thumb and forefinger, and give it to the tall man there next to you with the rifle. Is that musket on the mule loaded?"

The man nodded. "It is, though I ain't checked the load in a couple days." He slowly moved his hand to the pistol, jerking on it several times when the cylinder lodged on the leather.

Reuben heard Phillipe chuckle. "*Señor*, yours is not a very fast draw."

The man looked up from his focus on his Colt, his eyebrows raised. Then he laughed.

Reuben liked his laugh. *Genuine. Nervous, but not scared.*

"No," said the man still chuckling. "I ain't fast. Fact, I'm slower than molasses flowin' uphill. Only had this pistol for a bit more than a month, and only have three shells left."

Reuben twirled the Colt twice, then slipped it back in its Slim Jim. "Tell your wife she can drop her arms. You too. What are your names?"

"Thank you. I be Israel Thomas. That's my wife, Lucy, and this is our old mule, Sally. Picked her up in return for some leather work in the Nebraska Territories."

Philippe, now standing alongside Reuben, shoved his Colts back into his belt. Zeb picked up Israel's pistol from the grass, his grip on his Sharps now relaxed with one hand around the breach, the rifle dangling at his side. "Come on into the fire, Israel."

Philippe added in a friendly tone, "And señor, next time you come to *fuego,* call out long before you get as close as you did. Not everyone waits to see who's out there in the darkness before shooting."

Israel came closer, leading the mule. Reuben realized with a start that it was not the shadows of the night that made their features appear dark; it was their skin.

Israel extended his hand and Reuben shook it, surprised at the strength in the old man's grip. Over his shoulder, Israel said, "Say hello, Lucy." The woman on the mule half smiled, her eyes wide and white in the firelight, her lips pressed tightly, her gaze bouncing from Reuben to Philippe to Zeb to Michael, and then above their heads toward Sarah and Rebecca.

Israel dropped the lead rope. "I need to help her down. Her knee ain't too good and that chill these past few nights ain't helped much."

Reuben turned to Rebecca and Sarah. "Any food left?"

Rising from behind the log, Sarah gestured at the fire. "There's some helpings of that rabbit stew and two pieces of pan bread."

Reuben wheeled back to Israel. "If you're hungry, you're welcome to what's left."

The old man's tongue ran involuntarily over his upper lip,

his eyes locked on the pot at the side of the fire. "That would be mighty fine. We could use some fixins. Had the last of our smoked deer a few days ago and some fish yesterday morning before I lost my last hook...." His crinkled face puckered into a grimace and he shook his head.

Zeb chuckled. "I'll show you how to make 'em out of bone. Handy trick I had to learn since I tend to lose hooks, too."

Israel's teeth showed white against his dark skin. He turned stiffly. "Let me help Lucy off that mule...."

Philippe stepped forward, laying a hand on his shoulder. "*Amigo*, you go get the plates ready for you and your *esposa*. I will help her from the mule."

Israel's gray eyebrows shot up over the whites of his widened eyes. "Thank you."

"*De nada.*"

<hr />

LEANING ON PHILIPPE FOR SUPPORT, LUCY LIMPED TO ONE of the logs and, gritting her teeth, lowered herself next to Israel. Sarah and Rebecca heaped two plates full, emptying the pot and the bread pan.

They gathered around the couple in a loose semi-circle. Lucy and Israel were bent over their plates, wolfing down their meals but trying to be polite. *Hungrier than they let on.*

"Well, Lucy and Israel, I'm Reuben Frank. The gentleman who helped you from your mule, Lucy, is Philippe Reyes. The tall gentleman with the rifle, Zebarriah Taylor, and the young man over there by the log is Michael Sampson.

That beautiful, dark-haired woman there is my wife, Rebecca Frank...." Rebecca flashed him a smile, turning to greet Lucy and Israel. "And that pretty, redheaded lady who helped her serve you is Sarah Bonney."

Israel looked up chewing and nodded to all of them. Lucy stopped eating and gazed at each of them in turn, the corners of her mouth lifted, her stare lingering on Rebecca and Sarah.

Reuben saw her smile widen when her eyes dropped to their bellies. "I see you two are both getting ready to have chillin'."

Rebecca and Sarah exchanged puzzled looks until Zeb clarified, "Children."

Rebecca and Sarah's faces lit up. Sarah giggled, and Rebecca patted her stomach. "What gave us away, Lucy?" Everyone laughed.

Lucy inhaled another spoonful of rabbit stew. "So, you, Miss Rebecca, are married to Reuben." Her hand gestured at him. "I didn't quite catch who's your husband, Miss Sarah." Sarah's face reddened, her mouth opening and closing several times. Reuben sensed that looks were exchanged between Zeb and Philippe. *If she only knew.*

Clearing his throat, Zeb came to Sarah's rescue. "You could say, the father was killed."

*Good old Zeb.* Sarah flashed the mountain man a quick, grateful smile.

Lucy's eyes softened, the corners of her mouth drooping. She stared at Sarah, "Oh, child, I'm so sorry."

Sarah stood dumbfounded.

Rebecca bustled to the fire, grabbing two tin cups and the coffee kettle. "Would the two of you like some coffee to finish off supper?"

Israel nodded, still chewing, his plate almost empty.

Lucy wore a slightly bewildered look, her eyes darting around the circle, finally coming to rest on Reuben.

He smiled at her, "It's a long story." *Change the subject.* "How many nights since you folks slept under any cover?"

Israel's face lifted from his plate, "Don't rightly know. If little lean-tos with gutta-perchas hangin' over them don't count, reckon it's been a number of weeks."

"Months, Israel," Lucy corrected him, her tone sharp.

Philippe chortled.

Over their heads, Reuben caught Rebecca's eyes. *It was our night to have the wagon.* She smiled and nodded. "Well, why don't you sleep in the prairie schooner tonight."

Zeb was watching Israel, then Lucy, stroking his mustache where it dropped from his lips and hung to the stubble on his chin. "You folks slaves?"

The abruptness of the question surprised Reuben. The plate in Isreal's hand shook. He watched Lucy's face jerk toward Israel. The old man looked slowly up at Zeb; then he rose. His eyes moved to each of them in a silence filled only with the crackle of the fire, night sounds of the meadow and the murmur of the cows.

"We was, but we ain't no more." The man pressed his lips together, the muscles in his cheek twitching, waiting on their reaction.

Zeb stared at the old man for a moment, then nodded. "Good on you. I'll take that mule out and put her on the tether line with the horses." He slipped Israel's pistol from his belt and handed it to the old man who looked at him with a startled expression. "I see it's a Army Colt .44 caliber."

Israel nodded, sitting slowly back down on the log, his mouth open, his expression still one of surprise.

"You say you're good with leather?" Reuben asked.

Lucy patted Israel on the knee. "He's bein' modest. He's a full-fledged wizard with an awl. Not a bad carpenter either."

"Lucy!"

"Israel, you hush." She looked up at Reuben with a wide smile and earnest, anxious eyes. "Knows how to lay stone, too."

Rueben smiled at her. "Those skills might come in handy."

Lucy's teeth shone in a smile. She bobbed her head, her cheeks bouncing up and down with each nod. She looked over at Rebecca and Sarah and back to Reuben. "I knows a bit about midwifing, too."

Sarah and Rebecca's eyebrows raised, and they exchanged quick glances.

Reuben studied the old couple, thinking. "Where did you say you were headed?"

Lucy's eyes widened. Israel blinked, his gaze fixed on Reuben, then said slowly, "We didn't."

"We'll get all this sorted out in the morning. Seems you folks have traveled quite a spell and that's a pretty good climb up from the river to the ranch." Reuben gazed out into the darkness. "Or what we hope is going to be a ranch."

He watched Lucy and Israel turn to each other and exchange quick smiles. *You are right again, Father. There are no coincidences.*

# CHAPTER

## 36

September 25, 1855

# PROMISE OF THE UTE

ZEB HANDED THE FOOT BY FOOT-AND-A-HALF SLAB OF SOD to Michael standing three rungs up the makeshift ladder that Philippe had cobbled together. The sturdy climbing device was constructed of twin, twelve-foot fir poles joined by rungs of thick, two-foot-long branches of fir spaced a foot apart, lashed across the poles with rawhide.

The mountain man took several steps back watching Michael lift the root-bound slab of sod up to Philippe, who stood, his legs braced, one higher, one lower, over the eave on the staggered cross braces of limbed fir boughs nailed and tied across the top of the log rafters. The boughs served as the support framework for the slabs of sod, rapidly taking shape as the outermost layer of the roof.

Above Philippe, one foot on the ridge pole, the other several feet below down on the lattice of the sod support, Reuben was waiting for Philippe to take several steps up the rake of the roof with the next piece of sod.

Zeb watched Reuben place the slab of sod at the top of that course of green roof, fitting it tightly into the staggered, interlocking puzzle-like pattern that extended eight feet from the south gable end of the structure. *Almost a third done.*

Raising one hand to his mouth to amplify his voice, Zeb called up to Reuben, "Remember to get them as tight as you can to one another. Fall's the best time of year to be building a roof with them long grass roots."

Reuben straightened from placing the sod. "Zeb, are you sure this isn't going to leak?"

The mountain man laughed. "That grass should grow for a spell and bind them pieces together—kind of a natural thread. It won't be fully tight in a heavy rain or big snow that melts quick. And if I was you, the next four or five pieces, I would lay over the seams along the ridge pole where the two roof sides meet. Make sure them ridge caps extend below the high edge of the sod either side. That's where you'll have the biggest problems with leaks."

Reuben nodded as he lifted the next square of sod, almost losing his balance as he swung the heavy, four-inch-thick section of earth into place, its leading edge lapping over the top of the log ridge pole. Straightening up, Reuben removed his hat, wiping his forehead with a stroke of his forearm sleeve. He glanced out over Zeb's head toward where Dallas Creek rushed into the Uncompahgre, then did a double take, leaning forward, holding his hat in front of his head to break the sun. *Spotted something.*

Still looking out from the top of the roof, Reuben's voice was calm but quick. "Riders—looks like six or seven of them. Too far away to make out who they are. Zeb, pass my Sharps to Michael, and Philippe's Musketoon, too."

Zeb spun, looking down the faint trail that wound through the meadow before dropping off unseen to the Uncompahgre River. He lacked Reuben's elevated vantage point, and no riders were yet in his sight.

Taking two quick steps to the cabin wall, he grabbed Reuben's Sharps, tossing it to Michael. The boy reached up, handing it to Philippe, who turned and, in one smooth motion, pitched it to Reuben. Zeb repeated the process with Philippe's Musketoon, and then grabbed his Enfield, turning to face the still unseen visitors. Without taking his eyes off the line of meadow grass where it vanished in descent to the valley, he warned Michael, "You best come down, boy. Grab that pistol of yours and get inside the cabin. Hunker down next to a window, but don't let your face show, just one eye at the edge."

Zeb glanced quickly toward the creek near the prairie schooner. Lucy was by the fire fixing lunch. *Where's Sarah and Rebecca?* He spotted their shoulders and backs bent over in the grass on the edge of the meadow side of the willows that lined the watercourse. The women were cutting the next squares of sod, which he and Michael had been carrying over and stacking on either side of the cabin.

He started to call to them, but Reuben's voice rang out first, loud enough to be heard, but not a shout. "Rebecca, Sarah, riders coming. Rebecca, grab your rifle and get behind the wagon. Stay out of sight until we see how things evolve. Lucy, suggest you get away from that fire. The coffee will be fine. Get behind the wagon with the other women. Israel, stay in the shed where you're at. You have your Colt?"

Israel's thick drawl, muffled by the logs of the shed, came back faintly, "No, I don't. Left it in the wagon."

Behind him, Zeb heard Philippe chuckle.

Raising a hand to his forehead just under the rim of his coonskin hat, Zeb squinted past the glare of midmorning sun hanging low in the eastern sky. He could see movement, figures slowly emerging as they ascended the rise to the meadow. "Indians," he called out, "Ute, I think. Can't be sure just yet. Need to see the horses."

A minute later, the riders were in full view slightly over three hundred yards away. Zeb recognized the horses and felt the tension drain from the crook of his elbow where the Enfield rested. He looked up at Reuben and Philippe, both of them with rifles in position ready to raise to their shoulders. From the edge of one of the cabin windows, one round eye and pale, pudgy cheek poked from behind the frame. *Michael.*

"Looks like maybe Ouray and some braves. Might even have Black Mare and Chipeta with him. Two of them riders is mighty small."

The scuff of boots, slipping and catching on the sod furring strips, caused him to turn. Reuben was working his way down the roof toward the ladder. Philippe still sat cross-legged on the sod lattice support next to the last course of freshly laid sod, his Musketoon resting across his thighs, one hand on the grip, his finger across the trigger guard.

The riders were closing the distance between them at a steady but unhurried pace. Zeb recognized the stocky form of Ouray's shoulders. "Yep, Ouray for sure, and Chipeta and

Black Mare."

Behind him, Reuben jumped down with a thud from the second rung of the ladder. Seconds later, the young Prussian stood beside him. "What do you think he wants, Zeb?"

Zeb turned, taking the few steps back to the logs of the cabin wall, and laid his Enfield to rest against them. "Reuben," he said in a low voice, "lean that rifle against the wall next to mine." He moved his head slightly toward the wagon, speaking in a tone just loud enough to be heard by the women. "Rebecca, Sarah, Lucy—stay behind the wagon until I give a hint. Rebecca, keep that Sharps handy, but if I give the que, leave it behind the wagon when you come out. Don't be carrying it."

He glanced back toward the glassless window of the cabin. "Michael, you can come out. Leave your pistol right inside the door. Philippe...," he looked up at the vaquero who stared back at him with an amused grin, "you might want to lay that Enfield down in the sod next to you."

"I don't think so, *señor* Zeb," he said, his tone measured. *Mexican and Ute never did mix.*

The camp seemed approachable now, friendly even. Zeb spoke out of the side of his mouth to Reuben, never taking his eyes off the approaching riders, who were now close enough they could see faint facial features. "I reckon he's coming to see what you doing up here on Ute land."

Zeb felt the flash of Reuben's face turn toward him. "Easy, Reuben. I'm just saying it like they think. It's actually quite an honor for a sub-chief to visit your lodge, particularly with his woman folk along, but just know it ain't all friendly."

Reuben chuckled softly. "I'm glad they came up. I've been toying with an idea."

Zeb glanced at him quickly, then back to the approaching Ute. "An idea? Remember, don't you go offering him anything, or he'll have to give you something back. If he doesn't have anything, you might wind up with that Chipeta girl as your second wife."

Reuben chuckled again. "No, I have another idea. Didn't you tell me a couple of months ago not all our cattle were going to get through the winter? There is something he can give me."

"Reuben..."

"Don't worry, Zeb. I think I got this figured. And if you think I'm overstepping, just kick me in the leg."

Zeb shook his head. "Yep. They won't notice that."

Ouray was just fifty feet away, four braves trailing slightly behind him on one side, on the other, Black Mare parallel with him, but her horse a half step back. Behind her rode Chipeta. The Indians reined in, Ouray smiling and raising his hand, palm out toward them. When Reuben and Zeb returned the gesture of peace, Ouray dismounted, and the three men walked toward each other. They met, exchanging the customary Ute greeting, clasping each other's forearm and elbow, their arms moving once in unison—up, then down.

Ouray smiled and turned, looking toward the wagon. *"Donde es Ray-bec-ka."*

Reuben returned the stocky Indian's smile. "She's here somewhere close."

"Rebecca. Sarah," Zeb called out careful, not to shout

toward where he knew they were, "If you can hear me, come back to the fire. Ouray, Black Mare and Chipeta have come to visit."

Ouray smiled and nodded at the women as they appeared. Zeb noticed the Indian's eyebrows raise as he caught sight of Lucy. The sub-chief called out to Black Mare and Chipeta, "Come visit with Ray-bec-ka while Roo-bin, Zeb-Raih and I talk."

Ouray's eyes drifted above Zeb's shoulder, and he knew the Indian was looking at Philippe on the roof. Ouray's eyes narrowed. His facial muscles tensed. Then, he lowered his gaze to Reuben, and his lips stretched into a smile. "Roo-bin. This is your lodge?"

Reuben grinned. "We hope to have the roof done yet this week. He gestured at the pile of stones and mound of sand near the north gable wall. "Then, the fireplace." The Prussian turned back toward the cabin, one arm outstretched. "It's not much yet, but next year we'll expand it. With winter this close, this will just have to do to start."

Zeb watched Ouray's face as the Ute leader followed Reuben's movements, the Indian's eyes roving the cabin, the roof, the window openings, the horizontal lines of the logs and the two-stone-high foundation under the bottom course of timbers. Zeb thought he saw Ouray's eyes narrow momentarily, almost imperceptibly, when Reuben mentioned expanding the cabin.

Reuben turned back to Ouray, a wide smile on his face.

Ouray nodded and chuckled, "*Muy bien, pero* it will not fit on a *travois.* It is not movable."

Rebecca, Chipeta and Black Mare had ambled to the fire,

the three women seated on the logs, leaning toward one another talking earnestly and laughing. Sarah stood nearby with Lucy, listening, and occasionally chiming in.

Reuben interrupted his observation with a question. "Would you like to see the inside?"

Ouray grinned at him, took two long steps to the window opening, and leaned over the sill, his head in the shadow of the cabin interior, turning left, right and then up looking at the roof structure. After a moment, he raised his shoulders back from the windowsill, turning to Reuben and nodding. "*Muy bien.*" He spoke several sentences in Ute, a bit of Spanish mixed in. *Purposely cutting Philippe out of the conversation.*

Reuben turned to Zeb, his eyebrows arched in a question, not understanding the Ute. "Reuben, he said he will look forward to joining you at your lodge fire," Zeb chuckled as he interpreted, "but not until you have a lodge fire."

Reuben laughed, and Ouray nodded vigorously, laughing with him.

Reuben studied the Ute when the laughter subsided. "Ouray, we are very honored that you have come to see us, and that we are able to show you the fine things we are doing on the land where the Utes have allowed us to build our ranch."

Ouray's eyes were on Zeb's young friend, his features expressionless except for a slight upturn at the corners of his mouth. Reuben glanced at Zeb and continued, "You have given us something that has great value and is sacred, and we do not feel right receiving such a gift without returning a gift to you in thanks."

Zeb noticed the slight smile that had hovered on Ouray's lips had been replaced by a straight line, and his eyes had narrowed somewhat. *Careful Reuben.*

"Did you like the cow we left you as thank you for the wedding ceremony?"

Ouray patted his stomach. "*Si*—Roo-bin. We butchered it before moving the village to summer hunting grounds. Black Mare has fleshed the hide, and the cow's meat is salted. Different than buffalo and elk, but very good."

"Good!" Reuben smiled, "Just as we left you the cow in return for your gift of the wedding, Rebecca and I feel we should also give you something in return for your gift here...." The young man rotated his shoulders, sweeping his arm expansively across the lands. "I feel strange accepting such a gift from you and not giving you one back. I'm sure you understand." Ouray's features softened. His chin dipped once, his eyes remaining steady and unblinking on Reuben.

Zeb noticed Rebecca and Black Mare had walked from the fire, leaving the other women, Rebecca standing still, her hands on her belly, Black Mare close beside her, their heads tipped toward one another, the two of them conversing earnestly.

Reuben, who had paused, was speaking again, "We will always be friends with the Ute. I hope that our children grow strong together, share laughter, their lodges and the lands."

Zeb saw a shadow flit across Ouray's face at the mention of children. "And one day..." Reuben continued, "they can continue living side-by-side in friendship and peace.... I would like to give you and your village, if you think it a fair exchange for the use of these lands from now until our children take our place, thirty cows, so that our friends, the Tabequache, can enjoy the hides, bone and meat of the animals that we have brought to live on Ute land."

Zeb held his breath. *Could tip either way.* Ouray's eyes widened; his eyebrows raised into the wrinkles of the bronzed tan of his forehead. He stared at Reuben, then turned, looking toward the shapes with mottled color far out in the meadow, sun glistening on their turn of twisted horns. The stony set of his face eased, and a slow smile spread across his lips.

"*Treinta vaca? Para vente* winters?" Out in the meadow, a cow bawled, answered by another from the south. Ouray turned toward the sounds, then back to Reuben. He nodded. "*Si.* You shall have the promise of the Ute."

The knot in Zeb's belly untied itself with his slow, low exhale of air.

"*Beuno!*" exclaimed Reuben. "If you wish to take them now, Michael will help you," Reuben nodded with his chin at Michael twenty feet away at the far corner of the cabin. The young man's eyes were big as silver dollars, his face white, the flush gone even from his heavy cheeks.

"Michael is our best cowman. He can help your Braves cut out *trienta* of the *vacas* and show them some tricks in making them go where you wish. Can't you, Michael?" Reuben twisted toward the boy. Michael blinked rapidly, his eyes darting from Ouray to Reuben, briefly to Zeb and then back to the sub-chief and the Prussian. His open mouth closed partially and then opened again, without sound.

"Can't you, Michael?" Reuben's tone was kind, but there was a slight edge to the repeat of the question.

Michael nodded limply. "Thir, thirty c-c-cows?" The boy's voice was incredulous. *Like he's givin' away his family.*

"Yes, thirty cows, Michael. And you can show Ouray's warriors some tricks, maybe help them down the trail to where the creek meets the Uncompahgre."

Michael's eyes darted wildly between Reuben and Ouray and then to the four warriors, still mounted fifty feet away, who returned his stare impassively. His Adam's apple bobbed up and down several times, and he nodded, the fingers of one hand wringing the fingers of his other in front of the roll of his belly. The boy shot a beseeching look up at Philippe on the roof, "W-w-want to c-c-come, Philippe?" There was a tone of desperate hope in the boy's inquiry. Philippe's eyes rose briefly to Ouray and then drifted to the warriors. He shook his head. "No, muchacho. You can do this. You will be *bueno.*"

## *37*

October 3, 1855

# ℐECRETS

REBECCA WAS ENJOYING THE CASUAL CONVERSATION WITH Black Mare and Chipeta, especially since it gave her the chance to practice her Spanish. The women sat around the small fire discussing the finely polished wedding goblet adornments on the women's leather dresses, the cascading colors of late autumn and the coming winter. Sarah joined the conversation occasionally, and Lucy sat close by on the next log, nodding and exchanging smiles from time to time with Chipeta and Black Mare. Both of them regarded the portly negro woman with unabashed curiosity as Rebecca explained how she and Israel had come to be at the ranch. Chipeta was particularly impressed by the story, turning to Lucy and asking with admiration in her voice, "So, you were captured in a raid and managed to escape?"

Startled, Lucy stared at Chipeta, her expression perplexed. She began to answer but Rebecca, smiling, shot her a warning glance and answered instead. "Exactly, Chipeta! Wasn't that brave?" Lucy nodded, the sudden tension in her cheeks disappearing.

Black Mare glanced behind them toward the creek. "Ray-bec-ka, would you show me *Las Dallas* below the wagon? I have never before been to this spot with Ouray."

Rebecca tried to hide her surprise. Something in Black Mare's wide, nervous eyes and earnest stare as she posed the question led Rebecca to believe that perhaps she wished to discuss something more.

"I would love to stretch, Black Mare," Rebecca said, gesturing at the exposed square of earth where Sarah, Lucy and she had been cutting the sod slabs. "My legs are cramped." She patted her belly where it pushed above the top of the light-brown, wool skirt and against her heavy, beige, cotton shirt. "But we will have to walk slowly. I foolishly rode my horse ten days ago, and I'm a bit...well, a bit unstable."

Concerned wrinkles appeared at the corners of Black Mare's eyes, and Rebecca noticed that Sarah was staring at her, shaking her head, her lips pursed. *Sarah did tell me not to ride.*

Rebecca and Black Mare walked fifty feet from the other women, Lucy and Chipeta still visiting at the fire. Far off toward the Snaefel echoed the distant screeching of a bull elk, followed by a series of throaty grunts, barely audible over the distance. The bugle was answered faintly by another bull farther away. Rebecca smiled at Black Mare.

"That sound is truly remarkable. I had never heard an elk bugle until a month ago and had no idea what it was at first. Neither did anyone else, except Zeb, of course."

Black Mare returned her smile. "They are moving late today, heading lower to winter ground. "The call of the *wapiti* is a sound of Spirit. The cows talk, too." Her smile broadened. "And as with all things, it is the cows, usually the oldest and wisest of the herd, that makes decisions and is the first to spot danger."

Rebecca chuckled. "And of course, like us," she wagged her fingers back and forth between Black Mare and herself, "the men rarely know." Black Mare raised one hand to her lips to cover her giggle. She glanced over her shoulder back at the fire, then swung her head quickly to look toward Ouray, Zeb and Reuben.

The toe of Rebecca's boot caught in a particularly tough bunch of blue gamma grass, and she stumbled slightly, a sharp pain radiating through her midriff. She stopped, taking a deep breath and pressing both hands to the underside of her swollen belly. A step ahead, Black Mare turned quickly. Her eyes dropped to Rebecca's hands, spread wide around her abdomen. "Are you well, Ray-bec-ka?" she asked, lifting her gaze. "Are there problems with your child?" She glanced furtively again toward Ouray.

Rebecca pressed her lips together, exhaling slowly through her nose, the sharp twinges under her hands subsiding, and shook her head. "No, Black Mare. I believe I am fine, though, of course, I have no frame of reference."

Black Mare looked at her blankly, and Rebecca rephrased her response, "I've never been pregnant before, so I don't really know what's normal."

Black Mare nodded, her eyes sweeping the length of Rebecca's body before coming to rest on her pelvis. "You are very narrow there, Ray-bec-ka." She pressed her lips together and looked into Rebecca's eyes. "It is something to keep in mind." She paused, then added hastily, "but I'm sure everything will be good. When does your child expect to see the sun?"

It took Rebecca a moment to understand the question. "Oh! When is the baby due?" She giggled and leaned closer to Black Mare, her voice just above a whisper. "I'm not sure. I think in December or January—the winter months." Black Mare smiled, a slight blush coloring her cheeks. She gave a knowing nod.

"When we are with our men often, it is difficult to know exactly when life begins."

Rebecca blushed, a warmth rising up her throat as the image of Reuben's heated skin on hers flashed across her mind.

Black Mare glanced quickly over her shoulder, leaning still closer to Rebecca. "Since we are sharing secrets, and we are friends, I wish to share one with you, Ray-bec-ka." Her lower lip trembled, and a slight quiver came to her cheeks. "You said when you were leaving the village after your wedding that I would have children. One moon later, I was indeed with child."

Pleased, Rebecca smiled widely. "That's wonderful, Black Mare. See? I told you!"

The Indian woman wagged her head slowly, looking down at the tall grass around her moccasins. She raised her head, a tear slowly drifting down her cheek, her eyes blinking rapidly. "I am not with child anymore."

Despite herself, Rebecca gasped, raising her hand to her mouth "Oh, Black Mare, I'm so sorry."

Black Mare squeezed her eyes shut tightly. Her lids

opened slowly as she brushed away another tear with a finger. "No one knows of this, Ray-bec-ka—not even Ouray. You, my friend, and the *midiwiene,* Cougar Woman, only. She said this might happen." Black Mare swallowed and continued in a conspiratorial whisper, "I could not share, even with my husband, to spare him disappointment. I could not share with the other women in the tribe, or it will not remain a secret." She sighed deeply. "But I need to share." She lifted one hand, placing it gently against Rebecca's shoulder. "I hope you do not mind my burden."

Rebecca covered Black Mare's hand with her own, "I do not mind at all. I am honored I am your friend and that you trust me."

Black Mare nodded, her voice husky with the constriction of her throat. She took a deep breath, "Cougar Woman says that if I become with child again, or if this child had not left early, it is likely that one or both of us will die. There is something not right inside me."

Rebecca struggled to absorb the momentous, intensely personal information Black Mare had shared. She gazed into the distance at the dark-green masses of conifers, gray stone faces and golden aspen shimmer of the Uncompahgre, distracted by the thoughts she too had over the last several months. *Thoughts I have shared with no one.*

"Black Mare," Rebecca spoke slowly and carefully, "there is no assurance that things will turn out badly for either you or your baby if...when you get pregnant again." She leaned close to Black Mare, her voice a whisper, "I shall share a secret with you, also. I'm very worried. I know very little about these matters. Lucy," she gestured to the side with her chin toward the fire, "seems to know quite a bit. Sometimes, I see her watching me when she thinks I'm not looking. Her face is very serious and concerned, which increases my worry. And I have sharp pains often, particularly with any sudden movement, like just a few minutes ago when I tripped."

Black Mare blinked, slid her hand down Rebecca's arm to her hand and squeezed. She tried to smile, the trembling still in her lips distorting the attempt. She squeezed Rebecca's hand again.

Ouray's voice rang out from the cabin. "Black Mare, Chipeta—we leave to catch up with the village. Spotted Pony, Wolf Tooth and Four Arrows will be behind us," his voice boomed proudly, "moving our new cattle."

Black Mare turned back to Rebecca, locking eyes with hers." We share secrets, Ray-bec-ka—and worries. In the end, Spirit decides all things. I will likely not see you again until the season of the moon of thunderstorms. I hope all goes well. I will be thinking of you from winter camp in the Little Medicine.

Rebecca returned the pressure of Black Mare's hand. "Yes, my friend, we have shared secrets, and more, only as two women sharing trust can do. I will be thinking of you, too. You're right, Black Mare. In the end, God will determine."

# CHAPTER
## *38*

October 3, 1855

# *S*PIRIT PROVIDES

THE COOLING NIGHT AIR WAS TINGED WITH DAMPNESS. Drawing the blanket up to her chin, Sarah tilted her shoulders toward the fire as she watched Israel scrape the last of the venison and scallions from his plate. In the glow of the fire, his dark skin seemed framed in silver by his whiskers and curly salt-and-pepper hair.

The old man straightened his thin frame on the log and took a deep breath, exhaling it in a contented sigh, "Mr. Zeb, you shootin' that doe was a mighty tasty idea."

Zeb looked up from his plate from where he sat next to Israel, nodded once, smiled, then bent back down to his food.

"And Lordy, what a shot! One second that deer was just a shadow on the ridge sloping up from the cabin, and the next you was leaning up against the logs with that long-barreled rifle of yours."

Sarah smiled when Zeb muttered, "Enfield," as he raised another forkful to his mouth.

"Well, whatever that rifle is, that had to be three hundred yards."

Sitting close to Israel on his other side, Lucy chuckled mischievously. "Maybe you should tell Mr. Zeb about that deer you killed."

Israel's head snapped toward his wife; his eyebrows creased in a warning plea.

Lucy grinned back at Israel. "Don't you be looking at me that way, Israel. You don't want to hold nothing back from these fine folks." Lucy glanced around the fire at everyone to make sure she had their attention, her grin widening.

Sarah raised one hand over her mouth to stifle a laugh when Israel sighed deeply, shaking his head, his expression clearly one of distressed resignation. Tearing her eyes from Israel, Sarah looked around the fire. Except for Michael, all had stopped eating, their eyes shifting expectantly between the elderly couple.

Satisfied everyone was paying attention, Lucy cackled, "Let me tell you. First off we came down over some big ol' mountain. Then we followed this creek up from that river..." She looked at Israel, "What did you say the name of that river was?"

"The Yampa." Israel's tone was glum.

"It was muddy and high, so we was lookin' for clear water to catch some trout cause our supplies were about down to nothing. We ran into this man, tall, broad shouldered, had a scar over his lip, long brown hair, looked part Indian."

Sarah saw Zeb's head snap up. The mountain man bent forward to see around Israel, his eyes fixed on Lucy, who was continuing her story, her hands punctuating her words. "He had this young, blonde girl with him. We reckoned she was fourteen or fifteen. Pulled a gun on us at first, then invited us to share their fire and cook up their trout with ours."

"Pardon me, Lucy," Zeb interrupted, his eyes tense, his mouth a grim line under the fall of his mustache, "this man ever tell you what his name was?"

Lucy looked at him and blinked. "Sure enough did, Mr. Zeb. I was getting to that. He called himself Black Feather."

Reuben's fork fell to his plate with a clunk, "Black Feather?" He and Zeb exchanged looks. Rebecca's eyebrows arched over wide eyes, but she was too startled to speak.

Lucy peered around the fire, "Y'all know Mr. Black Feather?"

"Yep, we do." Zeb's voice was flat. "Keep on with the story, Lucy."

Lucy's fading smile indicated she sensed a shift in the mood around the fire. "Well, he said this girl was his niece, but me and Israel didn't believe that. She hadn't been tidied up, her hair combed or brushed in quite a spell. I fussed over her for a bit, got the tangles out of that pretty blonde hair and cleaned up her face."

Sarah glanced around the fire as Lucy spoke. Rebecca looked less startled, but she, Reuben and Zeb were all bent forward in rapt attention. Philippe appeared to be listening but disinterested. Michael was spooning food into his mouth, occasionally glancing over his plate at Lucy as he wolfed down his third helping.

"Please continue," Reuben urged.

"In return for me showing some kindness to that po' chile, Mr. Black Feather gave Israel that pistol, and ten bullets. Said that's all he had."

Zeb and Reuben exchanged looks.

"And that's all?" Zeb's voice was incredulous, "He didn't ask you for nothing? Didn't threaten you?"

Lucy shook her head.

"What happened then?" asked Rebecca.

"We went our separate ways," said Lucy slowly, her eyes drifting around the fire at her audience, "but what I was leading up to is Israel and that pistol."

Israel hunched forward, talking down to his cracked, worn boots, "And you make sure to tell them that I ain't never fired a gun before."

Lucy chortled. "He was maybe ten steps from a big ol' wide tree. Missed it the first time. Managed to hit it the next two, but nowhere near the knots he was aimin' at. Then, some days later, we was just settin' up camp, and this mama deer and her young'un walked right by us. The little one was maybe twenty feet away. Israel grabbed for that gun from his belt, finally got it unstuck and shot that little deer three times." She laid one thick hand on Israel's bony knee, gazing at him adoringly, "and it sure was tasty, though..." her voice had a tease in it, "a few days later, he missed a rabbit, even closer."

Israel smiled at her, patting her hand on his knee, then looked around the fire, "Now you knows why I only had three bullets that night we came up here."

Grinning now, Philippe tried to cover a laugh by pretending to cough.

"Is that the last you saw of Black Feather?" Zeb was *not* laughing, which didn't surprise Sarah.

Lucy's eyes widened at his hard tone. She opened her

mouth to speak, but Israel cut her off. "No, Mr. Zeb. It weren't. Might've been three weeks later or so. We was following a little creek off the White River; windy, fast, up a narrow valley with brushy hills; and we came upon where there been a fight. Five dead Indians. That Black Feather man was under a ledge tore up bad by two arrows."

And?" Zeb prompted.

"Well, Lucy patched him up, but we was both sure he was a goner. Somebody had been there not long before us. Little girl was gone, her horse dead, no saddle. I picked up that musket, tomahawk and knife off them Indians. We left him with food and water." Israel and Lucy exchanged glances, both of them wagging their heads. "But I doubt he ever got to eat or drink much."

Reuben leaned farther forward, "You say five Indians dead? Black Feather killed them all?"

Israel shook his head. "No, no. I don't know how many he got, but whoever was there before us surely kilt a few of them. One of them braves practically had his head cut off."

Sarah gasped. She sought out Zeb's eyes, but his gaze was pinned on Israel. Michael stopped eating, his eyes wide over his plate. The grin fell from Philippe's face. Reuben asked the question on everyone's mind. "By a sword or a saber?"

Israel nodded slowly, turning to Lucy with a puzzled expression.

"Did you see this other person?" Reuben pressed.

"Maybe. Before we got to that creek, we was headin' down the White. Far out, a mile or two, saw two riders— one small, one tall—on what we thought might've been Black Feather's black horse. Figured it to be him, till later."

*Johannes?* Sarah looked around the fire. Everyone was exchanging startled glances. Reuben slapped his knee. "Johannes!"

Zeb nodded. "Sure sounds like it." He glanced at Sarah way before locking his eyes back on Israel. "And you're sure Black Feather is dead?"

Israel shook his head. "No, I ain't sure. He was breathin' when we left, but not by much. We don't think he lasted the day."

Lucy nodded at her husband, the firelight glistening on a tear sliding down the thick roll of her cheek.

Israel's eyes darted around the fire. "How do you all know this Black Feather man?"

Zeb stood, tossing his plate next to the fire ring. The tin clanged as it bounced off the stones. "We run into him a time or two."

It was clear by Israel and Lucy's startled expressions that they wanted to know more. *How much,* Sarah wondered, *will Zeb tell them?*

Zeb pursed his lips. He stroked his mustache and stared out into the darkness. "We'll tell you about it sometime. Just know you folks is lucky."

Sarah shivered. Zeb was right to leave it be.

Zeb looked around the fire, a slight, forced smile playing on his lips. "More important, my bones tell me there's snow coming. By the look of those mare tail clouds to the west, and the damp in the chill tonight, snow'll be here in the next few days. Matter of fact, we're overdue."

He looked over at Reuben. "Lucky, too, since we just finished the last of them roofs on the shed and cabin yesterday."

Zeb's gaze shifted back to Lucy. "Lucy, I notice you've been out gathering roots and herbs. Looks like to me you're familiar with such things."

Lucy nodded. "With Miss Rebecca and Miss Sarah due here not too far off," she turned to smile at Rebecca, then Sarah, "I figured there might be a need for some cocklebur, black western chokecherry, prickly pear and yucca."

The medicinal uses of these plants were foreign to Sarah, but Lucy seemed to have some knowledge, and that was a comfort. Zeb glanced at Sarah before nodding at Lucy. "That was right smart. Might be a few other things growin' out there you're not familiar with, comin' from those flatlands like you have."

Zeb turned his attention to Reuben. "Maybe in the morning I'll spend a few hours with Lucy and show her some things that might come in handy for all of you. You're out of potatoes, and you're gonna need some plants, so you don't get scurvy. And there's some others that are medicines or good to touch up your food with."

He turned to Sarah. "I see you got a couple buckets of those chokecherries like I suggested."

His eyes softened as he looked at her. She was sure of it. She smiled up at him from across the fire. "I did, Zeb—two buckets full."

This time, there was no doubt that the mountain man's smile was for her.

"Good. I bet Lucy here can show you how to dry them, so they keep. You can mix them with that jerked meat, some of that rendered fat, make some pemmican, use them for toppings and all sorts of things. And since Israel has done such a good job of getting everything in the shed in its right place, the rest of you might want to get everything moved out of the prairie schooner and into the cabin."

Reuben rose from his log. "I was thinking the same, Zeb. Sarah and Rebecca can't lift much so me, Philippe, Michael and Israel can move everything out of the wagon, and get the heavy stuff in place in the cabin. Sarah and Rebecca can get the smaller things straightened out and put where they want them. We can get that R.R. Finch and Sons stove set up and run the flue. We got plenty of bits and pieces of logs to start a decent woodpile."

Still seated, Philippe peered up from under his sombrero. "*Señor* Reuben, what about the hay for the cows?"

Reuben's lips pressed together, and his cheeks tensed. His eyes flicked to Zeb, then Philippe. "I think we get that stove working, lay in a big supply of wood and hope this snow Zeb thinks is coming melts off quick. Then, we'll see what we can do on the hay. We have that thatch cover all set up."

Philippe shook his head. "But *señor* Reuben, *no tienen* any hay to put under it."

Zeb ignored the vaquero, instead speaking to Reuben. "You got one of the three things done you need to get through the winter, Reuben—the roof. Next thing you need is heat. The four of you, if you put in two or three long days. Ought to be able to stockpile enough to keep that place warm for two or three months at least, which brings us to the third thing you need to have...."

Sarah noticed Zeb had everyone's attention, even

Philippe's. "You need food." Zeb gestured at the fire, "The rest of your supplies are low, 'cept for flour and salt. That deer ain't gonna last you a week." Zeb stopped talking and stared at Reuben, who pressed his lips together and turned to Michael.

"Once we get that stove and fuel handled, then Michael, you pick out the two biggest, fattest cows out there." Reuben sighed. "Bring them back here close to camp, but downwind, and we'll butcher them. We'll salt part of the meat, smoke the rest and make some jerky like we did on the wagon train."

Michael looked like he was going to cry.

"You might want to make sure you kill them under a good stiff limb of a cottonwood or aspen," Zeb advised. "Makes it a sight easier if you can hang them quarters when you cut 'em up."

Sarah watched him gesture out at the dark mass of the cabin, struck by the realization of how intently she watched his every move, how much she valued his experience.

"You can use those pulleys we were using for the logs," he continued. "Anything you don't have butchered each night, you can raise up high with the pulley and tie it off at least ten to twelve feet off the ground, so a bear can't get at 'em, though I 'spect most of them are already holed up for the winter.

"I'll pitch in moving everything out of the prairie schooner. With all of us working, we ought to have it all in the cabin midday if we start at daybreak." His eyes fell to hers. This time, his look was genuinely warm. *Yes, a fine man.*

His eyes shifted to Reuben. "I'm headed up to my cabin, but you're comin' with me, Reuben. See if we can get into some elk on the way up, so I can show you how to kill them. There's a knack to it and a skill you got to learn. Most of them are already moving down, but I'm still hearin' a bugle here and there, so there's some stragglers still up high. That'll give you two cow hides and an elk hide, which will come in handy for all sorts of things, and that elk meat's mighty tasty."

Sarah caught Lucy and Israel exchanging a long, nervous look below Zeb. *They're wondering where they fit in.*

Reuben caught the old couple's shared glance. A kind smile played on his face. "Didn't you say you don't have any plans to be anywhere else, Israel?"

The old man returned his gaze across the fire. His wife was staring at him, her look anxious, the woman's grip on his knee tightening.

Israel rose, his stature short next to Zeb's. "No, Mr. Reuben, we got no plans." There was a slight, apprehensive crack in his voice. Lucy had moved her hand from his knee to her lap, her fingers now woven together, her eyes darting from Reuben to her husband.

Reuben's smile widened. "Well, the two of you have been a great help over the last two weeks. I think I speak for everyone," his head swiveled around the fire, "when I say we'd be pleased to have you stay at the ranch. Sounds like, Israel, we'll have some hide that needs tanning, you can sure help us with that fireplace, and there's woodwork to do on the windows, get the shutters in, figure out something to close them off with, cloth or skins maybe, keep the heat in and the wind out."

He looked quickly at Rebecca, adding, "since they don't yet have glass." Sarah noticed how he emphasized the word *yet*, the small, passing interaction triggering an acute awareness of how alone she was.

Reuben fastened another kindly look on Lucy. "It appears you might be just the help Sarah and Rebecca need. And you sure do make good biscuits." The worried press of Lucy's lips eased into a grin.

Reuben looked again at each of them around the fire. "If no one has any objections, and since the cabin will be more than a little crowded, I think with the prairie schooner cleaned out, fixed up with some bedding, some oil lamps and some extra blankets, it will work for Lucy and Israel till we get more built next year."

He smiled at the elderly couple. "You can come in the cabin for meals or anytime you want, and if those oil lamps can't keep the wagon warm when it's bitter cold, spend those nights with all of us."

Sarah liked Israel and Lucy; his steady disposition, common sense and apparently never-ending hard work, Lucy's jovial chatter and extensive womanly knowledge of all things. She felt an affirming stir in the mound of her belly, *and hopefully, she knows as much about birthing as she does about plants and food.*

Smiling at Lucy, she said, "I think that's a grand idea, Reuben."

All the other heads around the fire nodded. Philippe grinned, his teeth showing below the fire shadow of his hat. Michael smiled and stuttered, "Y-y-yes...and Is-Israel, c-c-can you sh-show me m-m-more of that wh-whittling?"

Israel threw a warm smile at Michael. "I sure enough can."

Lucy clasped her hands to her bosom, tears streaking down both cheeks. "Oh, thank you. We been plum worried. You people have been terribly kind to us, after we came here out of nowhere in the dark of night, sharing your food with us, letting us sleep in that wagon...." Her voice trailed off, and she sniffled. Israel laid a hand softly on her shoulder.

The rim of Philippe's sombrero rose, his face in full firelight. He wore a broad grin. "I agree with *señor* Reuben and *la señorita*. The two of you have brought smiles to this fire. You have courage to do what you have done, to come so far. I, Philippe Reyes, understand what it's like to be on the run." His eyes moved between the two of them, "*Y ustedes trabajan duro.*"

He looked up lazily at Zeb. To Sarah, his smile seemed more of a smirk. "*Señor* Zeb and I disagree on some things...." Both men shifted their eyes to her, and she suddenly felt embarrassed, pressured, even ashamed. Their stares drifted back to one another, Philippe completing his thought, "But we agree on this. You don't have to run anymore. You are home."

Her trembling lips pressed together, Lucy was trying not to cry. Israel, one hand still squeezing her shoulder, blinked several times rapidly, one dark cheek twitching. His eyes rose skyward, his lips mouthing, "Thank you, Lord."

Zeb squeezed the shorter man's shoulder. "Spirit provides, Israel."

Reuben stepped around the fire and extended his hand to

the old man. Israel took it, and they shook firmly, looking into one another's eyes. Reuben grinned, "I guess this is your official welcome to the ranch." He chuckled. "Such that it is. You and I can get together tomorrow and figure out your monthly pay."

Israel's head jerked. "Pay?"

The young Prussian pushed his broad-brimmed hat back on his forehead, stared at Israel for a moment and then at Lucy who was looking up at him, her mouth hanging open, watery eyes wide. "Yes, pay," said Reuben firmly. "You two are free men and Americans. Free men don't work for free." He smiled wryly. "And there's a pile of work."

Sarah thought Israel was about to speak, but he stopped, staring at Reuben, and then around the fire, the bottom rims of his eyes brimming. Sarah watched, transfixed. *Much has been resolved for you, tonight, Israel and Lucy.* She looked at Zeb, *so steady,* then Philippe, *so handsome* and finally at Rebecca, *my best friend.* All were engrossed in the emotional scene between Reuben, Lucy and Israel. Sarah sighed, looking down toward the ankle moccasins Zeb had given her when they were coming west, the double-stitched toes just visible under the roundness of her belly. *Philippe and Zeb, it is time I resolve things between us, too.*

CHAPTER

## 39

October 4, 1855

# CALL OF THE WAPITI

ZEB AND REUBEN RODE SIDE-BY-SIDE FOLLOWING THE TRAIL that wound with the course of Dallas Creek down to the river. Lahn and Buck walked in cadence four feet apart, their front shoulders parallel. Tendrils of thin, translucent mare's tail clouds stretched out over the looming Uncompahgre range, filtering the autumn sun.

Zeb stared at the feather edges of the clouds, tiny prisms shifting and shimmering in their wisps with each step and the changing angle of the sun. He glanced over at Reuben. The young man's head was turned away, looking downvalley toward the Wetterhorn. A heavier jacket wrapped around a long-handled axe was tied securely behind the Prussian's saddle. *Ain't no tenderfoot anymore, but still has lots of learning to do.* "Looks like to me we're right on time. I'd put it about midday."

Reuben turned his head to him. "Moving all that from the wagon to the cabin went faster than I thought." He grinned, partly at the way Buck flicked an ear back at the sound of his voice. "Once it was all spread out around the cabin, it didn't seem like much at all. Thanks for helping, Zeb. I know you're wanting to get back up to your place. I'm sure you have a lot to do."

Zeb nodded. "Wasn't much worried about moving all those goods with five of us plus Lucy, but where we picked up time was how quick that Mexican rigged that flue pipe for the stove. That thing was god awful solid and heavy. Four of us on those poles we put under it, and we had to stop twice in a hundred feet."

Reuben kept his eyes fixed on the trail in front of them while Zeb spoke, his jaw set thoughtfully and his voice colored with a tinge of concern.

"I was surprised at how small the fire chamber was," he said. "I don't think you can fit more than three to four small to medium-size logs in at a time. I sure hope it'll keep the inside of that place fairly warm."

Zeb threw him a quick glance. "No need worry, son. I've seen those stoves in action. Not that exact make and model but things real close. I think they was called Hopkins and Duff stoves. You get those logs going, and that iron heats up. You just may have to open the shutters on one of them windows except on the coldest days." He kept his eyes focused on the lower flanks of the mountains downstream as he rode. "It'll give you enough time to be slow and steady on the fireplace. It ain't life or death anymore. If you don't build it right, it'll smoke you out, and you'll be fighting it forever."

Reuben's palomino kept a steady pace alongside Buck. Zeb felt the young man turn to him as he spoke. "I thought the women did a nice job of setting the place up, too. I think it might just work."

Zeb kept his eyes on the opposite ridge. "It'll work just fine, Reuben—crowded, but just fine. What did you think of the Mexican's idea on trying to get up another real small, shed roof cabin for him and Michael, just a door and window before the big weather sets in?"

Reuben shifted in his saddle. "I think Philippe's idea was good. I just don't know if there's time, with no hay put up and snow if you're right. Although, with four of us working on it, now that you've taught us how, and we've done for ourselves, we might get it up in a week. I do like his idea of using it to store hand tools when we add to the cabin or build a house." He sighed. "Whenever that will be."

Zeb studied the Prussian's profile for a long moment. "It'll be what it'll be, Reuben. You get the basic cake baked, then you can worry about the icing and, yep, it's gonna snow. Mare's tails never lie. When we saw them last night, they were probably one hundred miles west of the Snaefel..." He raised his arm and pointed up and east. Buck flicked both ears forward. "Now, they are over the Uncompahgre. It's comin' quick. You've been awful lucky this far. If your luck holds, we'll get this snow and then we'll get a week or two of Indian summer. It'll melt off in time for that grass to dry since you can't cut or put it up wet, and you can get some feed in."

The young man's voice was level and calm but etched with unmistakable anxiety. "You told me a couple months ago you thought we were going to lose some cattle. How many do you think that might be?"

Zeb raised one hand and stroked his mustache. "I don't rightly know, son. Depends on the feed, how deep the snow, how cold the winter, how long it lasts." He glanced over at Reuben. "I don't think it will be less than half if you're lucky, and if you're not...could be most or all of them. That was right clever of you getting' rid of thirty of 'em and getting Ouray's promise on you staying there and not being bothered for twenty years." He chuckled. "Yep, right smart. Whatever happens to the rest of the herd, them thirty cows bought you a whole lot of value."

Reuben fell silent. *Probably thinking about having to go all the way east, buy more cows, move 'em way back here.* Zeb knew worry when he saw it. Below the shadow cast by the wide brim of his brown hat, already showing signs of wear, Reuben's lips were pursed and puckered, his cheek muscles working from side to side, no doubt pondering Zeb's words.

"And besides, that magic you did with Ouray, I was right pleased you decided to let Lucy and Israel stay."

Reuben's head jerked toward him. "Why wouldn't we? They work as hard as any of us. That Lucy is always making everyone laugh, and anyone with any of Israel's skills would be hard to come by in a town, never mind out here. With him knowin' how to do all the stuff he knows, I figure they are a gift to us, not vice versa."

"They have grit, no doubt. Been through all they been through, probably getting whipped, looked down on by folks, no pay, probably little food, some broken down hobble to live in, and then, at their age to come all this way." Zeb shook his head, thinking about it.

Reuben lifted his hat, holding it up against the sun.

"Wild country, ain't it?" Zeb said, following Reuben's gaze southeast toward the top of the peaks.

Reuben scrunched the hat back down, adjusting the brim with one hand. "It sure is—and beautiful. Father's scout tried to describe it in his letters, but he didn't come close."

"Just remember son...," Zeb turned to look at the younger man, and their eyes met, "it may be awful damn purty, but it can kill you in the blink of an eye. And, if you die, there ain't a single leaf on a single aspen tree that will so much as quiver. Kinda like a horse. Even the prettiest, fastest ones, the ones you've known forever and think are unflappable...they can change just that fast. Quicker 'n a woman and just as dangerous." An image of red hair framing blue eyes and freckles floated across Zeb's mind.

THE HORSES' HOOVES WERE STILL WET FROM CROSSING THE fast, shallow current of the Uncompahgre. Zeb watched Reuben edge Lahn southeast toward the trail leading to his cabin, and the young man was ahead thirty feet upstream when Zeb reined in Buck and called out, "No, Reuben, we're headin' north."

Reuben reined in Lahn, looking over his shoulder with a puzzled expression. He wheeled the palomino around and trotted twenty feet back. "Thought you said we were headed up toward the cabin?"

"That's what I said last night, but this is today. Elk have a habit of interfering with your plans since they got their own. You notice I stopped several times this morning, kind of facing off to the north?"

Reuben nodded. "I did."

"Well, them bugles I was hearing yesterday were southeast of us, more between us and my place, but this morning, they're north of us. Headed down, probably feel the snow comin'. Figure two herds. It's late for them bulls not to be in bachelor groups, but for whatever reason, these two bulls are still hanging with their cows. I think there's one herd the other side of the river, one group on this side movin' north. Late to be hearing bugling, too..." he grinned at Reuben, "but makes it a hell of a lot easier to kill them, particularly this time of year when they're headed to their winter grounds. Some of the herds up in this country go all the way down to the Gunnison. Don't mean nothing to an elk to travel with those long legs. They can go twenty miles overnight, easy."

Reuben looked at him, wide-eyed as a calf. Zeb flicked his reins and Buck started downstream, Reuben doing the same with Lahn.

Zeb constantly watched as they rode—to the front, to the side, above—reining in from time to time to take a closer look at something that caught his eye. He knew Reuben was watching, studying.

"When you're looking for critters, either in the flats or in the timber, look for horizontal lines. Just about everything else is vertical. And if you see them, stop. Don't move a muscle. If you got to move, move like time don't matter. Animals can see fast movement right off, but they don't pick up when you move extra slow. And keep the wind in your face."

"Even a boy from Prussia knows that much, Zeb."

"You don't know elk, Reuben. They're wilder than what you're used to."

"Wilder than a boar?"

"Different kind of wild. These critters don't much care for man stink, particularly elk. Their eyes aren't great, and they're so big they make lots of noise. Unless they're standing still or bedded, their ears don't help much. But they can smell you five miles away."

He shifted in the saddle toward Reuben. "And if they do, they're gone, and you'll almost never catch up. Now, if you're huntin' mule deer, that's a different story. They can smell you, but their noses aren't near as keen as an elk's. But they can see like an eagle. Sometimes, elk and mule deer will bunch up together in the same feeding or bedding area." He laughed. "You get that combination and you might as well set up camp till one or the other leaves, or just go home."

"Another thing, Reuben...this is important. Ain't no animal on the planet other than us that walks on two legs. And every other critter on earth knows what two legs means. Staying mounted helps, kneeling down right away if you spot something, keepin' your legs hid behind a tree if you stop when you're moving through the timber. If you've made yourself a stand, hoping to bushwhack them where they come for food or water, make sure everything from your chest down is behind something that sits between you and where you think they're gonna come out."

Reuben titled his face toward the timber, then shifted his gaze down along the toe of the rise they were following. "The deer around our farm were a bit more used to people."

Zeb laughed softly. "Yep, I imagine so."

Reuben chuckled.

Wafting up the river toward them came a shrill scream, starting low, its pitch rising, ending in a long trailing whistle, then followed by a series of throaty grunts. Zeb put out his hand, and they reined in. He leaned over to Reuben. "From now on, ain't no talking except for a low whisper. They generally take that just for wind. If they hear your voice, normal like, or any sound like metal on metal that ain't natural, it's almost as bad as them smellin' you."

Reuben's eyes were wide, a slight anticipatory smile playing on his lips. He moved his shoulders and head slowly from side to side, trying to see through the scattered trees in front of them.

Zeb beckoned with his finger, and Reuben leaned toward him, Zeb doing the same toward the Prussian, both of them tipped in their saddles, so their faces were less than a foot apart. "Nice and easy, draw that Sharps from the scabbard," Zeb whispered. "I'll do the same with mine. If we ride into them, won't be no time and if we stalk 'em on foot, it will be just one less movement when we get closer."

Zeb peered through the weaving branches of the cottonwood, tall alder, scattered pine and aspen. A fine snow of falling gold and red leaves sifted between the trees. "Figure we got three hours, maybe, till dark. These elk are likely bedded, though they will move early with this storm coming. Don't think that bull is a big one. Grunts just don't have enough chest to 'em. Since this is your first time on the trail of the wapiti, you take just the first elk you can, no matter bull or cow—even a calf, if that's all you have a clear shot at."

Reuben nodded, his eyes straining ahead of them. He brushed his heels gently against Lahn's flank, but Zeb reached out, indicating he should wait. Reuben flashed a look at him, an impatient twitch in the side of his face, his eyes narrowed as if to say, what are we waiting for?

"Listen, Reuben," Zeb's voice was barely a hiss, "remember what I'm telling you. Patience kills elk. Take your time. Be sure of your shot. These ain't no roe deer. These are big, tough animals. Shoot for the neck or the head. You will either kill 'em, or you'll miss. Anywhere else, unless you break both front shoulders, and you could be following them to some hellish hidey-hole five miles away. Ain't no fun, the meat will be tainted and gettin' them out is even worse."

They began to weave through the trees, the horses at a slow walk, Zeb taking the lead and slowly working Buck up the contours, the butts of their rifles perched on their thighs. The wind shifted more northwest, coming harder now, in pulses and spurts, twisting the increasing amount of airborne leaves in whirling spirals between gaps in the trees.

The wind shifted again, and Zeb smelled the sharp, pungent odor of the bull somewhere ahead of them. *Ain't too far, now.* He reined in Buck, motioning with just his hand down by his hip for Reuben to come up alongside. He raised a forefinger to his nose and tapped, and then pointed in front of them, his hand still by his face. Reuben raised his chin, sniffing, moving his head back and forth, then his eyes widened, and he nodded, his face animated, a slight flush rising up the tan of his neck.

Ahead of them in the broken timber, the bull bugled again, its winding scream and follow-up grunts echoing off the tree trunks. Zeb glanced at Reuben. The young man's eyes were wide, focused and searching ahead of them. Zeb raised one hand out slowly and tapped him on the thigh, raising the same hand slowly back to his face, raising one finger, then a second. *About two hundred yards.* He motioned Reuben to dismount. They tied the horses off and then slowly, Zeb leading, they moved between the trees, stopping every few steps behind one trunk or the other, peering ahead around the bark, listening, smelling, looking.

They crept through a small creek, making sure not to splash, and then up a gentle incline that formed the northern boundary of the drainage. Toward the top of the lightly timbered rise lay the trunk of a large, old pine, felled years before by age, wind and waterlogged roots.

Keeping his hand close to his chest, Zeb gestured toward the old trunk that lay catty corner across the top of the ridge. As they stole closer to the log, Zeb hunched down to a crouch, the palm of his hand parallel with the ground, raising and lowering it several times.

*Real easy now, Reuben. Step-by-step. Quiet.*

From over the rise, they could hear the occasional snap of breaking branches, and the mews of cow elk filtering faintly from the other side of the log. They moved, shoulders stooped toward the ground, one step at a time, stopping and listening, toward the log until they were hunkered down behind it. With hand signs, Zeb told Reuben to take off his hat.

Hat removed, Reuben started to raise up his shoulders, but Zeb pressed them down, shaking his head. He gave Reuben the hand sign for slow and pointed at the young man's Sharps, indicating to have it ready and slide it over the log first. Reuben's thumb moved to the hammer to cock it. Zeb covered his thumb with his hand, shaking his head again and then pointing at his ear. Reuben nodded that he understood.

Zeb counted on his fingers, one, two, three and together they rose, in slow motion, inch by inch up the near side of the log until just the tops of their heads and their eyes were above the smooth, gray, weathered wood of the dead pine. Fifty yards below them were twenty or more cows and calves, a spiked bull, and the herd bull, his antlers not large but wide and thick. One of the rear cows was larger, her gray hide darker than the others. *The lead cow, she's the one we have to fool.*

Reuben eased the Sharps over the log several inches at a time, its forestock brushing the curve of the wood. Zeb laid his Sharps down. *The less movement, the better.*

Reuben snugged the curved butt of the rifle into his shoulder, nestling his cheek tight to the stock. The barrel swung slightly, first at a cow and then with a slight shift toward the bull, whose neck and front quarters had become clearly visible seventy-five yards away between two aspen trees, the golden hue of his hide standing out against the dark, blue-green of several sapling spruces behind him.

Zeb whispered, his voice barely audible, even to him. "Remember, Reuben, the neck."

Reuben's thumb found the hammer, slowly pulling it back

until it cocked, the slight sound barely audible to Zeb, but the lead cow snapped up her head from where she had been warily grazing on fescue and gamma grass. *Looking right at us. Don't make a sound, Reuben. Don't move except that trigger finger. And don't be deedaddling.*

The Sharps roared in unison with the lead cow's sharp, loud alarm bark, followed by the sodden thwack of a bullet finding flesh. The bull's front quarters collapsed on folded front legs. The other elk scattered, yellow rumps disappearing in the trees, breaking limbs, panicked mews and alarm barks ricocheting through the timber.

Reuben started to rise, but Zeb pulled him down.

"Before you go down there, son, reload. Never want to go check on something you shot without another round ready. I seen them go down just like that, then jump up and hightail it for miles when you walk up."

Reuben's fingers shook slightly as he reloaded. *His hands don't tremble one bit when he shoots at another man, but just a tinge of buck fever with these animals.* Zeb chuckled to himself. *Just like me.*

---

ZEB LAID HIS KNIFE ON THE ELK'S NECK, THEN WIPED HIS bloody hands and forearms on the grass around the bull's body and stood. The elk's guts, rolled to the side of the spread-eagled carcass, steamed in the chill of descending dusk. The white bark of the aspen reflected the dying day's last burst of life and color in the same bright pink as the thickening clouds above them.

Reuben wiped his hands on the grass, too, then stood. Zeb slapped him on the back. "Congratulations, son, our first elk. I need to start skinning it while we still got a little light. Go back and get the horses and I'll show you why I had you bring that axe."

Zeb pointed, his finger running the length of the elk's body. "We'll take off his head up by the chin where we pulled his throat out. You don't do that, and that meat up there will spoil. Then, we'll take the top of his skull with them antlers. And then we'll split him lengthwise with that axe right down the middle of his spine. I'll take them legs off below the knees, and we'll lash one half over Buck and the other over Lahn."

A particularly strong, cold blast of wind shot through the trees, laying nearly flat the bloody grass around the elk.

"Get those horses, Reuben. Skinnin' in the dark ain't no fun. I need to get back to my cabin before the snow comes and you need to do the same. We can leave the half on Buck down toward the bottom of Dallas Creek and cover it with the hide. Have the men hang that first half when you get back and while they're doing that, you can ride down with Michael or Philippe and fetch that second half. Put the halves right next to them cattle quarters they should have strung up. Them antlers you can use for decorations in your new house, and if you ever need to make some tools or knives out of them, just take them off the wall." Zeb laughed. "Kinda handy that way."

Reuben bent, smoothing one hand down the long, coarse, golden-brown hair along the elk's ribs. Zeb squatted next to him. Reuben looked over to him in the fading light,

"Beautiful animals, Zeb."

"They are that, Reuben, and it's always good, just like you doing here, to take a moment and bond with their spirit. Show respect. Gives you more *puah* when you hunt them in the future, too. Now, let's get to going. We both have lots of work ahead of us...." He raised his eyes at the darkening sky above them. "That snow ain't gonna care much whether we're back in front of a fire, or wet, cold and in the dark."

October 17, 1855

# ESOLVED TO RESOLVE

SARAH STOOD WITH HANDS ON HER HIPS, APPRAISING ONE of Rebecca's three trunks, which she had just placed along the south wall of the cabin, end up and open for storage. The wooden shutters and wood-framed cloth interior "chill blockers" as Israel liked to call them, were open on two walls. This morning, there had been ice skim on the water buckets they left outside the previous night. The air was chilly, above freezing, but the cross breeze felt good and allowed the heat from the woodstove to escape to the wild lands beyond. *Zeb was right. That little stove more than heats this place, at least in this type of weather.*

The water bucket scraped on the stove behind her, and she turned. Rebecca was about to lift it off the stove. "Rebecca, let go of that bucket. I'll move it for you."

Rebecca stood erect slowly and smiled at her. "Thank you, Sarah." *Unlike her not to stubbornly persist about such things.* Sarah walked to the stove, took the two pieces of doubled-up cloth that served as hot pads from the brunette and began to lift the nearly full pail of scalding water.

Rebecca was walking toward the newly placed trunk when Sarah gasped at the sudden tightening and tingling of the outer walls of her abdomen. Her belly seemed to harden. She stood, hands still grasping the pail's cloth-protected handle, and took two slow, deep breaths. The strange spasm subsided.

From behind her, Rebecca said, "That trunk is perfect where you put it, Sarah, and we can..." There was a momentary silence, "Oh my, are you all right? Is there something wrong?"

Letting go of the handle, Sarah backed away from the stove. She swiped her forehead with her forearm, wiping the beads of sweat stinging her eyes. Rebecca walked anxiously toward her. "I'm fine. Perhaps you and I should not be lifting pails of water at this point."

Rebecca nodded. "Yes, I think you're right, Sarah. I feel foolish allowing you to even try it. You're twice as big as I am."

Sarah laughed and pretended a curtsy. "Why, Milady Frank, are you saying that you are less fat than I?"

Rebecca took a step toward her, put her hand on her shoulder and smiled tenderly. "You are, in fact, twice as round as I am. And, ironically, far more comfortable, it seems. Do you know how beautiful you look, Sarah? Almost glowing."

"Oh, Rebecca, and you are—"

Sarah was interrupted by Reuben's shout outside the door. "Rebecca, or Sarah, get this door for us, would you?"

Sarah turned, took the few steps to the door, followed by Rebecca, and pushed it open. Israel and Reuben were on either end of a three-foot by eight-foot slab fashioned from three-inch diameter poles, which had then been planed and adzed on one side to form a flat, uneven surface. The exterior edges were trimmed with slightly larger poles cut in half-rounded edges, joined with rough mitered cuts where they met at the corners.

Reuben grinned at her. "Look at this table Israel put together, and you should see the legs he built. Sturdy as can be!"

"Afternoon, Miss Sarah." Israel grinned at her, obviously pleased by Reuben's compliments. "Figured we needed a place to sit when we eat all that good food you, Miss Rebecca and Lucy whip up for us every day. Got some benches I'm working on, too. Probably have them done this afternoon."

The palm of one hand flew to Sarah's cheek as she stared at the tabletop, and then at Israel. "Oh my, Israel, that's beautiful! You truly are a man of many talents." She turned and swept her arm around the cabin. "And the way you built those interior, wood and cloth shutters, figured out the latches and hinges and storm hooks, is simply ingenious."

Israel beamed. Behind him, Reuben laughed. "He is far more skilled than this dumb Prussian farmer, I mean rancher. That's for sure. Ladies, stand aside. We'll bring the table in and set it against a wall. Then, I'll help Israel carry over the legs. He can put it all together. Then, we can set it upright and ready for those bench seats he's working on."

"We can do that," Rebecca said, glancing at Sarah and then Reuben.

Sarah exchanged looks with Israel. At Rebecca's suggestion, the old man's curly eyebrows curbed downward with disapproval. Apparently, Reuben thought the same.

"You'll do no such thing, Rebecca. Neither will you, Sarah. The table is heavy and awkward. And those benches won't be blown over by any wind, either. We'll get it set up."

Reuben bent to get a firm grip on the edge of the tabletop. "Ready Israel? On the count of three—one, two, three."

With slight grunts, the two men lifted the slab and moved it through the door, taking short steps, Reuben gauging his pace to match Israel's.

As Reuben huffed past Rebecca and Sarah, he commented, "Perfect timing, too. Ran into Zeb yesterday when I went down to the river to get that stray bull. He was just coming from downstream, a big, fat mule deer doe strapped over Buck. I invited him to dinner tonight for some of that elk. Told him he could spend the night if he wants."

Sarah was startled. *Zeb? Down here for dinner?*

Reuben grinned at Rebecca as he and Israel walked out the door. "Seems awful warm in here...." He pretended to fan his face, "Guess that stove was a good idea."

Rebecca contrived a sour look before laughing. "You've had worse, Mr. Frank."

Struck by an idea, Sarah reached out and grabbed Reuben's sleeve. "Reuben, could you grab that pail of hot water and carry it outside towards the corner where we usually do the dishes?" Trying to keep her voice nonchalant, she added, "When will Zeb be back down again, after tonight, I mean?"

Reuben was already busy folding the cloth to double over

the pail handle. "If this Indian summer ends and the weather comes in, we may not see Zeb until next spring." Reuben chuckled as he lifted the pail from the stove, "So, I'm glad he's coming for supper."

Sarah followed Reuben out the door. Israel was already half the way back to the shed. Bits of wood were leaning against the shed walls, and several short, half logs with triangular braces under them served as a sort of counter. *His worktable!*

She glanced over her shoulder. Rebecca was leaning down, running her hands along the edge of their new tabletop. Sarah looked at Reuben's retreating back and then out into the meadow. Nearly ten acres of what had been tall, waving meadow grasses a week prior, were now mown and piled hay. Out where the meadow was still tall, she could see the freight wagon brimming with golden-green hay and, at a little distance from it, the stiff scything, one-armed swings of Michael and Philippe. *This may be the last time for months that there will be an opportunity to resolve some outstanding issues. I shall have to think about the best way to do it.* She clamped her teeth. *And I am resolved to do so.*

Lost in thought, she jumped at Rebecca's voice behind her. "They're making good progress on the hay, don't you think? I believe Reuben said they had six heaping wagonfuls under that cover."

Without turning around, Sarah replied, "Yes. Yes, they seem to be coming along with the hay." She raised her eyes to a sky that stretched, royal blue, unblemished by a single cloud, from mountain range to mountain range. "I hope the weather holds. That first snow was over my ankles but melted by the next day. Quite remarkable."

"I'm going to gather up the dishes," came Rebecca's voice from behind her.

Sarah fixed her eyes on Philippe and the smooth, powerful motion of his shoulders as he swung the scythe. Her idea began to take shape, "I'll do the dishes, Rebecca. I have to finish up that chinking on the south side where you can still see daylight. Another day and that project will be done."

Her eyes found Philippe again.

*And by tomorrow morning, other matters will be done too.*

October 17, 1855

# DIVIDED LOYALTIES

SEVERAL HOURS LATER, SARAH STRAIGHTENED UP FROM where she had been squatting, smoothing the last of the mixture of sand, lime and clay into the rounded gaps between the logs. She stood back, holding the stick Israel had whittled to a flat spatula in one hand while eying her work critically. She bent forward, swiping the spatula across a clump of chinking protruding from the crack. She looked out at the field for the twentieth time. *Finally!* Philippe was walking toward the shed carrying his scythe. *Must need sharpening again.*

She took a deep breath and swallowed, ignoring the pounding of her heart. She raised her hand and waved at the vaquero, gesturing him to come over. He stopped, and then with a grin, she could see even at a hundred yards, changed course and walked toward her.

"*Buenos dias, señorita* Sarah. You look radiant." He flourished his hand at the chink lines, still glistening and wet, "and your chinking is like art."

Sarah conjured a giggle, "*Buena dias*, Philippe. I think the radiance is just sunburn, but you're very kind. I was wondering if you could carry these two buckets of chinking around to the east side of the cabin. There are still several touch-ups to do there."

Philippe peered down in surprise at the almost empty pails, but he flashed a dazzling smile, swept off his sombrero and bowed to her. "It would be my honor, *señorita* Sarah." She followed him around to the east side of the structure, and out of sight. "Right there, Philippe. That would be perfect."

The vaquero set the pails down, his eyes locking with hers, "And is there anything else I can do for you, *señorita?*" There was a suggestive current, subtle but palpable in his tone.

Sarah summoned her most beguiling smile. "In fact, there is, Philippe. There's something I need to talk to you about."

Philippe's eyebrows raised, and his eyes widened with a smoldering glitter. "*Si?*"

Sarah batted her eyes. "Not here, not now. We both have work to do. Would you meet me this evening? Perhaps on the other side of the willows behind the wagon by the creek?"

Philippe's grin widened. "It would be my privilege. *Cuando?*"

Sarah turned her head, coquettishly. "I think we're eating around sundown. Perhaps an hour before that?"

The vaquero bowed to her, again sweeping his sombrero from his head. He settled the hat back on his head, twisting the wide upturned brim with a flair. "I will see you at the creek before the sun sets *este noche.*"

Philippe disappeared around the corner of the cabin with a jaunty walk. Sarah's eyes dropped to the two almost empty chinking buckets. She smiled at them as she whispered, "Thank you, buckets. Well done."

IT WAS LATE AFTERNOON WHEN ZEB'S VOICE CAME FROM the open doorway to the cabin. "You ladies have sure done a fine job fixing this place up!"

Rebecca, Sarah and Lucy twisted toward the doorway from where they knelt by the second of the open trunks they had been carefully filling with folded clothes, but they all saw that Zeb's eyes were fixed on Sarah. She smiled at him warmly. Putting her hands on the top of the trunk, with Lucy and Rebecca looking on, she pulled herself up and walked toward him.

Lucy rose too, grinning and rubbing her hands together. "You ain't seen nothing, Mr. Zeb. You just give us a few more days, and this will be a mansion. The men just got that table that Israel built set up," she said, throwing a meaty hand toward the table and six short, log benches arranged around it. Her arm swept back toward the wall with the open trunk, Rebecca still kneeling in front of it.

"We'll have that last trunk of Miss Rebecca's set up, and Israel's going to build shelves to go there next to the stove for pots and pans, plates and cooking things as soon as he's done putting together that outhouse over the hole the men dug yesterday. Then, me and miss Sarah is going to take them flour sacks she's been keeping all the way out here, cut them so they open up, and then sew tick mattress covers and stuff them with some of that grass that's being cut. Then, Israel's going to build some beds, put one in each corner, attach two sides to the walls and one post on the corner that comes into the room. Then—"

Zeb held up his hands, laughing. "Leave the rest for a surprise, Lucy. Sounds to me like you women have it all figured out."

He took a step to their brand-new table and ran his fingers over it, then stooped down, looking at how the legs were attached underneath. His hand strayed to one of the benches, and he moved his head, so he could see underneath it, also. He straightened. "Israel's done some awful fine woodworking, Lucy, particularly given he doesn't have much to work with, and no dimensional lumber. I'm impressed."

Sarah took his hand. "Come see these indoor shutters that Israel fashioned," she said, walking him over to one of the windows.

He swung the shutter open and closed, inspecting the hinges and the latch. He shook his head. "That's right smart. I'm gonna have to do that up at my place." He chuckled. "Maybe Lucy will let Israel come on up and do it for me. He's way better with his hands than I am."

Lucy bobbed her head, her jowls stretched in a broad grin. "I think Israel would love to come up and help you, Mr. Zeb. You just gotta make sure he don't get eaten by no bear."

"Don't have to worry much about the bears, Lucy," Zeb said, Sarah the only one who could see the twinkle in his eyes. "It's the mountain lions."

Lucy's jovial expression vanished, replaced by a look of

horror.

Zeb pressed his lips together, trying in vain to maintain his serious expression. He burst out laughing. "Just teasing, Lucy. Just teasing."

Lucy put her hand to her chest. "You can't be funnin' an old lady like that, Mr. Zeb. I might just keel over." Everyone laughed.

Rebecca had struggled to her feet, using the trunk for leverage. "We're so glad you came down for dinner, Zeb. That elk meat is absolutely delicious. I think I like it better than beef...." She smiled at Lucy. "And Lucy has some wonderful recipes."

Lucy stood with her hands on her hips, her chin slightly elevated. "I do, indeed. And I was gonna do one of them for you tonight, Mr. Zeb, but after that mountain lion thing...I don't know." She shook her head.

Rebecca threw a quick glance at Sarah. "Lucy, why don't you take me over to the shed, and show me those flour sacks. I kept telling Sarah to throw them out all the way out here from St. Louis, but now I'm glad the seamstress in her just couldn't bear to part with the cloth."

She walked over, hooking an arm through Lucy's. "Just don't walk too fast."

Lucy grinned at her. "Chile, this old woman ain't walked fast in twenty years."

Rebecca threw a wink at Sarah as they passed her.

Framed by the door, the two women's figures receded toward the shed. Zeb watched them go, then turned to Sarah. "Sarah, I came for dinner tonight, and I'll probably spend the night, too. No sense working my way back up that hill in the dark, but it wasn't just for the food or to have a taste of Reuben's elk. I'm thinkin' you and I need to have a talk."

Sarah extended her arm, taking the mountain man's hand and squeezing it. "I think you're right, Zeb, but you never know who's going to be coming in and out of the cabin. I think we're eating about sundown." Her eyes roved the cabin. "I still have a few things to do here. Would you meet me on the other side of the willows by the creek behind the prairie schooner about an hour before sunset?"

Zeb's eyes widened, and the corners of his lips turned up toward the curve of his mustache. "Why...why, I would be pleased," he replied in a surprised stammer. Sarah felt a pang. *Drawn to his mountain man demeanor, but...*

She gestured at the stove. "Incredible," she said. "After dinner, I can make some coffee or some chokecherry tea for you."

Zeb was obviously pleased with the offer. "We'll see. Right now, you have things to do. I need to talk to Reuben, and see how that thatch cover we concocted for the hay is working...." He grinned. "And maybe get some pointers from Israel on building things like shutters."

He began to say something else, changed his mind and turned, walking toward the door. He paused in the doorway and looked back at her. "See you down by the creek."

*Now, I just hope they don't run into each other coming to meet me.*

A CHILL GRIPPED THE AIR AS THE BOTTOM OF THE SUN

kissed the top of the Snaefel. Sarah leaned on the long, stout walking stick Israel had cut and peeled for her, along with one for Rebecca and another for Lucy. If the temperature kept dropping, there'd be ice on the water buckets again in the morning.

An owl hooted somewhere up the creek, *cuhoo, cuhoo, cuhoo.* On the other side of the narrow current, two chipmunks chased each other, occasionally stopping at the scent of some delicacy, lifting it with their two front feet, popping it in their mouths and running to an old log with hollowed out rot holes in it, only to reappear and repeat the process. *Looks like we're all getting ready for winter.*

To the east, the evening star shone brightly against the pale, steel blue of receding day. Sarah tried to still the rapid beating of her heart. *This could go very wrong.* She fixed on the star and took a deep breath, exhaling slowly. *But it must be done.*

"Evening, Sarah."

She jumped at the sound of Zeb's voice just a few feet behind her. She spun, one hand pressed against her chest just below her throat. "Oh, Zeb. You startled me. I didn't hear you."

The mountain man grinned at her. "I move quiet." His eyes fell to her moccasins, his lips curling into a smile, "I see you're wearing those moccasins I gave you."

"I love them, Zeb, and thank you again. They are, without doubt, the most comfortable footwear I've ever had. I wear them constantly." The tall man's grin widened.

There was a rustle of willow branches behind them and the snap of a twig breaking. Zeb whirled, one hand reaching for the Colt in his belt.

Sarah hurriedly reached out her hand and covered his. "You won't need that, Zeb. It's fine."

A moment later, Philippe emerged from the tangle of willows, stopping short when he saw Zeb, his eyes darting rapidly between Sarah and the mountain man. Sarah could feel Zeb staring at her, too, and then at Philippe. She thought they might hear the pounding of her heart and hoped they did not notice how tightly her hand was squeezing the walking stick.

"Am I interrupting something, *señorita* Sarah?" Philippe's voice was colder than the evening air, his eyes narrowed, his chin tensed.

Zeb stared at her, his expression a gut-wrenching mixture of surprise and hurt.

Sarah suddenly felt terrible. *This is all wrong. I've made a big mistake.* She breathed in, leaning heavily on her walking stick, looking from one man to the other, both pairs of questioning, expectant eyes riveted on her. She gritted her teeth. *Well, we're here now. What does Reuben always say? It is what it is.*

She spoke slowly, hoping both men could hear the honest anguish and the earnest emotion in her tone and words. "I know what you both must be thinking. And I'm very sorry, but there are some things I need to say, not just to each of you, but to the two of you together. With winter coming, Zeb may not be back down here for months."

Neither set of eyes fixed on her seemed to soften.

She smoothed one hand over her belly. "And with me expecting," she swallowed, pressing her lips together, suddenly wanting to cry, "a child to whom neither of you is the father..." She heard the catch in her voice. Both men did, too. Philippe's stiff forward pose relaxed slightly and the tense lines under Zeb's eyes softened, just a bit.

"We are a small group in very tight quarters for a very long time," she took another deep breath, "and we must rely on one another."

Their faces blurred, and she felt the tremble in her lips. "Zeb, no one has ever been kinder to me. Philippe, you are always gallant. Both of you could not be more respectful or polite. I am drawn to each of you for different reasons, my loyalties divided. And I know that I have handled it poorly, causing friction between you, creating an unsettled feeling within our group and..."

She pressed her lips together, trying to steel herself. "I have not been honest with either one of you, and I have not been honest with myself."

The two men exchanged quick startled glances. Upstream, the owl hooted again. Behind them, the howl of a coyote cut the air. She looked toward the final light of the day. Only the top rim of the autumn sun still lived above the dark line of the Snaefel. *Sinking sun. Sinking spirits.*

"I know both of you, without saying it, have wished me, expected me, to make some kind of choice. Her eyes held Philippe's and then Zeb's. "I wanted the three of us to be together for this discussion. It is not right that I would've had a separate talk with either one of you. I have made a decision."

*Did either man care? She suddenly wondered if she'd imagined their interest. How foolish!* But Zeb raised his eyebrows in anxious anticipation, and Philippe's eyes widened, his head cocked slightly to the side, waiting. *No, she hadn't imagined it.*

"My decision is that I must focus on my baby, whenever its arrival might be, and I must focus on myself. I've been through much, quite a bit of it most unpleasant. I consider you both friends—very, very good friends." She felt the cool streak of a tear roll down her cheek. *I promised myself I wouldn't cry.* Zeb and Philippe exchanged sober glances.

"I mustn't let myself get distracted with romance, with womanly things. I must focus on motherhood. I hope that I can continue with both of you as good friends, and I don't wish to create any more friction between you."

Philippe's face relaxed, his lips puckered at one side of his mouth, his sombrero moving in a slight nod. One of Zeb's cheeks had a slight tremor, just above his handsome mustache. *Had she made a terrible mistake? Surely not.*

"I must also tell you that, though I have not reached a final decision, if the opportunity arises for me to perhaps leave this place and go to a city or a good-sized town where I can raise my child and potentially pursue my original dream of a seamstress shop, I may do that. When..." Sarah swallowed, "and if that time comes, and if that is my decision, I will tell you and the others."

A long silence hung like the dew forming in the air of the darkening evening. The sun was slowly disappearing over the western rim.

Philippe worked the toe of his boot against a tuft of grass, then looked up, a slight smile playing across his lips. "A *mujer* is always full of surprises, eh, *señor* Zeb?"

Zeb cleared his throat. "Seems like."

"Dinner must be about ready," the vaquero said softly. "Shall the two of us escort *la señorita* back to *la casa, señor* Zeb?"

Zeb's gaze rose to the evening star, which had been joined by countless twinkling cousins. He blinked twice, rapidly. "Suppose so, Philippe."

# CHAPTER

*42*

January 1, 1856

# *U*NANTICIPATED

THE SOFT GLOW OF THE OIL LAMPS CAST A RICH GOLDEN hue onto the curves of the cabin logs. Rebecca sat, savoring the aroma of fresh-baked pan bread on the warming shelf, and grilled wild scallions simmering with seasoned beef in the oven. Lucy stood at the stove, busy mixing batter for a celebratory New Year's cake and occasionally opening the oven door, a cloth folded in her hand. Bowls and pots were set on the corners of the stovetop, two of them on the warming tray covered with cloth, next to the bread. In the compartment next to the oven, kindling crackled in the firebox, the glowing embers beneath heating the oven. Sarah stood close, her cheeks red from the heat.

Rebecca turned to Reuben, seated next to her at the table. He was leaning forward on the bench, his fingertips drumming on the tabletop, his elbows and forearms planted on the uneven wood surface on either side of a cup of coffee untouched since Lucy had placed it before him twenty minutes prior. Rebecca watched his gaze alternate from his fingers to the stove and then to the door. *He has stared at that door twenty times.*

She covered his tapping fingers with her hand. Outside, the wind howled and moaned as it sifted through the jointed-log corners of the cabin. Pelting snow pummeled the window shutters.

"Philippe and Michael will be back any moment now," she said softly, hoping to comfort him.

Reuben swiveled his head sideways toward her, his eyes shadowed with worry. "I was out there all morning, Rebecca. It's miserable. Must be below zero, the snow's horizontal, coming so thick and hard there were times I couldn't make out Lahn's ears. A few times, I felt myself tipping over in the saddle, unsure of up from down. There were places the snow was higher than Lahn's belly. Some of the cows are pushed up against that jackleg fence we put around the hay," his voice was glum, "at least those that made it there. Who knows where the rest of the herd is."

Rebecca squeezed his hand, shifting her weight slightly on the bench at the movement and twinge in her belly. She had her own worries. *At least, under the table, how wide my knees are spread beneath my skirt can't be seen. Not ladylike. And I don't give a damn.*

"Reuben, the cattle will be fine. You were able to put up seventeen heaping wagons of hay before the weather set in November. That's a lot of grass!"

Reuben raised the coffee absent-mindedly to his lips and took a sip, setting it down just as slowly, his face puckered. "Cold." He looked at her, cheeks taut, lips pressed tightly together. "It's not near enough for all those cows, Rebecca, particularly now that we see what winter is like up here. And it's only New Year's." He chuckled without humor. "We have months of this to go. Zeb was not exaggerating."

He stared at the door again. "Philippe and the boy have been out too long in this miserable wet wind. It's freezing...and dangerous."

Rebecca noticed Lucy straighten at the stove and, like Reuben, throw a worried look at the door.

"This big ol' roast is just about done. I hope Mister Philippe and the boy get back soon." She turned toward Sarah, clucking like an annoyed hen. "Miss Sarah, I told you, don't you be standing near the stove. It's plenty warm enough anywhere in the cabin."

Sarah stared at her, her cheeks still flushed, her lips suddenly tightening, the outer corners of her eyes sagging in a wince.

Lucy reached out a hand to Sarah's arm. "I think you oughtta sit down, chile. I can finish up the fixins' just fine." Sarah grimaced, one hand spread over the heavy, rounded protrusion of her belly. She swayed slightly despite Lucy's steadying grip.

"Now, you go sit, Miss Sarah," Lucy said. "I'll bring you some water." She glanced at Reuben and Rebecca, her usual smile absent, her eyes lingering on Rebecca. "How you feelin'?" she asked.

Rebecca forced a smile to soften her deflection of the question. "Better than Sarah, it appears."

Sarah walked heavily, her feet oddly spread, her hips twisting with each step. With both hands flat on the tabletop for support, she eased herself gently to the bench at the head of the table.

Lucy's eyes followed Sarah's movements, one meaty hand still gripping the batter-covered spoon, her lips pursed. "Israel...," she looked toward the far corner of the cabin where her husband sat hunched forward on one of the corner beds he had built, reading one of the three books Rebecca had smuggled west in her trunks. Rebecca twisted to follow Lucy's stare. The old man held the book open on his knees, three fingers of one dark hand moving slowly across the page.

"Israel." Lucy's voice was uncharacteristically sharp.

Israel looked up, blinking, his hand paused in the middle of a page. "Yes, Lucy?"

"Did you bring over all them blankets from the wagon like I asked you?"

Israel nodded. "I did." He reached out a thin arm and pointed to where four or five blankets were neatly folded and stacked next to the trunks along the south wall, but out of Lucy's sight at the stove.

Lucy's eyes slid to Sarah, then back to Israel. Her chin dipped once. "Good." Her gaze lifted to the two, eight-foot-long branches that Israel had stripped of bark and hung with rawhide suspended from the rafters. The branches hovered level, six feet above and parallel to the tamped down dirt floor. *Curtain rods!*

Rebecca marveled at how he had been able to fashion primitive hooks from the antlers of Reuben's elk. The hooks were lashed every eighteen inches to two feet to the suspended rods running from the south to the east wall forming a square around the corner, which was home to Sarah's bed.

Lucy took the few steps to two pails of water against the wall, dipped in a tin cup, and limped to the table, placing the cup in front of Sarah, "There's some water, child." Sarah nodded, another wince stealing across her face.

A sudden pounding at the door caused them all to jump. "*Señor* Reuben," came a shout from Philippe, "open the door."

Reuben launched himself toward the door. He lifted the cross brace, which snugged the door closed against the wind and stepped back, swinging the heavy, half-cut-log slab open. A whirl of snow blasted into the cabin, flakes spiraling inside, hissing in the warm air as they fell to the floor.

Michael appeared first in the howl of wind and explosion of weather, snow clinging to his clothes, then Philippe, his dark eyebrows lines of ice. Even Philippe's olive complexion was reddened by the frigid bluster of the storm.

Pushing against the door, Reuben forced it shut against the wind, dropping the cross brace back in place. Michael flapped his arms and twisted around, brushing the snow off his stout young frame like a dog shaking itself after a fall in an icy river. Philippe peeled back the hood Lucy and Sarah had sewn to his gutta-percha and wiped one hand over his face, picking chunks of ice from his eyebrows and ears. Both of them peeled the wet, frozen outer layer of clothes from their shivering forms, dropping them in a heap near the door. Reuben bent and picked up the coats, hanging them on the wooden drying pegs near the stove.

Lucy flashed a relieved smile at Michael. "You be right in time for supper," she said, her smile disappearing as she fixed her gaze on Philippe. "You was out there an awful long time."

Philippe, bent brushing snow from his pants, looked at Reuben, then Rebecca and Sarah, where his gaze lingered. Straightening up, he stared at Lucy, his hand slapping his pants a few last times. "We were lucky we found the cabin, *señora*. Rode past it twice." He raised one arm in a backhanded gesture toward Michael. "That old mare of his went down in a dip filled with drifting snow. Took us an hour to get her out with Diablo pulling."

Reuben's voice was quiet. "Find any more cows?"

Philippe looked at him for a long moment, then shook his head slowly, "No, *senor* Reuben. We found one cow foundered and frozen in the same place *la muchacho's caballera* buried itself. Like you this morning, the only cows we see are those bunched around the hay fence."

Rebecca saw the worry in Reuben's face, the corners of his mouth pulling back, his cheeks taut. "And the horses?" he asked.

"*Las caballos es bien*—so far. They are bunched near the hay, using the willows for a windbreak."

Her hands on her hips and her chin in the air, Lucy broke the silence, "That soup ain't gonna have no water," she puffed, "and this cake ain't never gonna get baked until that roast is out of the oven and that ain't happenin' unless you all get set down."

Rebecca pulled her legs in and moved over on the bench to make room. As the others seated themselves, Lucy bustled around the table, laying out clothes folded up into squares between the plates at intervals, along with several thin slabs of rock for hotplates. She began moving the bubbling dishes to the table, frequently glancing at Sarah. Her friend's drawn face worried Rebecca. She didn't like the look of her flushed cheeks and pinched lips.

Rebecca started to rise to help, but Lucy looked at her sharply as she set down the roast. "You stay right there, chile. You don't move a muscle other than to lift your fork."

---

PURPOSELY SITTING NEXT TO SARAH, LUCY WATCHED WITH satisfaction as everyone voraciously consumed the New Year's meal she had prepared—except for Sarah. Lucy saw the telltale signs in the redhead's puffy red cheeks, the way she was just staring at her plate, not eating, her hands resting on top of the great rounded ball that was her belly.

The menfolk didn't seem to notice. They was just glad to have bellies full of food. Philippe sighed, his plate empty. "*Muy, muy, muy bien, señora.*"

His mouth full, Reuben nodded his assent.

Rebecca smiled at her. "Outstanding, Lucy."

Lucy could only see the top of Michael's head, his mouth lowered to his plate, the rise of his fork reminding her of the way she'd seen the wheels of a paddle steamer turn.

On the other side of her, Israel smacked his lips. "Now, I know why I married you, woman," he chuckled, his mouth half full.

Philippe stood. "I'm going to grab a cup of *kaffee*! *Nadie más quiere uno?*" Reuben and Israel raised their hands, their heads still bent over their plates.

Lucy started to get up, but her stiff knee almost buckled

on her. Philippe had the men's cups and his own filled and was perched again on the bench before she could rise.

"*Señor* Reuben," he said over the steam rising from the hot coffee, "although *mal tiempo ahora,* spring will come. We should begin putting together a list of supplies, building materials and goods we will need for next summer, adding onto this cabin, building the other, and to replenish *la cocina.*"

Reuben sipped his coffee and grimaced. "That's hot! ...I agree, Philippe. I've already started the list."

Everyone at the table chuckled, except Sarah. Both her hands were pressed into her back, down low. *More sure signs. Knees, don't you be failing me now.*

Philippe's teeth flashed in the lamplight. "Why am I not surprised, *señor*?"

Reuben continued. "But that'll leave us shorthanded. It has to be at least a month down to Santa Fe, load up, and back."

"*Si, quatro o cinco semanas.*" He stared back at Reuben, his eyes unblinking. "*Pero, señor,* I'm afraid it will not be as busy as you believe. You and Israel should be able to take care of the *vacas* that survive," his lips puckered grimly, "which I fear will not be that many. Michael and I can take both wagons down, doing in one run what would otherwise take two." He paused. "And we can inquire as to where to get *mas vacas.*"

The men's words blurred as Lucy reached for Sarah. She was gasping, her eyes pinned shut, her cheeks trembling, lines of pain radiating outward toward her temples.

"Breathe, chile. Deep," Lucy said. "Take the breath in

quickly. Let it out slow like, real slow."

Lucy waited for her to open her eyes. Still closed, Sarah's blue eyes found hers. "Ooh my... Ooh my." She leaned into Lucy, her eyes moving quickly around the table. "Lucy," she whispered, grimacing from the pain, "the spasm, I think I've dampened my dress. My legs are wet."

Lucy reached out and patted Sarah's arm. "No, Miss Sarah. That was likely your water breaking. Nothing to be nervous about. Happens to every woman with every birth."

She swiveled her head around the table. Everyone's eyes were fixed on the two of them. "I do believe Miss Sarah is about to have her chile. Earlier maybe than we expected, but no matter. Israel, take that cake out of the oven. No time to finish that now. Might be I can do something with it later. Then, help Philippe."

She was feeling her power now, thinking of all those babies she'd brought into the world. *Ain't nothin' unknown here.* "Mister Philippe," she ordered, "grab those blankets, and you can begin hanging them from them rods Israel's hung around Miss Sarah's bed. Mister Reuben, lift them water pails up to the stove and start heatin' up that water. Michael, take them two empty pails and fill 'em full of snow. No need to go to the creek. Bring 'em in here and set 'em next to the stove, so they start melting."

Everyone sat with surprised looks on their faces. Philippe's mouth was agape, Michael's eyes were wide as silver dollars, Rebecca's gaze was fixed on Sarah, her eyebrows curled in a worried frown. *They ain't never heard Lucy be the boss lady before.*

Lucy stood. "I'm gonna help Miss Sarah to her bed." She

looked around the table, keeping her voice firm. "This baby ain't gonna wait. Let's all git to goin'!"

Rebecca's eyes shifted from Sarah to hers. *She's thinking about when it's going be her time.* "What can I do, Lucy?"

"I don't want you doin' nothin', Miss Rebecca. You might be able to help me later when this is all further along, if you have the mind and stomach to. For right now, why don't you just gather up them herbs I done stockpiled over there on the far end of them shelves next to the stove. Lay them out here on the table so we can reach 'em quick and easy as we need to."

Lucy looked around the table. "Well?" There was a burst of activity as everyone scrambled simultaneously to tackle the tasks she had assigned them.

REBECCA SAT ANXIOUSLY AT THE TABLE, TRYING TO WILL her eyes to penetrate the drapes of blankets that now surrounded the corner of the cabin into which Lucy and Sarah had disappeared. Their tones were low, muffled by the wall of wool that hung from the frame Israel had fashioned, their voices competing with the crackle of the stove and the moan of the wind.

Israel was busy at the stove taking hot water from the pails, pouring it into bowls and mixing in some of the herbs, cocklebur, black chokecherry, prickly pear and yucca. Occasionally, he stood back from the iron stove, wiping his forehead with his sleeve. Lucy had cut cotton rags several weeks prior from clothes beyond wearing, and then washed and boiled them. Israel placed the folded pieces of cloth on a clean plate at the edge of the table nearest the blanket wall.

Michael and Philippe sat at the table hunched over their coffee cups, staring into them as if they contained some type of secret, every once in a while, raising their eyes and exchanging quick glances. Reuben sat next to Rebecca, the coffee cup still between his hands. *Embarrassed,* Rebecca knew. Except for a periodic quick glance from Reuben, none of the men looked at her.

Sarah and Lucy were talking again, their voices sifting from behind the blanket wall and Rebecca strained her ears, trying to pick up the conversation. "Now, you sit right there on the edge of the bed, Miss Sarah. Don't lie down. That's not good. I'm gonna have one of the men fetch one of them benches. Once you have your chile in your arms and it's nursing, we'll fix you up on the mattress and prop you up some."

There was a brief silence, then Sarah's anxious voice. "Lucy, it's starting again." Her voice rose in pitch. "I'm scared."

"Nothin' to be scared of, chile. This be done all the time. And you ain't had no problems up to now. Should be smooth. Don't you worry none. Lucy has delivered more than thirty chillun' They say I have the *mother wit*. Only one didn't make it, but that was a problem with the mama, not the baby. Even saved the life of the plantation mistress, her chile, too."

Rebecca could hear the tone of pride in Lucy's voice, even though diffused by the blankets.

A sudden groan ascended to a wailing cry. Rebecca jerked and felt her own small pain.

"Breath now, chile. Breath like I told ya. Deep. Breath out. Them bites will be comin' a little faster and then before you know it, your lil' chile be in your arms."

Sarah's wailing scream reverberated through the cabin again. The three men at the table exchanged looks and shifted uncomfortably. Reuben threw a rapid sideways glance at Rebecca, then looked back at his coffee cup as he reached out his hand, put it over hers and squeezed.

A minute passed. Another wail wound in increasing crescendo from behind the blankets, then Lucy's voice, soothing, instructing Sarah on how to breathe.

Philippe stood abruptly, glancing first at Reuben, then Michael. "*Muchacho*, let's go out and feed *las caballeros y vacas*."

Michael's face was white, his mouth wide open, his eyes darting from the blankets that hid the birthing process, to Philippe. "W-w-we al-already f-fed th-them."

Philippe stared at him. "*Muchacho, es muy frio.* They need more hay."

Michael threw a wild look at Reuben, his eyes growing even wider as yet another loud cry of pain, this time longer, rent the cabin. "B-b-but it's...d-dark."

Philippe's voice was firm. "We'll take one of the lanterns." He walked to the wall where their coats hung, not yet dry, grabbed his and held Michael's out to the boy. He nodded his head sideways at the door. "*Vamanos.*"

Lifting the latch, he swung the door open. The tumble of snow swirling in the door seemed less, and the wind had subsided somewhat. Philippe leaned his head back in the door before closing it. "*Señor* Reuben..."

Another wrenching cry coming from behind the blankets echoed in the cabin. Philippe's eyes shifted to the blankets, then back to Reuben. "Let us know when to come back in." He shut the door, and Reuben rose, putting the cross brace back in place.

Sarah cried out again, followed by Lucy's calm, empathetic murmur. The edge of a blanket against the logs curled back, Lucy poking just her head out. "Israel, bring me that black western chokecherry and cocklebur. Mister Reuben, take that smallest bench this side of the table. Bring it back here and set it by the blanket."

Reuben looked at her quizzically. "Do you need someplace to sit?"

Lucy looked at him, then shook her head and chortled. "No. That's for Miss Sarah. She'll be on that bench when the baby comes. Lying down ain't no way to birth a baby."

As Sarah's cries became louder and more frequent, Rebecca found her apprehension overtaken by curiosity. Soon, it would be she behind those blankets. Lucy's head and thickset, rounded shoulders poked out from the corner, two hands reaching out and dragging the bench behind the blankets. She looked up from her stooped position at Rebecca, "Baby's almost here, Miss Rebecca. Would you like to come in? Miss Sarah says it would be fine."

Sarah screamed. Lucy looked over her shoulder. "Breathe, chile. Breath like I told you. Clamp those teeth down on that rag I gave you. Keep pushin'. That little head's startin' to poke out. You're almost there."

Lucy didn't wait for an answer. She pulled the bench the last six inches behind the blankets and disappeared. Rebecca shook her head slowly and swallowed, her voice a hoarse whisper heard only by Reuben. "No.... No, thank you."

Sarah's wailing, muffled by the rag clenched in her teeth, was now almost constant, but there was a strength to it, *a determination.* Lucy's voice was audible in spurts between the ebb and flow of Sarah's cries. "There be the head.... Lookin' good Miss Sarah. Now, you rest. Take in a slow breath. That's it. Now, bear down. Keep pushin'. There is them shoulders. It gets way easier now. Keep breathing...."

Sarah's groaning diminished, then rose again, almost a growl.

"There you be, Miss Sarah, a beautiful baby girl, chile!" Rebecca heard several soft slaps of flesh on flesh, and then the high-toned cry of an infant.

Lucy began to speak. "Now, you can relax." But Sarah cried out again, her groan dying in a panicked sob. "The baby's not all the way out of me. I can feel it."

"Good Lord, Miss Sarah. There's another! And it's comin', too. Keep that breathin', keep the bite on that rag, and keep pushin'. I'll wrap this first chile up real quick, put her on the bed and we'll get her twin. You're havin' twins, chile!"

Lucy's voice bubbled with excitement, but Rebecca could only gasp. *Twins?*

Sarah cried out, then groaned, a different, more anguished tone than before. "Oooh, Lucy, it hurts. Oh...my...God. Hurts more than the first one." Sarah's voice was half sob, half frightened shout.

Reuben rose suddenly, bent over and kissed Rebecca. "I think I'm going to go help Philippe and Michael feed. We'll be back soon." He squeezed her shoulder and hurriedly put on his coat. "Shut that cross brace after me, Rebecca."

Israel's eyes lifted up from the stove where he was mixing yet more herbs and concocting some type of light-colored poultice. "I'll get the door, Mister Reuben." The old man's eyes shifted to Rebecca. *He looks worried.* As if reading her thoughts, the corners of his mouth curled in a slight, forced smile and he winked at her. "That black chokecherry is comin', Lucy."

As Sarah's wail escalated, both their eyes shifted to the fabric enclosure. "Lucy...Lucy...Oh my God..."

"Keep breathin', chile, but stop pushin'. Try not to push. This twin is kind of lodged. Turned his shoulder somehow. I'm gonna have to reach up and help get him straightened out. But don't push. Pant, just you pant, now."

Sarah screamed.

"That's okay, chile. Put that rag back in your mouth. Keep breathin'. Don't push."

Rebecca held her breath, unable to tear her stare from the blankets, her mind whirling, her imagination a wild thing.

Steady and in control now, Lucy's voice sifted through the wool. "Okay, chile, I got that shoulder straightened out. It ain't turned no more. You can start pushin'. Breathe and push." Seconds later, "Okay, one shoulder out now. Keep breathin'. Keep pushin'." Sarah screamed in a prolonged wailing cry, and Lucy raised her voice. "Israel, bring that black chokecherry. And bring the rest of them boiled rags and one of them pails of heated water. Quick, Israel."

There was a moment of silence. Sarah cried out again, then again.

"Here comes that there other shoulder." Rebecca could hear the relief in Lucy's voice. "You're on the easy part now, Miss Sarah. Keep up that breathin'. Keep pushin'," and then, "He was set on given us trouble there for a spell, but you got yourself a big baby boy now. Lookee here, one of each! Didn't figure on all that!"

Was Lucy holding the infant? Was she swaddling it? A boy and a girl? Rebecca blinked at the questions racing through her mind. *Twins. None of us ever anticipated twins.*

"Miss Sarah, let's get you cleaned up, get them cords cut and tied, and your two beautiful chillun' wrapped and nursing." Lucy laughed deeply, fully in control again. Sarah's voice drifted weakly through the blankets. "Somehow, I never imagined there would be *a boy.*"

"Well, that boy might've been a bigger problem. But don't matter now. You got yourself a healthy boy and a healthy girl. Two of God's miracles right there in your arms. Looks like that girl has red color hair like yours. That boy might turn out to be a towhead. What color hair did his pa have?"

Rebecca gasped. Sarah didn't answer. There was only silence.

## 43

March 13, 1856

# A CONSIDERED DELAY

SITTING CROSS-LEGGED NEXT TO WALKS WITH MOON BY their lodge fire, Eagle Talon grinned at his wife. She had lowered the shoulder of her dress, the leather bodice now gathered below one breast. In the crook of her elbow, she cradled their nursing son who was hungrily suckling, his tiny, pudgy hands kneading the smooth skin that draped her collar bone.

Eagle Talon adjusted the buffalo robe, snugging it over his shoulders. Poked by a stubborn winter wind, the leather walls of the tipi rattled against the lodge poles.

Walks With Moon looked down tenderly at the feeding boy, then raised shining eyes to Eagle Talon. "Dream Dancer likes to eat," she smiled tenderly, "like his father."

Eagle Talon allowed his gaze to caress his wife's bare flesh where it was exposed by the lowered dress. He grinned. "And he likes your body, too," he raised a teasing stare to his wife's eyes, "just like his father."

Walks With Moon giggled, her bronzed cheeks

reddening.

The baby's fat little arms pushed on Walks With Moon's chest as he raised his head from her breast, cooing. Eagle Talon laughed and pointed. "See, he agrees." He reached out both hands toward his wife. "Give our son to me. The rest, I can do."

Walks With Moon reached out, the infant wiggling in her arms. "I suggest, husband, that you remove the buffalo robe I worked so hard to tan for you from your shoulder. The hair is difficult to clean." She smiled at him, pulling her dress back over her shoulder.

"You are a wise woman," he answered, his voice as light as his heart. He slipped the thick leather hide from his left shoulder and reached out carefully, taking their son into his arms. He raised the baby high over his head toward the smoke hole. "One day, my son, you shall soar like an eagle!" Dream Dancer made several delighted sounds as his father lifted him, and then abruptly spit up a small portion of his mother's breast milk, several of the drops finding their way to Eagle Talon's upturned forehead.

Walks With Moon laughed heartily. "Perhaps, husband, you should put our son on your shoulder before making him think he's an eagle."

Eagle Talon cast a wry look at his wife, lowering the child's chest against the slope of his shoulder and softly patted the infant's back, his powerful hand stretching almost entirely across the baby.

Walks With Moon leaned forward, delicately wiping Eagle Talon's forehead with her fingers. She sat back, watching them. "Perhaps tap him a little higher up, between his shoulders, Eagle Talon. Then, I think we shall wrap him in the robes so he can nap while I prepare our midday meal. It seems men always have hunger in their bellies." She laughed. "But for you, it will take more than milk." Her eyes smoldered under suggestively lowered eyelids. "Pemmican and smoked meat from our brothers, perhaps?"

A loud voice outside the tipi interrupted them before Eagle Talon could reply. Three Cougars was standing near the door flap. "Eagle Talon, Flying Arrow wishes to see you."

The smile on Walks With Moon's face evaporated, her eyes rounding nervously.

Alarmed and annoyed, Eagle Talon answered from where he sat, still holding his son. "There is a Council meeting, today? In this weather?"

"No, Eagle Talon. It is just Flying Arrow and Tracks On Rock. In Flying Arrow's lodge."

"Three Cougars, tell them I will be there shortly."

A sudden gust of vicious wind muffled Three Cougars's words as he called out, "It is growing colder, and the wind is picking up. Bring your robe, Eagle Talon."

Walks With Moon stretched out a trembling hand, resting it on Eagle Talon's knee. "You are not supposed to leave to find Roo-bin and Zeb-Raih until at least one moon from now. You don't think they want you to leave early?"

Also perplexed, Eagle Talon did not wish to further worry his wife. He feigned a smile as he handed their son, the baby's stubby arms and legs flailing at the air, back to Walks With Moon. "I am sure it is nothing, woman. I would be surprised if they wished me to begin such a journey with

winter still upon us."

He rose, stooping over to kiss her on the head and close his thumb and forefinger gently around one plump little hand of their son. "I shall be back shortly. Do not worry."

---

AT THE FLAP TO FLYING ARROW'S TIPI, ONE HAND ON THE first rawhide tie, Eagle Talon paused. "Flying Arrow, it is I, Eagle Talon."

From inside the lodge came the old chief's deep voice. "Enter, Eagle Talon."

The lodge fire burned brightly. Tracks On Rock and Flying Arrow sat spaced in such a manner that there was an obvious third position at the fire. Gourds of pemmican were at each of their sides, and to Eagle Talon's surprise, he noticed a third gourd, also full of food.

Both of the tribal leaders smiled somberly at him, Tracks On Rock gesturing to the third position, equidistant and equal between he and Flying Arrow, next to the fire ring.

Eagle Talon sat, legs crossed. The tipi was warm with the crackling, high flames. He untied the rawhide fasteners that snugged the buffalo robe below his throat and across his chest and shrugged the cape from his leather shirt. It fell to a crumpled heap behind him.

Flying Arrow lifted the third gourd filled with pemmican, offering it around the side of the fire to Eagle Talon, who accepted it with a slight nod of his head. "Thank you, Flying Arrow. Thank you, Tracks On Rock."

Eagle Talon waited to dip his fingers in the pemmican, a

tightness in his chest. Flying Arrow spoke first. The creases and wrinkles radiating across the weathered skin around his eyes were more pronounced than in moons past.

"The Council met four suns ago. We have received word of an attack by the horse and foot soldiers of the hairy-faced ones on Little Thunder's village along the creek of the Little Blue, in the direction of the arcing sun. The hairy-faced ones killed more than eighty of the Brule." The old chief's eyes were unblinking, his face stony.

Tracks On Rock continued, "And they took more than seventy women and children prisoners." He spat the word "prisoners" contemptuously. "Little Thunder and most of his warriors were hunting buffalo. The village was scarcely defended. The leader of the hairy-faced ones, General Harney, has called a pow wow of all the Sioux, Cheyenne and Arapahoe to be held at the white man's Fort Pierre on the Missouri several moons from now."

Outside, the wind howled around the trembling skins of the tipi walls and moaned through the crossed tips of the lodgepoles lashed at the smoke hole. Flying Arrow raised some pemmican to his lips with two fingers and chewed slowly, his eyes never leaving Eagle Talon, who suddenly did not feel hungry.

"We did not sign the papers four winters ago as many of the other tribes did. The Council has decided that we will not attend the pow wow at the white man's fort. We shall stay to the side, perhaps not noticed, and see what develops between the hairy-faced ones and those tribes who do attend the pow wow."

Tracks On Rock smiled at him warmly. "How is my

grandson?" *He feels my discomfort.*

Eagle Talon smiled, though distracted by the disturbing news that had been shared with him. "He does well, Tracks On Rock. We have not decided if he will be tall or just fat." Flying Arrow and Tracks On Rock laughed. "Walks With Moon and I shall bring him in for a visit with you and Tree Dove soon, on a warmer day.

Tracks On Rock's smile broadened, and he nodded, then turned his head expectantly to Flying Arrow, who swallowed his pemmican before speaking. "After much consideration, the Council has also decided to delay, but not to abandon, your journey to where water turns rock red and your search for your hairy-faced brother, Roo-bin, and The People's friend, Zeb-Raih. It is too dangerous, this tension between the hairy-faced ones, The People, and other tribes. You will have enough to contend with evading the Ute. We will wait and see what news comes from the white man's pow wow. It is likely you will leave us from the trail we take toward the rising sun when we go in search of our brothers two or three moons from now."

Tracks On Rock nodded with his chin at the untouched gourd Eagle Talon held in his hand, the underside of the hollowed wood resting on one leg. Eagle Talon looked down at the pemmican, dipped two fingers into it and raised them to his mouth, his mind whirling. *More than eighty Brule killed. Surprise attack. Defenseless village. Seventy women and children taken.* He stopped chewing for a moment as he remembered what Walks With Moon had finally shared with him of Talks With Shadows's vision. *The future of The People is not bright.*

February 28, 1856

# $\mathscr{N}$O COINCIDENCES

FEELING A SHIFT IN THE MEAGER MATTRESS, REBECCA opened her eyes. Lucy had seated herself half-on half-off the mattress, at Rebecca's side.

Rebecca blinked. Lucy's features were unclear, her face a soft blur. Reaching up, Rebecca rubbed her eyes. Twenty feet from where she lay, the blankets still partially enclosed Sarah's bed area to afford her privacy when she was nursing. The redhead was singing softly. *A lullaby.* One of the infants was cooing, the other mixed its coos with periodic raucous screams, followed by fits of crying.

Rebecca closed her eyes tightly and then opened them again. Though still fuzzy, the unmistakably worried, creased brow and pursed lips on Lucy's features telegraphed her concern. "Would you like something to eat Miss Rebecca? You barely had a mouthful since last night."

"No, Lucy. Thank you. I'm not hungry. I'm just tired."

Lucy's frown deepened. She leaned toward Rebecca until only a foot separated their faces, her voice barely a whisper, "Been watching you. How are you feelin'?"

*Terrible.* "I'm feeling fine, Lucy." Rebecca reached out her hand and patted Lucy's forearm.

"Miss Rebecca, I hope you don't mind me asking again, but you've never said... When do you think you and Mister Reuben made this child?"

Rebecca's eyes, which she had lazily closed, snapped open. She stared at the underside of the latticework supporting the sod roof in the vault of the ceiling above her, thinking. "I have thought about that a hundred times, Lucy. It could have been as early as April."

Rebecca felt the heat creeping up her cheeks at the memory of her body on top of Reuben's, the two of them molded perfectly, desperately seeking solace and passion, all that he had and all that he was, in the wagon that night on the ridge northeast of Cherry Creek. *The evening I learned my mother had died.*

"But I think it was most probably the end of May last year."

Lucy held out one hand, her short thick fingers spread, her lips mouthing the names of the months as she counted on her fingertips. She stopped counting, her eyebrows furled, stared at Rebecca and then counted again.

On the other side of the hanging blankets, there was a satisfied coo from one baby, followed by a bellicose cry from the other.

Lucy's face seemed more relaxed, but there was a pensive shape to her eyes, and the press of her lips as she stared, unseeing, at the logs on the other side of Rebecca's bed, conveyed more worry than she was letting on.

*Change the subject.* "Where's Reuben?"

Lucy's eyes clicked back to hers. "Mister Philippe, him and the boy have gone out to look for cows. This thaw over the past few days has settled the snow some. They tryin' to get a feel for what's happening past where the hay is stored. Mister Philippe mentioned something about some of the cows look like they were ready to calf, and two already have." Lucy's eyes flowed down Rebecca's body. "Seems to be that season." She smiled.

Rebecca tried to remember the men leaving but couldn't. "When did they go out?"

Lucy's eyes squinted at her again. "Three or four hours ago."

"I've been asleep that long?"

Lucy nodded, her expression softening. "I watched you holding them chillun night before last."

Rebecca chuckled, then tried not to wince as the muscle compression of the laugh triggered something in her belly. She could tell in the sudden set of Lucy's jaw that it had not gone unnoticed. "Nancy is a delight. Cuddles right up to you, quiet, just happy to be touched. Richard, on the other hand, seems to want to be wherever he's not. If I hold him, he wants to be in Sarah's arms. If she holds him, he wants to be in your arms or mine. And such a wiggly little thing."

Lucy acknowledged Rebecca's words with a slight curl of her lips, and her head nodded, but it was apparent that her mind was not on Sarah's infants.

"How's your eyes?" the old woman asked suddenly.

Rebecca felt herself blink. "Just fine."

*Had Lucy nodded her head?*

The woman raised one thick, dark arm and pointed, "Can

you see that lil' ol' pot over on the table?"

Rebecca raised and turned her head, making a show of looking. "Oh, yes."

"You had any trouble breathin', Miss Rebecca?"

Rebecca felt her face blanch. "Just the normal when I first get up."

Lucy's eyes bored into hers. "Been studyin' you tryin' to write that letter. I think you said it was to your lawyer back there in England. You been workin' on it for a week, but you only got a few lines done."

Rebecca shrugged with a slight uplift of her shoulders against the mattress. "I found it difficult to focus on." She forced a distracting giggle. "All those matters are such a long ways away."

"You been rubbing your head a lot the last week or two," the old lady persisted. "Your head hurt?"

If Rebecca had been standing, she would have stomped her foot. "Really, Lucy? Is this twenty questions?"

Lucy leaned closer to her, so close she could feel the warm breath from her lips, "Chile, you can't fool ol' Lucy. Your head been hurtin'. Your breathin' is harder. We both know them pains in your belly have always been there, and the few times you been outside, it looks like the sun bothers you."

"Oh Lucy, your concern is appreciated, but needless."

Lucy shook her head emphatically. "And that pot over on the table you said you could see? There ain't no pot on the table." She paused, letting her words sink in.

"The good Lord sent me and Israel at this time, to this place to you good folks. It's part of his plan for me and

Israel, but it's part of his plan for all of you, too. It's a good thing I was here when Miss Sarah had that surprise of Richard on New Year's. I don't want to scare you chile, but I seen these things before, not likin' light, belly pains, not gettin' your brain to focus all too well, eyes blurry, head hurtin'. Some women get that way, particularly when it's their first. The mistress at the plantation? She had same things going on."

Rebecca was now listening carefully, butterflies of uneasiness stirring in her chest.

"She listened to me. She made it through, and her chile did, too, but barely. I seen others with the same things going on. They weren't so lucky. I'm pretty certain your baby's comin' sometime this month. I don't know if you're late or if you're early, but I do know that you need to stay in bed from this moment on, as much as you'll likely hate it."

Rebecca tried to sit up, but Lucy pushed her shoulder gently back down.

"You just gonna have to figure being on your back for the next two, three or four weeks." Lucy's lips pressed together tightly, the jaw muscles under her broad, dark face set in hard lines. "I ain't never going to lie to you. If what's going on is what I think, if you be real smart and you do what I say, your chances are still way less than certain that you and the baby will make it. You just gonna have to decide which means the most to you—you're not likin' stayin' in bed or your love for your man out there on his horse looking for his cows."

Rebecca had almost forgotten Sarah was close enough to be listening until her voice drifted toward them from her corner. "Lucy, could I impose on you to help me for just a minute. Richard soiled himself again, and I need you to hold Nancy, so I can get him cleaned up."

Lucy's expression turned tender. She raised her palm to Rebecca's face and gently stroked her cheek with her thumb. Leaning over just inches from her face, she whispered, "I'm right here, Miss Rebecca. And like your husband says, there ain't no coincidences."

Using both thick arms, Lucy pushed herself slowly off the bed and then called out, "Comin', Miss Sarah. That boy does his business about more'n any boy I've ever seen."

The old lady looked down at Rebecca without saying a word and then limped toward the blanket.

Rebecca watched the stocky, blurred image of Lucy's retreating figure, her mind whirling, the ever-present pain stirring in her belly, a sudden deep anxiety gnawing at her racing heart.

March 5, 1856

# *F*IRST CALVES

REUBEN LEANED FORWARD OVER LAHN'S SHOULDERS, BOTH forearms crossed over the saddle pommel. Next to him, on Diablo, Philippe did the same. A chilly breeze sifted through the aspens along the snow-covered meadow edge, their trunks marred by bulging black burls that stood out against the pristine whiteness and the deep blue sky. Reflecting off the snow, the sun warmed the meadow, transforming the landscape into an explosion of brightness. Reuben was glad he had remembered to smear charcoal from the cold stove across his cheek bones under his eyes. Philippe had done the same.

Next to him, the *vaquero* dejectedly lifted one finger from his crossed arms, flicking at the shapes of frozen front quarters, rear haunches and twisted horns jutting up from the snow. *"Otro seis vacas."*

Lahn and Diablo's heads and eyes shifted nervously in jerky movements. *They know what death is.* The thought only deepened his worry for Rebecca as he recalled her in bed that morning—eyes closed, face drawn, cheek muscles tight with pain.

Trying to focus on the scene in front of him, Reuben bent his head to the side, stretching his neck, then straightened in the saddle. "Yep, another six. That brings us to ninety-one head we've found over the last four days." Reuben's eyes followed the line of aspen to where it disappeared unevenly over the rise to the west, his eyes squinting against the assault of glaring light.

Across the meadow, the distant shape of another horse and rider worked their way slowly along the far, tree-lined edge a half-mile to the south. "You told Michael not to get off that horse, didn't you?"

Philippe nodded, "*Si, señor,* and I told him also if the ground is not level or there's the slightest hint of a dip, not to go through it. He almost lost that mare back on *el año nuevo.*"

Reuben shook his head. "We'll learn soon enough what he's found over there. But I doubt the outcome's gonna be any different on that side of the meadow."

Philippe craned around in his saddle, looking back northeast toward the cabin a mile below. "We counted *cuarenta y siete vacas* still alive down there by the hay, including that smart old lead cow. I think she and her bell got them down there early. Some are thin, and one or two are wheezing. I do not believe they will make it. Cold, wet weather is not good for their lungs. And there's the *dos toros* with them."

"Such a waste," Reuben said quietly, gesturing at the mounds of mottled carcasses protruding from the snow. "I'm not sure if we had more hay it would've made a difference.

Those cows that didn't make it down to the cabin, when that first set of storms came in, would've been stranded up here anyway. And there's no way to get feed to them."

He twisted in his saddle, following Philippe's stare back toward the cabin. "Some of those cows are stressed enough I doubt they'll make it, and it's going to be tough going for any calves that do drop. We lost one of the two calved yesterday, and we had to pull them both."

"Before next winter, *Señor* Reuben, we need to put up a fence maybe *cien* yards in all directions around the hay and bunch the cattle in there before that first snow hits. We can make the posts up here, but we'll figure out what else we need and pick it up in Santa Fe when Michael and I go down in May."

Reuben heard Philippe's voice, but not his words, his mind still on Rebecca.

"*Señor?*"

Reuben turned slowly back to the *vaquero*. "Sorry Philippe, I didn't hear you."

Philippe's eyes searched his face. He glanced back at the cabin. *He understands.*

"I think, *si tenemos suerte,* twenty or twenty-five calves will survive and maybe forty *de las vacas. Y el toros?* Both bulls should live, I think. And *la treinta vacas* you gave the Ute, he spat out the word, must be considered, too. They provided a great benefit for the ranch. But in the end, what lives and what doesn't will be determined by the weather...." He swept his arm up to the sky. "If this thaw remains and the spring snows are not as deep, we may be lucky. But on the other hand? *Quién sabe?*"

Reuben wheeled Lahn, backing the palomino until the horses were again side by side. "It is what it is, and it will be what it will be. Only thing we can do now is make sure those cows down by the hay keep getting fed. I think we have enough to get us to about mid-April with that few left."

He rotated his gaze across the expansive meadow, "Hopefully, by that time, there will be grass showing somewhere, even if it's between the snowdrifts." He swung his gaze to the vaquero. "And the unborn calves?"

Philippe shrugged. "*Quien sabe?* I think they will come in the next week."

Reuben nodded. week. *Maybe less for Rebecca.* The memory of Sarah's screams—the close call with the second baby—these were not easy to forget. He kept his thoughts to himself.

"Then, we're thinkin' alike on those calves," he said to Philippe. "We'll likely have to pull most of them as weak as those cows are and keep a close eye to see which mother cows are producing enough milk...then, figure out some way to supplement for those that need it."

Philippe sighed. "*Si.* When the snow goes down more we'll hook up the wagon team and drag whatever *vacas muerte* that get exposed off the meadows. We'll leave any like these that are up in the trees."

Reuben nodded. "There is a steep drop that begins before the bench falls off to the river. We can drag them there."

Philippe stared at him, reached out a hand and rested it momentarily on Reuben's upper arm. "Do not worry, *Señor* Reuben. We will find another place to get cows, and this year we will have the whole summer season to prepare. And your wife? She will be fine."

*His worries were not so private, after all.*

Far across the meadow, Michael and the mare began to pick their way back in the direction of the cabin, their forms dwarfed by the Uncompahgre and the Wetterhorn, the snow-covered facets of their faces above timberline winking bright, white and sparkling in jagged contrast to the blue sky.

Reuben's eyes drifted from Michael back to the cabin. Thin curls of gray smoke spiraled upward from the stove flue, as gray as the image of Lucy hovering over Rebecca's prostrate form.

He thought back to the previous summer, *seems so long ago,* and the first morning he had awakened as Rebecca's husband, the sounds of the Ute village dulled by the hide walls of the tipi, wisps of smoke spiraling from the embers of the lodge fire, the soft, smooth warmth of her back pressed against his chest, the flare of her hip beneath his thigh. Even the scent of their bodies satiated from lovemaking, and the earthy smell of tanned leather, still clung to his memory. How simple his naïve plans for building the ranch had been. *Nothing was as simple as it seemed.* Suddenly, all he wanted to do was kick Lahn into a lope down to Rebecca, but he couldn't risk it in the snow, slick with thaw.

Philippe was watching him closely, his eyes under the shadow of his sombrero dark and concerned.

"Go ahead down, Philippe. Nothing more we can do today. I will be right behind you."

Philippe hesitated, then nodded. Reuben watched the straight-backed *vaquero* and Diablo's muscular rear haunches sway as the stallion picked his cautious way downslope in the deep, slippery snow.

He stared at the cabin again, then swept the valley with his eyes, his gaze coming to rest finally southeast, toward the Wetterhorn and the Red Mountains, *where her land lay. And we thought the trail would be so smooth.*

Then, from the depth of his worry rose an image of Johannes, limping from the wounds inflicted by the grizzly bear, his features stern around the hard set of his blue eyes, handing him Zeb's note. "There may be no choice in trails," his friend had warned, "but trails always offer choices."

*Ah, Viking, you forgot to mention choice is sometimes out of one's hands. No trail is smooth, and no fork is without twists.*

# TO BE CONTINUED...

Coming next, Book Five of the
Threads West, An American Saga Series,
Footsteps

# $\mathscr{P}$REVIEW

## *Footsteps–Book 5*

ZEB GAZED ABSENTLY THROUGH THE OPEN SHUTTER OF HIS cabin sipping from a cup of cold coffee in one hand and stroking his mustache with the other. The deflated snows of winter lay in deepening hollows in the wells of the trees along the trail back down to the river. Heavy, melting snow dripped from branch to branch in the firs and spruce, triggering avalanches on the branches below, the fading remnants of winter rising in sodden piles at the base of the trees.

Zeb turned back to the table, his eyes first lingering on the crumpled note he had started to Sarah months prior and rescued from its resting place by the fire. He regarded the other paper next to it, smooth, clean and absent even a single word, then sighed. *Still two or three weeks till I can get back down there. I wonder how they have fared.* He stroked his mustache again. *I wonder how she has fared.*

ANNOYED AT THE TERRIFIED, DYING SCREAMS OF THE rabbit, Snake looked up from the fire and flung the contents of his half-empty coffee tin at Tex. He was even more annoyed by Tex's maniacal laughter and his bald head. "Ever think of killing them things before you peel the hide off 'em?" he growled.

Tex was bent over, one boot on the front paws of the hapless jackrabbit, both meaty hands gripping and peeling the skin from the animal's wreathing body. Tex turned his pudgy face toward Snake and stuck his tongue through the wide gap in his upper front teeth. *Crazier than an Injun after two bottles of whiskey.*

Rubbing the filthy stubble on his cheek, Snake shifted his attention back to the stocky Ute brave squatted next to him, speaking in a mixture of Spanish, English and Ute. "You think you have news I want to hear?"

The Indian nodded in return. "You want ball and powder for that musket?"

*Which you likely stole, you red bastard.* "*Si*. If the news *es muy importante* as you say, I will make that trade."

The Ute nodded and began speaking. When he finished, Snake tried not to show the sudden excitement churning in his gut. "You say, *el hombre de la pistole perla y dos mujers y dos o tres hombres* has built a cabin upstream on the Uncompahgre?"

The Indian nodded. Snake gazed into the fire, thinking. He reached toward a pile of branches next to the fire and threw on several larger ones. The hot blaze roared. He smiled into the flames. *Those cows mean you'll be far from the house most times. And now those old scores are doubled.*

SMOKE BILLOWED IN DARK, GRAY-BLACK COLUMNS ACROSS the river beyond two shallow hills several miles to the south, the thick boils climbing above a distant ridgeline, then rolling along its spine. Faint echoes of gunfire were audible above the gentle chug of Bear River current.

Shock and apprehension coursed through Joseph. *Smith's place!*

He turned, heart pounding, his limbs tingling with adrenaline, and began to run toward the one-story frame structure with the sod roof a hundred yards away. He raised one hand to the side of his mouth, cupping his fingers to amplify his shouts as his legs pumped through the high grass. "Roberta! Get my musket. Put the children under the beds and close the shutters."

THE AMBER GLOW OF DYING COALS CAST A FADING LIGHT in the tipi. The morning songbirds of spring had not yet begun their chorus. Behind Walks With Moon, his warm bare back touching hers, slept Eagle Talon, breathing deeply. To her other side, less than an arm's reach away, slept Dream Dancer, only his face exposed from the robes clustered around him, his soft breath that of infant slumber.

Walks With Moon reached out and stroked the long, coarse ends of buffalo hair around their son's face, her thoughts filled with the unsettling memories of the trancelike incantations of Talks With Shadows and her upsetting conversation with her husband from the previous evening.

*"But, Eagle Talon, why must you go alone? It would be far safer to go with one of the other braves."*

Eagle Talon had looked at her, a stubborn set to his jaw. *"I will not endanger one of my friends, nor leave one of your friends with a lodge with no man. Flying Arrow is right. A single warrior leaves only a single track, and I am the one who has bonded with Roo-bin. No one else."*

Walks With Moon had begun to reply but stopped when Eagle Talon looked up from the arrowheads he was sharpening, one eyebrow cocked higher than the other, a warning in the clench of his teeth and the glint in his eye.

—◆—

IN FRONT OF THE CABIN, REUBEN MOROSELY KICKED THE rock in the bare, muddy patch between lingering fingers of snow, dirty remnants of the last storm. The rock rolled into the melting snow and disappeared. He raised his eyes toward the Snaefel and took a deep breath, trying to clear the constriction in his chest.

He turned at Lucy's light touch on his arm. Tears streamed steadily down the dark, rounded wideness of her cheeks, the sinking sun glistening on the salty rivulets. "I'm so sorry, Mister Reuben. I did everything I could, and everything I know."

JOHANNES SWUNG OPEN THE DOOR TO THE ADMINISTRATION building at Fort Laramie and walked in. A harried-looking corporal, with two stacks of papers over a foot tall on his cluttered desk, looked up briefly at Johannes' question, rose partially from his chair, threw a quick sloppy salute and pointed. "She teaches down there—third door to the right." Then he buried his nose again in his reports.

*I'll let that salute pass for the moment.*

The chatter of children and the voice of their teacher filtered through the door. Johannes knocked lightly. After a moment, the door swung open. The woman was young, early twenties perhaps. Her feminine curves were unquestionably magnetic, her facial features highly attractive—full, shapely lips under a perfectly proportioned nose, a band of freckles running across its bridge. *Like Sarah,* topped by wide, bright-green eyes under thick, long auburn lashes, all framed by a cascade of strawberry-blonde hair.

As she swung open the door, she raised her eyes to meet his. Her lips parted, a flush rising from her throat to her cheeks.

Her eyes flicked to the rank patch on his shoulder, and she stammered, "Well, I... What can I do for you, lieutenant?"

Over her shoulder, Johannes saw youngsters, varying in age from five or six, he surmised, to fourteen or fifteen. And there was Dorothy—gazing at him over the teacher's shoulder, beaming. She raised her hand and waved, and he waved in reply.

The teacher turned and looked behind her. "Do you know Dorothy?"

Johannes smiled, "I'm kind of her godfather. I promised her I would come down and sit through a few of her lessons in the back of the classroom. I can stand back there. I assure you I will not be an imposition."

The woman's smile turned radiant, her blush deepening.

"How delightful. We have nine students. The little boy in the front row is my son...." A shadow passed across her face, "My husband was a corporal who served under Lieutenant Grattan. I am Susannah. Come, lieutenant, there's a desk in that far corner, though I am not sure your legs will fit."

She turned, pulling him by his hand. Dorothy's eyes flicked from him to her teacher, at their clasped hands, then back again, her smile deflating, a slight squint to her eyes.

THE YOUNG CLERK AT LIVINGSTON AND KINCADE IN SALT
Lake City watched the tall, angular figure with a pronounced
limp approach the counter. There was a bronzed undertone
to the man's sharp features and high cheekbones under
short, neatly cropped, dark-brown hair and a wide-brimmed,
beige hat. A .44 Army Colt was snugged in his belt. As he
moved closer, the clerk noticed the long white scar above his
lip.

"Good morning," the clerk said, looking up, his tone
cheerful. "May I help you today?"

The man nodded, pointing at the shelves behind the
counter. "Two hundred rounds of .44 caliber, Colt."

"Yes, sir."

The clerk turned, hurriedly pulling a stepstool down the
row of shelves and stood on it, grabbing boxes of ammunition
with one hand and cradling them on his opposite forearm
against his chest. He backed the two steps off the stepstool
and turned. "Haven't seen you in here before," he said,
placing the boxes of ammunition on the counter. "You live
in Salt Lake?"

There was no response.

The clerk stopped lowering the boxes into the sack he
had taken from under the counter. "Are you a member of the
Church?"

The man's lips turned up slightly underneath the scar, a
bemused glint in his eyes. "Sure." He threw several twenty-
dollar silver pieces on the counter, reached out and slid the
sack toward himself.

The clerk scooped up the coins. "Thank you. I didn't
catch your name."

The cold, black pools of the man's eyes flicked from the bag of ammunition to the clerk. There was a momentary pause. "Samuel." Then he turned and limped toward the door.

———

ISRAEL SHIFTED SLIGHTLY ON THE WEATHERED WOOD OF the old log, enjoying the weight and warmth of Lucy's cheek against his upper arm after a long day. She sighed. Behind them Sally blew in breathy response. Early summer grasses rose emerald green from the damp earth, and birds flitted between the aspens. *The smell of life and growin'.* Across the valley, the Uncompahgre, still crowned with the white of a stubborn winter, shimmered pale and dark green where the far-off groves of quakies and conifers danced their early summer waltz.

"Thank you for taking me up here, Israel," Lucy whispered. "With all that been goin' on, I ain't been out of that cabin for mo' than five minutes since New Year's..." Her voice cracked. "But I surely do believe we are finally home."

Israel raised his thin arm and wrapped it around her ample shoulders. "Amongst friends, and free," he said softly. "But there are many who ain't, Lucy. I think of that often, 'specially when I am prayin'...'" He turned his gaze to her from the evening glow of the peaks across valley. "Do you?"

"Yes, Israel, All the time. And all them thoughts always leads me to wonder 'bout our nephews. Do you think they be all right? Or even livin' after my brother got killed by their Massah?"

Below them, the two bulls that had survived the winter challenged each other, hurling deep throated grunts into the dusk. "I 'spect they is, Lucy," Israel answered. "And one day, good Lord willing, we might just know for sure."

STRAINING TO KEEP HIS TEMPER IN CHECK, ERIK SCRATCHED final touches on an invoice for a heavy man in a crumpled hat who had dumped an assortment of goods in a disorganized pile on the counter, and stood tapping his hand on the counter surface impatiently. He could hear Randy behind him, straightening a shelf.

Further down the counter stood a radiantly beautiful girl with long blonde hair and green eyes. "Erik?" she asked, smiling broadly.

The voice was young, feminine and very pleasant.

He jerked in astonishment. "Alecia?" Her eyes danced, and her smile widened.

"You ever going to finish up that invoice? I got places to be," snarled the heavy man on the other side of the counter.

Erik shifted his attention to the man, then back to the young woman. *Where's her father?* "*Mi Padre è ancora fuori dal carro,*" she said with twinkling eyes, reading his mind.

A large hand squeezed his shoulder. Randy's eyes narrowed at the overweight patron. His voice was terse. "Erik, go see that young lady friend of yours. I'll finish up this invoice, or maybe I won't. In which case, this customer can travel two hundred miles north or south to get what he needs."

The man's puffy jowls reddened. Grateful, Erik moved down the counter to Alecia.

The girl had a small pad of paper and a pencil. She smiled at him. *Dazzling. That same feeling as on the ship.*

She scribbled hurriedly on the pad and then pushed it over to him. *I cannot yet speak English, but I can write some.*

Erik lifted his eyes from the note and grinned at her, reaching out his hand. She handed him her pencil. *How did you get here? And where are you going?* he quickly wrote, pushing the pad back to her. She slowly traced each word with her finger, then bent over the counter writing furiously again.

Erik read the words upside down as the pencil moved. *Going to Santa Fe. Padre has business there.* She was returning the pad to him when the light from the window next to the counter was shadowed by an unusually tall man in a blue Army uniform. The window glare prevented Erik from gleaning much more, but he knew the man was an officer by the saber dangling from his belt.

The officer entered the store. He had blond hair and piercing blue eyes and wore an amused smile. Shifting his eyes from Alecia to Erik, he asked with a chuckle in his voice and a distinctly Scandinavian accent, "Am I interrupting anything?"

The gripping, sizzling, heart rending reads of the *Threads West, An American Epic Saga* unfold over the course of five eras (series):

**1854 to 1875—The Maps of Fate Era**

Book One, *Threads West, An American Saga*
Book Two, *Maps of Fate*
Book Three, *Uncompahgre—Where water turns rocks red*
Book Four, *Moccasin Track*
Book Five, *Footsteps*
Book Six, *Blood at Glorieta Pass*
Book Seven, *The Bond*
Book Eight, *Cache Valley*

**1875 to 1900—The North to Wyoming Era**

Book Nine, *North to Wyoming*
This era includes seven other novels

**1900 to 1939—The Canyons Era**

Book Fifteen, *Canyons*
This era includes five other novels

**1939 to 1980—The Coming Thunder Era**

Book Twenty-One, *Coming Thunder* This era includes five other novels

**1980 to present—The Summits Era**

Book Twenty-Seven, *Summits* This era includes three other novels

*An American Saga*

# The *Threads West, An American Saga* series now Honored with Twenty-Eight National Awards!

## A Sweep of the Major Categories!

The Threads West Series is the proud recipient of twenty-eight national awards as of the date of this printing, including Best Book of the Year award or finalist designations in the categories of Western, Historical Fiction, Multi-Cultural, Romance, West/Mountain Regional Fiction, Historical Western, Western Romance and Design! Thank you readers, and USA Book Review Awards, Next Generation Indies Awards, Independent Book Publishers Association— IBPA Ben Franklin, Forward National Literature Award, International Book Awards, and Independent Publisher Book Awards (IPPYs).

### Winner / Gold Medalist

- (BEST) Western (two Winners in three years!) (USA Book News Awards)
- (BEST) Romance (Next Generation Indies Awards)
- (BEST) Historical Fiction (IBPA—Ben Franklin Awards)

- (BEST) Design (IBPA—Ben Franklin Awards)
- (BEST) Overall Design (Next Generation Indies Awards)
- (BEST) Cover Design (Next Generation Indies Awards)
- (BEST) Western Romance (True West Magazine)

## Silver Medalist
- (BEST) Regional Fiction/West/Mountains (IPPYs)
- (BEST) Historical Western (True West Magazine)
- (BEST) Historical Fiction (two Winners in three years!) (USA Book News Awards)
- (BEST) Historical Fiction (eLit Award)

## Finalist
- Historical Fiction (IBPA—Ben Franklin Awards)
- Romance (Forward National Literature Awards)
- Romance (International Book Awards)
- Romance (two Winners in three years!) (USA Book News Awards)
- Best Multi-Cultural Fiction Novel of the Year (two Winners in three years!) (USA Book News Awards)

# Be part of the Threads West Stampede!

Hop on board the Threads West Express! The adventure and romance of America, her people, her spirit and the West is comin' down the tracks at ya! Keep your ear to the rail for upcoming specials, excerpts, videos, audio book excerpts (Great!) and announcements *only* for Threads West Express members!

Sign up to receive insider information, updates, the <u>only</u> accurate information on upcoming releases and contests at:

## www.ThreadsWestSeries.com

Follow the conversation, enjoy Reid's great ranch photos, stay abreast of new releases, and participate in the promotions at:

## www.facebook.com/ThreadsWest

## Throw Us A Like!

Have questions, suggestions or comments about the series? Contact us at:

## ThreadsWest.Media@gmail.com

# Shop the Threads West Express!

As a thank you for buying this book and being a part of the Threads West Stampede, we invite you to join the Threads West Express. Send us your comments/feedback and receive discount coupons that can be used at the Threads West Express store!

Canvas Tote Bag

Limited Edition Prints

Photos of
Threads West Country

Or shop at:
## www.ThreadsWestExpress.com

## Want the fun of helping us get the word out?
## Become a Deputy in the
## Threads West Posse!
## threadswestposse@gmail.com